DRIVEN BY
LOVE AND FATE...

Mary Saville
She worked a lifetime to make up for a mistake long buried in the past. But nothing could protect Mary—or the child she loved—from the consequences of that one terrible night so long ago....

Kay Terrell
Held fast in a glittering prison of wealth and privilege, desperate to save her family's name from disgrace, Kay dreamed of simple joy—and simple truth.

BOUND BY A
SHARED DESTINY...

Lily Saville
Gifted child of love, shining with a promise too great to be contained by the small minds of a small town, she lived her life haunted by secrets—her own and others'....

Jack Terrell
Restless son of a proud and troubled family, he was determined to make his own way in the world, and to have the only woman he had ever wanted—even if it took a lifetime.

Books by Patricia Coughlin

Silhouette Special Edition

Shady Lady #438
The Bargain #485
Some Like It Hot #523
The Spirit Is Willing #602
Her Brother's Keeper #726

Silhouette Books

Silhouette Summer Sizzlers 1990
"Easy Come..."
Love Child

PATRICIA COUGHLIN,

also known to romance fans as Liz Grady, lives in Rhode Island with her husband and two sons. A former schoolteacher, she says she started writing to fill her hours at home after her second son was born. Her hard work paid off, and she accomplished the rare feat of having her very first manuscript published. Early in her career she was named Best New Series Writer by *Romantic Times,* and has since gone on to publish nineteen novels. Patricia has also won *Romantic Times* awards for Best Romantic Adventure, as well as an award for Best Silhouette Special Edition with *The Spirit Is Willing* (SE#602) in 1990.

Patricia's next book, *Gypsy Summer,* is due out from Silhouette Special Edition in December 1992.

PATRICIA COUGHLIN

LOVE CHILD

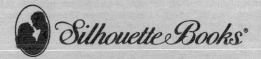

Silhouette Books®

Published by Silhouette Books New York

America's Publisher of Contemporary Romance

SILHOUETTE BOOKS
300 East 42nd St., New York, N.Y. 10017

LOVE CHILD

ISBN: 0-373-48245-0

First Silhouette Books printing July 1992

All the characters in this book have no existence outside the imagination of the author and have no relation whatsoever to anyone bearing the same name or names. They are not even distantly inspired by any individual known or unknown to the author, and all incidents are pure invention.

®: Trademarks used under license and registered in the United States Patent and Trademark Office, and in other countries.

Printed in the U.S.A.

Acknowledgments

I owe thanks to many people for their patience, advice and assistance while I wrote this book.

To my parents, Tom and Eileen Madden, who lived through the forties.

To my sister, Kathie Walaska, and to Carolyn Malluck and Julie Blanchette, who were the first ones I told this story to.

To Ken Malluck, who knows about the jewelry business, and Michael Blanchette, who knows about medicine.

To Leslie Kazanjian, for her loyalty and her belief in me.

To Janeen Costello, Pam Mazzuchelli and Karen Fontaine, for their constant friendship and support.

To Linda Barlow, who read an early version and encouraged me.

To Kristine Rolofson, who also read and encouraged, and traded secrets.

To Nancy Bulk and Pat Viall, for late nights and good advice.

To Tara Gavin, for help in fitting it all between the covers.

Special thanks to Eileen Fallon, who was with me every step of the way....

And to Bill, for the same reason.

For Billy and Ryan

PROLOGUE

Westerly, Rhode Island, 1991

Mary Saville walked every evening at dusk. Her route was always the same. She walked the long, climbing length of Hazel Street, crossed to the other side and slowly made her way back. She did it partly because after her heart attack a year ago the doctor had ordered her to exercise, but mostly for this moment on the way back when she paused on the curb to look across at her own house.

It was important that it be dark outside because then the lamp she'd left burning in the front window made the small gray bungalow seem to glow from within. It beckoned, looking warm and full of life. As Mary stood there, her jacket fastened against a chill wind that felt more like March than April, it was easy to picture her husband, Rusty, sitting in the brown tweed recliner just to the right of the window, poring over a seed catalogue, figuring what was the best buy. The four boys would be sprawled out on the braided rug at their father's feet watching television. Mary's mouth curved. And just as likely they would be squabbling over whose turn it was to choose a program.

Lily, of course, would be in her bedroom at the top of the stairs with her nose stuck in some book. Or else bent over a drawing at her desk, a relic Rusty had happened upon one trash day and dragged home in the back of the station wagon. He'd hidden it in the basement and for weeks, each night after the kids were in bed, he would sneak down and work on it, fixing the broken drawers, sanding the top smooth as satin, finally painting it white and gold just like the one in the Sears catalogue that Lily had fallen in love with, but which they couldn't possibly afford.

Instinctively Mary lifted her eyes to the window above the front door. Lily's room. There was no light there, of course, just as there were no longer any seed catalogues stacked beside the recliner and no canned laughter blaring from the TV. In the darkness the panes of glass appeared nearly black. By straining she could just make out the ruffled shadow of curtains bowing out at exactly the same angle on both sides of the window, as if they had been painstakingly arranged and then not touched for a long time. All the windows on the second floor looked the same.

With a sigh, she stepped off the curb and started toward her empty house, the fragile spell of the past broken for tonight. She moved slowly, favoring her left side, since her sciatica was acting up again. She probably shouldn't have tried flipping that mattress all by herself at the nursing home this afternoon. She probably shouldn't be working there at all.

She was sixty-five years old. After her heart attack she'd agreed to retire from Our Lady of Hope Hospital where she'd been a nurse for over forty years. The mortgage on the house was paid, and if she was careful she could get by on her pension. The kids were always telling her to quit the nursing home, too, to stay home and enjoy life. She told them she wasn't such an old lady she couldn't manage two days a week. It kept her hand in nursing and gave her a few extra dollars to buy presents for her grandchildren or treat them to a movie now and then. Things she hadn't been able to do when her own were small.

Money was only part of it, though. Mostly she liked having a reason to get out of the house a couple of days a week. Not that she didn't love this old place. It was home, the only one she'd ever known, really. One of her regrets in life was that she had so few snapshots of the kids growing up. This house was her scrapbook. Her memories were all preserved here, in the scorch mark Lily's first attempt at frying bacon had left on the counter beside the stove and in the scratches the boys' toy cars had carved in the wood floors. This was where she belonged.

The kids could talk till they were blue in the face about moving her someplace more secure, someplace newer, maybe condo with all the conveniences. She shook her head, wondering what went on in their minds to think she'd trade her home for a garbage disposal. The floorboards groaned as she crossed the porch, and the spring on the screen door whined. To Mary they were the sounds of coming home, as familiar to her as her own breathing. No, sir, when she left here for good it would be feet first and not for some fancy condo.

Inside, the house was silent and smelled faintly of vanilla from the cake cooling on the counter.

Tossing her jacket onto the hook in the back hall, she went straight to the small dinette adjoining the kitchen and turned on the television. She never could stand a quiet house. It made the thoughts inside her head too loud.

Tomorrow at this time the house would be far from silent, she thought with satisfaction. The boys and their wives and all the grandchildren would be here for her granddaughter Lori's birthday party. Lily was coming, too, although she would be late getting here on account of her big job over at Delaney Silver.

They would eat and tell jokes and linger over coffee. There was half a bottle of apricot brandy left over from Christmas. Maybe Ben's wife, Carol, would make apricot sours again. The kids would bang on the old piano in the living room, and when it got dark enough they would rush outside to play flashlight tag, their shouts and laughter ringing through the yard, turning back the clock for Mary. For tonight, though, she would have to settle for listening to the familiar voice of the local anchorman delivering the six o'clock news while she frosted the cake.

She put the butter for the frosting on the back of the stove to soften and went to change into her housecoat, only half listening to the headlines. What did it matter to her if the Middle East tore itself apart or the stock market regained a hundred of the record points it had dropped the day before? Tomorrow's weather forecast—now that interested her. She hoped it didn't rain.

As she hurried from her bedroom still tugging at the zipper on her old pink flannel housecoat, the mention of the nearby town of Richmond drew her attention to the TV. She paused to listen, wondering what on earth sort of treasure anyone could have found in that hole-in-the-wall place.

The anchorman cut away to a young reporter at the scene of the discovery who smiled into the camera as he spoke:

"Little did Tom and Claire McGurty suspect when they bought their dream house six months ago that they were getting more than they bargained for. After moving into what was once the home of the late Mr. and Mrs. Anthony DiCarlo, the young couple came across several overlooked belongings of the retired postman and his wife, but nothing as interesting as what Tom uncovered early this morning in the old toolshed out back. This discovery even has the federal government interested and it might well prove to hold a lost treasure for some lucky person.

"What Tom found was *mail*, at least a dozen bags full, some postmarked nearly forty years ago. No one is yet sure exactly how many letters are in the canvas bags, which had been carefully concealed behind the shed's rear wall, but a spokesman for the postal department said a preliminary examination of the contents suggests the bags contain mostly Christmas cards, which, for whatever reason, DiCarlo never bothered to deliver. Still, it's too early to discount the possibility that there might be something more momentous in there somewhere.

"One thing is certain. The postal service has announced it will make an all-out effort to deliver each and every piece of the long-overdue mail, along with its apologies. So if you've ever been told the check is in the mail, you might want to heed postmaster Larry Cohen's advice and watch your mailbox for further developments."

Mary could feel panic building inside her all through the news report, coming in waves of hot and cold, and in the eruption of bile in her throat, as if a steady stream of it was being pumped up there by the erratic pounding of her heart. Yet she couldn't tear herself away from the television until she had heard everything.

As soon as the report ended, she staggered into the kitchen and grabbed her purse from the counter. Eyes squeezed shut, she plunged her hand inside, searching frantically for her medicine bottle. Finally she turned the purse upside down, dumping the contents half onto the counter and half on the floor, and spied the small amber bottle amidst the loose change and tissue.

Her fingertips plucked at the plastic cap and then at last the tiny white nitroglycerin tablet was under her tongue, just the bitter taste of it bringing the first flutter of relief. She gripped the counter for support while her breathing and pulse gradually slowed, until it was only her thoughts left spinning uncontrollably.

Oh, God, why now? After so many years? She had prayed that letter would never turn up; she had thought that she was safe. No. No, that wasn't true. Never in all these years had she ever felt *truly* safe. A part of her had always feared this day would come. Yet she had dared to hope that her secret would die with her.

What would happen to her now, she wondered, and to her poor Lily? Or maybe it would be lucky Lily in the end. Who could predict how the folks at Delaney Place would react to the news? Either way, her little girl would never forgive her.

Little girl. A snort of bleak laughter escaped as she wiped at the tears flowing along the crevices in her cheeks. She felt in her pocket for a tissue, not seeing those spilled on the counter before her, and finally resorted to using the edge of her sleeve. She must stop thinking of Lily as a girl. She would be thirty-eight this year, older than Mary had been when it happened. And Lily's life was so different from hers, so full of promise. How could she hope Lily might understand why she had made the choices she had?

She'd done what she thought she had to do and had accepted the awful guilt and the nightmares as the price to be paid. Only now the price would be so much higher than she could have imagined. It was like Rusty always used to say... what goes around comes around.

Mary knew in her heart that the letter she'd written to Kay Delaney Terrell so long ago was in one of the bags of mail found hidden in that shed.

Closing her eyes, she was able to recall every word of the letter as clearly as if she'd just that moment put the pen down.

She remembered debating whether or not she ought to sign her name and then stuffing the envelope into the mailbox before she lost her nerve. She remembered everything. She was the only one left who did. The only one who knew what really happened that night and afterward. Soon everyone would know.

The very thought of it was like a slow ticking inside her head that Mary couldn't stop and couldn't shut out. All she could do was wait.

PART ONE

ONE

The last sound Mary wanted to hear tonight was a newborn baby crying. She didn't want to see or hear or think about anything having to do with babies. Which was unfortunate, considering she worked as a nurse on the maternity ward at Our Lady of Hope Hospital.

Usually there were two nurses to cover the three to eleven shift, but the snowstorm howling outside had left the entire hospital short staffed. Both Mary and Florence, the RN in charge, had been pressed into working a double shift. Then, sometime around ten, Florence had been called to help in the emergency room, where heavy snow always meant more business. That left Mary alone to care for a handful of sleeping patients and three newborns.

When the faint crying persisted, she sighed and pushed away from the desk. It just wasn't in her to let a baby's cry go unanswered, no matter how rotten a mood she was in. She quickly crossed to the nursery, her white, rubber-soled oxfords making a soft squishing noise on the polished linoleum floor. Rusty had driven her to work today and as she'd stepped from the car she missed the curb, landing ankle deep in the icy gray slush in the gutter. As the car pulled away still more slush had sprayed onto her coat. She'd stood there, dutifully waving goodbye to the kids huddled in the back of the old station wagon, and felt tears forming. It didn't take much these days.

Of course if she had been wearing boots it wouldn't have happened. But her boots, like so many other things in her life, were a sorry sight to behold. She'd rather work all night with wet feet than be seen in them outside of her own backyard. Her uniforms might be mended and her stockings twisted to hide the runs, but she still had her pride.

Stepping inside the nursery, Mary had to smile. Just as she suspected, the crying was coming from the baby in the crib closest to the door, the only boy in the group. Wrapped snugly in a flannel blanket, his round face red and puckered, he reminded Mary of a papoose doll she'd had when she was a little girl. She placed her hand on his back and rubbed gently. If she was lucky he might fall asleep again without a bottle.

Usually feeding the babies was her favorite part of her job. Sitting in the old rocker in the corner, she would nestle their feather weight against her, watching their tiny faces with their eyes still squeezed shut and their mouths working furiously, remembering when her own children were newborns. Tonight she didn't want to remember.

After a minute or so the baby quieted into a deep sleep and Mary tiptoed to her desk. She slipped off her shoes and stretched her legs so her feet were as close as possible to the radiator. Her wet toes reminded her again of how the boys had looked as they waved goodbye to her earlier. They hated her leaving them to go to work, and Mary hated doing it, but it couldn't be helped. With Rusty unable to hold a job for longer than a few weeks at a stretch, she couldn't afford to quit hers. She only hoped Cliff's cough didn't get worse from being out in this cold and that Rusty had remembered to stop for milk on the way home. She'd meant to call and check on them, but she'd been busy earlier and now it was too late. All four boys would be in bed and odds were that Rusty would be passed out in front of the television. Although she had to admit that after the other night and Joey's black eye, Rusty had been on his best behavior. Still, she'd count herself ahead of the game if he'd simply bothered to put a diaper on the baby before putting him to bed.

There it was again. *Babies.* Her own, other people's. They filled her life. Automatically her hand went to her stomach and the black swell of desperation always at the back of her mind threatened to overwhelm her. Once again she tried telling herself that it was God's will, that this was the life He wanted for her. But try as she did to squelch it, the same question kept bubbling to the surface . . . *what about what she wanted?*

No one ever asked about that. It was as if it never occurred to anyone, not Rusty or her friends from the neighborhood or the women she worked with, that plain old Mary Saville might want more out of life than washing dishes and emptying bedpans. Truth be told, until a couple of years ago it hadn't even occurred to her. Once it did, however, the notion took root and grew.

She had already started saving every cent she could spare and as soon as the children were finally all in school, she was going back to school herself to become an RN. Once she had that black stripe on her cap she would earn enough money that it wouldn't matter how many jobs Rusty lost because he drank too much and talked too much and couldn't get over the fact that a stupid accident had cost him the use of one arm and along with it his promising future as a mechanic. It wouldn't be easy, but she could do it. She had to.

As if to underscore her determination she quickly removed the hand that had been pressed to her stomach. Glancing around for something to distract her from the dark funnel of her thoughts, she reached for the dog-eared copy of a woman's magazine someone had left at the nurse's station and tried to lose herself in an article about fifty new ways to thrill your family with hamburger. The ringing of the telephone a short while later was a welcome intrusion.

"East Three," she answered.

"Mary, this is Evelyn down in admitting. We've got one for you. Her name's Dolly Martin, twenty years old. She's on her way up now, as a matter of fact... Dr. Lagasse's orders."

"She's a patient of Dr. Lagasse?" asked Mary, tensing.

"That's right, although even if she weren't he'd probably end up handling her delivery tonight, what with this storm and all. Anyway, he's already examined her in ER and given me his admitting report. I've got charts backed up like nobody's business down here so I'll have to get it up to you when I can."

"That's fine, Evelyn, but as long as you have Dr. Lagasse's report, can you tell me how far along she is?"

"Let's see... It was right here a minute ago." Mary heard her heave a disgusted sigh accompanied by the rustle of papers. "Aha, right under my nose. Let's see now, says here she's six centimeters."

"Thanks, Evelyn."

"All righty."

Six centimeters. A little more than halfway along. Which meant she could deliver within minutes or hang on for hours.

Wrinkling her nose as she stuffed her feet into her soggy shoes, Mary hurried to prepare the labor room. She was turning down the bed covers when she heard the sound of rubber wheels rolling along the corridor.

As the orderly pushed the wheelchair into the room Mary turned and smiled at the young woman huddled in it. She was pale, with hair the softest shade of red Mary had ever seen. Beneath the blanket wrapped around her shoulders she was wearing only a faded blue cotton hospital johnny. It didn't take a genius to figure out that she was hunched over because she was cold.

"Here you go, honey," said Mary, "a nice warm bed all ready for you. You just hop in... Here, let me give you a hand."

Though petite, Dolly Martin was still as bulky as any woman nine months pregnant and she smiled gratefully as Mary helped her out of the chair, motioning for the orderly to put her coat and other things on the table by the bed.

"There now. You just lay back, Dolly... It's Dolly, right? You lay back and relax for a minute, and I'll run and get you a hot water bottle. That'll warm you up in a hurry."

When Mary returned it seemed to her that the other woman hadn't moved a muscle. Beneath her chin her fingers were tightly clenched on the sheet and bleached just as white. She looked so young to Mary. Her hair was spread out on the pillow, framing her pretty, heart-shaped face with waves, and her blue eyes were very wide and very frightened.

"Is this your first baby?" Mary asked, knowing the answer even before Dolly nodded. "Well, don't worry. I've had four. The way I see it that's plenty of experience for both of us and I'll be right here with you for the rest of the night. My name's Mary."

The woman in the bed let out a long breath, as if she'd been holding it for a while, and her grip on the sheet relaxed a little. "You're the first nice person I've met here, Mary."

"I'm sure it just seems that way because they're so busy downstairs. Nothing like a snowstorm for filling up an emergency room."

"Will I... will it be soon now, do you think? The baby, I mean."

"I can't say. How far apart are your pains?"

"About ten minutes or so. Maybe a little less. I was afraid to wait any longer to come because of the storm."

"You did the right thing. Now, you lift up and I'll slide this under you..." The young woman obediently lifted her hips, propping both hands on the mattress to accomplish it, and Mary slipped the hot water bottle under the small of her back. "Feel good?"

"Yes. Thank you."

"You're welcome, honey. Now, we'll have to wait until your chart gets here and we see what Dr. Lagasse has ordered before we can see about prepping you and all." Mary saw the quick flash of panic in her eyes. "Now, now, don't worry about any of that. He'll order some medication for you and you'll be just fine. Twilight sleep, we call it. You won't care a fig what's happening and by the time you wake up again, you'll have a brand-new baby to hold in your arms."

A tentative smile brightened Dolly's face. "Yes, my baby."

"That will make it all worthwhile, you'll see," promised Mary, moving to hang Dolly's coat in the narrow closet between her bed and the next. For the first time she noticed the brown paper bag on the nightstand. Mary felt a twinge of sympathy. Her own suitcase was frayed and battered enough to shame her, but it was a step up from a paper bag.

"Let's get this all put away. The last thing you want when you aren't feeling good is to be looking at a messy room." She talked quickly so Dolly might think she hadn't even noticed the bag. "Well, isn't this a pretty nightie?" she exclaimed, as she pulled from the bag a waltz-length nightgown with a wide band of lace trim. "Satin, right? And just the shade of peach to show off your skin."

"It *is* beautiful, isn't it?" agreed Dolly. "It was a gift."

Mary couldn't help seeing the way Dolly brightened when she said it, any more than she could help seeing the label as she slipped the nightgown over a hanger. Francine's. The elegant little lingerie shop was a fixture in the exclusive Watch Hill section of town. No one Mary knew could afford to do more than drool over the display windows. The rest of the things in the bag, as well as the clothes Dolly had worn to the hospital, were decidedly less elegant.

"I think that takes care of everything except for your purse," Mary told her a few minutes later. "If you like I can lock that in the file cabinet out by the nurses' station, along with your jewelry. Did they tell you downstairs that you'll have to take off your wedding ring and any other jewelry you're wearing?''

"No, I..." Dolly's pale face reddened. "I'm not wearing any jewelry...except for this." Her slender fingers moved to the base of her throat where a silver medallion hung from a fine silver chain.

No wedding ring? Mary, already curious about this pretty young woman who wore hand-me-down clothes and carried in a paper bag a nightgown that cost more than her week's salary, was suddenly filled with questions, and compassion.

"Well, then, let's just have that necklace of yours. I'll slip it inside your purse and lock them both up so they'll be safe. Close your eyes now, and I'll be back to check on you in a few minutes. If you have a contraction before then," she added, wrapping the cord with the call button around the bed rail close to Dolly's hand, "all you have to do is push this button, and I'll come running."

Mary was at the desk making some notes to copy into the chart later when she heard footsteps coming down the corridor from the elevator. She knew who it was even before he rounded the corner. Dr. Lagasse. Blood rushed to her face as she recalled their meeting in his office just hours ago.

Working in a hospital as long as she had, you heard things, rumors, talk about which doctors did what for a few extra dollars on the side, about who had been known to help out a woman in a jam like the one she was in. She had come in early today hoping for a chance to speak privately with Dr. Lagasse, praying that what she'd heard about him years ago was still true. It had taken every scrap of her courage to approach him, and his harsh refusal had left her shaking and humiliated.

"I am the assistant director of obstetrics at this hospital," he had shouted almost before hearing her out. "And I resent your attempt to involve me in an illegal medical procedure."

Wearing a contemptuous sneer, he had stopped her as she fled his office to deliver a parting shot. "You made your bed and evidently enjoyed lying in it, now the consequences are yours to deal with."

As his footsteps drew closer, Mary tried to clear her head of the insulting words she would never be able to forget. Nor would she ever forget the cold look in his eyes as he dismissed her. She couldn't imagine ever again looking him in the eye, never mind assisting him in a delivery. Yet amazingly, as he strode up to the desk, his brief glance gave no indication that anything out of the ordinary had passed between them.

"Has the Martin woman arrived?" he asked, his gaze fixed on the papers in his hand.

"Yes, Doctor. She's in the labor room. Bed one," she added nervously—and unnecessarily, she realized, as it would be clear to him that there was no one in any of the room's other seven beds. "I haven't had a chance to take her vital signs yet, but I'll get right to—"

He waved his hand impatiently. "Never mind that now. I have some papers for her to sign. I'll need a pen."

"Of course, Doctor." She placed a pen in his outstretched palm and he walked away, leaving Mary puzzled. The hospital must be short staffed indeed if the mighty Dr. Lagasse was handling routine paperwork.

Minutes later, he reappeared at the desk, his narrow face rigid with anger, the papers bunched in his closed fist.

"Hand me the telephone," he demanded.

Mary hurriedly placed the phone where he could reach it easily.

Yanking an address book from the pocket of his coat, he impatiently flipped pages, then grabbed the telephone receiver. Almost as an afterthought he glanced her way. "I need to speak privately, if you don't mind."

"Of course, Dr. Lagasse. I'll see to Miss Martin's vital signs now." She was already out of her seat and reaching for the nurse's cart parked by the side of the desk as he began to dial.

She heard Dolly crying even before she set foot in the room. She was lying curled up on her side, her shoulders shaking. Mary touched her lightly.

"Dolly, what is it? What happened?"

She drew a deep breath, her words vibrating between sobs. "He just got so angry all of a sudden."

"Dr. Lagasse?"

Dolly nodded, her face pressed into the pillow.

"Angry at you?" Mary glanced warily at the door, wanting to comfort Dolly if she could and at the same time not wanting to say anything to get the doctor angry with her. Not tonight of all nights.

"Yes." Dolly sniffled and shifted to look at her. "Because I wouldn't sign the papers. I thought I could. I tried, but when he actually put them in front of me and held out that pen, I knew that no matter what happens I can't do it. I can't give up my baby.''

TWO

Mary stared at her in surprise. "Give up your baby? Why on earth would you do that?"

Dolly's lips were pressed tightly together, her frail shoulders squared against the pillow. "I was so scared I couldn't think straight. I couldn't see any other way. But now I know I can't do it. It makes me sick just thinking about my baby in some orphanage or being raised by strangers."

"Heavens. I should think so," said Mary, empathizing more than the other woman could possibly know.

"Somehow or other I'll find a way to take care of my baby. I'll be a good mother and Gloria promised to help...she's my landlady. She said she'd baby-sit so I can go back to work."

"But what about your baby's father?" asked Mary.

Dolly shook her head, her lips pressed tightly together. "Don't get me wrong," she said quickly, "he's a good man...a real good man, and he loves me. I know he does. This just isn't a good time for him and..." She trailed off, wiping her eyes with the back of her hand in a way that reminded Mary of a child. "It doesn't matter, though. I know that once he sees the baby, he'll want it every bit as much as I do. Everything will be all right. It just has to be."

Plucking a tissue from the box on the nightstand, Mary handed it to her. "Of course it will. Now don't cry. Crying won't help anything."

"They can't make me do it, can they?" Dolly asked her, her determination of a minute ago lost somewhere behind her trembling lower lip.

"No, I shouldn't think so," Mary replied, "but you shouldn't be worrying over this right now. You're going to have your hands full just having this baby, never mind crying and getting yourself all worked up about what's going to happen afterward."

"But Dr. Lagasse wants me to sign those papers tonight. He says he doesn't want any loose ends."

"I can't understand that at all. Whenever a baby is sent to the Good Shepherd Home, Sister Maura herself comes in and takes care of all the arrangements, and it's done after the baby is born. I just can't see a doctor getting so involved, especially not Dr. Lagasse... Unless he's arranged some sort of private adoption for you?" she added quizzically.

"No. No, it's nothing like that," Dolly replied, but she rolled onto her back, looking at the ceiling instead of at Mary.

Mary had the feeling there was more to the situation than Dolly was revealing. One thing Mary always remembered being taught in nursing school, though, was that a patient's private life was just that, private.

She reached for a thermometer on the nurse's chart, forcing a reassuring smile. "Then I would try to put it out of my mind. Dr. Lagasse has a stern manner, but I'm sure he didn't mean to upset you."

Not much, she thought as she stuck the thermometer under Dolly's tongue. Dr. Lagasse was a man who did exactly what he wanted to do and nothing he didn't.

When she returned to the nurse's station, Dr. Lagasse was gone. Mary barely had time to breathe a sigh of relief when another man rounded the corner by the elevator. There was something about the way he carried himself, about his loose stride and the way his open coat flared behind him when he walked, that made her take notice. The man was...rakish—that was the word she was looking for. She couldn't put into words exactly what the word meant, but she knew it fit this fellow to a T.

One thing was certain—he wasn't a doctor or one of the hospital administrators who sometimes stopped by to make spot checks. So why did he seem so familiar? Even as she struggled to figure it out, the professional side of her remembered that whoever he was he didn't belong here at this time of night.

"May I help you, sir?" she asked, moving to the center of the corridor to prevent him from going any farther.

"I hope so," he replied. "I'm here to see Dolly Martin."

"I'm sorry, but she's still in labor. Besides, visiting hours are long over. You'll have to come back tomorrow at two."

He looked crestfallen. "Please, it's important I talk to her for just a minute."

"That's impossible."

"Impossible?" he countered, his smile gentle, "or simply against the rules? I'm sure if you really wanted to you could make an exception just this once."

"I really shouldn't...." Mary felt herself wavering. She wasn't particularly susceptible to men or their lines, but when this one smiled, darned if she didn't feel it right in the pit of her stomach.

He was wearing a camel hair topcoat and brown leather gloves, but no hat, so that melting snowflakes glistened in his dark brown hair. He must be the father of Dolly's baby, Mary decided. So he had come after all, braving the snowstorm to be with her. It was so romantic. Maybe what Dolly said about him was true. Maybe he *was* a good man who just needed a fire lit under him to get him to do right by her. And what a handsome couple he and Dolly would make.

"Please," he said softly. "It would mean a lot to me—and to Dolly—if you could do this for me."

"All right," Mary heard herself say. "But just for a minute."

Not until she was leading him down the corridor did she remember Dr. Lagasse and have second thoughts. They worsened when she stopped at the door to motion him inside and noticed that unlike the woman dozing in the bed he *was* wearing a wedding band.

"Remember," she whispered as he pushed the door shut behind him, "only a minute."

She told herself she was crazy for allowing even that. It was strictly against hospital rules to permit fathers into the labor room at any hour. If anyone found out...Mary didn't even want to think what might happen to her.

She looked at the clock. One minute and she would go back and get him out of there. What good did his coming do when it was as plain as the nose on her face he was going home to another woman and Dolly would be left to have his baby all alone?

It was the thought of him with another woman that brought back to Mary where she'd seen his handsome smiling face before. Not on the cover of a movie magazine, but in the society pages of the *Westerly Sun*. She could see him now, in his white dinner jacket, standing with his arm around his wife, Kay Delaney Terrell. She shook her head, stunned at the realization that the father of Dolly's baby was none other than James Terrell.

Kay Delaney was like a princess, beautiful and regal, a real lady, and with more money than anyone could know what to do with. The Delaneys' millions came from silver, not mining it, but turning it into spoons and vases and anything else their wealthy clientele might desire. Delaney Silver was one of the biggest silver manufacturers in the world, and just about every family in town had someone working at the Delaney plant.

Kay Delaney and James Terrell had been married right after the war, around the same time as she and Rusty, and Mary knew almost as much about their wedding as she did her own. Why wouldn't she? People had talked about it for weeks afterward, saying the whole affair was straight out of a fairy tale.

She'd heard that Kay's gown was a vision, all trimmed with lace and tiny pearls, each one sewn on by hand. The groom had worn his uniform, of course, and the newspaper story had told how the sun glinting off his medals had been blinding.

She'd always figured James Terrell for a Gary Cooper type, and she was right. That was a little thing she did, matching people she knew with a particular movie star. Kay Terrell—now there was a Grace Kelly type for you. Mary shook her head, glancing again at the clock. Some fairy tale. She wondered if Kay Terrell with all her money and fancy clothes and jewelry knew where her handsome war-hero husband was right this minute.

Suddenly the sound of shouting pierced the silence and sent Mary running to the labor room.

"What in heaven's name is going on here?" she demanded as she swung open the door.

"Nothing," snapped James Terrell, stepping back from where he'd been looming over the bed. He didn't look so rakish now, simply angry, with bright red splotches staining both cheeks. Sad, she thought, for all his smooth talking and shiny medals he was no more of a prince than Rusty.

"You'll have to leave," Mary told him. Dolly lay with the sheet clutched to her chest, looking anything but pleased by the surprise visit.

"Don't worry, I'm going," he said, backing away from the bed with a strange expression. Pausing briefly in the doorway, he added, "For your own sake, Dolly, remember what I said."

Dolly turned her head away, moaning and clutching her stomach. "The pains . . . they're worse," she cried. "I feel awful. I can't . . . I think I'm going to throw up."

"No, you're not," Mary said firmly. "That's just the baby pressing down."

"My back, it burns." She twisted in the bed, panting. "It burns."

"I know it does, honey. Try to lay still. Think about something else if you can," she urged, knowing how useless that suggestion was. "I'm going to leave you for just a minute to page the doctor," Mary told her, not knowing if Dolly even heard her through the pain. Her face and the wispy strands of hair around it were wet with perspiration. Her eyes were glazed. "I'll be right back."

She ran to the desk and was reaching for the phone when she realized that Dr. Lagasse was already there, standing at the far end of the corridor talking to James Terrell. For a second Mary panicked, knowing she would be held responsible for allowing him on the floor after hours. Then it occurred to her that the two men were talking for far too long for Dr. Lagasse to simply be questioning him about his presence there.

There was something odd about the way they were talking, as well. Mary could not hear anything, but she couldn't help noticing the way Mr. Terrell was gesturing so emphatically. Dr. Lagasse was nodding. Maybe they knew each other, but Mary's instincts told her this wasn't a casual chat.

She was about to interrupt when Terrell suddenly reached inside his topcoat for something and handed it to Dr. Lagasse, who just as quickly tucked it away. A second later Terrell was gone, and Dr. Lagasse was heading straight toward Mary.

The last thing Mary wanted was for him to think she'd been standing there watching them, but it was as if her feet were rooted in the floor. She remained where she was at the front of the desk, and there was the slightest hesitation in his step when he glanced up and saw her as if he wondered how long she'd been there and how much she'd seen. All he said was, "How is she?"

"Pretty far along," Mary replied. "She says she feels nauseous."

She followed him into the room and assisted while he examined Dolly. Dolly winced, gripping Mary's hand. Mary squeezed tight and stroked her forehead, knowing from experience how uncomfortable it was to have someone poking into you at a moment like this.

Withdrawing from beneath the draped sheet, the doctor stripped off his rubber gloves. "Well, Miss Martin, it seems you're nearly ready to deliver."

Mary wondered if she'd only imagined the way he seemed to stress the *miss*.

"We'll get you to the delivery room and put you to sleep so you don't feel any more pain," he continued. "Won't that be nice? But first I must insist you sign these papers for me."

Mary looked on in disbelief as he pulled the same crumpled papers from the pocket of his jacket and smoothed them on the bedside table. "I have the pen right here. If you'll just lift up a little . . ."

"No!" Dolly's shrill cry reverberated in the quiet room. "No, I already told him no. I want my baby."

"Are you crazy, woman?" he demanded, his tone exasperated. "Think. You have no husband, no way to support a child. This gravy train you're riding will end as soon as the baby is born. You'll be on the street in no time. Is that what you want for your baby? Is it?"

Mary stood by, her throat burning with the urge to speak out and tell him to stop badgering the poor woman, but she didn't dare.

"No. No." Dolly's head tossed on the pillow. Damp strands of hair covered her face like a web.

He shoved the table closer to the bed. "Then do as I said. Sit up and—"

"*No.*"

Dr. Lagasse's head whipped around in response to Mary's sharp tone, but he couldn't be any more surprised than she herself was by the bold way she'd spoken out.

"I'm sorry, Doctor," she said in a hurried attempt to smooth over the fact that she'd openly opposed him. She just hadn't been able to stop herself. "But I don't think she can sit up. Can't this matter wait until afterward?"

"This matter," he said softly, "is none of your damn business. Leave the room please and page a nurse . . . a *real* nurse," he added pointedly, "to assist me with the delivery."

"Yes, sir," Mary whispered and for the second time that night fled from his disparaging glare. What else could she do? she asked herself. Still, she felt like a coward for leaving Dolly alone with him.

Florence quickly arrived from emergency, along with the anesthesiologist on duty and an orderly to help move Dolly to the delivery room. Mary didn't have a chance to tell her anything about what had gone on in her absence. As Florence entered Dolly's room, Mary hung back, waiting in the doorway as Dr. Lagasse barked out a few orders before stalking off to scrub for the delivery. As he passed her she peeked sideways at him. He didn't look happy, and although she didn't dare let it show, that pleased her. It meant that Dolly had won for now, at least.

"Oh, God, please," Dolly cried out as they moved her from the bed to the hard narrow surface of the stretcher.

"There, there," soothed Florence, "don't you worry, it will all be over soon now, very soon."

Mary said nothing, but squeezed Dolly's hand as they hurried her to the delivery room. She knew what the others didn't, that Dolly was tormented by a fear far greater than simply a first-time mother's natural anxiety.

Suddenly Dolly gripped Mary's hand so tightly her knuckles cracked. "Please," she said, staring at her with wild pain-glazed eyes. "Please, promise me if anything happens, my baby won't go to strangers...."

In spite of the interrupting contraction that made Dolly wince, Mary knew exactly what Dolly was asking her to promise, and she knew that ultimately it was way beyond her control. She had a sick premonition that when all was said and done, Dr. Lagasse would have things his way. However, she was far too sensible and kindhearted to let Dolly even suspect such an outcome at this moment.

"I promise you, Dolly," she whispered, leaning down and brushing the hair from her damp forehead. "Everything will be all right, you'll see."

Dolly's eyes closed, but over and over for the rest of the way to the delivery room, she murmured the same plea. "Please, God, let me keep my baby, please let me keep my baby, please...."

Her words tore at Mary's heart even after the delivery room door had swung shut, leaving her standing there alone. How could God be so unfair? she thought miserably. Here was poor Dolly, being bullied into giving up the baby she wanted desperately, while Mary was carrying one she couldn't allow herself to keep.

THREE

Mary's first suspicion that things weren't going smoothly for Dolly came when fifteen minutes stretched to twenty, a half hour, longer, and still no one emerged from the delivery room.

She didn't want to believe that anything was wrong. In the space of a few hours she'd developed a special feeling for the other woman. Like her, Dolly was in a tight spot because of a man. In a strange way, it felt as if their fates were linked. If things worked out for Dolly then maybe they would for her, too, and so Mary was pulling for her even harder than she would ordinarily.

She clung to her optimism right up to the moment Florence stuck her head out the delivery room door and yelled for her to call downstairs for three units of blood *stat*. As a precaution all obstetrical patients had their blood typed and cross matched some time prior to admission, and now it took the blood bank only minutes to get blood up there, if necessary.

Standing just outside the delivery room door in case she was needed, Mary blessed herself, then flattened her hand over her pounding heart while she raced through one Hail Mary after another.

She'd been present at enough deliveries to piece together what was happening from the clipped conversation taking place on the other side of the door, and it scared her to death. As the baby turned, the cord had become tightly wrapped around its neck, forcing Dr. Lagasse to perform an emergency cesarean. Now he was having trouble stopping the bleeding, and Dolly was losing blood into her abdominal cavity faster than it could be replaced.

Mary listened in horror as he snapped orders for drainage tubes and clamps and the anesthesiologist called out Dolly's

rapidly falling blood pressure. "Ninety over sixty-eight. Over
sixty."

Mary pressed her clenched fists against her lips so hard i
hurt. It was almost a physical relief when at last a weak, high-
pitched newborn wail pierced the night.

"Oh, thank God, thank God," she murmured.

The crying went on, growing louder. Above it she heard Dr
Lagasse's voice, loud and unmistakably worried. "Get respi-
ratory up here right away," he ordered. And then, "Damn it—
we're losing her. Call a code—*now*, woman—and get that
damned baby out of here."

The door swung open and Florence thrust the baby at Mary
still wet with blood and haphazardly wrapped in a cotton
blanket.

"Call a—"

"I heard," Mary interrupted, already moving toward the
phone at the nurse's desk.

Her arms shaking, she pressed the baby to her chest as she
dialed the operator. "Code Blue, East Three," she said and
instantly heard the operator repeat the words over the hospital's public address system.

Code Blue was only used to summon assistance in the most
critical, life-threatening emergencies. Within a minute came the
sound of running footsteps and equipment being pushed along
the no-longer-quiet corridors. The baby in her arms was shuddering from the force of her own cries, and call lights went on
outside one room after another as patients woke and wondered what all the commotion was about.

Mary stood outside the delivery room long enough to direct
the doctors and others arriving with more blood and a respi-
rator, then hurried the baby into the newborn nursery and laid
it on a changing table to at last peel away the wet, stained
blanket.

A girl, a beautiful baby girl. Mary's eyes filled with tears as
it occurred to her that she'd never even asked Dolly whether she
wanted a girl or a boy. Most likely she would have said either
one, that all she wanted was to keep her baby no matter what.

Using tepid water and baby oil, she cleaned the tiny infant
and from long practice went about the routine of weighing and
measuring her. The baby cried harder than ever when the silver nitrate drops were put in her eyes, but Mary just kept right
on talking to her in the low voice that always worked with her

own babies. As she powdered her and dressed her in a warm flannel nightgown, she couldn't help thinking of how often she'd done this with her own babies, and of the baby inside her.

Gradually the infant's sobs eased until, by the time Mary lay her on her side in one of the newborn cribs, she wasn't crying at all. She wedged a rolled up blanket behind the baby for support and rubbed her back, marveling at how quickly her breathing became smooth and regular. All this time her eyes had been squeezed tightly shut. Now, as she relaxed, the wrinkles at their corners disappeared and her tiny mouth puckered into an O, flexing in an instinctive rooting motion.

Soon she would wake up hungry and they would have to do something about it, thought Mary. But for now the little angel was exhausted enough to sleep peacefully, totally oblivious to the fact that in the next room the most important person in her world was fighting for her life.

The second she stepped from the nursery Mary knew Dolly's fight was over. The air was no longer charged and two of the interns who had responded to the code were heading toward the elevator, their pace slow, as if there was no longer any need to hurry. Florence sat at the desk, her head bent low. Mary knew she was crying. A few patients, dressed in robes and looking sleepy, huddled nearby, talking in hushed tones.

Mary stopped beside Florence. "She's gone?"

The older woman nodded, dabbing at her eyes with her handkerchief. "Yes." She made a clicking noise with her tongue. "She was such a pretty little thing, and so young. It's a sin."

All Mary could manage was a nod. Her head throbbed, and the tears she was fighting to hold back made her eyes feel like they were on fire.

"Her poor baby," Florence continued. "My heart goes out to her . . . and to her poor husband, too. Is he out in the waiting room?"

"No. She wasn't married."

Florence was a woman of granite principle. Her lips thinned in disapproval. "I see. Then I suppose we'll have to notify her family."

"I'm not sure she has . . . had any family. The only name she gave to admitting was a friend, her landlady, actually."

"Landlady?" Florence exclaimed. "Well, she can hardly be expected to take this baby. There must be someone closer to her."

Mary thought of James Terrell. "Well, there is—"

"No one."

She whirled around to find Dr. Lagasse behind her. For the briefest instant his dark eyes bored into Mary, chilling her. Then he shifted his gaze past her to Florence, his expression instantly becoming what you would expect from a doctor who had just lost a patient, grim and compassionate.

"I overheard your question about Miss Martin's family. I've been treating her throughout her pregnancy, and I know for a fact that she has no one. As a matter of fact she intended to give her baby up for adoption."

Mary gasped softly. Lagasse didn't even glance her way.

"It was the wisest course," he went on, "considering her unfortunate situation."

"Yes." Florence nodded. "So sad."

Mary couldn't help herself. "Her situation was that she made a mistake and got herself in trouble, but she wanted to keep her baby. She told me that."

"Really?" Lagasse's tone was polite, but clearly disbelieving. "Well, that's not what she told me. In fact I have the adoption papers right here, all signed. I witnessed the signing myself."

Mary watched, stunned, as he pulled the now familiar wrinkled papers from the pocket of the jacket slung over his arm and handed them to Florence.

"I know it's not usually handled this way, but the poor girl was so upset, kept telling me that she didn't want any loose ends. You will see to it that these forms are included in her chart and that the nun at the home is notified, won't you?"

"Of course, Doctor," Florence replied. "Right away." She smoothed the papers on the desk, shaking her head. "Maybe the poor woman could feel what was coming—I've heard it said that you do—and she wanted to be sure her baby would be in good hands."

Lagasse smiled, a small, regretful smile that turned Mary's stomach. "I'm sure that was it."

And Mary was sure that he was lying through his teeth. She didn't care about the nearly illegible signature scrawled on those papers, looking just like what you'd expect from someone in a great deal of pain. Of course Florence was swallowing his story and would no doubt reprimand her if she opened her mouth to say otherwise. It would be Mary's word against his, after all, and within the walls of this hospital a doctor's word was second only to God's.

Heartsick, Mary recalled her promise to Dolly. Not that she'd ever promised anything specific in so many words, but she had sensed what Dolly wanted and what she hadn't wanted. And she definitely hadn't wanted her baby to go to strangers, never even to know who her real mother and father were. Still, promise or not, there wasn't much Mary could do about it now.

She tried to put it from her mind, keeping herself busy until the first of the morning shift began to arrive. From the kitchenette across the hall came the aroma of coffee perking, and gradually the ward came alive with the routine sounds of bedpans clanging and the nurse's cart being wheeled along the corridor. As saddened as every nurse on the unit would be to hear of Dolly Martin's tragic death, that crisis was past. They had jobs to do, and around here the most important emergency was the one lurking right around the corner.

At last it was time to go home. Taking her coat and purse from the nurses' lounge, she paused by the window for her first glance at the snow that had fallen overnight. It blanketed everything, creating soft white sculptures that made it hard to tell exactly what was hidden underneath. In the distance a plow slowly cut a path across the parking lot. Out there, like in here, life went on. There ought to be some comfort in that, she thought, without finding any.

Life. Instinctively her hand went to her stomach but she stopped herself short of touching it. She thought instead of the kids. They would be getting up, seeing the snow and wanting to go out to play even before they had breakfast. She remembered that the zipper on Cliff's snowsuit was broken and that she'd wanted to fix it before going to work last night. Suddenly she was overcome with the feeling that everything was spinning out of control, that her world was coming apart just like Dolly's had, and that she had to get home to hold everything together.

As she hurried past the delivery room on her way out she purposely kept her eyes straight ahead, not wanting to think about Dolly, lying cold and still beneath a sheet in there. With the snow it would probably be hours before the undertaker came for her. As hard as she tried it was no use. She couldn't think of anything else, and with a sigh Mary gave in to the compulsion to peek into the newborn nursery and check on Dolly's baby for her. She found the baby still asleep, lying just the way she'd left her.

Mary touched her, lightly so she wouldn't wake, and the second she did, she knew there was no way she could just walk out of there and forget what she had seen. She'd never broken a promise in her life, and she wasn't going to start now. But it was more than that. Mary knew firsthand about orphanages and she knew that some family, any real family, was better than that. Sure, maybe this poor little angel would eventually be taken in by good folks who wanted her. But maybe she wouldn't. Mary wasn't willing to take that chance.

"It will be all right," she whispered to the baby, flushing as she remembered those were the same words she'd said to Dolly as they rushed her along the corridor. "I'll make it all right for you, little one. Somehow or other I will. I promise."

Not even pausing at the elevator, she headed straight for the stairs, taking them two at a time. When she reached the third floor she was out of breath, but it was from nerves, not from running. She caught Dr. Lagasse as he was leaving his office.

"Dr. Lagasse, may I speak with you for a minute?"

Looking not at all pleased to see her, he yanked the office door shut behind him, a clear signal that he didn't plan on giving her any longer than a minute.

"What is it?" he demanded, with no pretense of politeness now that they were alone. "If you've come to ask me to reconsider your request for an abortion, the answer is still the same as last night—"

"That's not it," she interrupted. "I've come to tell you that I . . . That I know Dolly Martin didn't sign those adoption papers."

His eyes narrowed to dark slits. He didn't look surprised or alarmed, she thought, but he wasn't dismissing her, either.

"And just how do you come by this knowledge?"

"She told me. We talked a lot last night and she told me she wanted to keep her baby no matter how hard things were for her."

"If that's so, then how do you suppose those papers got signed?"

Mary hesitated. "I don't know for sure. I guess someone else must have signed them."

"Forged them, you mean. You seem predisposed to making unfounded accusations, Nurse Saville. Are you by any chance accusing *me* of forging her signature?"

"I don't know anything about that, Dr. Lagasse," she said, her voice beginning to shake. "I only know that Dolly Martin didn't want her baby to be sent to the home, and she should at least get her last wish. I grew up in an orphanage," she said, racing desperately to say what she had to say before he cut her off. "My mother died when I was barely ten, and my father couldn't manage so he put all of us there. It's no place for a baby. A baby needs a real home, with a mother and a—"

"The mother of this baby is dead," he reminded her harshly.

"She still has a *father*. He has a duty to care for her now that her mother is gone."

"And how do you propose we track down this father? Especially if he's not willing to do his duty by her, which seems to be the case, or else he would have married her a long time ago. Hmm?" he prodded, his mouth twitching, as if amused by her stupidity.

Recalling the way he and James Terrell had been huddled together talking, she was sure it wouldn't do her much good to blurt out the obvious, that Terrell had to be the father of Dolly's baby.

"The Martin woman certainly never mentioned this man's name to me," he continued. "More than likely she wasn't even sure who he was herself. The woman was a cocktail waitress, you know."

The sly insinuation in his tone made Mary burn. "That doesn't change anything for that little baby downstairs," she said, finding it hard to keep the anger from her voice. "Even if the father's not man enough to come forward, there must be someone willing to make a home for Dolly's baby. Maybe she had a sister or brother that she never mentioned. Somebody. All I know is that with her signature on those papers no one will even bother looking for any real family."

"Which is exactly the way the Martin woman wanted it. Good day, Nurse Saville."

"Wait," she insisted.

He turned slowly.

"I . . . I think I should warn you that I plan to let someone know what went on last night, I mean how you tried to badger Dolly into signing those adoption papers and how she tried to tell you no, you and the man who came to see her," she added.

"What man is that?" he asked, the tight set of his jaw telling Mary he wasn't as unconcerned as he sounded.

"I don't know his name. But," she added pointedly, "I'm sure I could find out if I had to. He looked very familiar to me."

He stiffened. "And just who do you plan to tell all this to?"

Mary thought quickly. "My supervisor. Or maybe the hospital board. Or Sister Maura. Whoever will listen. I have to, because I know that Dolly didn't want her baby to go to the home. You know it, too."

"I know nothing of the sort. Which means that if you go ahead with this foolishness it will all boil down to a question of your word against mine. Without any concrete evidence to support your wild claim, whom do you suppose will be believed?"

Her word against his. Hadn't she known that all along?

"But it's wrong. What you've done is wrong."

"No. It would be wrong to create a stir that would call public attention to the fact that this baby is a bastard, perhaps ruining her chances for adoption by any decent family. Not to mention the fact that once your accusations are proven false I will do everything in my power to see that you never work in nursing again—in this hospital or any other. Is that really what you want?"

What Mary wanted at that moment was to run away, as fast and as far away as she could.

"Of course it's not what I want." Her voice cracked. She had to draw a deep breath before she could go on. "You know how badly I need this job."

He shrugged. "Well, I can't see how you could be kept on after causing a scandal of this sort. Better stop and think of the repercussions, Nurse Saville. And then consider that you were under tremendous strain working all alone last evening. It's easy to become confused under such circumstances, to misinterpret what a patient says or think you saw visitors when there weren't any. I understand that, and I am perfectly willing to forgive your impudence and forget this conversation ever took place."

Their talk had taken on the atmosphere of a nightmare. He was standing there telling her she was wrong while the hostility in his eyes and the tightness in his voice were unmistakable proof that she was right.

Mary shivered. "You want me to go along with what you did. To just close my eyes and let that poor baby be sent to an orphanage when—"

"What I want," he snapped, "is for you to mind your own business. If you do, then perhaps I can help you out of that mess you are in after all."

Mary's head jerked up, her eyes wide. Her mouth was so parched she swore she could hear her tongue scraping nervously across her dry lips. "You mean you'll . . . take care of what we discussed in your office?"

"I mean I'll get rid of the baby in your belly for you," he said with disdain. "That is what you want, isn't it?"

She shook her head. "I don't know. It's a sin."

He snickered. "Life's a sin, my dear woman. When you're given a chance to fight back you grab it. If you don't, if you insist on making an issue out of what you *think* happened last night, no good will come of it for anyone. Keep your mouth shut and everyone wins."

Mary could hardly think with the sudden pounding in her head. Is this how her fate was linked to Dolly's? If she somehow found the courage to speak up and tell the truth about what Dolly had wanted for her baby she would lose her job. If she kept quiet she would get her chance to make a better life for her own children. But what a price to pay. One sin on top of another.

"What's it going to be?" he snapped. "I don't have all day to stand here while you wrestle with your conscience. Face it, you really don't have any choice."

So what else was new? Without meaning to Mary shoved her hands deeper into her pockets, pulling her coat tightly across her stomach.

"How soon?" she asked softly. "How soon can you do it?"

FOUR

Kay Delaney Terrell wasn't drunk, but she was getting there. She really ought to know better than to guzzle champagne on an empty stomach, she thought, helping herself to another glass from the tray of a passing waiter.

Dinner had been a fiasco. Not the meal itself. Perish the thought. Her mother would never permit that. Marian Delaney was an exquisite hostess, and this evening's Silver Bells Ball was her biggest bash of the year.

Her mother had spent most of the day personally overseeing the decor of Delaney Place, the family home majestically situated atop a cliff overlooking the Atlantic Ocean. With its marble fireplaces and silk wall coverings, the rambling Victorian was one of the grandest of Watch Hill's renowned seaside "cottages" and the perfect setting for a woman with her mother's passion for throwing lavish parties.

For this evening Marian had chosen a color scheme of silver and white. With the dramatic exception of the fifteen-foot-high red poinsettia tree in the ballroom, everything was the color of snowflakes and starlight...tables draped in white lace, white candles in silver candelabra, centerpieces of white roses and baby's breath sprayed silver.

Her mother's gown was also white and she had strongly suggested that Kay follow suit. Instead, Kay had chosen to wear a strapless, ankle-length Dior gown of midnight blue velvet. She'd had her long blond hair pinned up for the occasion and threaded with silver ribbons that sparkled in the soft light.

The menu for the party had received the same scrupulous attention from the hostess. When Kay arrived a few minutes early, she'd found her mother in the kitchen, a white apron over her white silk moiré, checking to see that the borscht was properly seasoned, the lobster tails and the shrimp for the flambé thoroughly cleaned and the white chocolate and strawberry tortes precisely ten inches high.

As always at Delaney Place, the meal had been perfection. The reason Kay hadn't been able to swallow a bite of it was that smack dab in her line of vision, if she leaned forward and craned her neck to the left, that is, had been her husband, James, seated next to the Viscountess Olivia de Roussel.

It hadn't been planned that way, but then, what's a little thing like a seating plan to a viscountess? The woman, whom Kay had known and disliked when she was still just Livvy Peckham, had blithely rearranged place cards to suit herself and then proceeded to rub James's leg with her foot all through dinner. It had been nauseatingly obvious to Kay what the viscountess was up to. As obvious as the fact that her own darling James hadn't gone out of his way to discourage the little game. In her opinion there had been precious little conversation between him and his dinner companion and entirely too much eye contact. Not surprising, since James could say more to a woman with a look and a raised eyebrow than most men could armed with Shakespeare's sonnets.

Only her mother's aversion to public scenes had held Kay in her seat. Then, afterward, when Kay was about to confront James, he'd been called to the phone and had to leave the party to check on some emergency at the plant. Convenient, but not a reprieve by any means, thought Kay. She would deal with James later. And, in her own good time, with the viscountess, as well.

Perhaps, she mused, eyeing the other woman over the rim of her glass, she ought to sashay over there right now and do the poor thing a favor by pointing out that a feather-trimmed gown was a mistake on someone so thin, making her resemble nothing so much as a chicken.

"Care to share the joke?"

Kay turned to find Drew Goddard beside her.

"I'd better not," she demurred. "I'm sure no one but me would appreciate this particular one."

"Try me."

She shook her head, taking another sip of champagne.

"All right," said Drew, "if you won't share your joke, you can at least dance with me."

"Deal."

Drew smiled as Kay automatically handed him her empty glass to deal with, then led him across the crowded dance floor to a spot of her choosing. At twenty-two, he was seven years younger than Kay, the same age as her brother Ted, who had been his best friend since prep school. He took her into his arms carefully, but her dress was cut low in the back and there was no way he could prevent his hand from resting on her soft golden skin.

"So what do you hear from Ted these days?" he asked after they'd taken a few slow steps without exchanging a word. He'd have preferred to dance the whole number in silence, savoring the brush of her body against his and the scent of her, sweet and dark at once, like no other woman he'd ever known. Opportunities like this were rare, but manners dictated small talk.

"Hmm?" responded Kay, with a disheartening lack of attention. "Oh, Ted. He seems to be doing fine, although he's not allowed to write any specifics about where in Korea he is or what he's doing, only that he's still on special assignment. I have this awful image of him in a jungle foxhole somewhere."

Drew chuckled, taking advantage of her small shudder as an excuse to pull her a little closer. "Not likely, since he's in the Navy. But even if he was in a foxhole, I guarantee you he would greatly prefer it to being stuck in an office at Delaney Silver for the rest of his life."

"I know. I just wish my parents could accept that. They still haven't forgiven him for enlisting without so much as telling them he was considering it or asking anyone's advice."

"Ted's over twenty-one, Kay. He hardly needed their permission. Besides, he did ask someone's advice."

"Yours?"

"No," he said, recalling how uncharacteristically quiet and preoccupied Ted had been the last few times they were together. "Actually, he consulted your husband."

Kay appeared startled. "Ted discussed enlisting with James?"

Drew nodded. "He told me James was all in favor of the idea. And I think you know how much Ted has always looked up to James . . . his brother-in-law, the war hero."

"Yes, of course, I should have guessed." Her green eyes were thoughtful.

"I take it James never mentioned it to you," he remarked, wanting to underscore that point in her mind.

She shook her head, seemingly dismissing the matter with a delicate shrug. "With all the hoopla Ted's enlistment caused, James probably didn't want to be blamed for encouraging him."

"Cagey man, your husband. I guess it's a good thing he's around. With Ted out of the picture your father needs someone to groom to take over the company."

"Daddy doesn't see it that way. Both he and Mother are convinced Ted will come to his senses and return home the conquering hero to take the helm of Delaney Silver. The very thought of an outsider running it gives Daddy conniptions."

The fact that Charles and Marian considered their son-in-law an outsider didn't come as a surprise to Drew. Kay's brother was his closest friend, after all. He'd known from the start that her parents had vehemently opposed Kay's choice of a husband and had only given in when Kay made it clear she intended to marry him with or without their approval. That they had chosen to present a united front to the world, even providing James with a position at Delaney Silver, didn't change the fact that behind closed doors he would always be an outsider.

From a family with very similar traditions, Drew knew all about the importance of appearances and family loyalty. He also knew that Kay wouldn't have hinted at anything less than utter harmony tonight if the champagne hadn't loosened her tongue. Still he took perverse pleasure in any hints of discord, and so he continued the conversation.

"If your father has his heart set on a Delaney running the company, why doesn't he groom *you* for the job?" he asked.

Kay tipped her head to look at him. "Very funny."

"It wasn't meant to be," he told her honestly. "You're bright and talented, and you're a Delaney."

"In case you haven't noticed, I'm also a woman."

Drew longed to tell her exactly how much he'd noticed and for how long. Instead he shrugged and said, "It seems to me that could be an asset. Besides, I remember when you used to tease Ted that he'd never head Delaney Silver because you planned to beat him to it. At the time I thought you meant it."

Kay lowered her gaze till she was staring at his bow tie, her expression wistful. "At the time I thought I did, too."

"What happened?"

For a second she looked stricken by the question, and Drew would have given anything to take it back. Then came the familiar toss of her head and the smile that had bewitched him for years.

"James happened, of course. Ted might not have his eye on the president's chair, but my husband definitely does."

"And James is a man who always gets what he wants."

"He likes to win," she agreed. "And I like winners."

"It must be in the blood," replied Drew, deciding it was time to change the subject. He didn't need to hear how she felt about the man she'd married—it had been clear from the way her eyes sparked when he walked into the ballroom a moment ago. At her quizzical expression, he explained, "I meant that your father likes to win, too. He showed me the silver filigree panels he finally persuaded the Vatican to sell to him."

"Oh, yes. My great-grandfather designed those for the Pope's private railroad car, and Daddy's been trying to get them back for years."

"That's quite a collection of original Delaney silver he's put together."

Kay nodded. "His pride and joy. That's one reason tonight is especially important to him. It's his last chance to show it off before donating it to the museum in Providence."

"My hands-down favorite piece," Drew told her, purposely spinning her around to thwart her frequent glances in her husband's direction, "is the maharaja's bed."

Kay winced. "Oh, God, Drew, that's perfectly ghastly."

The bed, according to Charles Delaney, designed and commissioned by a maharaja in 1878, had required 639 pounds of silver. The bedposts were four life-size statues of nude women, each holding an ostrich feather, which together formed a canopy over whoever slept in it.

"Ghastly?" Drew's expression grew pensive. "I don't know about that. I picture that bed shrouded with miles of sheer netting, covered with something soft and furry... What kind of animals do they hunt in India?"

"I don't know. Only that it's not cows."

"Okay, llamas, then."

"I think llamas are from South America."

"Close enough. Covered with a nice llama spread and silk sheets spun by the maharaja's personal battalion of silkworms." He nodded, his thoughtful gaze holding hers. "Under the right circumstances sleeping in that bed could be a very memorable experience."

"Why, Drew, I had no idea you were such a romantic. Although," she added, tilting her head to study him in a way that made it hard for him to breathe, "you always have reminded me a little bit of Lord Byron, with this curly black hair," she said, running her fingers through it at the nape of his neck, "and those dark, brooding eyes. The wire glasses add an intellectual touch. And of course, as a kid you were a little . . . well, frail."

"Thanks."

"Don't sulk," she said. "Actually you've filled out very nicely."

"Thank you," he said again, this time with a smile. "I wasn't aware you had noticed." In a rush he added, "Or that you were so familiar with Lord Byron."

"I'm not really," she admitted. "I read a few of his poems for senior lit class, and his name always struck me as perfect for a dark, brooding poetic figure."

"Like me?"

"Exactly," she teased. "How did a dark brooding guy like you ever become such good friends with my little brother, anyway?"

Drew shrugged. "Opposites attract, I guess. And since sailing was about the only sport I was allowed to take part in back then, we were thrown together a lot."

"That's right, the Moses Brown sailing club. I remember watching your crew race along Narragansett Bay. I could always spot your boat because your black hair and Ted's blond hair would be flying in the breeze like flags."

"And I remember . . ."

Buoyed by the easy flow of conversation, he was about to tell her that he remembered seeing her there on shore looking like an angel in white shorts and sweater, her pale hair blowing around her head like a halo, and being so mesmerized he could barely work the ropes. But right then the music ended, and her gaze instantly slid past him. Even her smile grew distracted.

"Please excuse me, will you, Drew? I want to see how James made out with the problem at the plant." As she spoke her eyes remained fixed on James standing a short distance away, his head bent to listen to whatever Livvy de Roussel was saying.

Drew touched her arm lightly and she turned back, the smile she offered him bland compared to her impassioned expression when she looked at her husband. He cleared his throat and said, "You don't have any cause to worry, you know."

Kay's brows lifted. "I beg your pardon?"

"Livvy," he said. "A man would have to be a fool to think she's any match for you."

"I know that," she said, smiling that wonderful, wicked smile that had been the center of so many of his daydreams. "But just the same, you're a good kid for saying so. And thanks for the dance," she tossed over her shoulder, leaving Drew alone with absolutely the last words he wanted to hear from her.

You're a good kid. Suddenly the magic of the dance was gone and he felt fifteen years old again, all pimples and washboard ribs, tripping over his tongue every time Ted's sister walked into the room.

It wasn't her fault, of course, now or then. How could it be her fault that she wasn't merely beautiful, she was everything a woman ought to be, smart and funny and nice? That was what impressed him more than anything else. She didn't have to be nice. Because of her beauty and who she was people would flock to her anyway. Kay Delaney was, had always been, the most lovely woman he knew.

James Terrell watched his wife approach, aware that heads, especially male heads, turned as she passed. It didn't bother him. In fact, he enjoyed watching other men watch her. For the same reason, he supposed, that he liked racing his Jaguar around town; because he owned it and they didn't.

At the moment, that was about the only thing he was enjoying. He certainly didn't enjoy having Olivia de Roussel clutching at him and whining in his ear about her husband's lack of attention. Who could blame the poor bastard? And he didn't enjoy the gnawing feeling that had been in his gut ever since he'd left the hospital, as if he'd been sucker punched.

In a way he had been. Damn Dolly Martin. Leading him on, pretending to go along with what he wanted and taking his money right up until the last second. Of course, what he'd really wanted was to arrange a quick solution when she first came to him with the news that she was pregnant. She wouldn't hear of an abortion, however, so he had been forced to settle for her word that she would give the brat up for adoption as soon as it was born, he hoped to a family far away from Watch Hill and the Delaneys.

Now she was reneging, or was pretending to. He hoped it was simply a ploy to bleed more money out of him. It would be worth any amount to keep Kay and her parents from finding out about the baby. Any amount. That's why he'd told Lagasse to go ahead and make whatever deal necessary to get her signature on those adoption papers. It was in the doctor's hands now, and for the price he was being paid he damn well better pull it off.

James tensed as Kay drew close enough for him to see the anger in her eyes. She had been smoldering ever since dinner. At the time it had amused him to use Olivia to provoke her. Women were a lot like the brightly colored balls on a billiard table; they responded in an utterly predictable way to the strokes of a master. And he was a master. Since dinner, however, his mood had changed. Accepting that a scene was now inevitable, he decided to try to minimize the damage as much as possible by disentangling himself from Olivia and stepping forward to meet his wife.

"I was looking for you," he said.

Kay smiled. "Tell me another."

So much for diplomacy. "I need a drink."

She followed him to the bar, stood at his elbow while he downed most of a vodka tonic and waited for him to turn and face her before saying another word.

"It certainly didn't take you long to handle that big emergency at the plant."

"Are you timing me now?"

"Of course not. I was simply remarking that you're back sooner than I expected." After a short silence she said, "Well, aren't you going to tell me what happened?"

"It doesn't concern you."

"Really? Last time I checked, it was my name on the company letterhead."

"Last time I checked, your name was the same as mine."

She rolled her eyes while managing to keep up her smile for anyone who might be watching. "Here we go again."

"What's the matter?" he asked, laughing harshly as he tossed down what remained in his glass. "Don't you like being reminded that your last name is no longer Delaney? Maybe I should have taken your name when we got married. Maybe you would have liked that better.''

"*You* certainly would have. At least it would have made you legitimate.'' Instantly a look of regret flashed in her eyes. "James, I didn't mean that the way it sounded.''

"Didn't you? Well, I'll tell you something,'' he said, the liquor adding to the feeling of hot wires wrapped around his belly, "I'm damn sick of people who don't say what they mean and don't do what they say they'll do.''

"James, what are you talking about? What happened tonight?''

"Nothing." He shoved his glass toward the bartender for a refill. "It was a false alarm. Now you know. Happy?''

"They called you away from the party for no reason?''

"Not for no reason,'' he said, wishing she'd let it drop. "Some guy cut his finger, and the stupid night foreman thought he should report it. By the time I got there they'd already driven the guy to the emergency room.''

"Is he going to be all right?''

"Yeah, he's fine. If you don't believe me, why don't you call the hospital and check?''

"Of course I'm not going to check. I don't understand why you're acting this way.''

"Maybe because I'm tired and a little ticked off at being called out on some wild-goose chase and then grilled about it afterward.'' He emptied the glass again. "This party stinks. I'm going home.''

"Fine. Don't bother to wait up.''

She whirled and walked away. James knew that for his own sake he ought to go after her. Kay was a spoiled woman. The longer she stewed the harder he would have to work to get back in her good graces. Unfortunately, with everything else on his mind tonight, he didn't have the energy for her games.

Leaving the party without her had been an idle threat, but the more he thought about it, the better it sounded. After all, home was only a hundred yards away, in the renovated guest house that had been a wedding present from his in-laws. Maybe he would walk over and give Lagasse a call to see if he'd done what he was supposed to do. If he had, maybe James would feel more like indulging his wife's whims.

As James was heading for the door he was stopped by Clarke, the family's faithful butler.

"Mr. Terrell," he said without smiling. Clarke never smiled at James. "There's another phone call for you, sir."

"Who is it?" he demanded.

"The caller didn't identify himself."

Lagasse? wondered James. And if so, was he calling with good news or bad?

"Shall I say you're unavailable, sir?"

James shook his head, too preoccupied even for the usual fun of giving Clarke a hard time. "No, I'll take it in the den."

From across the ballroom Kay watched James hurry off, wondering where he was going this time and wondering what had happened to put him in such a black mood. As curious as she was, she knew better than to ask. When he was like this, James withdrew into himself, and no amount of talking or pleading could bring him out until he was ready.

It was too bad. Usually after an evening out, they made love for hours when they got home. Disappointed, Kay acknowledged that that was not going to happen tonight. Unlike Kay, who found comfort in making love when she was sad or after an argument, James only enjoyed sex when he was feeling good. It irked Kay that he only got around to her when everything else in his life had been taken care of.

She was surprised when James entered the ballroom a moment later. So, he'd decided not to leave after all. Perhaps his mood was improving. There was one sure way to find out.

The uniformed guard posted outside the door to the reception room recognized Kay and nodded, standing aside as she swept past him. On display inside the room was well over a million dollars in silver works of art. The maharaja's bed caught her eye as soon as she walked in. It was hard to overlook. She smiled as she trailed her fingertip along the arc of one silver feather, wondering what on earth a llama bedspread would feel like, anyway.

Bending to reach under the headboard, she found the key on the music box concealed there. She had to hand it the maharaja, he'd thought of everything. Just as the first notes of the unfamiliar melody tinkled forth she felt a hand on her backside, moving in a slow, bold caress.

"Ah, so here you are."

The voice was deep and scarred by years of cigarette smoke. Kay didn't jump. She'd been expecting this voice, this touch.

Her tone was intentionally nonchalant. "Were you looking for me... again?"

"Wasn't that the whole point of disappearing? So that I'd come looking for you? Again."

At last she turned, meeting her husband's knowing smile with one of her own. "Yes," she admitted, "and it worked."

"Just like you knew it would."

"I wasn't sure," she lied. "I thought you might decide to go looking for the viscountess instead. You seemed to be having such fun with her earlier."

"The viscountess is a bore. And she has a bony ass," he added, cupping that same part of Kay's anatomy with both hands and grinning with approval as he yanked her hard against him.

"I knew that, but I wasn't sure you did. You appeared quite absorbed with her."

"Appeared being the operative word," countered James. He bent his head to play his lips along the side of her throat, biting at her earlobe. "Bear in mind that your father is counting on her husband to make a hefty contribution to the new museum wing."

"And you think he'll contribute if you flirt with his wife?"

"I think he'll contribute if she jerks his leash in that direction."

"The way I just jerked yours?" she asked, eyes innocently wide.

James's rough chuckle tickled her neck. "No. No, my spoiled brat, this is very, very different. You see, with us, while you might get to choose the game, I always decide how rough we play."

His fingers plunged into her hair and for about a half a second Kay considered how long it had taken Lucy, her hairdresser, to arrange it and how James, with his usual enthusiasm for things of this sort, would probably dismantle it in a fraction of the time. Then his lips pushed hers open and she stopped thinking about anything but the way he kissed. Hard and hot and wet, not like anything she'd ever felt with anyone else or ever seen in any movie.

"Right?" he asked, his mouth still on hers, his tongue still between her lips, for heaven's sake. How could he expect her to answer questions now?

"That's right, isn't it, Kat?" he prodded, using the name only he ever called her. Because, he said, her dark green eyes reminded him of a cat's. "When it comes to this, I call the shots. Right?"

"Mmm. Right."

"Good." His hands slid over her bare shoulders and dipped inside her dress in back. "Now that that's out of the way, there's something I'd really appreciate your doing for me."

"What's that?"

"Take off your dress."

"You're crazy."

"And you love it."

"Okay, I love it. But not enough to take off my dress in the middle of the biggest party my parents throw all year."

"Considering that we're not exactly in the middle of the party anymore," he reasoned, "there's no reason for you not to do this for me."

James came from the south, some hole-in-the-wall town—his words—outside Charleston that he didn't like to talk about. He'd left most of that world behind, but traces of it still lingered in his voice and at moments like this, the slow, rich cadence of it was like a drug she had never grown immune to.

"C'mon, Kat. Take it off for me."

"What happened to your bad mood?"

"I came to my senses."

"Just like that?"

"Just like that. Now take it off."

"Here?" she breathed, twisting with pleasure as his hands slid lower to stroke the backs of her thighs.

"Right here. Right now."

She shook her head, but she didn't actually say no. Why was it that no matter how wild, how outrageous he was, she could never actually say no to him?

"Anyone might walk in," she said instead.

"I'll lock the door."

He did. Turning back, he stood for a moment watching her, his shoulders resting on the solid oak door, hands hitched in the pockets of his black tuxedo trousers. He wore his dark brown hair combed straight back, but a clump at the front inevitably found its way forward. That, along with the dimple that slashed his left cheek when he smiled, was what had first caught Kay's eye.

He wasn't very handsome or very tall or muscular. What he was, she had determined long ago, was reckless. Looking into his golden brown eyes a woman, and probably most men as well, understood that here was a man who would do anything, risk anything, dare anything, if he wanted something or *someone* badly enough. What woman could resist being wanted that way?

Certainly not Kay. As he slowly made his way to her he loosened his bow tie with a lazy, utterly confident tug. Everything about him was loose, unhurried, everything but the look in his eye. The intensity burning there made her weak.

"Someone still might come along," she protested feebly as he reached around her for her zipper. "They'll find the door locked, with us in here, and they'll *know.*"

"Who cares?" he said, giving the zipper a sudden jerk so that her dress fell to her waist. The velvet bodice was lined so she hadn't needed to wear a bra. Now he stared at her naked breasts until the tips hardened before pressing his palms to them.

It had happened before like this, dozens of times since that first night in New York City, when with that same half smile and speculative look he'd dared her to walk out on her own twenty-first birthday dinner in the Waldorf's Wedgwood Room. They'd left a note with the maître d' to be delivered to the table where her parents and James's commanding officer were waiting for them to return from the dance floor so they could cut the cake.

Alone, they had walked for a while and then taken a ride through Central Park. In the back of the horse-drawn carriage she had let him unbutton her coat and blouse and had come alive to the feel of the cold February air and his warm rough hands on her skin.

It was always the same. First the dare. His black gaze asking if she had the guts to say to hell with everyone and do as she pleased. Followed by her breathless, heart-pounding rise to meet the challenge.

Of course, it had never before happened exactly like this, in her parents' house with over a hundred guests just down the hall. The added risk only heightened the excitement. James craved excitement, she knew. And, God help her, after years of doing what she was supposed to do, what she was expected to do, he'd taught her that she craved it, too.

"You taste like champagne," he whispered as he tumbled her onto her back on the maharaja's bed. He bent his head and flicked her nipple with his tongue and Kay arched off the antique silk coverlet that felt cool and smooth against her bare back. His chest, when she shoved his shirt up to drag her hands across it, was warm and rough.

James's hands raced over her body, pushing aside the barrier of gown and panties to drive her to the very edge of control and keep her there. She heard the rasp of his zipper and when he moved on top of her Kay felt his desire and lifted to meet it, so aroused that with his first deep thrust inside her she exploded with a rough gasp. Seconds later he collapsed on top of her, damp and panting. Then the weight lifted.

She groaned as he jumped to his feet, something he did with annoying frequency even when they had just finished making love in their own bed.

"I wish we could stay right here," she told him.

"So do I. But just think, the sooner we say our goodbyes, the sooner we can go home. Alone. Now up." He dragged her to her feet.

Quickly straightening his clothes, he helped with hers, spinning her around to get at the zipper. Kay felt like some floozy being hurried out of a room rented by the hour, and she didn't like it. Suddenly the one percent of her that wasn't absolutely sure of him took center stage.

"James," she said, twisting her head around to see his face. "I do love you."

"And I," he answered, punctuating it with a kiss between her shoulder blades, "love you. All set?"

On their way out he grabbed an unopen bottle of champagne from the bar.

"For later," he whispered to Kay. "Our own private celebration."

"Exactly what are we celebrating?" she asked, snuggling close to his side.

He thought a moment before breaking into a satisfied smile. "Happy endings," he said. "We're celebrating happy endings."

FIVE

Four days after she'd struck her unholy bargain with Dr. Lagasse, Mary took a bus across town to his office. Getting off in front of a corner drugstore a few blocks away, she checked her watch. He'd told her to be there at ten. That meant she had twenty minutes to do what she had to do.

As she stepped toward the drugstore entrance her fingers closed around the damp, balled-up handkerchief in her coat pocket. Only by biting hard on the inside of her lip did she manage not to need it for the time being. For days now her emotions had been so close to the surface it was hard to keep them in check at the best of moments. Sometimes when she got too buried in her own thoughts the pressure to scream became so overwhelming that she found herself looking around to see if people were staring at her, afraid maybe she really had screamed out loud.

At night she would wake in a panic for a reason she couldn't pinpoint. Gradually, as she came fully awake, she would remember. Then came the all too familiar feelings of guilt and regret and anger. She was angry with Rusty, with herself and life in general. And she was desperate.

She'd made up her mind once and for all on the long bus ride over here that if she ever wanted any peace at all, she had to do something to set things right for Dolly's poor little girl. And she was determined to go ahead and do it before she lost her nerve. She'd given her word to Dr. Lagasse that she wouldn't tell anyone connected with the hospital about what had happened that night, but she'd never said anything about telling someone *outside* the hospital.

She'd given this a lot of thought, going over in her mind how adamant Dolly had been about not wanting to give up her baby and about what a decent man the father was. Mary wasn't so sure she would describe James Terrell as decent, but Dolly had thought well of him and that's what counted. That, and of course the fact that he was the only blood relative that baby had.

He owed his daughter something, that was for sure, and if he wasn't man enough to come forward on his own, something would have to be done. That poor baby needed a home, a real home, and at least with James and Kay Terrell she would have that. You didn't get much fancier than Delaney Place, and maybe someday there would even be half brothers and sisters to keep her company. Mary knew for a fact that Kay Terrell wanted children, that she'd had at least two miscarriages, and in the end that's what made her decide that Mrs. Terrell was the one person she could go to. The one person who, if she knew the whole story, just might be able to rise above her husband's infidelity and be moved to help his poor, innocent baby. The problem was that Mary didn't have the courage to confront her face-to-face.

Inside the small drugstore she kept her head down, worried she might run into someone she knew and have to answer questions about what she was doing on this side of town. The drugstore's shelves were crammed with holiday decorations and gift sets of powder and cologne wrapped in bright red and green foil... reminders that Christmas was only three weeks away, which added to Mary's misery.

She paced the aisles quickly, searching for the stationery section. She needed only one sheet of writing paper and an envelope, but all they had were boxed sets, and the cheapest of those cost a dollar.

Anxious to get out of there as quickly as possible she grabbed the first Christmas card her hand fell on and hurried to pay for it. Too late she noticed the wreath and big red bow on the front and the message written in gold inside: Merry Christmas and Happy New Year. The message she had to deliver was anything but happy, but the card, already bought and paid for, would have to do.

Using a corner of the counter for support, she wrote as quickly as she could, expecting that any second the clerk who was glaring at her over the top of her half spectacles would tell her to go fill out her card somewhere else. It was just as well she had to hurry. If she'd had time she would have agonized over every word. This way she just wrote what came to her.

Dear Mrs. Terrell,

We've never met, but I'm a nurse on the obstetrics ward at Our Lady of Hope Hospital. I think you should know that last Friday night your husband came to the hospital to see a young woman....

Once she got going the words came easily. Too easily. Restricting herself to only a few words about how beautiful her husband's baby girl was, she hurriedly sealed the envelope and with a short prayer that she was doing the right thing, dropped it into the mailbox outside.

By nearly running all the way, she made it to Dr. Lagasse's office with a few minutes to spare.

His office was located in a brown house squeezed between a pair of three-story tenements. The place suited him, she decided. Like everything about him it was long and narrow; not ugly exactly, but unappealing. Stepping into the empty waiting room, Mary noticed Dr. Lagasse in the office beyond. He was standing with his back to her, shirtless except for a sleeveless undershirt. His head was bent, his arms cocked at a curious angle.

She cleared her throat. "Hello, Dr. Lagasse."

At the sound of her voice he jerked around, then halted abruptly, standing so his hands remained hidden from her view.

"I told you ten o'clock," he snapped, his expression making it clear that her efforts to be punctual were not appreciated.

"I know I'm a few minutes early," she said. "But this is the time the bus got me here. I couldn't very well ask my husband to drive me."

"Oh, all right, all right," he said. "Wait out there. I'll call you when I'm ready for you."

Still not facing her, he pushed the door shut.

Coming here alone had been scary; his angry reception had Mary cowering inside her old brown tweed coat. She hated him more than she could remember ever hating anyone. From the start he seemed to have gone out of his way to make this even more horrible than it was already. He was a doctor, for heaven's sake. He must know how hard this was for her, yet even this morning he offered no gentle word, no reassuring look.

Nervously she paced the waiting room, ignoring the straight-backed chairs lined up against the wall and the nicked maple coffee table with its neat pile of out of date magazines, and peered out the window. What was taking him so long? Belatedly it occurred to her to wonder why he'd been standing there in only an undershirt when she walked in and why he'd reacted so guiltily. Maybe he'd come straight from a messy delivery and was changing into a fresh shirt. Then again, maybe Mrs. Lagasse had put him out and he'd spent the night in the office. The possibility that he had problems of his own brought Mary a certain satisfaction. She only hoped that whatever they were, they didn't interfere with his work this morning. At the moment, he was her only hope.

Whatever was keeping him, Mary wished he would hurry up. She was so nervous she felt like a balloon that had been over-inflated and might explode any second. *One step at a time,* she reminded herself silently. That had become her creed: take it one step at a time, and you'll make it. But surely this step had to be the hardest one of all.

At last the office door opened and Dr. Lagasse appeared in the waiting room.

"You can come in now." Nodding toward the room at the very rear of the house, he added, "In there, all the way back."

Mary clutched the front edges of her coat to keep her hands from shaking as she walked where he directed. The fluorescent light overhead made the room unnaturally bright in spite of the fact that all the window shades were tightly drawn.

Another light, attached to a metal accordion bracket, hung on the wall above the gynecological examining table. A small round stool was positioned at one end of the table. Along the opposite wall stood a tall metal cabinet and a machine for sterilizing instruments. Not for the first time Mary reminded herself that she was lucky Dr. Lagasse was a qualified physician and not the sort of back-room butcher many women resorted to in her situation.

He instructed her to strip from her waist down without offering her a johnny or even a draw sheet to cover herself with. As she took off her skirt and underwear she glanced around, but didn't see any draw sheets and didn't dare to ask for one. Lying on the tissue-covered table, her feet obediently propped up in the metal stirrups, her face was so hot with embarrassment she felt as if it was on fire.

"Roll to your side facing the wall," he ordered, brandishing a hypodermic needle. "This will take the edge off the pain. I won't have you squirming around while I'm working."

He administered the shot, then left the room for a few minutes while it took effect. While he was gone Mary studied the other instruments arranged there. There was a stainless steel bowl, several curettes and a pair of polyps tongs. They were all familiar, things she'd handled many times. She knew that the technical name for the procedure he was about to perform was a D and C, dilation and curettage. It was treated as a routine matter in the hospital, but this time it wasn't routine. This time she was lying there, and the sight of those steel instruments made her tremble.

When he returned, Mary gathered all the courage she could muster and asked, "Will it hurt very much?"

"Of course it will hurt. But it will solve your problem. That's what you want, isn't it?"

She nodded. "Yes, it's what I want," she said, thinking that she had never wanted anything more or, perversely, less, in her whole life. She closed her eyes then and kept them closed until she heard him toss the curette into the steel bowl and peel off his rubber gloves. She knew then that it was finally over.

It had taken thirty minutes, and in spite of the shot he had given her, the pain from the cramps that had started almost immediately had been excruciating. Throughout she kept telling herself what she always told her patients, that her tension was only making it worse, but she couldn't relax. Her fingers gripped the sides of the table so tightly the metal edges left deep indentions in her skin. Not caring if it was adding blasphemy to all her other sins, she did what she had done at moments like this since she was a little girl and had been frightened to walk home from school because of the unleashed German shepherd down the street. She recited the Hail Mary to herself, over and over again.

"Finished," was all Dr. Lagasse said at the end, standing and carrying the bowl into the adjacent bathroom to empty it. He called out to her, "There are pads on the bottom shelf of the table. You'll need them. The bleeding may last up to a week."

Mary scrambled to get into her clothes while he was out of the room, but with the sound of the toilet flushing came the full realization of what she had done, and with it such a flood of tears it was impossible to see what she was doing. She was fumbling with the button on the waistband of her skirt when he returned. Her legs were still bare, but she shoved her feet into her boots anyway. She'd rather freeze on the way home than struggle to get her stockings on straight with him standing right there.

At the moment he had his back to her, loading the used instruments in the sterilizer and turning it on. Mary hastily dabbed at her eyes with her balled-up stockings, then stuffed them into her purse. As she bent over to pick up her coat from the chair where she'd left it she felt suddenly woozy and grabbed the back of the chair to steady herself.

The sterilizer hummed loudly, and when she heard Dr. Lagasse say something from behind her, she was certain she had misunderstood. As soon as she felt steady enough, she turned to him.

"I'm sorry, Doctor, I didn't hear what you said."

"I said my fee is one hundred and fifty dollars."

She *had* heard correctly. If the bottom of everything hadn't already been cut away from her it would have fallen then. "But... that can't be. We had a bargain."

"A bargain?" A faint smirk shaped his mouth, but his eyes were cold, narrowed as if he hadn't the slightest idea what she was talking about. "What possible sort of bargain could I have made with you?"

"That you would help me, and..." She fought a rush of guilt recalling her stop on the way here. He would find out about that soon enough. "And that I wouldn't report to my supervisor what happened the other night."

At that, even his smirk disappeared. "What you *think* happened the other night."

"No, I know what I saw."

"Really, madam, I have no intention of standing here discussing your absurd accusations. One hundred and fifty dollars, please."

"But I don't have that kind of money. I certainly don't have it with me."

"Well, I can hardly be expected to send a bill for this sort of service, can I? And you're getting a bargain as it is. Anyone else would charge twice that, or more. I'm extending you a professional courtesy."

Mary longed to tell him that there was nothing the least bit courteous or professional about his actions, but years of training forbade her from saying such a thing to a doctor.

"I'm not sure how much cash I have on me," she said instead, certain only that it was nowhere near one hundred and fifty dollars. From behind the lining of her worn billfold she extracted forty-one dollars, money saved a quarter or fifty cents at a time to buy Christmas presents for the boys. She had another eighty-seven cents in loose change and six dollars tucked away in an envelope marked Groceries that was supposed to last until the end of the week. Aside from the twenty or so dollars in her college fund, it was all the money she had in the world. She held the bills out to him.

"Here, this is forty-seven dollars. I can send you twenty more first thing tomorrow and pay you the rest a little out of each check."

"Pay me a little out of each check?"

"Yes." Mary nodded, the woozy feeling growing worse. "Or something."

Closing her eyes, she struggled to hold the queasiness at bay. She opened them to find him regarding her in a new, blatantly assessing manner. His eyes were no color at all, she noted, unable to stop staring into them. Yet they glittered in a way that sent a strange sensation through her.

"Maybe we can strike a bargain after all." His tone was slow and deliberate. "Now that I think about it, forty-seven dollars may be just enough." He moved closer as he spoke. When he reached out and touched her hair, Mary felt even sicker. Shivers danced along her spine.

"You're a pretty little thing in your own way. Such a pretty mouth. Maybe I can teach you a trick or two." Unbelievably his hand dropped to his zipper. Mary was afraid to look down, but there was no mistaking the metallic hiss it made as he lowered it, or his intention as he fumbled with his clothes. "I'll show you a way you can please your husband without getting yourself in a jam like this one all over again." His fingers slithered through her hair, pushing her head down. "Come here."

The top of Mary's head brushed his chest before she completely understood what it was he intended for her to do. Horrified, she stiffened and twisted to free herself from the painful pressure of his hand. "No, stop. What kind of a pig are you?"

She tried to move away from him but the examining table was a solid barrier behind her. To her right was the smaller metal table, blocking that route, and if anything, although he had released her, he had come even closer in response to her outraged protest. There was nowhere to go.

"How dare you call me a pig?" he asked, sneering. "It seems to me you're the one who fits that description, behaving no better than an animal, breeding like a damn rabbit, having to impose on an honest person's kindheartedness to get you out of trouble."

"Honest?" gasped Mary.

His insults shamed her, but miraculously that feeling took a back seat to the anger she felt at hearing him describe himself as honest and kind. It was as if all the rage that had been building and simmering within her had finally found its proper target. "You *are* a pig. You're disgusting, not even human. You think you're so high-and-mighty, as if you have a right to order other people around and control their lives just to get what you want. But you don't. You can't." She was panting between words, out of breath from the sheer force of her anger. "It's wrong, and you deserve whatever happens to you."

"And what do you deserve? Do you fancy yourself an innocent in all of this? Do I need to remind you that abortion is against the law?"

Mary shook her head, her chin held high. "No. I know I'm not innocent. I deserve whatever happens just like you do. But that baby in the hospital *is* innocent, and at least I fixed it so now she might have a chance."

His twisted smile faded. The contempt in his eyes slowly gave way to suspicion. "What are you ranting about now, woman? I told you . . ."

"And I told you that I know what I saw. I know you tried to bully Dolly Martin into giving up her baby and when she refused you forged her signature on those papers. And I know that James Terrell was the man who came to see her that night. He's the father of that baby. I know it, and I couldn't live with myself if I didn't say something or do something to help her."

He grasped her shoulders so tightly Mary could feel each separate point of pain. "Shut up, do you hear me? You're not going to say anything to anyone. I won't allow you—"

"I have. You can't stop me because I already have. And I'm glad I did because now you'll have to— Let go of me!"

"Who?" he shouted, tightening his hold. "Who did you tell?"

"His wife, that's who. Mrs. Terrell."

Mary spat the words at him. Tears ran from her eyes, partly because he was hurting her and partly because of the sudden sense of freedom rushing through her. For the first time in days she felt something besides frightened and guilty. She felt as if she was striking back.

"I wrote her a letter and told her everything that happened, then I mailed it before I could change my mind. There's nothing you can do about it now. They'll take a closer look at those papers and they'll question Mr. Terrell and the truth will come out. They'll have to believe me. You'll see."

"You fool, what have you done?" For a few seconds he stared at her, his eyes no longer colorless, but black and burning with an emotion beyond anger.

Mary's burst of spirit played out and she became afraid of what he might do to her. As soon as she made a move to free herself, though, he dug his fingers into her once more, shaking her roughly. "Fool, little fool, you've ruined everything. All of it. What right do the likes of you have to interfere with me? Fool."

Mary was too weak to resist. She felt feverish all over, but she couldn't stop shivering. Down low in her stomach the cramps were so bad she wanted to bend over and clutch her middle to hold herself together. All she knew was that she had to get away from him, and yet, if he let her go now, she was afraid she would collapse. "Please, you have to stop...."

Please, she pleaded again, but this time no sound came from her throat. There were only his grunts and mutterings.

Suddenly the room began to turn dark around the edges, like a photograph tossed into a fire. Then, just as suddenly, she was free. His hands fell away, releasing her so abruptly she struggled for balance. Seconds passed before she realized that he hadn't let her go willingly, but was himself falling, clutching at his shirtfront.

Mary knew instantly that he was having a heart attack. Yet instead of plunging into action as she'd been trained to do, she froze.

Somewhere deep in her subconscious a rapid-fire string of images was recorded that would be with her forever after. A bone-chilling gasp from low in his chest. His open mouth, red and slack against his too-white face. His eyes bright and hollow. The expression in them changed as quickly as the flickering scenes in a cartoon, from anger to confusion, then panic, disbelief, accusation.

Or did it happen so quickly he never knew what hit him and she just imagined all that? She didn't, however, imagine the crushing weight of him as he collapsed against her and slowly sank to the floor at her feet. For the life of her, Mary could think of nothing but the scene in *The Wizard of Oz* when the wicked witch melts into oblivion.

Dr. Lagasse didn't melt, however. He lay facedown on the gray linoleum in front of her, a widening puddle of blood oozing from the place where his head struck the floor. Mary stared at the blood, feeling numb and trying to think what to do next. Call an ambulance? Automatically she bent and felt for his pulse, but she knew even before checking that he was already dead.

The tiny room suddenly seemed unbearably noisy. The sterilizer was still humming. But she finally realized it was her own moaning she heard, as harsh and droning as an airplane flying low overhead, circling endlessly. Pushing to get past the moans were screams, and Mary quickly pressed her knuckles to her lips to silence herself. It wasn't the first time she'd witnessed a death, but it was the first time it had happened so violently, the first time she had just stood by, frozen and useless, and watched it happen.

What now? What now? Drawing a deep breath she told herself she had to move, do something. She couldn't go on standing there like a statue forever. She had to get out of there. If anyone found her there... She bit her lips, tasting blood.

If she was found, there would be all sorts of questions. And she would have to answer them, explain why she had gone there this morning, tell about the deal she had made with Dr. Lagasse. There would be talk. Rusty would find out, and the boys. Everyone would know what she had done, and no one would really know why. They would know what kind of woman she was, someone who would agree to a lie in order to get what she wanted. She whimpered softly. Oh, God, she couldn't think about that now. She had to get out of there.... It was the only way.... No one must ever know she had been there this morning.

Carefully, still trembling, she stepped around him to get her coat. At the door she stopped and glanced around to make sure she hadn't forgotten anything that would connect her with this place or with Dr. Lagasse. Her gaze fell on the money. She couldn't recall which one of them had been holding it, or if maybe he had already placed it on the table before he came at her. Now it lay scattered around his body like some sort of obscene confetti.

Forty-seven dollars. Every instinct for survival urged Mary to pick it up, yet she stared at it, unable to move. The truth was that the money was no longer hers. No matter what had happened, no matter how despicable a man Paul Lagasse had been, he had performed a service for her and had demanded payment. She might be guilty of a lot of things, but stealing money from a dead man wasn't one of them.

Outside the clouds had lifted, leaving behind a brilliant winter sun that glared down on her like a spotlight as she hurried along the sidewalk, making her huddle guiltily behind the collar of her coat. The wind, which hadn't seemed nearly as strong earlier, lashed at her bare legs.

With each step the pain inside her grew stronger, her thoughts more confused. Each time her foot hit the pavement a thousand hot knives slashed between her legs. She wasn't going to make it. The world was pared down to the distance between her and the bus stop. All she could think about was sitting down before her stomach dropped onto the sidewalk. Images of the kids and Rusty flashed before her. God, she wanted to get home to them.

Finally she reached the corner and counted the telephone poles between her and the bus stop. Eight. She could do it. When at last she reached the stop she stood leaning against the last pole, nearly crying with relief when the bus rolled into sight. Hauling herself up the few steps, she collapsed into the first empty seat. It was almost over. She was going to make it home. No one ever had to know what she had done. Of course she knew and she would have to bear the guilt and shame, but she'd make sure her kids didn't suffer because of it. Dr. Lagasse was gone. Only she ever had to know the whole truth.

It wasn't until the bus was moving that she remembered the letter she'd written to Kay Terrell.

SIX

As the bus rolled along, oily-smelling gusts of hot air shot up from the heater beside Mary's feet, making her stomach reel.

To get home she had to take one bus into downtown Westerly and buy a transfer to take another out to Misquamicut, then walk the six blocks from the bus stop to Hazel Street. The town of Westerly was divided into small villages based on fire districts. Though some were little more than a crossroads, each village had its own unique personality. Nowhere was this more obvious than in Misquamicut and its neighbor along the coastline, Watch Hill.

Watch Hill was private beach clubs and old money; seaside Victorian cottages with servants' quarters and white-wickered verandas. Misquamicut was food stands along a public boardwalk, air heavy with the odor of fried food and cotton candy; it was tattoo parlors and Madam Michele, who for a dollar would tell your fortune behind the purple silk curtain of her beachfront shack—and who would for five dollars do considerably more. Misquamicut was Mary; Watch Hill was Kay Terrell.

Mary couldn't stop thinking about the letter. Just a few hours ago it had seemed the right and noble thing to do. Now it seemed like the biggest mistake of her life.

She was going to have to tell Rusty, she decided. No matter how things stood between them, he was still her husband. But she sure wasn't looking forward to the discussion. She stared out the grimy window at the dirt-streaked snow piled along the roadside and wished, among a host of other things, that she was going home to someone else. Someone like Ozzie Nelson, she thought, knowing it was ridiculous to be fantasizing about a television actor when her world was crumbling around her.

Still, that was what she wished. She wished Rusty would listen to her the way Ozzie listened to Harriet, and smile that gentle smile and tell her he understood and that no matter how bad things got they would make it because they were a family. Even Ricky Ricardo, after throwing a fit, always took Lucy in his arms in the end. She wished she was going home to Ozzie Nelson or Ricky Ricardo, but even more than that, she wished she was going home to the Rusty she had married.

For at least the thousandth time since his accident she thought about how different everything would be if only Rusty hadn't been the one working on that car when its engine exploded, if he still had two good hands, and if Tony, Rusty's old boss down at the station, still smiled whenever he saw her and told her she was married to the best mechanic he'd ever come across.

Things might be different in spite of the accident if they hadn't had the kids—or at least not so many so fast. Sometimes she thought that maybe if they'd talked more after it happened, talked the way they used to a long time ago, Rusty would have gotten over it better. But who had time to talk? When she wasn't at work or doing things around the house she was so tired she couldn't keep her eyes open, let alone hold a conversation. The trouble was she'd been too busy tending to the needs of her real babies to cater to his.

Mary was suddenly stuck by an absurd image of their life together, with her paddling ferociously to keep herself and her four little chicks above water, while Rusty drifted along behind, searching for someone or something to blame for each small squall that came their way. This time, however, the trouble was no squall, but rather a full-blown hurricane, and she knew exactly who he was going to blame.

It was after noon by the time she got home. As she dragged herself the last block she quit wishing for Ozzie Nelson and simply wished that Rusty had already fixed lunch for the children so she wouldn't have to. Frightened, exhausted, aching right down to the frozen tips of her toes, she pushed open the back door and her heart sank at the sight of the breakfast dishes still piled in the sink where she had left them.

Cliff was at school, but Greg and Joey came running at the sound of her footsteps. For their sake she did her best to hide what she was feeling. Somehow she managed to fix a smile on her face and get them and the baby fed and tucked in for afternoon naps. She longed for a nap, but that would have to wait. She'd become a master of suppressing her own wants and needs, and that's what she did now. Now that she'd made up her mind to tell Rusty, she wanted to get it over with.

As she struggled to find the right words she automatically went about making him a cheese sandwich, cutting it into triangles and placing two pickle slices on the plate beside it just like every other day. She poured him a glass of beer from the open quart in the refrigerator, just like always. She couldn't seem to stop going through the motions.

Finally, when there was nothing left to do she sat down across from him and cleared her throat. "Rusty, I didn't go to the hospital this morning like I said I was going to. I went somewhere else, to see a doctor..."

"Why?" he asked with his mouth full. "You sick or something?"

"No. It's worse than that."

Everything came tumbling out. Once Rusty realized this wasn't the usual lecture about finding a job or fixing the screen door he started listening more closely. As what she was saying began to sink in, he pushed aside his half-eaten sandwich and his beer and listened intently.

His usually ruddy face paled as he took it all in, looking even whiter next to his thick hair, which through the years had darkened from the red that gave him his nickname to the deep russet of autumn leaves. Again and again he stuck his fingers inside the collar of his blue plaid flannel shirt as if to loosen it, the way he always did on Sundays when he had to wear a tie to Mass.

As she spoke the tears finally rolled from her eyes. She wiped them with the handkerchief she was clutching until that was as wet as her face and then just gave up and talked around her sobs.

"God, Mary," he said when she was through. "God."

He looked away from her, scrubbing his face with his palm as if he could wipe away what he'd just heard. Getting to his feet he crossed to the refrigerator, his steps heavy in his old tan work boots. With his good left arm he took the open bottle of beer from the refrigerator, then stood with it forgotten in his hand, the refrigerator door ajar. Instinctively Mary opened her mouth to tell him to shut it before all the cold air got out, but she lost heart before the words even formed.

Finally shutting it on his own, he moved to lean against the sink, facing her but staring at the spot between his feet where her hours of standing and washing dishes had worn an ugly black patch in the linoleum.

"What are we going to do?" she asked.

"What are we going to do?" He shook his head and repeated it again. "What are we going to do?"

His voice startled Mary, and she realized she hadn't really been asking him, just asking.

"I thought," she began, "that we should make some plans. You know, in case anyone saw me there today and mentions it to the police.... I think they'll look into this, don't you? With all that money laying around and the table he tipped over. Oh, I don't know...." She knotted her hands on the table in front of her. "Maybe I ought to just call the police and have it over with."

Rusty was shaking his head, an odd, almost bewildered expression on his face. Mary left her chair as he came at her, not knowing what to expect from him, but all he did was grab her by the elbow, tight, but not so tight he hurt her. He was much taller than she was, and until Mary tilted her head all she could see was his flannel-covered chest.

"Do you know what you've done?" he asked, his soft tone catching her by surprise, confusing her.

"I know. I know it's real bad, Rusty. Oh, God, he's dead, a man is dead, and I was fighting with him when it happened. They might think it's all my fault. Maybe in a way it is."

"No." He shook his head again. His breath was dragging in and out and his eyes were narrowed to such slits Mary could barely make out a tinge of blue between his dark lashes. "No. That wasn't your fault...."

"Oh, I know it was an accident," she interrupted. "But I'm a trained nurse. I should—"

"No." He gripped her harder, but his voice remained low, weary almost, as if even shouting was beyond him. "Forget it. I don't give a damn what happened to him." His eyes widened so that she could see the familiar deep blue, glistening brightly, and the pain. "Mary, you killed our baby."

Before she had fully comprehended that he wasn't going to lash out at her, that what he was feeling wasn't anger, but grief, he had let her go. Turning away he stumbled on the leg of a chair that stood between him and the back door.

"I got to get out of here," he said, without looking at her.

The door slammed behind him so hard the venetian blind hanging on the window came loose at the bottom. For several seconds after he left it rattled against the glass. Mary automatically walked over and stilled it so that the noise wouldn't wake the children. She stood looking at the closed door, past tears now.

She thought about how things had happened one after the other to get her where she was now and found herself remembering how when she and Rusty were dating they used to drive to that little lake up north. He would stand on the bank and skip stones into the water in just such a way that they made rings on the still surface, each ring bigger than the last. That's what this was like. If Dolly hadn't died, none of this would have happened.

Dr. Lagasse never would have changed his mind about doing the abortion, and she never would have written that letter to Kay Terrell. She wouldn't have had any reason to go to his office and never would have struggled with him. He would still be alive. And she would be standing here now still pregnant with Rusty's baby.

But it had happened. Rusty's quiet words thundered inside her. *You killed our baby.* For the first time in her life, Mary fully comprehended what the word *final* meant. This was final. No matter what she said or did or how many babies she might yet have, this one was gone forever.

The ache that shot through her was sharper and more wrenching than anything Lagasse had done to her. It was total, suffocating, imbedding itself in places deeper inside her than she had known existed. Was this why she had been so obsessed with Dolly's baby these past days, she wondered, to keep from thinking of her own in any real way? Had she somehow instinctively known that if she thought about it, about the reality of it, she wouldn't have been able to go through with it? How could she bear never seeing or touching that baby? Her baby? Never holding it in her arms and smelling that sweet, soft baby smell that Ben was already losing.

You killed our baby.

Suddenly just standing demanded more strength than she had. Leaving the dishes in the sink, she made her way to the bedroom and collapsed on the bed. She tried to think about Dr. Lagasse, about how long it would be before he was found lying there. Please, God, she thought, don't let his wife be the one to go looking for him. Mary tried to pray for him, but in her head the words kept getting tangled up with the sound of the toilet flushing after he'd carried that metal basin into the bathroom and with the look on Rusty's face as he walked out.

It wasn't a familiar look. It wasn't the way he used to look before the accident, sort of brazen and sure of himself. Sure in a good way, a way that made you think, yes, this man really can do whatever he sets his mind to. But it wasn't the way he usually looked lately, either, angry and sullen. He'd looked...*lost*, she decided, and at last she slept.

She stirred once, when the boys woke from their naps and came running down the stairs. She called to them, opening her eyes just enough to ask them to please let Mommy rest a few minutes longer because she wasn't feeling well and to please, please not wake up Ben. They nodded, looking vaguely confused to find her in bed in the middle of the day and at the same time intrigued by the prospect of playing unsupervised.

It was risky, Mary knew. She thought of all the things they could get into and started to lift her head off the pillow. When she did, pain waved through her, forcing her flat on her back again. She curled into it, squeezing her eyes shut until everything went black and numb.

When she woke the next time it was to a quiet clattering sound by the bed. The room was dark, the only light a yellow wedge at the doorway, which came from the living room lamp. It was night. My God, she thought, struggling to get up, the kids, dinner, the baby...

Her legs got caught in something and she realized that someone had covered her with a blanket while she slept. She became aware of a shadow moving beside her.

"Rusty?"

"Shh."

Her eyes focused enough for her to see him turn on the nightstand lamp. She immediately looked at the alarm clock beside it.

"Six-thirty. Oh, my gosh, I can't believe I slept so long. The kids must be starving. Cliff... Did Cliff get home from school all right? Where's Ben? And—"

"Shh," Rusty said again. Laying his hand on her shoulder, he gently held her in the bed. "Stay right where you are."

"But I have to feed the kids."

"I already fed them."

She stopped struggling to get up and looked at him. "You fed them?"

He nodded. "It was just soup. But I toasted some bread to make croutons for them like you do. Joey doesn't like alphabet soup," he added.

"No. Only chicken noodle."

"I made him a peanut butter and jelly sandwich. Now they're watching television."

"What about Ben?"

"He's in the playpen and he's already changed for bed so there's nothing you have to do except lay right where you are and get your strength back." He gestured toward the nightstand. "I brought you a bowl of soup and a cup of tea. I thought you might be hungry and, well, you were so still I needed to come in and make sure you were all right."

"I'm all right. Some tea would taste good," she said, trying to come to grips with the strange way he was treating her as she shimmied up against the headboard. Rusty reached across her for the pillow from his side of the bed and tucked that behind her, as well, before handing her the cup of tea.

Taking the cup and saucer from him, Mary froze with it in her hands, looking from it to Rusty, not understanding at all. The cup he'd used for her tea was one of a set of six his aunt Bessie had given them as a wedding present. It was fine white china edged with gold and decorated with roses. The cups and saucers were the only truly fine things they owned, Mary's pride and joy. She used to serve morning coffee in them on their anniversary, but for the past few years they hadn't left the top shelf of the china cabinet.

"Rusty? Why?"

"I know how you like pretty things and all and I thought that besides the soup and tea maybe you could use some cheering up, too," he said, his deep voice rough, as if something were caught in his throat.

Cheering up? Mary winced as she put the cup aside. "Oh, Rusty, I don't deserve cheering up."

"Well, you sure as hell don't deserve what you got. A no-good loser like me for a husband and more kids than you know what to do with, so many you—" He broke off, turning away.

"Rusty, I love the kids. They're my whole life."

"I know that, Mary," he said, still facing the wall. "That's how I know how bad things must have seemed to you for you to...to..."

He spun around, going down on his knees next to the bed. Rusty was a big man, and strong. Mary had seen him push a stalled car six blocks all by himself. She'd seen him hurl a beer bottle against the wall in anger and she'd seen him smile at her in a slow, teasing way that made her all tingly inside, but in all the years she'd known him she had never seen him cry.

The sight of his head bent, his broad shoulders shaking, brought on an emotional earthquake. It shattered the wall she'd spent years building to keep from being hurt by him, and all at once the love that had always been in her came rushing like a spring river. It shook her voice as she whispered, "Oh, Rusty..."

He lifted himself up to sit on the edge of the bed, his stiff and scarred right arm clumsy as he tried to hold her, getting her and the blanket and the pillow and drawing them all against him. His head fell to her shoulder and his words were muffled against her throat.

"What, Rusty? What did you say?"

He lifted his head. His cheeks were wet, his eyes still brimming with tears, but he met her gaze without trying to hide them.

"I said I'm sorry."

"You? I'm the one who—"

"No." Fingers to her lips, he silenced her. "No, I'm the one who caused all this, Mary. I'm the one who drove you to do what you did with the way I've been acting, not being any help and all, and I'm the one who has to take responsibility for what's happened. No, please, Mary," he said when she tried to protest. "Let me talk. I did a lot of walking and thinking this afternoon. Let me say what I have to say, then it will be your turn."

She nodded, watching the cords in his throat flex as he struggled for the words he wanted.

"After the accident," he said finally, "I felt like it was all over for me. Engines are about all I know and nobody wants a mechanic with only one good arm. I had such plans for us, Mary, and just like that, it was all over. I kept thinking, why me? It was so unfair. I wanted to get back at the world, and at myself for screwing everything up. Instead the only one I really hurt was you. You and the boys.

"It's not like I didn't know things weren't right," he went on. "All along I knew. Sometimes I'd even try and make a fresh start. Like the time I got that job at the lace factory. I'd swear that this was it, no more drinking, and I'd think about how I could start to make things better for us, make things the way they used to be, you know?"

Mary nodded. She knew. The memory of how things used to be was what got her through the worst times.

"Then the job wouldn't work out again, and I'd be right back where I was, hating myself and everybody else."

"Hating me, too, Rusty?"

"No," he said emphatically. "Never you, Mary. I love you. I've always loved you, but somehow that got lost in everything bad that I was feeling. I can see that now. I can see how bad I let it get for you to decide it was better not to bring our baby into the world with me for a father."

"Rusty, please . . ."

"It's all right. I know what I've done, just like you do. We're both going to have to live with that. That doesn't mean we can't change things from now on. You and the kids are the only good thing in my life, Mary, and I almost destroyed it." He swallowed hard. "Maybe I did destroy it. I guess that's for you to say."

"I don't know," Mary replied. "I don't know what's going to happen when they find Dr. Lagasse's body and when Kay Terrell gets that letter. It connects me to him, to the whole sorry affair. How will I . . ."

"Shh," he admonished. "I'm not talking about that. Whatever happens we'll get through it. I'm talking about you and me, Mary." Unconsciously he touched his damaged arm. "I can't ever be the man I was, the man you married, but I know I can be a better man than I've been. A better husband and a better father. I want to be, if you'll stand by me."

"Oh, Rusty, can't you see it's you who'll be standing by me after all that's happened?"

"That's what I want to do, Mary, if you'll let me. Will you give me a second chance?"

Under his pleading gaze the weight in her stomach lightened, just a little, but it was enough to permit her to smile.

"I will, of course, I will," she said, clinging to him, thinking that it was really a second chance for both of them. Then reality intruded. "But what about the rest of it?"

"Lagasse had a heart attack, period. That had nothing to do with you."

"I was there. We fought."

"It was an accident," he insisted, a trace of the old confidence in his voice. "If it comes to it, that's what we'll tell them."

"What do you mean, if it comes to it?"

"I thought about this, too, Mary, and I think if they don't ask, we shouldn't tell them anything. You said you cleaned that place up real good, right?"

She nodded.

"Then maybe no one ever has to know what really happened. Think about it, Mary, what good would it do? It won't bring Lagasse back. Think what it would do to the kids . . . and to you."

"But what about the letter? As soon as the police see that letter, they're bound to come around asking me all sorts of questions."

"Maybe. And maybe they won't ever see that letter. Whatever Kay Terrell decides to do about the baby, I don't think a lady like her will want to make public a letter telling how her husband was shacking up with someone else."

"Of course, you're right." Mary breathed with her first twinge of real hope.

"And don't forget, that letter is just your say-so. It's no real proof of anything. It would be the easiest thing in the world for her to just rip it up and throw it in the trash."

"Even after she hears about Dr. Lagasse? I said right in the letter that he was involved, and now he turns up dead, with his office all topsy-turvy. She'll have to tell the police about the letter then."

"She might, and she might not. Rich folks are different from us, Mary. They play by different rules. We just have to wait and see what happens."

"Rusty, I don't know . . . I'm so scared."

"I know. I'm scared, too." His smile was forced, but at least it was there. Familiar, more precious to her right then than the fortune they used to dream about. "But you know what, Mary?

As bad as things are right now, I feel better than I have in a long, long time. I don't feel alone anymore.''

She just looked at him, wondering if she should trust his sudden turnaround, deciding she didn't have any choice and didn't really want any.

"Me, either," she said at last, dropping her head to his shoulder. It fit perfectly into the crook of his neck, just like it always had. His skin was warm, his old shirt soft against her cheek, and beneath it his shoulder was solid, blessedly solid. "Me, either."

SEVEN

Ordinarily Marian Delaney received visitors in the sitting room off the front hallway, but today she asked Clarke to show the callers directly to the parlor, where she and Kay were putting the finishing touches on the family Christmas tree. A photographer from the Providence *Journal* was coming by in an hour to take photos for a feature story on local holiday traditions. It had long been a Delaney family tradition to trim the tree with white candles, red satin bows and the family's heirloom silver ornaments.

Each ornament was one of a kind, especially designed and created through the years by the artists at Delaney Silver. The photographer's phone call yesterday had forced Marian to get the tree up and decorated. Ordinarily it was already up by now, but she'd been delaying it in hopes that by some miracle Ted might surprise them by coming home in time to help.

Usually it was Ted, and not Kay, who volunteered for this job. In fact, this was the first year since he toddled that Marian was doing it without him. Last year, though already in the Navy, he had been attending Officers' Candidate School in Newport and was able to come home for Christmas. This year he was half a world away, she thought, holding in her hand the perfectly crafted sterling train that had been designed especially for his first Christmas. Along the side of the engine was engraved his name and the year, 1930.

She turned as she heard Clarke enter the parlor, the two navy officers following behind him. When Clarke first told her that Captain Ingraham and Lieutenant Fontaine from the base in Newport were here to see her, Marian had assumed their visit was connected with the Navy's Toys for Needy Children drive, of which she was honorary chairwoman. Now, as Clarke announced them, her eyes met Captain Ingraham's, and she knew instantly that was not the case. Maternal instinct? Sixth sense? It was as if her heart knew the truth even before it was spoken.

"Tell me," she demanded, not bothering with greetings. Her voice was very small in the big room.

"Mrs. Delaney, is your husband at home? If not, perhaps you would rather—"

"Tell me," she said again.

"I'm here about Edward."

"Ted," Marian murmured softly, squeezing her fingers around the tiny silver train.

"Ted," Captain Ingraham agreed with a nod, clearly ill-at-ease. "I'm sorry to have to inform you that Ted has been killed in the line of duty in Korea. You will, of course, be given a full report of the circumstances as soon as . . ."

Marian didn't hear whatever else he said. She did feel Kay rush to her side and grab her arm, crying out, "Oh, Mom, no, no," and it took Marian a few seconds to realize Kay was reacting not only to the news about Ted, but to the fact that the sharp point of the train's steam stack had punctured the palm of her hand. Blood seeped from her tightly closed fist onto the ivory Oriental carpet, marking it with a dark stain that would fade in time, but never completely disappear.

It wasn't really him, Marian told herself again and again. It wasn't Ted in that gleaming mahogany box with its ornate carving and white satin lining. Ted was somewhere else now.

For a while after being told that her son had been killed in action, she had refused to believe it at all. It wasn't him, period. It was a mistake, she kept insisting to Charles and Kay, it couldn't be him, not Ted. It was possible the Navy had made a mistake, wasn't it? Weren't mistakes like that made all the time? Maybe, Kay would say, her face pale and hopeful. Charles only shook his head.

Then the body arrived, sooner than promised after Charles made a phone call to Washington. *The* body. Not Ted's body; she refused to think of it like that. Even when Charles came out of that room where he had to go to identify the remains, she had refused to think Ted could really be lying in there. She hadn't been able to make herself go in, but she had smelled the cool darkness when the door opened.

"Did you look closely?" she demanded of Charles. "At his face? They said it was a grenade...and people can look totally different after they die. Maybe..."

"It's him," Charles said.

"What about his medallion? Did you check for that? You know Ted would never take off that medallion...."

He'd gripped her shoulders hard and made her look at him. "It's Ted, Marian. Ted is gone." And at last she'd had to stop pretending.

Ever since then she'd been hoping that today would turn out to be cold. She wanted to be numb for the funeral, forever, really, but at least through the funeral. She wanted to be so cold that she could block out everything.

It wasn't cold, though. Actually the temperature was quite mild for December. Warm enough to melt the snow into gray slush. Here and there throughout the cemetery patches of brown grass showed through the disappearing snow, and muddy rivulets of water ran along the edge of the road. Altogether an ugly day. A perfect day for an ugly ending to such a beautiful life, thought Marian.

It wasn't an ending for the rest of them, though, and as grief-stricken as she was over Ted's death she couldn't help wondering where they would all go from here. She knew Charles was worried about it, as well. She knew when she lay there beside him in the dark, both of them unable to sleep, that he was thinking about Ted and what might have been, what *should* have been. His death shone a spotlight on the future, and there was a hole in it where he should be. The most obvious person to try to fill that hole was James, of course, and the very thought of it fired Marian with resentment.

If only, she thought, as she had many times during the past nine years. If only they had never made that damn trip to New York City. If only Naval Officer James Terrell hadn't been injured in the line of duty so that he had to return to the States to recuperate, a heroic, romantic figure in Kay's eyes. If only she herself had stood her ground that long-ago day when Kay had come to them and told them she wanted to marry him. She'd tried, but perhaps not hard enough, she thought now. Then again, if she had followed her instincts and forbidden Kay to marry James, the way they had forbidden Ted to join the Navy, maybe they would have lost her, as well.

Marian shivered, at last getting her wish. The cold was beginning to crawl up her legs from the damp earth. She had an impression of it spreading from that deep, gaping hole they had gathered around to say goodbye to Ted.

"Ashes to ashes and dust to dust," the minister intoned from his position at the head of the coffin. Instinctively Marian reached for her husband's hand and held it tightly, needing his strength at that moment more than she ever had.

The gesture was observed rather cynically by James, who had a great view from where he'd positioned himself a little behind and to the right of Kay. Touching. And so typical, he thought. In times of trouble the Delaneys always presented a united front. He understood, had always been made to understand, that no such show of unity would ever really include him.

To someone further on the outside than he was it might not be apparent, but the truth was that in spite of Kay and the cushy job her folks had been forced to give him and the fact that he lived on their damn doorstep, he was still an outsider. Just as surely as if the word was tattooed across his forehead.

At first he felt as if there were a secret password they all knew and he didn't. He'd since learned that in this world he'd married into there were hundreds of passwords. They came in the form of old school nicknames like Bish or Hatsy, private jokes that had their beginnings in a particular weekend they had all shared at a particular ski resort, knowing instinctively the exact shade of navy blue blazer to wear.

By watching and listening he'd finally gotten the clothes part straight. Of course, as Kay's husband, he was invited to all the right parties, but the history—that was something he didn't have and never would.

Sometimes the frustration of knowing that made him feel like he was burning up from the inside out. Only recently had it started to fade. Very recently. After all, Ted had had the right history and known all the secret passwords. But Ted was gone, and he was still here.

The irony of that had to be killing Kay's mother. He'd lay ten-to-one odds that old Marian felt like she was burning up now. He could tell because in the past few days she'd stopped looking through him the way she usually did and started looking *at* him. It wasn't a really friendly look. Not that he expected one after all this time. It was a look that told James she was thinking the same thing he was, that it had taken a long time, but he had finally won.

Their quiet tug-of-war had begun even before he and Kay were married, the morning he had been summoned to Delaney Place to meet with Marian before that first big important lunch with Charles.

He thought back to that day and how he'd been shaking in his boots as he rang the bell. It was the first time he'd ever been in that house without Kay and he'd felt her absence keenly, as if he were about to walk a tightrope without a net.

He remembered following Clarke, the family's somber-faced butler, into the sitting room just inside the front door and accepting his terse offer of a cup of coffee, mostly to have something to do with his hands. The sumptuousness of the surroundings had unnerved him even as it had dazzled him. Back then he simply wasn't accustomed to sitting on a silk brocade love seat or drinking from a Limoges cup so fine it was nearly translucent. He'd gotten very familiar with those things since, however.

After keeping him waiting long enough to start him sweating, Marian had finally swept into the room, looking pretty much the same as she did now. That was another thing he'd learned, that the rich don't age as fast as the poor.

"Good morning, James," she said, and he shot to his feet as if she had cracked a whip.

Dressed in a black skirt and ivory crepe blouse, she looked serene and pampered, representative of a breed of women he hadn't known existed until he met Kay.

"Good morning, Mrs. Delaney," he replied, unconsciously straightening his tie and second-guessing whether his best dark blue suit had been the right choice after all.

"I'm sorry I've kept you waiting, but I'm chairwoman for the fashion show at the club next month, and I seem to spend every waking moment on the phone with the caterer or the dressmaker or someone else who needs assistance doing the very thing they are being paid to do."

Stopping directly in front of James, she smiled at him in a way that made him wonder how he could ever have thought there was a strong resemblance between her and Kay. The eyes were the same, and perhaps the fine bone structure, but the essence of the two women, what lay beneath the flawless skin and polished demeanor, was totally different. If Marian Delaney possessed any of her daughter's sweet vulnerability it was clearly inaccessible to him.

Her gaze didn't waver or her smile warm as she asked, "How do you suppose a person ends up in a position for which he is so ill-suited, James?"

Surprise showed on his face. He'd come here expecting to be subjected to the art of gentle persuasion, not a game of hard-ball in which the first pitch was aimed at his gut without him being granted any time to warm up.

"I don't know enough about fashion shows or dressmakers to even venture a guess," he replied, "only that a lady as lovely as yourself is worth any wait."

"What a charming thing to say—but then charming remarks are your forte." As she spoke she slipped into the gold velvet side chair to his right, its seat high enough so they were eye to eye when he sat, and lifted the silver coffee pot. "More coffee, James?"

"Please."

"Cream?"

"No, thank you. Black is fine."

She took an unhurried sip from her own cup before putting it aside. "Do you have any idea why I asked you here for this little chat on the very day you're to have lunch with my husband?"

He eyed her levelly. "Several, actually."

"Good. Then we won't need to waste any time posturing. Are you also aware of what Charles intends to discuss with you later?"

"Only what Kay told me. She believes he's going to offer me a job with Delaney Silver."

"A job you want no part of, I understand."

Her smile was making him increasingly uneasy. "That's true."

"So I can assume that you'll refuse any offer Charles makes?"

"Not exactly. Kay has persuaded me to reconsider my opposition to working for Delaney Silver. If it will make Kay happy, I'm willing to give it a try."

"How noble of you."

"With all due respect, Mrs. Delaney, I think you're hinting that I might have ulterior motives, and I don't like it."

Her gaze was cool, direct. "Then we finally have something in common, because I don't like this entire scenario. In the interest of putting it behind us as quickly as possible, I'm going to get straight to the point. You said a moment ago that you're prepared to take a job at Delaney Silver for the sake of Kay's happiness. I'm prepared to do quite a bit more."

James felt the muscles of his throat contract.

"Twenty-five thousand dollars." The words fell from her lips like chips of ice. "That's how much I'm willing to pay you to break your engagement to Kay and leave Rhode Island."

He shook his head as if dazed. He'd thought himself well-prepared for the meeting, ready to withstand pleas and even threats. But it hadn't occurred to him that a lady like Mrs. Delaney would try to bribe him outright. Twenty-five thousand dollars. It was more money than he could imagine possessing, yet at least it was a currency he understood, and for the first time he realized exactly how much he wasn't wanted there.

"All right," she continued, with less emotion than he'd seen among housewives back home when haggling with a street vendor over the price of a pound of catfish. "Fifty thousand dollars. That's a great deal of money, James, and truthfully, as much as I could lay my hands on immediately and still insure that this matter remain strictly between the two of us . . . as, of course, I will insist it must."

James forced his fingers to unclench. He couldn't help imagining what fifty thousand dollars would look like. Once he'd won eight hundred and seventeen dollars playing poker and thought he had the world on a string, and here this woman could just *lay her hands*, as she put it, on fifty thousand at a pop, no questions asked. She could gamble with it or give it away or buy anything she wanted, even somebody else's dreams.

"Think about it, James," she urged with her precise, fancy diction. "You're no fool, you know that with that much money you could buy your own business somewhere. I'm sure a man like you would prefer that to starting at the bottom at Delaney, which is certainly what Charles will demand."

She paused, watching him, waiting for the answer he couldn't seem to formulate, finally prodding, "So? Do we have a deal?"

James would have liked for her to look shocked when he stood, or maybe display a little reluctant admiration, but all she did was go on gazing at him with that faintly smiling, unmistakably superior expression, which seemed to say that no matter what was said or done here today she would always be the winner and he the loser.

"No deal, Mrs. Delaney. No payoff, no broken engagement. Not even for a million dollars. In fact, the only part of your little deal I want any part of is your stipulation that this remain our little secret. I wouldn't want to break Kay's heart by telling her what you've done."

"No, I imagine you'll find numerous other ways to break her heart all by yourself."

"You just can't admit you were wrong about me, can you? Or accept the fact that I love Kay for herself alone?"

"On the contrary, James," she said, getting to her feet, one hand automatically smoothing the already impeccable line of her skirt, "I'd be thrilled to admit such a thing if I believed it. But I don't believe it. I don't believe you love my daughter any more than she loves you . . . Oh, please, spare us both a show of indignation."

Her request was accompanied by a wave of her hand, as if she meant to ward off the sudden anger in his expression. "The fact is the two of you have nothing on which to base a lasting love. I won't offend you a second time by mentioning what I think attracts you to my daughter. As for Kay . . ."

She hesitated, looking past him, a soft blend of affection and sadness in her gaze before it returned to him and frosted over once again. "Kay is a romantic at heart. She looks at you and sees a hero, handsome and dashing. The role suits you well. But medals tarnish in time, Lieutenant, and even the best, most carefully contrived facades have a tendency to slip. You are not the man Kay thinks you are, and you will never be able to love her the way she needs to be loved."

"I can try, Mrs. Delaney."

There was a flash of undisguised hostility in her eyes. "You'd better try, James. That's the only warning I'll ever give you. If you are to be a member of this family—as I am forced to concede you probably will be—you'll be expected to meet the same standards as the rest of us, and I'll be there, always, to see that you do."

Drawing a deep breath, she took the first step away, signaling she was through with him. "Now, I've already detained you long enough on what is certain to be an eventful day for you. I'll have Clarke show you out."

"That's not necessary," he said, following her from the room. The faithful Clarke was standing guard in the hallway outside. James bet the old coot would be counting the teaspoons before he even got his car started. "I can find the way out." *Same as I found the way in,* he thought.

It wasn't until he was behind the wheel of his old Ford that it fully hit him that he had just been offered fifty thousand dollars, free and clear, and had barely been tempted. Amazing. He was smiling as he steered the car toward the street....

There had been times since when he'd wondered if he shouldn't have taken the money and run. Now, watching Ted's body being lowered into the ground, he was thanking God he hadn't. He'd bided his time, paid his dues, and he was being rewarded. He hadn't wished Ted any harm, had certainly never wished him dead—just out of the way for a little while. But what was done was done. Ted was no longer a factor, which meant that as Kay's husband, he was left holding the only ticket to the whole shooting match.

Until then James had been barely paying attention to the prayers being said, merely keeping his head respectfully bent and moving his lips whenever it seemed appropriate. Now the booming words of the minister caught his attention and his imagination. "For thine is the power and the glory...."

Yes, the power and the glory. Taking a cue from his in-laws, James reached for Kay's hand and held it clasped between his own.

Incredibly, Kay, who usually longed for such spontaneous shows of affection from her husband, felt only irritated by the contact. If there weren't so many people watching she would have succumbed to the urge to snatch her hand away from his.

This was the saddest day of her life, and all she wanted was to be left alone. Her sadness was bigger than anything she'd ever felt. She was feeling grief, to be sure, a rawness all through her and an emptiness she kept trying to fill up with memories of Ted. It didn't work. It was like when she was small and tried to fill a hole she'd dug on the beach with water. As quickly as she poured the water in it disappeared, leaving the hole just as deep and empty as before.

Her hold on her own life suddenly felt very tenuous. Perhaps it had to do with the way Ted had died, so suddenly and far away, just disappearing from their lives with no chance for them to say goodbye or see him one last time, no time to fix forever in their minds his smile or the way he talked with his eyes as much as his mouth. During the awful wait for Ted's body to be flown home she had seen, for the first time in her life, how vulnerable her mother and father could be. How vulnerable they all really were.

But no matter how she tried to explain what she was feeling, she couldn't put aside the fact that these uneasy feelings inside her had been there even before Ted's death. His dying had forced her to confront what had been growing beneath the smooth surface of her life.

The furthest she could trace it back was to the Silver Bells Ball. Ever since that night disturbing thoughts had been cropping up at odd moments. Some of them stemmed from the fact that when she'd stopped by the plant to see Daddy last week and had inquired—quite innocently—about the man who'd injured his hand, no one could recall any such incident taking place. She kept thinking about that and about what Drew had told her about how James had encouraged Ted to enlist. His encouragement wasn't so odd, considering James's military record, but she'd have thought he would at least have mentioned to her that he and Ted had discussed the matter. At the time James had seemed as surprised as the rest of them by Ted's decision. Obviously that had been an act. But why?

She had to ask herself how much James had influenced Ted's decision to enlist, and how things might be different if he hadn't. Perhaps Ted would be here right now. And her ambitious husband would still be doomed to play second fiddle at Delaney Silver. Something sharp and close to guilt made Kay tremble. She fought for control of her emotions.

There was probably a perfectly plausible explanation for everything. So why didn't she ask James for it? Maybe because no matter how she phrased the questions in her mind, they still smacked of accusation and were sure to precipitate a scene. And maybe because she wasn't ready to know. At the moment she had all she could handle emotionally.

When she first met James, Kay had known right away that something big was happening. She'd been filled with the awareness that although it was too soon to know exactly how, everything had changed for her. It was as if some powerful, invisible hand had lifted the red carpet of her life, given it a hard shake and laid it down again in a totally new direction. She couldn't explain why, but she had that same feeling now.

EIGHT

In the days following Paul Lagasse's death, Mary combed the local paper for news of it. She kept waiting to hear that a woman had been seen hurrying from the scene, that foul play was suspected, that the police were launching an all-out investigation. It didn't happen. His death was ruled a heart attack. Case closed.

Only through the hospital grapevine did she later hear that the autopsy had turned up traces of morphine in his blood and evidence of long-term use. Mary recalled how irritated he'd been when she arrived early and startled him. Privately it was assumed the drug played a factor in his death; publicly it was all hushed up. If the money scattered on his office floor raised suspicions, they were never mentioned.

Mary was beginning to relax when news came of Ted Delaney's death in Korea. Her heart ached for his family, yet she couldn't help wondering how the tragedy would affect her situation. Would a woman like Kay Terrell open her mail at such a time? If she did, would she be more or less likely to dismiss Mary's card as a crank?

It was Rusty who first suggested that the letter might have gotten lost. It had been two full weeks since she had mailed it. Even with the delay caused by the extra Christmas mail, that was far too long for a letter to get across town.

"Is that possible?" she asked, glancing at him over her shoulder as she continued to wash dishes in the sink. Rusty was sitting at the table, straddling the chair the way she was constantly telling the boys not to. "Do letters really get lost in the mail?"

He shrugged. "Sure. Anything is possible."

Mary clapped her hands together in excitement. Foamy white soap bubbles filled the air in front of her, clinging in lacy puffs to the red calico ruffle on the kitchen curtains. Even before they disappeared she was having second thoughts. She whirled to face Rusty, for once not caring about the dishwater dripping on the clean, waxed floor. "Oh no, Rusty, that would be even worse. We could never be sure if the letter would be found, and the not knowing would be like . . . like living with an ax hanging over our heads forever."

"Relax, Mary," he said, crossing the kitchen to take her into his arms. "Worrying isn't going to change anything."

She knew that well enough because he told her so all the time. Still, whenever Mary truly began to relax it would all suddenly come back to her, the memory like the touch of a live electrical wire, causing her to jerk and stiffen wherever she happened to be. She woke in the mornings with a sore jaw and eventually figured out that it was from grinding her teeth in her sleep, on edge even then.

The nightmares came and went . . . lulling her into thinking it was safe to close her eyes and then returning sharper and more vivid than ever. She heard Dr. Lagasse's last gasp, saw the flash of white, his face, and those black eyes staring at her. She would wake up sweating and rush frantically from room to room, making sure each one of the children was safe. Only then could she go back to bed. It was as if, as long as they were safe, there was some purpose to it all.

When more days passed with no word of the letter, she began to feel more like herself. Still it took some doing to convince Rusty she was strong enough to go back to work. He fussed over her as if they were dating again, fixing her tea, asking her if she was warm enough, carrying the laundry basket for her. Most astonishing of all, he listened to her when she talked, looking right at her and listening instead of interrupting halfway through or turning away to catch the score of the ball game on the radio, as if that was more important than anything she could possibly have to say.

And he had found a job. Not a one-shot deal cleaning out someone's cellar or something flimsy like picking up bottles to sell, but a real job at a nursery. Rusty was always good at growing things, and he liked it there. He said it smelled a hundred times better than the garage had, and made the boys laugh by insisting the dirt he got under his nails now was clean dirt.

The job didn't pay much to start, it was true, but at least he went to work every morning and came home every afternoon, and at the end of his first week when he handed Mary his pay-check his eyes sparkled like they hadn't in years. He went to bed early because he had to be at the nursery at six, and these days the only bottles lined up in the icebox were Ben's. If things were different, thought Mary, she would be walking on clouds. The baby that had been growing inside her had been replaced by a sorrow she knew would never go away.

Some moments were worse than others. For a while the hardest time was when she was caring for Dolly's baby in the hospital nursery. An allergic reaction to the formula had kept her there past the time she was to have been transferred to the orphanage. "Baby Martin," the ID card on her crib still read. There was no one to give her a real name.

She was a fretful baby, waking often during the night. The official policy was that if a baby was dry and fed, you let it cry and went about your duties. But Mary didn't have the heart to ignore this particular infant no matter how much work she had to do. Holding her in the dark, silent nursery, she often felt tense and jittery. At those moments it was impossible not to think about Dolly and everything that had happened.

Gradually, however, feelings of tenderness overcame her uneasiness around the baby. She found herself looking forward to seeing Baby Martin when she came on duty and enjoying the quiet moments while she rocked her back to sleep, feeling her small body nestled trustingly against her own. Somehow the ever-present thoughts of her lost baby weren't so painful when she held Dolly's baby in her arms.

The idea first came to her in one of those quiet moments. It was so perfect, like coming full circle, that Mary couldn't believe it hadn't occurred to her sooner. She called the Good Shepherd Home that same night and spoke with Sister Maura, who not only approved the idea, she welcomed it. She told Mary that the hospital pediatrician had said the baby was ready to be discharged and that she planned to come for her first thing Thursday morning unless the situation changed.

Now, thought Mary, all she had to do was convince Rusty to go along with her plan.

At first he resisted. She'd waited until they were alone, with the children asleep, and he had polished off a big piece of his favorite chocolate cake before broaching the subject. Even then she knew it would not be easy.

"Mary," he said, his strong face sober, "do you honestly think you can bring that baby in here after all that's gone on and love her like one of our own?"

"Yes, exactly like one of our own," she told him, leaning forward in her chair. "Don't you see? It would be almost like . . ."

"I know what you're thinking," he said when she faltered. His voice was gentle. "But, Mary, she won't be our baby. And having her here won't undo anything that's been done."

"I know that. That's not the reason I want to adopt her."

"Then what is the reason?"

"Because she needs me." The answer came without thought. It wasn't one of her carefully rehearsed arguments, which all seemed to have fled now that the moment of truth was at hand. "I should have spoken up for Dolly that night, but I was too afraid for myself, for my job. Afterward I felt so ashamed. That's why I wrote that letter to Kay Terrell. It was a long shot, but I told myself that at least I was doing something to try to help her baby. I promised Dolly."

"So you're doing this to pay some kind of guilty debt you think you owe? Mary, that's—"

"No," she broke in. "That's not all. It's not just Dolly I'm thinking about, or the baby. Remember last Saturday when you took me to confession?"

She'd had him drive her all the way into Providence so she could go to confession at Saint Francis's Chapel downtown instead of to Father Coletti, their parish priest.

Rusty nodded.

"When I finished telling the priest everything, he blessed me, but he didn't give me any penance. He said my guilt was punishment enough and that I had to find my own way to atone for this sin. He told me God would let me know what he wanted me to do. I know now that this is what he meant. Rusty, I want this baby. I want to love her and make a home for her so that she doesn't suffer any more for something that wasn't her fault. And I . . . I need her, maybe even more than she needs me."

When she finished a smile slowly creased his face. "Then what are we standing here jawing for, woman?" he asked her in that wonderful teasing voice. "Get on the phone and call that sister before it gets any later. Tell her that starting right now that baby's a Saville."

"Really? You mean it?"

"Really. I mean it."

"And you really want her? You're not just doing it for me?"

"I'm doing it for us." He handed her the receiver. "Now call."

"There is one other thing," she said, pausing with the phone book open to the number. "I can't help wondering what the neighbors will think, and your family. Here we are without two nickels to rub together and we're taking in another baby."

"I don't really give a tinker's damn what they think," he scoffed, throwing his shoulders back.

Smiling, Mary began to dial. He was more like his old self everyday.

Sister Maura was delighted and promised to see to the paperwork right away. Mary hung up and turned to find Rusty grinning at her. She grinned back.

"Now we have to think of a name for her," she said.

"How about Lily?"

"Be serious."

"I am."

"I don't think Lily is even a saint's name."

His grin widened. "All the better, 'cause we sure ain't saints." She laughed as he looped his arms around her waist. "C'mon, Mary, what do you say?"

"I say there are lots of better names for a baby than Lily."

"Such as?"

"Elizabeth."

He made a face.

"After your aunt Bessie," she added.

"Fine, if you want her to be an old maid."

"Well, that's better than being a . . . a Lily."

"I've always thought Lily was a beautiful name, but there's another reason it came to mind tonight." His expression grew a little sheepish. "While you were at work the boys helped me clean up that pile of leaves and wood in the backyard, you know, the one you've been nagging me about for about a year or so?"

She gave him a dubious look. "The boys helped?"

"Let's just say they tried. Anyway, when I got to the bottom of it, damned if there wasn't a lily beginning to sprout there underneath it all. I figure it's that one you bought last Easter. It must have gotten tossed out there afterward and taken root.

I moved it inside, down by the furnace. The boys are hoping it'll bloom in time to be a Christmas present for you.''

"That's so sweet," she said, knowing who must have planted that hope in their heads. "So you want to name our new daughter after a Christmas lily."

He smiled, pulling her a little closer. "Why not? Any flower that can bloom under snow has to be pretty scrappy, and any little girl in a house with four big brothers better be scrappy, too.''

"We would have to give her a saint's name for her middle name," she pointed out.

"Of course," Rusty agreed with mock seriousness as he danced her across the kitchen floor, already knowing he'd won. "How about Bartholomew?"

"Stop. I was thinking of Marie. Lily Marie Saville. It does sound sort of pretty, doesn't it?"

"Real pretty," he agreed. He stopped dancing and just held her, his gaze moving over her face as reverently as if it was a rare and beautiful painting. "Real pretty. Just like her mama," he added softly, and for the first time since the night he'd cried in her arms, the first time in a long time, his lips gently touched hers.

They brought Lily Marie Saville home on the afternoon of Christmas Eve. The nurses at the hospital had chipped in and bought a pink outfit for Lily to wear home, then topped it off with a big red Christmas bow. Rusty teased that they ought to put her under the tree and tell the boys Santa had brought her instead of the horse they wanted.

"That's a surefire way to make them resent her," Mary told him.

But the boys were nothing but thrilled by her arrival. She and Rusty had already decided they were too young for complicated explanations. The easiest and safest approach was to keep the story simple and stick with it. She was their new baby sister. Period. She fit in well enough, with hair the same reddish shade as Rusty's—and as Dolly's had been. It looked as if her eyes were going to stay blue, although today when she'd opened them outside in the sunlight Mary thought she caught a glint of deep jade.

"Whose is she?" Cliff asked when Mary stopped right inside the back door and stooped down with the baby in her arms so they could all get a good look at her.

"She's ours," she told them.

"Does she have a name?" he asked.

"Of course. Her name is Lily. Lily Marie Saville."

As he absorbed the connection between him and this tiny baby, Cliff's eyes widened, reflecting the amber glow from the candles Rusty had put in all the windows. "Can we keep her?" he asked. "Forever and ever?"

Mary met Rusty's gaze over their heads and smiled.

PART TWO

NINE

December, 1964

The shopping trip to downtown Providence was an annual tradition for Mary and Lily, begun five years ago when Lily was six and her first-grade teacher reported that she was having trouble seeing the blackboard.

The ophthalmologist had confirmed that she needed glasses. Lily hated the clear blue plastic frames, which tilted slightly up at the corners, but she liked being able to see everything going on around her, so she wore the glasses without complaining.

Not everyone had been so agreeable.

"Heck, Mary, she looks like a miniature Mata Hari," Rusty had grumbled, seeing Lily in the new glasses. "Didn't they have any that don't look like cats' eyes?"

Mary silenced him with a glare, but it was too late. Lily stood with her bottom lip trembling, her eyes rapidly filling with tears behind the offending glasses, while the boys closed in, singing, "Cats' eyes, cats' eyes."

She didn't cry, though, not that night or in the days that followed when their teasing continued. As the only girl in the family Lily had learned early that whimpering or any other sign of weakness has the same effect on young males that the scent of blood has on sharks, arousing their inborn instinct to attack. She had dug in and held her ground, wearing the glasses like a badge of honor.

Finally Rusty had grown tired of listening to their teasing and decreed that the words "cats" and "eyes" were not to be used in conjunction in his house ever again. After that the boys settled for a quiet but eloquent "meow" whenever they thought they could get away with it.

Then had come the day when Mary was hanging out laundry and she heard a boy from down the street harassing Lily with the familiar taunt. "Cats' eyes, cats' eyes." For all her resolve never to get involved in the kids' squabbles, Mary had been tempted to teach the child a thing or two about good manners when Ben beat her to it.

"So what?" he'd shouted. "At least she's not a white-bellied, sap-sucking toad face like you. You're going to need glasses *and* crutches if you don't shut up."

Mary had snapped the next clothespin into place with a little extra zip, smiling broadly at how Ben, the closest to Lily in age, had jumped to his sister's defense, and also because Lily, in her own strong, quiet way, had once again emerged triumphant.

In Mary's opinion the worst thing about the glasses was that they hid the deep green eyes that she considered Lily's most beautiful feature. Not that everything about her wasn't beautiful. She had curly red hair, like her daddy, some people said—and when they did Mary would just smile and change the subject. Summer and winter her pale skin glowed, as if lit from within by apricot light, and she possessed a natural gracefulness, which always served her well in baseball games and wrestling matches with her four big brothers.

Looks weren't everything, of course, and Lily was also smart and a hard worker. If Mary worried about her at all it was because Lily so often had her head in the clouds. She was a dreamer, and Mary knew firsthand what insubstantial stuff dreams could be, especially when you dreamed about things you had no right to.

She and Rusty had had their share of dreams once, and so, she recalled with great anxiety from time to time, had Dolly Martin. And not one of those dreams had come to any good. Not that she would trade her family for a nursing degree or a fancy job for Rusty, or anything else they had once dreamed about, but there had been many hard lessons—and regrets—along the way.

If she could make Lily understand anything it would be that in this life it's best to keep your feet planted on the ground and never mind chasing after dreams. But she might as well save her breath. Every time she caught Lily staring off into space with that faraway look in her eyes, she tightened up inside, just knowing that Lily's thoughts were on all those highfalutin things and places she was always reading about in books.

Rusty was no help. He just kept telling Mary not to worry, that there was nothing wrong with a little culture. Culture my eye, thought Mary. She couldn't help remembering Dolly and worrying about where Lily's taste for culture and fancy things had come from, and where it might lead her.

At the moment it was leading Mary and her tired feet all over downtown Providence. They always scheduled Lily's eye examination for first thing Saturday morning so they would have the rest of the day to themselves, supposedly to Christmas shop. The fact was they did more browsing than shopping, which suited both of them just fine. Mary because she didn't relish the prospect of lugging along bundles on the bus ride home and Lily because it meant they could spend their time looking at things they could never actually afford to buy.

From Garr's Fabric Shop, where Lily loved to look through the Vogue pattern books and run her hand along the bolts of deep-toned velvet, to the long perfume counter at Cherry and Webb, they had hit all her favorite haunts. Their last stop was always the toy department at the Outlet Department Store, the place Mary supposed would be number one on any other child's list. It certainly would have been for any of the boys when they were Lily's age, but she had different priorities. It never failed to surprise Mary that Lily remembered not only what stores they had visited a whole year ago, but what they had seen in each.

"Look, Mom," she said now, as they stood in front of the ivory satin-lined window of Goddard's, Providence's most exclusive jeweler, "there are no dresser sets this year."

"No," Mary agreed. The disappointment in Lily's tone jogged her memory, and she vaguely recalled the silver filigree trays and dainty hairbrushes and combs that had been displayed there last year. Lily had stared at them with eyes full of longing. "Now there are only dishes."

"China," Lily corrected quietly, studying the place setting with its hand-painted poinsettia and gold-beaded edging.

Mary stamped her feet on the frozen pavement. Surely Lily wouldn't want to stand around looking at dishes...*china*...for as long as she had the silver brushes and combs. "It's nice," she said, "but who would pay all that money for china they could only use at Christmastime?"

Lily turned her head to look at her, blinking as if coming out of a trance. "It's Royal Copenhagen," Lily said.

"How do you know that's what it is?"

"Because that's the Royal Copenhagen crest." She pointed to the crown above three waves on the small engraved card discreetly positioned in a corner of the window. "And because I saw this same china in an advertisement in *House Beautiful* magazine at the library."

Mary didn't bat an eyelash at hearing that her eleven-year-old daughter read *House Beautiful*. "Oh. Well, I still think it's a waste of good, hard-earned money."

"I think it's beautiful," countered Lily, a familiar stubborn note in her voice.

No, it wasn't stubbornness, exactly, though Lord knows she could be that. It was . . . resolution, as if nothing and no one could change her opinion on this matter now that it had been set. Mary had no doubt Lily was standing there, her breath fogging the cold glass, imagining how on some future Christmas she would set her own table with that fancy, useless china.

Mary sighed, feeling the same old tug-of-war in her heart between a mother's natural yearning for all her daughter's dreams to come true, no matter how farfetched they might be, and the more practical impulse to shake them out of her for her own good.

"Brr. It's cold standing still," she said, pulling her scarf a little closer. "What do you say we head on over to the Outlet. We'll spend a while in the toy department and then we can have lunch."

"Mom, if it's okay with you, I'd just as soon skip the toy department this year."

Mary took a deep breath. Just last year they had spent forever admiring the dolls and the packaged outfits that came with accessories like tiny fur muffs and high heels. The more straps and sequins the better, as far as Lily was concerned. Afterward they would always wait in line to visit Santa Claus and for a quarter Lily would get to fish a grab bag out of the open mouth of the big clown face beside him. She would clasp the brown-paper-wrapped package close to her chest and make an occasion of opening it over lunch, uncovering a coloring book or some other small toy.

Of course, now Lily's own drawings were far more clever and detailed than those in any coloring book, but it was still a shock for Mary to see her baby eyeing her a little worriedly as she announced she had outgrown all that.

"All right, then," she said, forcing a smile, "lunch it is."

"McGarry's?" Lily countered, her smile tinged with relief.

"No, I have a surprise planned. We're going to Shepherd's Tearoom."

Lily's eyes widened behind the glasses that lent her still childlike face such a serious look. "A tearoom? Really? A tearoom in Shepherd's?"

"Not actually in the store—it's behind it. Just a few blocks over from here. But it is run by Shepherd's."

Shepherd's was one of the nicest stores in Providence and Mary was certain that lunch there would cost considerably more than a hamburger in a basket at McGarry's, but she didn't care. She'd been planning this surprise for weeks, and it was worth every cent it might cost to see Lily light up the way she had. She'd known that lunch in a tearoom would be Lily's idea of something special.

When she was younger Lily would arrange her dolls around the kitchen table for tea parties, and sometimes after school she still asked Mary to have tea with her. Occasionally, between getting supper ready and getting herself ready for work, Mary even had time to say yes. On those days they would have tea and Lorna Doones, or maybe toast sprinkled with cinnamon sugar and cut in triangles. Once she'd surprised Lily with scones from the bakery. But inside Mary always knew that no matter what she did it never quite measured up to Lily's cherished memory of the day she had tea at Delaney Place.

That had been Kay Terrell's doing, one Saturday afternoon when Lily accompanied Rusty while he set up the flowers and plants for a garden party to be held the following day. No doubt Mrs. Terrell had taken pity on Lily, hanging around in the hot sun waiting for her father, and had invited her to tea to entertain her. Little did she know how just being there was heaven for Lily, or how she pleaded and wheedled to be taken along whenever her father had to work on Saturday. Lily had once confided to Mary that Delaney Place was like a castle in a fairy tale and how she would sit on the wide green lawn and pretend she was the princess who lived there. Mary had smiled, but inside an old fear had turned her spine to ice.

From the start she had been opposed to Rusty taking the job as grounds keeper at Delaney Place, even if it did pay more than the nursery and meant that for the most part he was his own boss. And she had certainly never wanted him to take Lily there and risk having her rub elbows with those people, even though none of them had any hint of Lily's background. Neighbors had come and gone through the years, and if any of them even remembered that Lily was not Rusty's and her own daughter, they never mentioned it. Mary lulled herself with the thought that everyone had forgotten all about it, the way even she was sometimes able to do.

But after Lily had gone along with Rusty just once, the damage was done. Lily had glimpsed the Delaney house with its gardens and pool and stables and never ceased pleading with her father to take her again. Rusty never could say no to Lily. And so from that day on everything in Lily's life was measured against the glittering yardstick of Delaney Place and especially of Kay Terrell, who Lily insisted she wanted to be exactly like when she grew up.

Well, thought Mary as they hurried along, she might not be as glamorous as Kay Terrell or have all the fancy clothes and jewelry that Lily was always going on and on about, and she might not be able to give Lily silver combs or Royal Copenhagen china, but she could treat her to lunch in an honest-to-goodness tearoom—and by God she was going to do it.

Lily was beside herself with excitement. Mary could tell by the way she was half skipping, half running in her hurry to get there.

"At Delaney Place they serve little sandwiches with tea," she told Mary. "Some have chicken salad inside and some have cream cheese and cucumber slices shaped like stars."

"Mmm?" Mary responded distractedly. She had heard it all before, at least a hundred times.

"And for dessert they have date squares with these sweet little crumbs sprinkled on top, and cheesecake. I didn't think I would like cheesecake, but I did. And you could have milk with your tea or lemon or these little sprigs of mint. I had milk, but I think I might try the mint today. What are you going to have, Mom?"

"Milk, same as I always do," Mary replied quickly, a little too quickly. She made sure to give Lily an extra warm smile as she held open the door of the tearoom. It wasn't poor Lily's fault that Mary wasn't more like Kay Terrell.

They walked through the small entry and paused beside the sign that read Please Wait To Be Seated. Mary took a quick look around, then turned to see Lily's reaction. Her smile wilted. She'd had no idea what to expect and no idea what Lily had expected, only that the green-walled restaurant with its high-backed booths and counter running the length of one wall wasn't it.

There was no lace. That was Lily's first thought when she stepped inside and looked around. A hundred other thoughts crowded her mind after that, but that was the most crushing. There were no lace tablecloths on the Formica-topped tables, no lace-trimmed napkins, no lace anywhere.

Lace was what she remembered best about that wonderful long-ago afternoon at Delaney Place. There had been a beautiful lace cloth on the small round table where she and Mrs. Terrell had sat, and lace doilies lining the silver trays of sandwiches and sweets.

Sweets, that's what Mrs. Terrell had called the date squares and cheesecakes. Sweets. There had been flowers on the table, too, and a beautiful teapot and a teacup made of china so fragile she'd been afraid if her teeth bumped the rim, it would shatter, and so she had made sure to be extra special careful before each sip. She wouldn't have to do that today. The cups here were as heavy as the mugs at home, white with a narrow band of brown around the top and a brown S on the side. Only not a whole S because some of it had peeled off.

"Maybe I was wrong."

At her mother's anxious whisper, Lily looked up to find Mary watching her with a look that made Lily feel guilty.

"Maybe we should go somewhere else," her mother said. "Across the street I noticed..."

"No," interrupted Lily. "I like it here. Really," she added, grasping the sleeve of her mother's old tweed coat to keep her there.

"Two?" inquired the hostess, barely glancing at them as she plucked that number of menus from the pile beside the cash register.

Still looking doubtful, Mary nodded and motioned for Lily to follow as the woman led the way to a booth about halfway down the side aisle of the crowded restaurant. They ordered tea. It was served with milk. After carefully studying the menu Lily decided not to ask about the mint sprigs. She didn't think this was that kind of tearoom. They both had chicken croquettes for lunch, the specialty of the house, her mother said, with chocolate cream pie for dessert. Lily ate every bite and smiled as hard as she could. It seemed the only thing she had to offer in reply to the question that never left the back of her mother's eyes.

"Did you like your pie?" Mary asked as Lily wiped her mouth with the crumpled paper napkin.

"Yes."

"And your croquettes?"

"They were good, too. Very good."

"You're sure?" Her mother glanced around. "This place isn't quite as fancy as I thought it would be. I hope you weren't disappointed."

"Oh, no. It was wonderful. Really."

Her mother seemed to relax a little. "It's nicer than McGarry's, that's for sure."

"Much nicer," agreed Lily. It was much nicer than McGarry's, that was true, but like so many things lately, it just hadn't been what she hoped it would be. Not at all.

TEN

A few weeks after the trip to Providence, Mary received an early morning call from the hospital, asking her to work a double shift. With Christmas right around the corner she was glad for the overtime. Only after she hung up did she remember Rusty telling her he had to spend his day off at Delaney Place to help with the floral arrangements for a big party that evening.

Disappointed at having to give up the extra pay, she explained to him that she didn't want to leave Lily alone all day. It was Saturday and the boys were all off playing hockey at a nearby pond. She knew from experience that they wouldn't return until darkness or hunger forced them to.

"Nonsense," Rusty insisted. "Lily can come along with me."

Lily immediately began hopping around the kitchen with excitement. Mary glared at him, receiving only a good-natured shrug for her trouble. If he hadn't said it in front of Lily, she might have had a chance to put her foot down without a lot of questions and explanations. The fact was she'd rather quit her job entirely than have Lily hanging around Delaney Place and James Terrell.

She often wondered if he knew, or even cared, what had happened to the little girl he didn't want. Just as she wondered what had happened to the letter she'd sent to his wife. Had Kay Terrell believed what she'd had to say and chosen not to pursue the matter? Had she simply dismissed it as the work of a crackpot? Or had the letter never reached her at all?

If that was the case, what would happen if they were to find out about Lily now? Find out that she was living just a few miles away, the daughter of their gardener? Would they want to take her away from the only home she'd ever known? Could they? Just thinking about it caused Mary to shiver—and the chill stayed with her long after she watched Rusty and Lily drive away in his old pickup truck.

In the front seat of the truck, Lily sat clutching her sketch pad and pencil case with mittened hands, playing the game she always played on these wondrous, all too rare occasions that she was permitted to accompany her father to Delaney Place. She pretended she was going home.

In her game her father was transformed into the family chauffeur, complete with black cap and uniform, who had been sent to pick her up at boarding school. She closed her eyes and the truck became the dark green Bentley she'd seen Kay Terrell riding in and her old coat became the soft white wool coat she wished was hers. She kept her eyes closed as they drove along the curving ocean road, past finer and finer homes. It was all part of the game. She wouldn't open her eyes until they had turned onto the drive at Delaney Place. She didn't have to see to know when they had made that turn—she could always feel it in her bones. As if she really was coming home.

As she opened her eyes the house lay before her, every bit as magnificent as in her daydreams, its tall windows looking out over acres of snow-covered lawn on three sides and the Atlantic Ocean on the fourth. The twin turrets that held round rooms at the top of the house beckoned, filling her with thoughts of princesses and knights in shining armor. What would it be like for a kid to really live in such a place? she wondered.

The Terrells had only one son who was four years older than Lily. He was away at boarding school and camp during the summer. From things her parents had said, Lily had learned that he had been adopted, and adoption had suddenly seemed a much more glamorous fate. She loved her own family, of course, but sometimes when she was angry with them she imagined that she was the one Mrs. Terrell had chosen to adopt and that she lived here and her room was the one at the top of the stairs with the pink ruffled curtains and canopy bed.

Mr. Terrell never figured into any of her daydreams, however, mostly because he frightened Lily with the mean way he stared at her. It was as if she'd just done something wrong, which she never did, of course, because before she set foot out of the house to come here she was warned and lectured and warned again by her mother about the proper way to behave. Forget being seen and not heard. Around here she did her best to be neither seen nor heard.

Most of the time when her father brought her along the weather was warm and she stayed outside, sitting on the lawn and sketching. Today they went straight to the greenhouses where he gathered the pots of white poinsettias and carnations he'd forced into bloom for the occasion, then told her to follow along to the house and stay with him every minute.

Lily could have burst with joy. The house. She'd been in the kitchen on several occasions, but only once, the day she'd shared tea with Mrs. Terrell, had she been any farther. That was the day she'd glimpsed the beautiful pink bedroom that had become her own in her heart. She wouldn't dare venture up there alone, of course, but at least she was going inside. And today was even more special because the house was being decorated for tonight's party. Her father had told her that the Delaneys' Christmas tree stood fifteen feet high and was decorated with hundreds of tiny white lights and one-of-a-kind silver ornaments. If she only got to glimpse that tree she would be happy.

Unfortunately, most of her father's work was in the front hall, itself bigger than their parlor at home. He arranged the flowers in brass urns and climbed a ladder to string white lights along the banister of the split staircase and the balcony above.

"Daddy, the tree," Lily prodded as often as she dared.

"In a minute, honey," he replied each time, without taking his eyes off what he was doing.

The minutes stretched. Lily paced to the door of the living room where the tree was just an enticing blur in a faraway corner. She knew better than to step inside for a closer look unless her father brought her. When Hilda, the Delaneys' cook, saw that she was there and invited her to the kitchen for cookies and hot chocolate, Lily figured that was the next best thing. She liked Hilda, who smelled of vanilla and always had a smudge of flour on her chin. Besides, if she chewed real slowly, maybe by the time she finished her father would be ready to take a break and bring her to see the tree.

When she finished, she carried her plate and cup to the sink and thanked Hilda. The older woman seemed just as preoccupied as her father, but at least she took time to look up from her mixing bowl to smile at Lily.

"You're welcome, Lily. You come see me again real soon, yes?"

"Yes," agreed Lily eagerly.

She hurried to the front of the house only to find her father and the ladder gone. He had probably returned to the greenhouse for the rest of the flowers, thought Lily. She passed the time waiting for him by tracing the veins in the marble floor as if they were trails. No matter where she started, however, they all led her to the same spot...the door of the living room. Someone had turned on the tree lights while she was gone, making it all the more tempting.

It wasn't as if she was going to harm it, Lily reasoned. She would simply walk in, take a look and walk right straight back out. She'd pretend she was a mummy, she promised herself, already gliding across the thick crimson-toned rug. She'd keep her hands plastered to her sides the whole time. She wouldn't touch a thing; wouldn't even breathe.

That part was easy. As she approached the glittering tree that was three times as tall as she was, her breath caught in her throat at the beauty of it. She stepped closer, mesmerized. Aglow with hundreds of white lights buried deep within its full branches, this was the Christmas tree of her dreams.

There was no tinsel adorning these branches, no hodgepodge of dime-store glass ornaments. Aside from the white lights and a sprinkling of red satin balls, all the ornaments were silver. Silver icicles and snowflakes and pinecones, and even— hung close to the star atop the highest branch—a tiny silver train. Lily stared at the train for a long time, wishing it was closer to her.

Locking her hands behind her back to keep from touching anything, she examined one ornament after another, awed by the fine craftsmanship and attention to such small details as the braided tails on the horses pulling a tiny silver sled. She slowly made her way around the tree until she came to the most magnificent ornament of all. It was a clear glass ball the size of a large orange; inside, cast in silver and suspended as if it was floating in air, was a perfect replica of Delaney Place.

At last she'd seen everything and told herself it was time to get back to the hallway. A little guiltily, she thought that if she didn't say anything, she could get her father to bring her to see it a second time. It was then that she spotted the ship in the bottle resting on a table and stopped to look at it. The bottle was only as long as her hand and half as wide, but the ship inside was complete with sails and rigging and flags of color. Tiny gold letters on the stern read *HMS St. James.*

"Her Majesty's ship, the St. James," Lily whispered softly, smiling in delight. She'd read about the laborious process involved in building such a ship, but had never actually seen one. In her fascination she forgot all about being a mummy and reached for it.

She'd barely lifted it from its wooden stand when someone grabbed her shoulder.

"What the hell is going on here?" demanded a deep voice.

If she'd had time to get a better grip, she might have been able to catch the bottle even after it began to slip from her fingers. A sickening feeling washed over her as she saw it go, and her fingers automatically clenched, closing on air.

She cried out as it landed at her feet, on a strip of polished wood floor between two Oriental carpets. The delicate glass shattered into a million fine slivers and the tiny ship's mast snapped as it tottered for a second, then finally came to rest on its side.

"Oh, no, oh, no." Lily felt a thundering urge to run, to get out of there as fast as she could, but her feet might as well have been cement blocks. Her father would be furious, and her mother... Her stomach clenched. This was exactly the sort of trouble her mother always warned her to stay out of when she came here.

"Now look what you've done," said the same harsh voice.

Lily forced herself to turn and look up, already knowing who she would see. Mr. Terrell. She was trembling as if the devil himself was gripping her shoulder. He was still wearing his coat, as if he'd just walked inside, but Lily had a feeling his face wasn't dark red because it was cold out, but because he was furious—furious with her.

He shook her hard. "I asked what you were doing, and I want an answer."

"I was just looking at it," she said finally, softly.

"Hasn't anyone ever told you that you don't look with your hands?"

Lily nodded. Hundreds of times. As recently as a few hours ago, as a matter of fact.

"I'm sorry. It... it slipped."

"Slipped?" That one word seemed to suck all the air from the room. Lily's lungs ached for a breath. "All by itself?"

Her eyes widened. He had to know it hadn't happened all by itself. It probably wouldn't have happened at all if he hadn't surprised her by grabbing her the way he had. Something inside screamed that it was his fault as much as hers, maybe more. Something else warned that she had better not say so.

"I came in to look at the tree and then I saw the ship and . . . I just wanted to look at it. I picked it up and then it fell. I'm sorry," she said again.

"Do you have any idea of the value of that ship, young lady? Do you? Of course not, how could you? You don't belong here, and you have no business touching things that cost more than your old man makes in a month."

Lily stared at the floor as he continued. She was mortified by the things he was saying about her and her father and stung by the unfairness of it. She had the feeling, somehow, that he was pleased to have finally caught her doing something wrong.

There were footsteps in the hallway.

"Excuse me, Mr. Terrell. Hilda called me. She said there's some kind of trouble in here."

Lily recognized her father's voice in spite of the strangely hesitant note she'd never heard in it before, and she almost cried out loud with relief. Her father had a way of getting to the bottom of things so that it all came out fair in the end. He would ask questions and discover that what had happened wasn't all her fault. Of course he would still be upset at her for coming in here where she didn't belong, but that didn't matter. At that moment he represented all that was safe and secure in her world.

"Yes, there's trouble, and your daughter is responsible for it," Mr. Terrell told him in a mean voice Lily thought he would only dare to use on kids.

"I'm sorry, Mr. Terrell. If I've told her once I've told her a hundred times not to be in here underfoot. I thought she was in the kitchen with Hilda having some hot cocoa." As he spoke his gaze moved jerkily around the room, touching first on Lily and then on the shattered glass at her feet. "Lily, you didn't..."

"She certainly did," snapped James Terrell even as Lily was opening her mouth and shaking her head. "She doesn't belong here. I told her that, and now I'm telling you."

Her father nodded. "Yes, sir. I'm sorry about this, Mr. Terrell, and you can be sure I'll pay for whatever it is she broke."

"Oh, I'm sure of it, all right. That ship was a one-of-a-kind replica that I waited months to get my hands on. I'll see that the cost of replacing it is deducted from your salary."

Horrified, Lily took a step toward her father. "Daddy, I..."

"Quiet," he said, and even though he spoke softly Lily knew better than to ignore the warning look in his eyes.

Mr. Terrell paused on his way out and glanced back. "One more thing, Saville. Clean up that mess before you get on with your other duties."

"Right away, Mr. Terrell," her father replied with another quick nod, but this time it seemed to Lily that his head stayed bowed even after the other man had left the room.

Hilda had already brought a dustpan and brush from the kitchen, but when she tried to sweep up the broken glass Lily's father intervened with a small smile, saying, "I'll take care of it."

Without another word he knelt and painstakingly swept up every last sliver of glass from the floor and beneath the edges of the rugs, using his damaged right arm to hold the dustpan. Looking on, Lily felt a crushing ache in her chest, knowing it was her fault that her father was on his knees obeying another man's order.

Her father had always been a heroic figure to her. He was bigger and stronger than anyone else's dad, big and strong enough to chase away the monsters of her nightmares and to hold her safely above the waves when they went to the beach. He didn't work in a factory or a stuffy old office like other kids' fathers. He worked here at Delaney Place, outside in the fresh air. He was responsible for the velvet green lawns and the greenhouses full of flowers. He could coax a thing of beauty from a shriveled-up brown seed and a little dirt. He was everything safe and secure and magical.

Now, in a matter of minutes Lily's illusions were ripped away, forcing her to a full understanding of the way things really were. In this world of glamor and beauty her strong, kind, wonderful father was one who served. He was as powerless here as she had been a few moments ago.

Lily stood by in silence as he cleaned up the mess, then followed him to the greenhouse to wait until it was time to go home. She hated James Terrell and she hated ships in bottles and most of all she hated herself. She should have known better than to touch it in the first place.

Huddled inside her coat she tried and tried to think of some way to put everything back the way it was, but inside she knew there was no way. It was while sitting there in the cold that she decided she didn't want to come here again even if she had the chance. Somehow after today it would never be the same.

It was just starting to get dark outside when the greenhouse door opened and Mrs. Terrell walked in. At first Lily was frightened, thinking maybe she'd come out to yell at her some more for breaking what must have been a very valuable treasure. Then she surprised Lily by smiling the same friendly smile as always. Feeling a little less afraid, Lily slid from the bench to her feet.

"Mrs. Terrell, I'm sorry about—"

"Shh." Kay Terrell reached out and stroked her hair. "Whatever happened was an accident. I'm only sorry that my husband was . . . well, harsh with you. He can be a bit impatient at times, I'm afraid. I came looking for you to tell you that . . . and because I wanted to give you this."

She held out a small package wrapped in tissue paper. Lily had never before seen pale pink tissue paper.

"Go on, take it," she urged, laughing softly as Lily just stared at it with her eyes wide and her arms tightly clamped to her sides. "It's for you, Lily."

"But. . ." But why? wondered Lily. Why was Mrs. Terrell giving her a present when everyone, including her own father, believed she was responsible for what had happened? Lily didn't know how to ask without revealing the truth, and she wasn't sure that Mrs. Terrell would go on smiling at her after she accused her husband of hurting her shoulder and causing the accident in the first place. Admiring her the way she did, Lily would rather have Mrs. Terrell think she was clumsy than a snitch or even worse, a liar, and so she said nothing.

Feeling guilty and excited at the same time, she finally reached out and took the package, opening the box wrapped inside to uncover the glass ornament that had been her favorite.

"It's the house," she exclaimed in amazement.

"Your father mentioned you had gone in to look at the tree, and I had a hunch that particular ornament would catch your eye."

"It's Delaney Place."

Mrs. Terrell smiled approvingly. "You're very observant, but then I suppose that goes along with being an artist. Oh, yes, I've seen you working away, sketching the house and gardens."

"I didn't think anyone would mind," Lily said quickly.

"Of course I don't mind. I think it's wonderful that you have something you love to do. And now you have your own little model to use on those days when you can't be here."

Lily nodded, thinking how that would be everyday from now on. "Thank you, Mrs. Terrell, but you should keep this. After all, Delaney Place is your house."

"I can replace it, Lily. I'm sure the original mold still exists. But even if it doesn't, you deserve to have this for all the unpleasantness you put up with this afternoon."

The way she said it made Lily think that maybe Kay Terrell suspected a little of the truth after all.

"I just don't think my father will let me take it from you," Lily told her. "Especially not after..."

Mrs. Terrell closed Lily's hands gently around the box. "Don't worry, Lily, I'll take care of things with your father."

She did as she promised. Lily got to keep the ornament and when later, driving home, she asked if the ship in the bottle had cost a lot of money her father swallowed hard and said that he didn't know, that Mrs. Terrell had told him she had no more intention of charging him for it than she did of charging Hilda every time she broke an egg or spilled a little sugar.

After a minute or so he cleared his throat and said there was no need to tell her mother about the whole sorry affair or about how Mrs. Terrell had come to give her the ornament. They would just say it was an early Christmas present and leave it at that.

Lily knew he was saying that so her mother wouldn't blame her for what had happened, and at last she found the words to tell him the truth about how Mr. Terrell had grabbed her and made her lose her hold on the bottle. He asked her to tell the story twice, as if he couldn't believe anyone would do something so horrible.

"Damn him," he said finally, staring straight ahead. "Sweetheart, I'm sorry I didn't listen to you back there or ask for your side of the story. You see, Lily..."

"It's all right," she said quickly, nearly as shaken by the quiver in his voice as she had been by the sight of him sweeping up the broken glass.

"No, it's not all right. But don't you worry." He reached over to rub her shoulder. "We both learned a lesson today. I won't let anything like that happen to my little girl ever again."

Lily desperately wanted to believe his promise. Just a few hours ago she would have, heart and soul. Now she wasn't sure.

Even so, she understood how he felt and recognized the determined tremor in his voice. The same determination was beating inside her. She didn't know how or when, but she was going to see to it that someday things were different.

Someday *she* was going to be the one with a big house and enough money to arrange things so that her father never had to bow his head and take orders from anyone ever again, especially not from someone as mean as James Terrell.

ELEVEN

January, 1971

Lily needed money and she needed it in a hurry. The senior class trip was scheduled for the last week of April, barely two months away. She'd been saving for the trip since September, but had secretly dipped into the fund when she made up her mind to apply to the Rhode Island School of Design.

RISD, whose campus was located next door to Brown University in the historic section of Providence known as College Hill, was one of the most prestigious art schools in the country, and competition for admission was stiff. In addition to the usual request for high-school transcripts, SAT scores and recommendations, the college required each applicant to submit a portfolio of between ten and twenty original works that best represented the applicant's artistic interest and expertise. The unexpected expense of having her paintings professionally photographed had eaten up most of what Lily had saved for the trip.

Flopping onto her back on her bed, she stared grimly at the faded water stain on the ceiling above her and wished the class trip had never been changed from Bermuda to New York City. Theresa's was a Catholic high school attended by girls from all over Westerly. When the Sisters of Mercy, who ran the school, had, in surprisingly democratic fashion, allowed the senior class to vote on the destination of their traditional class trip, the small but persuasive Watch Hill clique had lobbied for Bermuda and won.

Lily had been relieved. The cost of a trip to Bermuda was so far out of her reach it wasn't worth thinking about. Besides, she wasn't particularly tempted by the prospect of lying on a beach all day and spending her nights plotting how to escape the chaperon's watchful eye long enough to sneak a rum swizzle at the hotel patio bar. Then Sister Assumption, the school's principal, had proved to be not so open-minded after all. She had vetoed the Bermuda trip in favor of the class's second choice, New York City.

For Lily, that was more than tempting. Broadway shows, Greenwich Village, shopping on Fifth Avenue. Saks, Bloomingdale's, Tiffany's.... As if all that wasn't enough, Sister Dominic had promised to take the girls in the art club on a special tour of the Museum of Modern Art. Lily was determined to do whatever she had to do to go on that trip, and right now the biggest obstacle was money.

There was no way she could ask her parents for help. For one thing, they had all they could do paying their own bills and her tuition. Besides, she didn't want to raise questions about what she had done with the money she'd saved. She still didn't know if she'd be accepted by RISD, and until she did know for sure, she wasn't about to confess to her folks that she'd ignored their objections and gone ahead with the application. Telling them wasn't a scene she was looking forward to. They were convinced RISD was crawling with long-haired weirdos who spent their time smoking pot and painting nude models.

Of course, her mother was convinced that her dream of studying art was just that...a crazy, impractical pipe dream that Lily should have outgrown long ago. Mary had no patience with dreams, or dreamers, for that matter. Someday she would see that Lily wasn't only a dreamer, but a doer, as well, willing to work hard to make her dreams come true. But for now, Mary would only frown and say, "Dreams don't pay the bills, young lady."

As much as she hated to admit it, at the moment, Lily was forced to agree. She had exactly forty-six dollars in her savings account and another eleven dollars and thirty-seven cents in the bank on her dresser. Even if she added in what she earned babysitting it was still a long way from what she needed.

One of her brothers might be good for a loan, but Lily dismissed that possibility as soon as it occurred to her. Cliff, the oldest, was halfway through a year-long tour of duty in Vietnam and had more to worry about than college or Broadway shows and window-shopping. The summer after high school, Greg had grown his hair to his shoulders, packed a knapsack and taken off to "find himself." Judging from his sporadic phone calls and postcards home, he wasn't even warm yet.

Joey was still living at home, but out of work because of a recurrent back injury, a souvenir from his high school football days. That left Ben. He would be willing to help, Lily knew, but until he graduated from the State Police Academy, he was earning next to nothing and saving every cent of that to buy an engagement ring for his girlfriend, Carol.

There was only one possible solution that would provide her with the cash she needed and help her save toward her next year's tuition. She had to find a job.

But first she had to convince her parents—correction, convince her *mother*—that she could handle a part-time job without letting her grades slide and jeopardizing her chance for a scholarship. It was an old battle and one Lily invariably lost. Until tonight, she told herself firmly.

Downstairs, her mother was sweeping the kitchen floor and her father was sprawled in his favorite chair, one leg thrown over the arm, halfway through his after-dinner cigar. Ben and Joey were there, as well, watching "I've Got A Secret." Lily would have preferred to make her case without them for an audience, but it couldn't be helped.

She sauntered into the room, trying to appear as nonchalant as possible. Joey, in particular, could smell nervousness a mile away and would do anything he could to make her sweat. She positioned herself in the archway leading to the kitchen so she could talk to both her parents at once. Her best hope was to get her father to say yes before her mother said no.

"Mom, Dad," she began, "I have to talk to you about something."

The broom in her mother's hand froze midstroke. "What's the matter?" Her eyes crinkled at the edges. "And where on earth did you get that blouse?"

Lily squared her shoulders inside the blouse her mother was eyeing with such distaste. It was a great blouse, vintage forties with a shawl collar and shoulder pads and made of real silk in a gorgeous silvery gray. Her parents' fear that she would turn into a tomboy had been alleviated years ago. Lily not only preferred wearing dresses, she preferred wearing dresses from another, more glamorous era.

She'd been thirteen when she saw the movie *Bonnie and Clyde* and fell in love with the clothes Faye Dunaway wore in her role as Bonnie Parker. Sophisticated hats with veils and sexy silk stockings and suits tightly nipped at the waist; clothes that swished when she walked and clung when she stopped and kept tantalizing secrets about the woman inside. Sleek, blond Bonnie was—at least in the Hollywood version of things—a woman of beauty and style and grace. Lily had no doubt her blouse was something Bonnie would have worn, and the fact that no one else she knew would be caught dead in it didn't bother her a bit.

"Chandra gave it to me," she explained.

Mary rolled her eyes. "Of course, who else?"

Chandra Gibbons lived next door. Her real name was Karen, but, like a lot of other things in life, her given name wasn't flamboyant enough for Chandra, who had run away from home when she was sixteen to join the Rockettes. Now in her forties, she wore miniskirts and fringed suede vests like most of Lily's contemporaries, but saw nothing wrong with Lily's passion for the glamour of a bygone era and was happy to feed it with treasures from the boxes in her attic.

"Where's the nice new sweater I bought you for Christmas?" her mother asked her. "You know, the pink one with the fancy stitching around the neck. You don't need to be afraid to wear pink with your hair, Lily. I keep telling you it's not red anymore, it's auburn. Pink looks beautiful on girls with auburn hair and green eyes."

"I'm not afraid to wear pink. It just so happens I like this blouse." Lily ignored the snort that came from the general direction of where her brother Joey was sprawled on the sofa.

Her mother's forehead puckered. "You like wearing clothes that are out of style?"

"They're not out of style," Lily argued, knowing that trying to explain was about as promising as gathering feathers in a stiff wind. "They're out of *fashion*."

"There's a big difference?"

"Yes, a big difference. Chandra says that fashion says, *me, too*, but style says, *only me*. I want to have my own style."

"Then keep working at it, kid," Joey called out, without taking his eyes off the TV, "because the style you got now is half Twiggy's and half Lucille Ball's."

He and Ben both laughed uproariously. Lily didn't especially care what they said about her clothes—if she did she would wear jeans and skirts and sweaters like everyone else—

but she hated when they made fun of her for being skinny, especially since she wasn't anymore.

Slanting her most condescending look Joey's way, she said, "Twiggy and Lucille Ball? My, my, that's quite an inspired observation coming from someone who thinks Saturday afternoon wrestling is a cultural event."

"You mean it isn't?" exclaimed Ben, comically wide-eyed as he joined the fray.

Joey guffawed and punched his brother's shoulder in a show of solidarity Lily was well accustomed to. She and Ben were close, but Ben and Joey shared a much stronger bond—they were both male. She was convinced there was some bizarre chemical attribute of male genes that enabled guys to appear to be perfectly normal human beings when they were alone with you, then instantly regress to their lowest common denominator whenever two or more of them were in the same room.

"Why don't you grow up?" she asked, quickly turning her back to them. Her father had tuned out the routine squabbling and was again engrossed in the gardening catalogue open on his lap.

He'd begun growing irises as a hobby years ago, but gradually it had evolved into a passionate quest to produce a hybrid never before seen. The house was always filled with seedling trays strategically placed near radiators and potted plants growing beneath fluorescent lights in the cellar in an attempt to persuade the flowers to defy nature's clock and bloom out of season.

"I'm close," he had announced to the family just last week, marking off an indescribably small distance with his fingertips. "I'm just this far from producing a beauty, an all-white Siberian miniature with just a hint of silver green in its ruffle. I started with Dreaming Meadows and White Bliss and their baby is going to be the sweetest flower you ever saw. That's what I'm going to call it, Sweet Saville."

"Sweet Saville." He had savored the words on his tongue. "And when I sell her, she's going to make us a fortune. Five, maybe ten thousand dollars. Think of it, Mary, we'll pay off this place and put Lily through college with no worries. We'll be on easy street."

"People really pay money for these things?" her mother had asked skeptically.

"Not always. But they will for this one."

"Who? Who in their right mind would pay thousands of dollars for this fancy new flower of yours?"

"Not just for a flower, for the thrill of owning something new and rare. Other growers will buy the bulbs. Maybe some seed company will even want an exclusive on it. What the heck, if you're going to dream you might as well dream big." He'd grinned at Lily's mother until she couldn't help smiling back. "You'll see, Mary, you'll see."

Now, peering over his shoulder at the pictures of an endless variety of blooms and at the figures scribbled in the margins, Lily felt a rush of affection for her father. Maybe the reason he was the only one who didn't scoff at her dream was that he had one of his own. She was convinced her mother had never once in her whole life dreamed of doing something or being anything other than exactly what she was, an overworked wife and mother.

"Dad," she said, resting her hand on his shoulder, "can I please talk to you and Mom for a second?"

He flipped the catalogue shut. "Sure, sweetheart, what's up?"

Her mother came to a stop a few feet away, broom in hand. "What's the matter, Lily?"

Lily felt the familiar tightening at the back of her neck and took a deep breath not to let her irritation show. "Nothing. Why does something have to be the matter just because I want to talk to you?"

"Because it does, that's why. Now out with it." Before Lily could say anything her mother went on. "It's algebra, isn't it? I told you if you stayed up late every night painting instead of studying you would fail that test and you went and failed it. Oh, Lily, you know Sister Assumption said it had be straight As for your whole senior year if you want to have a chance at that Kettering scholarship. Now you'll—"

"Will you stop?" Exasperated, Lily straightened from where she'd been leaning on her father's chair. "I got an A on the test. I have As in everything and a better chance at the scholarship than anyone else in the senior class."

Lily didn't need to be prodded to study. She desperately wanted to win the Kettering Award, a two-thousand-dollar scholarship established by the late Kettering sisters and awarded to the senior with the highest grade point average and the highest moral standards. Since the sisters at St. Theresa's didn't give "their girls" a chance at anything short of the highest moral standards, it came down to a race for high marks.

Lily knew her mother was counting on the scholarship to cover all her expenses at either of the two state colleges. Privately, Lily figured it would pay about half the cost of attending RISD, where she had every intention of going if she was accepted. But that battle could wait until another day.

"Then what is the matter?" asked her mother, a sharp, worried V forming between her eyebrows.

"Nothing," Lily repeated, then added in a rush. "I just wanted to tell you that I've decided to look for a part-time job."

"No." Her mother began sweeping again.

"Daddy..." Lily threw a pleading look his way, and he smiled.

"What sort of job?" he asked.

"Rusty," admonished his wife.

"Well, it seems to me we can at least hear her out, Mary."

"Why? She's not getting any job, part-time or otherwise." She swung her gaze to Lily. "You need to spend all your time hitting the books. That's your job."

"Plenty of kids work part-time and still get good grades. Lisa DeBellis works every afternoon at Clemson's Pharmacy and she made state and national honor societies same as I did."

"Good for Lisa DeBellis. She can afford to take chances. Her father's an undertaker. He makes good money. Don't you see that without that scholarship you can kiss college goodbye?"

"Yes. Why can't you see that working a few hours a week isn't going to ruin my grades? I already baby-sit and fold clothes at the stupid laundromat."

"And that's enough. Pocket money, that's all you need."

"No, it isn't. You don't even know what I need or what I want."

"Then tell me." Her mother stabbed the floor as if the broom was a pitchfork and stood gripping it tightly as she glared at Lily. "You tell me what's so all-fired important that you need to get a job and maybe ruin your whole life."

Lily lifted her gaze to the ceiling. "Oh, please."

"Tell me. Tell me what you need."

"Things," Lily shouted, hands spread wide before her. "I need—" She stopped abruptly, knowing she had about as much chance of convincing her mother of her need to paint or wander through a museum or see a play as she had of convincing her the moon was made of green cheese. When it came to agreeing on what mattered in life they were more like creatures from different planets than mother and daughter. "Nothing. Forget it. You wouldn't understand."

"I understand more than you'll ever know," declared her mother. She took a step toward Lily and stopped. "I understand that the things you want now, all these things you think are so important, won't matter to you at all when you grow up and have to make your own way in the world. Security, that's what's important."

Lily listened with her jaw rigid, doing her best not to smirk at the lecture she'd heard at least a thousand times. It was always the same—study, work hard, get a good job with a good pension. Her mother didn't care about any of the things Lily really wanted out of life, like travel, adventure, beauty, fun. After all, thought Lily cynically, what was a visit to the Louvre compared to a pension plan?

"You'll thank me some day, Lily, you'll see. If you get that scholarship and go to college, you can—"

"I know," Lily interrupted, recalling how this little talk invariably wound up. "I can be whatever I want to be, even a teacher or a registered nurse."

"That's right. You'll see." Her mother beamed as if she'd said she could be the first woman president. The woman was hopeless, Lily thought.

"Then if I'm so smart, smart enough to be whatever I want to be," Lily countered, "isn't it possible I'm smart enough to work a few hours a week and still get good grades?" She looked directly, appealingly, at her father.

He released a deep sigh as he shifted his gaze from Lily to her mother and back. "How many hours?"

"Not many," she hedged, "and only on weekend nights."

"It sounds like you have a job already picked out," he observed.

Lily nodded. "A girl at school told me the country club is looking for a waitress weekends—"

"No," Mary interjected. She couldn't help noticing that her husband looked as surprised as Lily by her emphatic refusal.

"Now, Mary, there's nothing wrong with being a waitress," he said.

She glared at him, thinking that he, of all people, should know it wasn't the waiting tables that worried her, but where Lily wanted to do it.

"Please, Mom," Lily pleaded. "At least let me give it a try."

Mary made a few useless sweeps with the broom before glancing at Rusty again. This time she could tell from his expression that he knew exactly what she was thinking, just as he always seemed to know, and like always his eyes held one strong, constant message: *Relax. Everything will be all right.*

"Please, Mom," Lily said again. "I'll take the bus straight there after school on Friday and Dad can pick me up later."

"How much later?"

"I'll find out when I go to fill out an application and if it's too late, I won't take it."

"What about your homework?"

"Come on, Mom, you know I never do homework until Saturday or Sunday afternoon, anyway." She perched on the arm of her father's chair. "I can handle it. Just give me a chance to prove it! You have to, Daddy, you just have to."

"Why?" asked Mary. "Why has this business about getting a job come up all of a sudden?"

"It isn't all of a sudden," Lily reminded her. "I've asked before, and you've said no. But the class trip is coming up, and I really want some new clothes, and I'm going to need—"

"Well, if that's what this is all about..." began her father.

"No." Lily stood up. "No, I won't take the money from you and Mom. I'm determined to pay my own way. I figure if I get the job at the club I can earn all the money I need between now and the end of April. It's only for a couple of months, Daddy."

"A couple of months." He puffed his cigar. "And once the trip is over, you'll give up this job?"

The smell of victory was strong enough for Lily to risk pressing her luck. "*If* my grades slide I'll give it up. If I prove I can handle the job and school you'll think about letting me stay on. Deal?"

He looked past Lily to where her mother was sweeping the pile of dust and crumbs into the dustpan. She met his gaze and sighed. "I suppose it won't hurt to let you try it for a while. If we don't give in, you'll just pester us to death," she added, as Lily threw her arms around her in an enthusiastic hug.

"Oh, thank you, Mom. I love you." She leaned down to kiss her father's cheek, inhaling the familiar blend of cigar smoke and the specially blended iris food that clung to all his clothes and stained his hands a deep violet-blue. "I love you both. And I won't let you down, I promise."

TWELVE

The next day at school dragged for Lily. As soon as her last class was over, she took the bus into the village of Watch Hill where the country club was located.

During the afternoon the temperature had climbed into the fifties, unseasonably warm for February in New England. The bus's heating system was oblivious to such gifts of nature, however. It delivered the same noxious gusts of heat as if it was freezing outside. By the time Lily got off in front of the club she was sweating inside the heavy fur coat that was her most prized possession.

The coat had belonged to Chandra's mother, another relic unearthed from the far reaches of her friendly neighbor's attic. Lily had grumbled when Mary forbade her to buy a used fur coat at the Salvation Army, but it had turned out to be a blessing in disguise. The twenty-dollar coats she had sneaked down there to try on had all been made of ratty-looking raccoon, while hers was sheared beaver, dark brown and as soft as an angora kitten. The black silk lining was frayed in places, but the garland of red roses embroidered along both sides of the inside front more than made up for that.

Not until she approached the club did she have second thoughts about the coat, wondering if, in deference to the old adage about first impressions, she should have worn instead what her mother invariably referred to as *the perfectly fine navy blue pea coat hanging in the front hall closet*. No, she decided. For better or worse, this was the real her.

She walked through the club's wrought-iron gates and along the drive, canopied now with bare oak branches, thinking of all the times she had longed to be doing exactly this. When she was younger and the entire family piled into the station wagon for Sunday afternoon drives, their route often took them past the club. Her brothers liked to look at the yachts docked at the private marina, but her favorite part was gazing along the wide front drive, which was invariably lined with sports cars, their tops down, reminding her of a string of brightly colored beads.

Sometimes she would glimpse members strolling around the club grounds—the men in white slacks and navy blazers, the women in pastel dresses or short white tennis skirts with rackets tucked under their arms and all the confidence in the world in their step. As the car went slowly past, she would twist around in her seat to peer out the back window until there was nothing left to see.

The clubhouse, with its blend of brick and white clapboard, was quintessential New England. A wide porch with a spindled railing ran almost all the way around the sprawling two-story main building. Tall French doors opened onto the porch at regular intervals, and copper-roofed bay windows overlooked the ocean and golf course.

The entrance Lily used led directly into what she guessed was the club's cocktail lounge, which at the moment was dark and deserted. In the winter obviously most of the club's activities took place in the evening. After a few seconds, her eyes adjusted enough for Lily to notice the man sitting across the room. He was smoking a cigarette, his feet propped on the table before him, his chair tipped backward to balance on its hind legs. He watched as Lily approached, her footsteps on the plush burgundy carpet as silent as he was.

"Excuse me," she said, "I'm looking for Mr. Ben Higgins." The classmate who told her about the opening had suggested Lily speak directly with the manager.

He exhaled a stream of smoke, but didn't bother to sit up. "What can I do for you?"

"Mr. Higgins, I'm here to apply for a job," Lily replied, concealing her surprise.

There were no lights on, and between the cloud of smoke hanging in the air and the glare from the late afternoon sun angling through the window at his back, it was hard to make out more than dark hair and a lean masculine frame, but she had the vague impression that he was young, at least younger than she expected the manager of a place like this to be.

"What is it you do?" he asked.

"Waitress—at least that's what I want to do."

"Well, you're sure pretty enough to be a waitress," he told her. "The members like something pretty to look at. That's real important around here, keeping the members happy."

Lily nodded eagerly. "Yes, I'm sure I could do that."

"I'm sure, too," he said in a tone threaded with soft laughter. Lily found it unsettling not being able to look him in the eye while they talked.

"Why do you want to work at the club?" he asked as she did her best not to fidget.

It was a question she'd anticipated. "Because of its reputation. Everyone knows the club is just about the nicest place in Watch Hill. *The* nicest, actually. It has a tradition of quality and tastefulness, and I'd be proud to be associated with that tradition even in a very small way."

Silence. She shifted her feet, intensely aware that he was not simply looking at her, or having a conversation with her, but *watching* her in a way that made her feel suffocated. Belatedly it occurred to her that the sun's glare, which prevented her from seeing him clearly, was working to his advantage.

"Let me see you walk," he said without preamble.

"I beg your pardon?"

"I said, let me see you walk."

His words were unhurried, as if it didn't matter if it took him the rest of the day to decide about hiring her, and his tone was deep and textured, the sort of voice she could feel as well as hear. His every word reverberated in the pit of Lily's stomach. God, she was nervous.

"You already saw me walk," she pointed out. "I walked in here."

"That was from the front. I'm going to have to see you walk from the back."

His tone was innocuous enough, but she had a hunch that if she could read his expression she would let him see her walk straight out the door. She thought about doing just that. Then she thought about the trip to New York and how just stepping inside this place had whetted her appetite for more of it.

Tossing her hair over her shoulders, she stood with her hand on one hip and asked, "Where do you want me to walk to?"

"Over to the bar and back. Here. You can carry this." He nodded at the table where three empty beer bottles were lined up on a tray. As she reached for it, he added, "Take your coat off first."

Hesitating for only a second, she slipped off her coat and laid it over the back of a chair. Reaching for the tray, she told herself that even if Higgins's manner was a little unnerving, his request might not be all that unreasonable. After all, he had a right to know if she was a total klutz before he armed her with a tray of dirty dishes and sent her scurrying through a room full of club members in formal wear.

She carried the tray to the bar, careful to keep her back straight and head high. Walking as quickly as she dared, she prayed all the while that she wouldn't stumble. Back at her original spot, she waited in silence for him to say something. She couldn't help wondering if he had any other little tests in mind and if she wanted the job badly enough to go along with them, too.

"Nice," he said finally. "Very nice."

She smiled with relief. "Does that mean I can have the job?"

"Actually, I think . . ."

"Jack? Are you still here?" inquired a man's voice from somewhere across the room. "I thought we agreed you ought to go home."

Lily automatically turned in the direction of the newcomer, so she heard rather than saw the man at the table drop his chair onto all fours. Who was Jack?

"I thought so too," he replied. "But I got . . . sidetracked. Pleasantly sidetracked. I've decided to hire this young lady."

She *did* have the job! Lily's heart lifted even as the other man asked, "To do what?" He had moved close enough for her to see that his impeccably trimmed hair matched the steel gray of his suit. He was watching Ben Higgins with a look that was somewhere between amused and exasperated.

Higgins made a sweeping gesture. "Waitress, golf pro, whatever she wants to do is okay with me."

"Waitress," Lily reminded him, slightly unnerved. "Waitress will be fine."

"And she'll make a fine waitress. You'll see. And you don't have to worry about all that formality crap, Ben. I already interviewed her . . . and administered a road test. She passed."

"Jack, I think you really ought . . ."

At that moment the phone behind the bar rang and he moved to answer it, leaving Lily wondering what was going on. If this man's name was Ben, as in Higgins, and the man beside her answered to the name Jack, it didn't take a genius to figure out that he wasn't who he said he was. So who was he? As confused as she was, Lily had a feeling that whoever he was, he had nothing to do with the hiring around there.

In the time it took her to turn to him, he'd gotten to his feet. He was as young as she'd suspected, probably only a few years older than she was. The confusion in her eyes was quickly replaced with an accusation. "You're not Ben Higgins."

He smiled, not apologetically, but rather complacently. "I never said I was."

"You sure as hell let me think it. Of all the...walk for me," she mimicked as she snatched her coat off the chair. "Take your coat off. What a jerk."

"Don't be so hard on yourself. Anyone would have made the same mistake."

"*You're* the jerk I was referring to. And there was no mistake—you purposely misled me."

"That's gratitude for you."

"What should I be grateful to you for? Lying? Amusing yourself at my expense? Did you get a big thrill out of watching me walk?"

"The truth?" he said, doing a poor job of controlling the twitch at the corner of his mouth. "Yeah, I did. That's one thing I wasn't *misleading* you about, you do walk real nice. C'mon, don't be mad. Think of it as a dress rehearsal for your interview with the real Mr. Higgins."

The real Mr. Higgins finished his phone conversation and rejoined them.

"Jack—"

"I'm going, I'm going," the imposter interrupted. "You don't have to tell me to get lost more than five or six times." He turned to grin at Lily. "Good luck, and do yourself a favor and can that crap about being proud to be associated with this joint. Old Ben here is sharp; he'll see right through it."

Lily's face flamed. The nerve of him. As if she wanted or needed his advice. Still, when she was seated in Ben Higgins's office and he asked why she wanted to work there, she found herself canning her prepared spiel in favor of the truth. She needed a job.

For a minute she thought it had worked. He recalled how badly he had needed a job at her age and went on about how important it was to continue her education. Then, glancing again at her application, he frowned so deeply his dark brows formed a V. He said something about her total lack of experience and about how demanding the members were about the quality of service at the club.

Lily leaned forward, determined to convince him to take a chance on her, when she was interrupted by the ringing of the telephone. Fists clenched, she sat going over her arguments in her head and paying little attention to what Higgins was saying to the caller.

"Totally inappropriate...proper channels...how about the fact that she has absolutely no experience?"

That got her attention. Was there someone else around there totally lacking in experience? Something told her no.

"Yes, yes," Mr. Higgins continued with a long sigh. "I realize that." A pause. "Don't you always?" he queried in a dry tone, then hung up. Folding his hands on top of her application, he met her gaze with a placid expression.

"Miss Saville, it appears I will be able to offer you a position after all," he said. "How soon can you start?"

Lily was stunned, but somehow she managed to gather her senses before he came to his. "Right away."

"All right. See my secretary about filling out the application forms."

Mr. Higgins brought her over to his secretary who gave her a stack of employment forms to complete. By the time Lily was finished, it was dark outside. She briefly considered calling home for a ride, then decided to take the bus instead. Calling was bound to invite questions and she'd prefer to do all her explaining at once and in person.

Her hours at the club were going to be later than her parents had agreed to and would include several school nights. Lily knew that wasn't going to make her mother very happy, but she'd been so grateful for Mr. Higgins's startling change of heart that she wasn't about to quibble over her hours. The phone call he received seemed linked to his decision to hire her, but she couldn't figure out how. No one besides her family knew she was coming here this afternoon, and none of them had the clout to intercede on her behalf.

On the bright side, her salary would also be better than she had supposed. She decided she would tell her parents about that first, then remind her mother that it was only going to be for a few weeks. At least officially. Lily was already imagining what it was going to be like working at the club during the summer when everything was in full swing.

She was halfway down the drive when a black Corvette streaked from out of the darkness and screeched to a halt beside her. The driver leaned over and rolled down the passenger side window. "Hi."

Instinctively Lily moved to the inside of the walk and walked faster.

"Whoa, slow down."

She recognized his voice the way a blind person can identify certain objects, from texture alone. Relief rippled through her, only to disappear as she turned to find him smiling at her much the way she'd caught him smiling at her a while ago when he'd watched her walk.

She gave him a blank stare. "Do I know you?"

He chuckled. "No, technically, I guess you don't. If you'll hold still a second I'll introduce myself."

She kept walking and he kept the car rolling along beside her.

"My name's Jack," he said.

Lily kept walking.

"It's your turn. You see. I told you my name, now you're supposed to say I'm . . ." He trailed off expectantly.

She couldn't resist. "I'm . . . too smart to waste time talking to a jerk like you."

"Charming. Very charming. I just thought that since you're going to be working here—"

She swung around to face him so quickly he stalled the engine. "How do you know I'm going to be working here?" She wouldn't be surprised if he'd hung around outside Mr. Higgins's office, eavesdropping.

"I checked with Higgins's secretary."

Just as sneaky, thought Lily.

"Not that I had to," he went on. "I knew you were a shoo-in as soon as I saw you walk across that room. Old Ben's a butt man, you know."

"For your information, *Old Ben* was a perfect gentleman. He certainly didn't do anything as sleazy as watching me walk."

"Oh, he watched all right, he just didn't ask permission first. At least I was honest about it."

"Honest? Don't make me laugh."

"All right," he called out, hurriedly shifting into first as she resumed walking. "I don't blame you for being ticked off. But at least I tipped you off to be straight with Higgins. He really goes for that honesty stuff.''

"It so happens I'm always honest," she said pointedly.

"I could tell," he said. "That's why I didn't bother telling you upfront to lie about not having any experience."

She stopped a second time, eyes narrowed with suspicion. "How did you know I don't have any experience?"

His smile curled slowly, suggestively, enough to make Lily's cheeks heat before he'd even uttered a word. "I could tell that, too, just by looking at you."

"Really? I think it's more like you could tell because Mr. Higgins told you so during your little phone chat a while ago."

"What phone chat?"

His sudden blank look only convinced Lily she was right. "When you called to tell him to hire me, remember?"

He shook his head, chuckling. "That's a good one." He gestured toward his leather jacket and worn jeans. "Do I really look to you like the sort of person who could twist Higgins's arm and get him to do something he didn't want to do?"

She peered at him, taking in the upward thrust of his jaw and the hand draped carelessly over the leather-wrapped steering wheel. She nodded slowly. "Yes, you do."

He shrugged with the same absence of regret as when she'd confronted him inside. "All right, so I made a quick call to put in a good word for you. You ought to thank me."

"I'd rather have gotten the job on my own merit."

"Or have lost it the same way?" he shot back. "Higgins never would have hired someone with no experience."

"I would have found a way to convince him. When I want something badly enough I always find a way."

He met her fiery stare and nodded. "Yeah, I'll bet you do, at that. Look, saying I'm sorry won't change anything. How about if I make amends by giving you a lift home?"

Lily ignored him.

"That was an invitation. It requires a response of some sort."

She turned and smiled. "Drop dead. How's that?"

"Ah, a classic case of cutting off your nose to spite your face."

"I fail to see how just jumping into your noisy rattletrap of a car is comparable to cutting off my nose."

"It wouldn't be this noisy if I could shift out of first," he pointed out dryly. "Besides, you have to consider the fact that it's getting colder out there by the minute. Weatherman said it might even snow. And then there's the simple fact that even my noisy rattletrap of a car beats walking.''

"It so happens I plan to take the bus."

"The bus, huh? Gas fumes, fighting for a seat...a ripped plastic seat at that, with the dirty stuffing all coming out and sticking to that great coat you're wearing... Yeah, I can see how that's too tempting to pass up. How about if you let me drive you as far as the bus stop?"

"Forget it." Once more she stopped, forcing him to clutch and brake in a hurry. "This is all a big joke to you, but not to me. What you did was childish and embarrassing. You might have completely blown my chances of getting the job and..."

As she was talking she heard a familiar heavy roar and turned to see the bus speed past the deserted bus stop still five hundred feet away. "No, wait," she shouted, waving her hand in the air and running a few steps before realizing it was futile. "Now see what you've done? I'm going to be even later. Damn."

"You don't have to be late. You can let me drive you home." He secured the stick shift and got out of the car, leaving the engine idling as he faced her over the black convertible top. He was wearing a blue oxford cloth shirt beneath the leather jacket. Lily had a thing for blue oxford cloth shirts. His eyes were also blue, the clear, unbelievable blue of an amateur artist's landscapes.

"Look," he said, "you're going to freeze your pretty ass off waiting for another bus...just so you can teach me a lesson, when teachers have been saying for years that I'm a lost cause. Why not use me instead?" When she didn't immediately refuse, he smiled. "What do you say?"

This time Lily was caught off guard by a smile as shiny and dangerous as a knife. Not the sort of danger that lurked in dark alleys. Something more subtle.

The streetlights revealed everything the shadows inside had hidden—dark wavy hair, granite jaw, broad shoulders, all the prerequisites for your average, everyday drop-dead gorgeous guy. The embarrassment she had felt parading before him in her plaid school uniform suddenly returned threefold.

Get a grip, she told herself. So he was gorgeous. And he was standing there offering to drive her home. No, *begging* to drive her. That was no reason for her to stop breathing.

She hesitated, considering her alternatives. They weren't very appealing. She could either wait for the next bus and be later still, or look for a phone booth, call home for a ride and risk having to answer over the phone the million questions her mother was bound to ask.

"All right," she said finally. "On one condition."

"Name it and we'll see."

"Promise me you'll never tell another soul how you tricked me this afternoon."

"You got it," he agreed, grinning and ducking into the car to swing the door open for her. "Hop in."

Lily gripped the door handle as he took the turn at the end of the drive on what felt like two wheels. She couldn't be sure if it was simply that she wasn't accustomed to riding in a car so low slung or if he really did drive like a maniac. Either way, in a surprisingly short time she adjusted enough to carry on a conversation.

"I don't remember ever seeing you at the club before," he said once they'd gotten the directions to her house out of the way.

"Probably because I've never been there before. I don't exactly travel in country club circles."

"What circles do you travel in?" He flashed her a grin. "Besides those of the infamous Sisters of Mercy, that is."

Lily rolled her eyes as she drew her coat more tightly over the hideous plaid jumper that branded her as one of St. Theresa's finest. "I was hoping maybe you hadn't noticed the uniform."

"You mean you were hoping maybe I was blind?"

"Either that or that you're so lacking in fashion sense you mistook it for a very avant garde designer original."

He turned to meet her gaze again, this time without the teasing grin. "I think you're an original, does that count?"

Lily just laughed. Living with four teasing older brothers had taught her that when your tongue gets tied, the safest course is silence.

Soon they had left Watch Hill behind and were zipping through the side streets of the considerably less picturesque village of Misquamicut, where her neighborhood was located. For a variety of reasons Lily found herself wishing the ride had taken a lot longer. For one thing, she wasn't looking forward to telling her mother that she was going to have to work later hours and more nights than they'd agreed on. But mostly she was starting to really enjoy the ride, the roar of the powerful engine, the suggestion of control and agility in the effortless way his long brown fingers manipulated the stick shift.

"Am I that boring?" he asked.

She glanced at him quizzically.

"That long-suffering sigh a second ago," he explained. "Am I really boring you that much?"

"No. I mean you're not boring me at all. I was thinking about something else entirely."

"Oh, that makes me feel infinitely better. Not boring, but not riveting, either."

"Sorry," she said, with a laugh. "It so happens I was thinking about my mother."

He groaned until she explained about the extra hours on school nights and how it was the thought of breaking the news at home that had prompted her sigh.

"I take it your folks aren't happy about your applying for the job?"

"My father was pretty reasonable, but my mother..." She shook her head. "Reason isn't always her strong suit."

"She thinks working will interfere with school?"

"That's her excuse. She says she's afraid my grades will slip and I'll jeopardize the scholarship I need to go to college. But that isn't likely to happen this late in my senior year. I think what she objected to most was where I was applying for a job."

"She has something against the club?" he asked.

"I think she has something against country clubs in general and with anyone in her family having anything to do with them or with the sort of people who belong to them."

"Reverse snobbery?"

"Something like that. Sometimes I think that in a previous life she must have been a scullery maid left at the altar by one of the landed gentry, and she has this subconscious fear that history will repeat itself. She's always saying things like *know your place, stick to your own kind.*" She shook her head. "It's weird."

"I'll tell you what's weird," he countered. "The fact that I still don't know your name."

"It's Lily. Lily Saville."

"Saville?" he echoed softly, his brow wrinkling. "Are you related to a guy named Rusty Saville?"

"Sure. That's my house there." She pointed. "Next one on the right...with the porch." As he swung close to the curb and braked, she said, "Rusty Saville is my father. Do you know him?"

He shrugged. "I've heard the name before. I think my parents might know him."

She paused with her hand on the door handle. "Now you have an advantage over me. I still don't know your last name."

"Daniels," he said after a few seconds. "Jack Daniels."

"Like the whiskey?"

"Yeah. It's an old family joke."

"I'll bet no one ever forgets your name."

"That's for sure," he agreed dryly. "No one ever forgets my name."

She turned the handle. The overhead light came on. "Well, I guess I better go in and get it over with."

Jack smiled. "Good luck."

"Thanks. Thanks for the ride, too."

He shrugged. "I owed you."

"Yes, well, good night."

"See you."

The unfamiliar buoyant feeling that had blossomed during the ride home faded as Lily made her way to the back door. "See you," he had said. Not that she had expected anything more. But just because she hadn't expected more didn't mean she hadn't hoped. Jack Daniels was the kind of guy who made silly feminine hopes inevitable.

And impossible. At least as far as she was concerned.

Without knowing a single substantial thing about Jack, she knew he was out of her league. It wasn't only the fact that he drove an expensive sports car and obviously had the kind of influence only money can buy; it was everything about him.

He was the groom on the top of the wedding cake, the man in the Coppertone ads, the smile that sells a million tubes of toothpaste. What he wasn't was the kind of guy who went for girls in wire-rim glasses and secondhand fur coats.

Through the back door she heard the familiar sound of pots rattling as her mother hurried to get dinner on the table, and her thoughts abruptly shifted to the more important matter of convincing her parents to let her take the job at the club in spite of the hours.

"I'm home," she called out as she opened the door.

"And just in time," her mother said, looking up from the pan of boiled potatoes she was straining. Her face was pink from the steam and a stray brownish gray curl clung to her forehead. "Well, don't keep me in suspense. Did you get the job or didn't you?"

"I got it," Lily replied brightly.

"Congratulations, honey," said her father, grinning at her over his shoulder as he scrubbed at the plant food stains on his arms.

Her mother's smile wasn't nearly as enthusiastic. "Just remember what I said."

"I will," promised Lily. "It won't effect my grades at all. You'll see."

Her mother made an unconvinced sound as she dumped the potatoes into a bowl. "So when do you start?"

"Thursday," Lily mumbled.

"Thursday?" her mother echoed. "That's not a weekend night."

"I know, but..." Lily took the bowl from her hands. "Here, let me help with that. In fact, you just sit right down here and let me do everything tonight... It will be good practice for me."

"You won't be needing any practice if they expect you to work on school nights."

Lily placed the bowl on the table and hustled her mother to her seat before returning with the pot roast and vegetables. Her father finished washing up and took his place, bellowing for Joey and Ben to come to supper.

After grace was said and everyone's plate was filled, her mother met her gaze across the table. "I'm still waiting to hear about Thursday."

"It's sort of a long story," Lily told her.

Her mother sighed. She wasn't smiling, but her mouth didn't have that pinched, unreasonable look either, Lily noted with relief. "It always is," Mary said.

After dropping Lily off, Jack made a U-turn at the corner and sped past her house hoping to sneak one last look at her, but she was already inside. Damn. He'd been half hoping another look would reveal something to snap him out of the hormonal overdrive he'd been in since she walked into the club. He couldn't figure it out. She wasn't at all like the girls he usually went after. She wasn't petite, she wasn't blond and she didn't gaze at him like he was the answer to prayers she hadn't even thought of yet.

Maybe that was it. Maybe it was because of his gut-level certainty that he was not the answer to Lily Saville's prayers that he was so attracted to her. He was always swimming upstream.

It wasn't just the way Lily looked that grabbed his attention, although he liked that, too. She looked smart and foxy at the same time. Her long hair and long legs tempted a guy to reach out and grab, while those self-assured green eyes that stared out at the world from behind oversize wire-rimmed glasses warned him to think twice before trying.

Smart and foxy. Especially smart. He cursed the afternoon beers that had fogged his brain enough that the best he could come up with was a name like Jack Daniels. It wouldn't take long for her to figure out that he had lied, if she hadn't already. The question was, why had he done it? To protect Lily? Or himself?

He shook his head to clear it. Ben Higgins had been right. It was time for him to stop trying to drown his problem and go home and confront it. And what a problem it was. Tossed out of college with only ten weeks to go until graduation. Not that the dismissal was irrevocable. The dean, no doubt recalling his family's hefty contributions to the alumni fund, had assured him that all that stood between him and reinstatement was an apology to old Professor Chabot. Screw it. They might as well ask him to swallow the Grand Canyon.

The reason he'd stopped off at the club before going home to deliver the bad news was that aside from knowing that he wasn't going to apologize for telling the truth—Chabot *was* a bigot—he hadn't decided what he was going to do next. He knew what he wanted to do, just as he knew what he was expected to do. In his family there had never been any doubt about that, he thought grimly. And between what he wanted and what was expected lurked one huge hassle on the home front.

Plugging in his favorite Rolling Stones tape, he cranked up the volume. He was in too good a mood to think about all that right now. Lily had put him in a good mood, an expectant mood. Tapping the wheel in time to the music he thought about her legs, and her smile. Then he thought about her father. Rusty Saville. So much for his good mood. It sure was turning out to be his week for unlucky breaks.

THIRTEEN

Convincing her mother she could handle working the longer hours wasn't as tough as Lily feared. It was as if, having already made the major concession of allowing her daughter to waitress at the club, Mary could only muster a halfhearted protest when the terms of their deal changed. And even that was cut short by Joey, who wanted to know who had driven Lily home. It quickly became clear that he was more interested in Jack's car than in the company his sister was keeping.

Not so her mother.

"What do you mean *just some guy?*" she demanded, echoing Lily's evasive reply. "Since when do you climb into a car with some guy you don't even know?"

"Not just a car," Joey inserted. "A 'Vette."

"That's something special?"

"It is if you consider a car worth as much as this whole house special."

"What kind of work at the club pays a boy enough to drive a car like that?" Mary wondered out loud.

"I'm not sure he works at the club," said Lily. "I think he might be a member. As a matter of fact he even put in a good word for me with the manager."

"Leather interior?" inquired Joey.

"How should I know?"

"You sat on it, didn't you?"

"So why would he put in a good word for a perfect stranger he just met?" asked her mother, not one to be sidetracked.

Lily cursed herself for mentioning Jack's assistance. "I don't know why. He just did, that's all."

"How much horsepower?"

Lily glared at her brother. "Double the number of your IQ."

"Touchy, touchy."

"Well, I know why he did it," declared her mother. "Driving around in a fancy car and hanging around a country club in the middle of the day... There's only one reason a boy like that would be nice to a girl like you. Stay away from him."

Meeting Ben's amused gaze across the table, Lily fought the impulse to argue the matter with her mother. What was the point when common sense told her she would have a lot more trouble getting close to Jack than staying away from him? Besides, she could afford to be agreeable. She'd already won the battle that really counted.

Working at the club was more exciting than Lily had dreamed, and twice as exhausting. She worked Tuesday through Saturday nights, with Sundays and Mondays off. There were no easy nights.

If there wasn't a private party or club function going on, the dining room was operated as an ordinary restaurant, with guests ordering from the full menu. Waitresses weren't allowed to use order pads, and Lily quickly learned to concentrate so as not to forget that Mrs. Winston Pierpont wanted the house dressing for her salad, sour cream for her baked potato and sauce all served to her on the side, and that Clinton Maxwell III wanted every speck of skin removed from his chicken before it left the kitchen. Some members were gracious when she slipped up, and others were very vocal in their displeasure. She discovered that the very rich were pretty much like the very poor—good and bad, nice and nasty—only with lots more money.

On special function nights when all the guests were served the same meal she had other problems, namely seeing to it that everyone seated at the same table was served at the same time. No easy feat when trays had to be carried from the kitchen individually so as not to inconvenience the guests by cluttering the aisles with serving carts.

By the time Lily got off work sometime around eleven, she was bone-weary and usually felt aftershocks of fatigue the next morning in class... Something she vehemently denied whenever her mother approached, wearing a worried frown, to ask if the job was getting to be too much for her. Even if the work was a hundred times harder, she wouldn't give it up.

Each night at the club was like attending a fashion show featuring jewels and furs and designer clothes that until now had existed for Lily only as glossy magazine photos. Even the snatches of conversation she overheard as she carefully replaced consommé bowls with salad plates were like peepholes into a different world.

Watch Hill's location and yacht-docking facilities made it a popular getaway spot for wealthy New Yorkers, and the names of famous people and places peppered their conversation. Lily marveled at how they spoke of attending an opera at the Met or a Broadway opening as casually as her mother talked about picking up hamburger on sale at the local grocery store. They discussed important, fascinating things that were happening in the world right now.

Lily was in heaven. She wanted to see and do and experience everything that was out there. It wasn't a new feeling; she had always felt the desire to see things and go places that no one else around her seemed to care about. It was a hunger that in her family, her school, her neighborhood, seemed to exist only in her, making her an outsider even in her own home. She'd learned young that it was possible to feel well-loved and utterly alone at the same time. There had been times when she worried that maybe it wasn't simply a matter of hearing a different drummer, that maybe the life she dreamed about was pure fantasy. That maybe she should just give up her grandiose ideas and follow her mother's advice to settle for a career that would guarantee security. Working at the club had ruled out that possibility forever.

This was a world she had always known existed. Now, having come close enough to see and smell and touch it, her yearning to be part of it was stronger than ever. She read the *New York Times* as if it was bread and she was starving. She read reviews so that she recognized the books and plays and events she heard mentioned, and she formed opinions on them, such strong opinions that sometimes she had to keep her lips pressed tightly together to keep from serving them along with the crème de menthe parfaits.

Someday, she vowed, she wouldn't have to stay quiet. Someday she would be sitting at one of these tables wearing something gorgeous that had been designed for her alone and discussing important art exhibits and the latest Broadway plays.

Ambition beat inside her as steadily as her heart, until she felt she would go crazy if she couldn't stop marking time at school, at home, at work, and get on with her life. She clung to the hope that she would be accepted at RISD, the first step toward her future. Each night she returned home both praying and dreading that she would find waiting on the kitchen counter a letter from the admissions office. Early acceptances from both state colleges had arrived weeks ago, and it was assumed she would decide between them. She still hadn't dared tell anyone about applying to RISD.

After working at the club a month, she had earned enough to pay for the class trip and was saving toward spending money and some new clothes to bring along. She wouldn't buy anything fancy—that way she would be able to use the clothes for school next year, as well—but she had promised herself she would splurge on at least one absolutely wonderful outfit that she ordinarily wouldn't dream of buying. With that in mind, she stopped on the way to work one day to window-shop along Bay Street in Watch Hill.

Some of the shops, especially those catering to tourists, closed for the winter, but now, at the end of April, most of them had reopened. Not that it mattered to Lily. The neon bikinis and fishnet cover-ups displayed to tempt those who spilled from nearby yachts were not what came to mind when she thought of something "absolutely wonderful." A simple white knit dress in the window of Derring Do—now *that* was wonderful . . . classic . . . perfect. Still, she would have to stroll by several more times to be sure before going in to ask the price, much less try it on. Splurging wasn't something she did often, and she intended to wring every drop of pleasure from it.

With the possibility of the dress weighing delightfully on her mind, she perused the cluttered window of Yesterday's Gone, the antique shop that was a favorite haunt of hers even when she didn't have money to spend. The shop was so tiny she could see nearly everything in it through the front window. There were antique watches and jewelry and small intricately beaded handbags that made Lily think of flappers in fringed dresses doing the Charleston.

"What's so fascinating?"

The words sent a shiver of excitement along her spine. No, not the words themselves. Those she barely registered. It was the voice that uttered those words, deep and familiar to her in the way the William Tell Overture was. Having heard it once, she remembered it forever.

She hadn't seen Jack since the day she got the job. She'd even abandoned her offhand inquiries about him when one of the other waitresses smirked and told her to wake up, that the only member named Jack Daniels was standing on a shelf behind the bar. Her curiosity didn't fade, however. Sometimes it was so strong she almost got up the courage to ask Mr. Higgins himself. Other times she wondered if Jack Daniels, or whatever his name was, had been simply a figment of her imagination. A too-good-to-be-true fantasy.

Now here he was, wearing jeans and a faded navy polo shirt beneath the same leather jacket. Careless chic. He was real, all right, as real as the funny hollow feeling in the pit of her stomach, a feeling Lily had never experienced before meeting him. She had begun to think she'd imagined that, too.

She returned his smile; it was impossible not to. His dark hair was longer than she recalled. About four weeks longer. And he needed a shave. He looked terrific. And expectant. An answer, he was waiting for an answer, she realized in sudden panic. Now what was the question?

"I asked what was so fascinating," he prodded, amusement in his eyes.

Lily gestured toward the window. "Everything. I love this place."

He glanced skeptically over her shoulder. "Yeah? It all looks sort of dusty to me."

"That's part of its charm."

"If you say so."

"Just look," she urged, turning so they were side by side staring into the antique shop window. "There are hundreds of different stories in this window." She pointed to a silver pocket watch. "I look at that watch and wonder what sort of man carried it and where he was when he pulled it out of his pin-striped vest pocket to check the time. And this bag, the one with the fringe, that had to belong to a lady of the evening. Maybe more than one."

"More than one lady or more than one evening?"

"Take your pick," she said with a laugh. She touched the glass. "And look at this beautiful mirror over here in the corner." He followed her gaze to the etched silver hand mirror in the corner. "I'll bet if you look into that mirror hard enough you can see the ghosts of all the people who've ever owned it. Ladies primping for fancy balls and little girls sneaking in to sit at their mothers' dressing tables.''

"Personally when I look into a mirror I'd rather just see me.''

"Well, I wouldn't," Lily countered emphatically. "I'd rather see ghosts."

He stared at her in silence, an odd expression in the dark blue eyes that held hers. "I was right," he said at last, quietly, as if talking to himself.

"About what?"

"You. The way you make me feel."

"How do I make you feel?" she found breath to ask.

His sudden grin held mischief. "Interested. Very interested.''

The tilt of her head suggested an offhandedness Lily was far from feeling. "Really? I would have thought otherwise. Considering.''

"Considering?" He fell into step beside her as she began walking slowly.

"Considering that I haven't seen you around for four weeks. I wonder how you act when you're not interested."

"Sounds like I'm not the only one who's interested. I mean, considering that you went to the trouble to count the weeks and all.''

"I hardly had to count them. I simply know that I was hired four weeks ago."

"Of course."

"It's true."

"I'm sure it is. But just in case you are mildly interested, the reason I haven't been around to see you is that I was away at school.''

"What school do you go to?"

"Princeton."

"I'm impressed. What year?"

"Senior, but don't get carried away. The last time I saw you my college career was hanging by a thread. I went back to snap it.''

"You mean . . ."

"I mean I'm out," he finished for her with a nonchalance she found remarkable. "No 'Pomp and Circumstance,' no stupid tassled hat . . ."

"No degree for four years of hard work."

"I didn't work all that hard."

Lily shook her head, startled and intrigued by his attitude. "My folks would kill me."

"Mine would like to," he responded agreeably.

"What did you do to get kicked out at the end of your senior year?"

She listened as he explained about a bitter classroom argument with a tenured professor. He spoke quickly, his tone bored, as if he was weary of talking about it.

"So the dean said I'd be welcome back as soon as I apologize to the jerk," he concluded.

Lily glanced at him in amazement. "That's it? That's all they wanted, an apology? So why didn't you?"

His impossibly square jaw suddenly got more so. "Because I never say I'm sorry. Especially not when I'm right." He shrugged hands resting in the pockets of his jacket. "Besides, I have better things to do."

"Such as?"

He hesitated. Lily saw him consider the question and then close himself off from it. "See you, of course."

"Right. You got yourself tossed out of Princeton just so you could come home and see me."

He stopped in the middle of the sidewalk and turned to face her, forcing the stray pedestrians to walk around them. His hand lifted to brush her cheek. He spoke quietly.

"You'd be surprised, Lily."

She was. Stunned, in fact, that a touch no more substantial than a falling snowflake could make her knees shaky and her throat dry.

"I . . . I have to get to work," she said, although she still had plenty of time to make the ten-minute walk to the club.

Jack nodded. "I'll drive you."

"Two blocks?"

"Okay, I'll walk you."

At the corner they stopped to let a car pass before crossing the street, and Lily recognized Andrea Evans, her chief competition for the Kettering scholarship, in the passenger seat. Andrea did a double take at the sight of Lily walking side by side with Jack.

It wouldn't take long for the word to spread through school, thought Lily, unable to keep from enjoying the prospect. After all, it wasn't every day she was seen in the company of a great-looking guy. More like never, actually. She suspected that on Monday she would be asked more than once who he was.

Which was a question she wouldn't mind having answered herself.

Backing into it as subtly as possible, she said, "You did mention that your family belongs to the club, didn't you, Jack?"

"No. I didn't," he replied with a sideways glance. "But they do."

"That's strange, because no one I've spoken with recalls any members by the name Daniels."

If her pointed tone made him uncomfortable, it didn't show. Flashing her a grin, he said, "Talk about me at work, do you?"

Lily shrugged. "I asked around. Not that it did me any good, since I was asking about someone named Jack Daniels."

"Not very original, huh?"

"Not to mention truthful."

"Would it help if I told you I had my reasons for not telling you my name?"

"It would help more if you just told me the truth."

"I did, to an extent. My name *is* Jack."

"What's your last name?"

"Why does it matter so much what my last name is?" he countered, his voice taking on a hard edge.

"It doesn't matter so much. So why not tell me?"

He hesitated.

"For heaven's sake, it's not like you're Jack the Ripper . . . Or are you?"

"Believe me, it might be simpler for both of us if I were."

Lily stared at him, more curious than ever. "Why? What's the big mystery about your name?"

"It's not a big mystery. It's just that by talking about it this way we've blown it all out of proportion. Do me a favor, will you? I told you that the Jack part is true. Could we just leave it at that for a little while longer? Just Jack?"

"But . . ." The almost desperately wistful look in his eyes cut her protest short. "Sure, why not? It's no big deal."

They walked in silence for a moment, then Jack steered the conversation to her, asking questions about work and about school. Lily startled herself by confiding in him what she hadn't told another living soul, that she had applied to RISD and that she felt like she would die if she didn't get in.

"Of course every day that goes by without a letter, I become more convinced that I'm not good enough to make it," she told him, exposing her most secret fear.

"Of course you're good enough."

"How would you know?"

"I was almost a Princeton graduate, remember?" he said, jostling her playfully with his shoulder. "I know these things."

"Thanks," she said dryly. "I feel much better now."

"All right, so maybe it would help me form an opinion if I saw something you've done."

She chewed her lip for a few seconds, then slipped her canvas tote from her shoulder. "You asked for it."

"You carry paintings in your purse?"

"Book bag, not purse. And it's not a painting, it's my sketchbook. And I can count on one hand the people I've ever let look at it."

Lily appreciated the fact that he didn't fire back a clever retort. His expression solemn, he took the sketchbook from her and walked to a nearby stone wall where he carefully laid it down and opened it.

Lily leaned against the wall, her stomach in knots, her hands tucked behind her to keep from fidgeting as he slowly flipped the pages. She couldn't remember ever wanting anyone's approval as much as she wanted Jack's at that moment.

He spent a long time studying her favorite drawing, a charcoal study of an old staircase at school that began in sharp focus, becoming hazier and less detailed as the eye was drawn upward until it faded completely into shadow with just the suggestion of a lady's long skirt trailing at the top. He returned to it again after looking at all the others. When he lifted his head, his expression was still somber, but his eyes were filled with admiration.

"More ghosts?" he asked, indicating the sketch of the staircase.

She gave a nervous shrug. "I draw what I see."

"Lily, you can't honestly be worried that you might not be accepted by RISD. These are terrific. I'm no art expert, but some of these gave me shivers."

"Does that mean they're good?"

"I think it means they're great. Relax. You've got nothing to worry about, kid."

"I hope so," she countered excitedly, then sighed as she packed the sketchbook away again. "Of course, if I do get accepted my real problems begin."

"How's that?"

She briefly explained about her mother's determination that she should pursue a career that was secure and practical and about her parents' assumption that she would win the Kettering scholarship and go meekly off to one of the state colleges to major in nursing or education.

Jack chuckled sympathetically. "I guess they really discouraged you from applying to RISD."

"Actually they forbade it."

"And you just went ahead anyway?"

"I had to. If this was a whim or a last-minute decision, things might be different, but it's not like that." She stopped walking, overwhelmed with relief at finally being able to present her arguments to someone other than her own conscience. "This is what I want to do with my life, the only thing I want to do, the only thing I care about and the only thing that will make me happy. Have you ever known in your heart that you're right about something, even when everyone else is telling you that you're crazy?"

He stared at her without saying anything for so long that Lily began to worry that maybe he thought she was crazy, too. Finally he gave a small nod. "I think so."

"Well, that's what this is like for me. And I believe that at times like that, you have to listen to your heart and go after what you want."

"But don't you worry about the consequences? About letting your parents down?"

"Of course I do," she said quietly. "I love them and I want them to be proud of me, but I want to be proud of me, too."

"So you just went for it. You know, that's pretty gutsy."

"Not all that gutsy," she confessed sheepishly. "Sure, I took the plunge and applied, but I didn't tell anyone about it. At least not until a few minutes ago."

"You mean I'm the only one who knows about this?"

Lily nodded.

"But why?"

"There was no one I felt I could trust to understand."

Jack nodded, registering the implication of that, but mercifully not pressing her about why she had felt she could trust him. Lily didn't have an explanation she could put in to words.

"Actually I didn't intend to ever tell anyone if I was rejected, and if I was accepted..." She shrugged. "I figured I would worry about that when the time comes."

"I'm sure when you do finally tell your folks and they see how much this means to you, they'll come around."

"You really think so?"

He glanced at her, his mouth twisting. "Based on personal experience? Not really. If your parents are anything like mine they have their own agenda. You're another piece on their chessboard."

She sighed, absently breaking a leaf off a budding azalea bush at the edge of the club's walk. "Sometimes I think maybe I should just take the path of least resistance and go to the state school. I could always minor in art, maybe become an art teacher."

Jack turned suddenly, surprising Lily by grasping her tightly by the elbows. "Don't say that. I don't want to hear you say that. It makes it sound like you don't have any guts after all. And I don't want to think that."

"Why not?"

After a second's hesitation, he grinned and released her. "Because I hate being wrong. I want to go on thinking that you're the type who goes after what you want with both guns blasting."

"That's me," countered Lily, playfully forming a gun with her fingers and blowing on the tip of the barrel. "A regular Annie Oakley."

"Go to work, Annie." Jack laughed. "But first tell me what time you take your break."

"Around nine-thirty."

"How about meeting me on the porch overlooking the eighteenth hole?"

"Okay," Lily said, doing her best not to sound as excited as she felt.

For the first time in years her vision of the future extended no further than the next few hours.

FOURTEEN

Lily's spirit was infectious, Jack discovered. After leaving her at the club, he went home and took the stairs to the second floor two at a time in search of his mother. He had been tiptoeing around the matter of his future for weeks, years actually, not wanting to agree to his mother's plans for him and not ready to declare open warfare by revealing his own. Now, thanks to Lily, he was ready.

Listen to your heart, she'd said. It sounded like a line from a bad song or from one of those sappy soft-focus cards girls liked to send, but for some reason when Lily said them, the words hit him where it counted. If he listened to his heart he wouldn't be returning to Princeton with his tail tucked between his legs or assuming what his mother referred to as his rightful place in the family business.

His father was always accusing him of having no ambition, but, as he was about so many things, he was wrong about that, too. Jack had ambition, plenty of it, but it lay in a different direction than the one he was expected to follow. He tried telling his parents so, but either they didn't listen or he'd never found the right words. Today he was going to change all that.

He found his mother in her bedroom, seated at the dressing table. Jack took one look at the clothes and shoes strewn around the usually tidy room and at the matching disarray in his mother's expression and knew this wasn't the time for the talk he had planned.

Concealing his disappointment, he crossed the large room with its tall mullioned windows and stood behind her. She met his gaze in the mirror.

"Hello, Mother," he said. "What's wrong?"

She tossed aside the silver hairbrush that had been designed expressly for her on her eighteenth birthday. "What isn't? Tonight's the night of the Pattersons' party. I accepted the invitation ages ago, and now—''

"Let me guess," Jack interjected, quirking an eyebrow as he glanced around the room. "You have nothing to wear?"

That brought a small smile to his mother's lips. He almost always managed to make her smile. There was an unusually strong bond between them, in spite of the fact that he was adopted. Oh, he'd heard all about how adopted children were special because they were *chosen* and how they grew *not under their mothers' hearts, but in them.* Jack didn't totally buy it, maybe because he was raised in social circles that left no doubt about the importance of bloodlines.

"I suppose I could rummage up some old rag," she returned playfully, gesturing at the careless heaps of velvet and satin, enough to dress half the female guests at tonight's party, he was sure. "What I don't have is an escort."

"Where's Dad?"

"Working late," she replied, as he'd known she would.

Retrieving the brush, she dragged it through her shoulder-length blond hair, carefully avoiding his gaze in the mirror. She needn't have bothered. Jack had long ago stopped asking why it was necessary for the president of Delaney Silver to spend so many late evenings handling business-related "emergencies." They both knew why, and it only added to his mother's pain.

When his grandfather was still alive and running the company he'd rarely put business ahead of his family. Jack recalled his grandfather with a loving warmth he did not feel for his adoptive father. Charles Delaney, more than anyone else, had always made him feel like an important member of the family. But Charles was gone now, along with the grandmother Jack had also loved. Sometimes he wondered if the strong bond between his mother and himself was the result of the fact that in the closed triangle of what was left of their family, they had only each other.

"Can't you cancel?" he asked her now.

"At the last minute?" She moved to face him. "I suppose I could say I have a headache, but I used that excuse two weeks ago when we were scheduled to have dinner with the Fontaines. Anne Patterson and Louise Fontaine are sisters, and I just know they call each other and compare notes every morning."

She sighed, the slight tremble at the corners of her smile revealing a vulnerability most people never saw in her. Jack's fists clenched reflexively. His father was a jerk. His mother was beautiful and fun and generous, everything a man could want in a woman. And James Terrell wanted every woman but her.

"There's no way out of it," she said sadly. "I have to go."

"Alone?"

She gave a small nod, then lifted her gaze to meet his. "Unless..."

She let the unspoken suggestion hang in the air. Jack could have kicked himself for coming home and landing himself in this. Not that he would ordinarily mind spending a free evening doing his mother a favor. God knows, she'd done him enough through the years, interceding with his father and school officials whenever his free spiritedness got him into trouble. But strictly speaking he wasn't free this evening. He had plans to meet Lily later. For about fifteen minutes, his conscience reminded him, as his mother began to turn away.

"I have a great idea," he said, as if it had just occurred to him. "Why don't I take you to the Pattersons' party?"

She played along, fluttering her lashes. "Oh, Jack, what a fabulous idea. Not only will I have an escort, but I'll get a chance to show off my handsome son...a pleasure I have all too rarely these days. And I promise we'll bow out before you absolutely die of boredom."

"No problem," he assured her, thinking he would have to call the club and leave a message for Lily. "I'll take a shower and get dressed. What time are you supposed to be at the Pattersons'?"

"Eight or so will be fine," she replied, heading for the bathroom. Over her shoulder, she tossed, "It's formal, so I hope you remembered to have your tux cleaned. And it's not at the Patterson's—it's at the club."

Jack felt as if he was walking a tightrope. His only way out of this jam of his own making was to find Lily before she found him and tell her the truth. That wasn't as simple as it sounded.

True to her words, his mother was basking in the glory of having him with her. She dragged him along to say hello to one old friend after another, glossing over the less than flattering details about what he was doing home weeks before graduation. Each time he had to bite his tongue. His plan for his future wasn't anything to be ashamed of, and the urge to have it all out in the open had grown steadily stronger since this afternoon.

Several times he spotted Lily across the crowded dining room, her concentration apparent from the expression on her face. It didn't surprise him that Lily would bring the same serious determination to waiting tables as she did to everything else. The urge to talk to her kept him on the edge of his seat, as he only half-listened to the conversation at the table. But he could hardly walk over there and say what he had to say while she was serving the salad. As time passed, he began to think the best course was to meet her on her break as planned.

At nine twenty-five, he excused himself and headed for the door. He was in the club's foyer when he caught sight of Lily in the pass-through between the dining room and kitchen and called to her.

"Jack," she said, a smile brightening her face as she hurried toward him. "I was just going to grab my coat and go out to meet you."

"Hurry. I have something I want to tell you."

Her head tilted. "Sounds ominous."

"It's not . . . at least not as far as I'm concerned. I just hope you agree."

"Now you have me—"

"Jack? There you are, darling."

Jack recognized his mother's voice but didn't turn around. He was afraid of what he was going to see on Lily's face when she figured out the truth, and yet perversely he had to see it.

At first she looked bewildered. A second later, as his mother approached and Lily recognized her, her eyes glowed almost as if she was in the presence of royalty. His mother had that effect on people. Flicking a glance sideways at her, Jack understood why. The light from the chandelier fell in a circle around her, igniting the fine gold threads in the white off-the-shoulder gown she'd finally decided to wear. Her upswept hair and diamond jewelry added to the regal impression.

"They told me you were going to step outside for a moment. I'm so glad I caught you." She placed her hand lightly on his arm. "For the past half hour I've been trying to catch your eye to tell you that you absolutely have to ask June

McAllister's daughter to dance. The poor girl is languishing there all by herself."

"I'll be back in a while," he replied. "I'll dance with her then."

"That's all right, Jack," said Lily. "Don't let me keep you from the party."

"You're not keeping me," he told her, surprised by her blasé reaction.

For the first time his mother seemed to notice that there was someone else there. Her slight smile was courteous.

"Hello, Mrs. Terrell," said Lily. "You probably don't remember me."

A question flickered across his mother's face and was quickly replaced by a genuine smile. "Of course I do." She held out both hands to clasp Lily's. "How are you, Lily? Rusty didn't mention that you were working here at the club."

"I started only a few weeks ago."

"How do you like it so far?" she asked, the hint of impatience gone from her tone and her expression radiating interest, as if how Lily liked waiting on tables was a matter of great importance to her.

"It's fine," Lily replied. "Everyone is very nice."

"That's good. You must still be in school, of course. Let's see, if I remember correctly you must be seventeen or eighteen. That makes you . . . a senior?"

"Yes. At St. Theresa's."

"Do you have plans for next year?"

"Yes, I'm hoping to go to Rhode Island School of Design."

Jack felt a stab of resentment that he was no longer the only one who shared her secret.

"That's wonderful," his mother responded. "I remember how you always had a pencil and pad in your hand when you came to visit. I wish you the very best of luck, Lily. And I know a few people on the admissions board at RISD. If you need a letter of recommendation, I'd be happy to write one."

"Oh, thank you, Mrs. Terrell."

Lily sounded thrilled, no, downright blessed by his mother's offhand offer. Jack had a petty urge to ask her what had happened to wanting to get places on her own merit.

"It's been wonderful seeing you again, Lily. Now don't let my son get you fired by keeping you out here talking all night. I'll see you inside, Jack."

As she walked away Lily's horrified gaze swung to meet Jack's and suddenly he knew why she had reacted so placidly earlier. Until his mother's parting remark, she'd had no idea that Kay Terrell was his mother.

"Listen, Lily, I know how this must seem to you."

She was shaking her head, her expression no longer shocked, but angry. "No, you can't possibly, because if you knew how incredibly slimy this makes you look you never would have done it."

Jack felt his whole body get hot inside in the black tux. "I didn't . . ."

"Of course, maybe you don't give a damn how you look to me. Why should you? I'm only the gardener's daughter."

"That has nothing to do with this."

"Doesn't it? You mean if I was some sorority princess you met at one of these posh parties, you still would have told me that your name was Jack Daniels?" She laughed bitterly. "I don't think so, Jack."

"I already admitted to you that that was a stupid lie, one I regretted as soon as the words were out of my mouth."

"But obviously you didn't regret it enough to tell me the truth, that you're Jack Terrell, that your father is my father's boss."

"I was going to tell you."

"When?"

"Tonight."

"I don't believe you. If your mother hadn't happened to come along when she did, I think you'd still be stringing me along and laughing behind my back at how clever you are."

"No." He grabbed her arm. "Don't you remember me saying I had something I wanted to tell you? Well, this was it."

Her rigid expression wavered, then turned icy again. "Why didn't you tell me who you were in the first place? What were you after?"

"Nothing," he said, still holding on to her arm.

"People like you don't do anything for nothing."

He felt a familiar resentment rise inside, suffocating him. "What's that supposed to mean? People like me? You hardly know me."

"I know you as well as I want to." She tried unsuccessfully to pull free. "Please let go of my arm."

"I'm not through talking with you."

"But I am through talking with you. Besides," she added, glancing pointedly in the direction of the guests who had gathered in the lobby for after-dinner cigarettes, "we're creating a scene."

"I don't give a damn."

"You don't have to," she said, jerking loose. "I do."

Jack stood and watched her go. Usually when a girl walked away from him, which wasn't too often, he said good riddance. Right now it would be tough to say anything, the way frustration was burning a path straight through the center of the chest.

He fought the urge to go after her. She needed time to cool off. Hell, they both did. He'd expected her to be angry, but deep down he'd also been confident he could charm her out of it. Something told him that charming Lily wasn't going to be that easy; that a glib explanation wasn't going to do the trick. She was going to want the truth. All right, he could handle that. She was probably also going to want an apology.

Loosening the starched collar that suddenly felt like it was choking him, Jack headed to the party and to June McAllister's poor languishing daughter, but his thoughts were still on Lily. And the prospect of apologizing. He had time. He'd think of something.

It was after midnight when they left the party. Several times Jack tried to catch Lily alone, but she avoided him. Obviously that didn't improve his mood any.

He had driven the old Bentley tonight, his mother's choice. Not that he minded. He considered it a privilege to drive his grandfather's cherished automobile. The car always brought back memories of special times with his grandfather: tagging along with him to the silver plant and Sunday afternoon trips to ride the carousel in the village.

Tonight it also roused some not-so-pleasant memories. He kept thinking of the time when he was six and he'd scratched the side of his father's car with his first two-wheel bike. His father's anger had terrified him and taught him a lesson. That was the last time he'd ever said he was sorry for anything to anyone.

Later, his grandfather had come to his room. There had been no criticism or lectures. Charles had simply said, "Be more careful next time. Think first and try always to do things in a way that you won't have to be sorry for later." His bright eyes crinkling at the corners, he'd tousled Jack's hair and added, "But do them, and follow your instincts. Good instincts are what makes a man a winner."

The recollection of his grandfather's words was all it took to spur Jack to speaking his mind.

"Mother, there's something I want to discuss with you."

"Of course, darling." He sensed her hopefulness as she half-turned in the passenger seat to face him. "Have you finally made up your mind to forget this stubborn nonsense and return to school?"

"I've made up my mind, all right, but not to return to school."

"Oh Jack, you—"

"Don't you even want to hear what I've decided?" he interrupted.

"Of course," she said, then without pausing added, "I'm sure you've decided that you don't need an official degree to take your place at Delaney Silver, and of course, you don't. But it's the principle of the matter. Darling—"

"I'm not going to take my place at Delaney Silver," he said, speaking over her in a rough manner he would never use with her if an accumulation of rage and frustration hadn't made it feel like he was about to explode.

"What did you say?" she asked, staring at him.

"I'm not going to work for Delaney Silver." He took a deep breath. "I'm going to enlist in the Air Force instead."

"Don't be ridiculous." The panic in her voice assured Jack that she understood the determination in his. He tried to be more gentle.

"It's not ridiculous, Mother. I want to fly."

"Flying is a hobby."

"It was a hobby for Grandfather. It's more to me."

"Jack, please, it's always been my dream for you—"

"That's right," he cut in. "*Your* dream for me. What about my dreams?"

"All boys have dreams, darling. We're talking about what you want to do with the rest of your life."

"Flying *is* what I want to do with my life. It's all I want to do," he added.

"Surely there are opportunities to fly airplanes outside of the military?"

Jack took no pleasure in her weakening to the point of compromise. On the contrary, he wished he could make this painless for her. He knew that he couldn't. "Not opportunities to fly state-of-the-art jets," he said.

"For God's sake, Jack, there's a war going on. You could get killed."

"I won't." He flashed her a grin to try to break the tension. "Only the good die young."

"Don't you know that every young soldier who's ever been shot or blown to bits has said that very same thing?" There were tears just beneath her words now. "Please, Ted—" She stopped abruptly, looking as if she'd seen a ghost instead of called on one.

"That's it, isn't it?" Jack asked softly. They had pulled into the driveway and stopped. He reached across the back of the seat to touch her shoulder and felt her trembling. "It's because of what happened to your brother, Ted. But I'm not him."

"No, but you're too much like him for your own good. You're headstrong and impulsive and you take too many chances."

"I admit that by enlisting I'm taking a chance, but it's a chance I want to take. Can you understand that?"

"No," she said, drawing herself into the aloof posture not even he could penetrate. "I don't understand and I don't care to discuss it any further. Ever."

"We have to discuss it, because I'm not going to change my mind. I'm signing up as soon as they'll take me."

"I forbid it."

She reached for the door handle to do the unthinkable, open her own car door, and Jack let her. He wouldn't force her to talk about it anymore tonight. But he also wouldn't back down now that it was out in the open. Part of him felt relieved, part apprehensive. And part of him was only concerned with how he was going to make peace with Lily.

He glanced at his watch. The hangar at the airfield would be locked, but he had his own key. Turning the car around, he drove out of the driveway to do what he always did when he needed to think things through. Fly.

FIFTEEN

Kay ran up the walk to the house, chased by an echo from the past. *I forbid it.* Miserably, she realized that the words she'd hurled at Jack were the same words her father had used when she announced that she was going to marry James Terrell.

She slammed the door and stood with her back pressed against it, coming to terms with the absolute silence inside the house. Sometimes she wished they had never moved from the guest house. She'd dragged her feet over the move until James insisted that it was ridiculous for the three of them to be crowded into a bungalow with a mansion standing empty a few hundred yards away. Although why they needed more room when she was usually the only one home was beyond her. A bigger house meant a bigger silence.

Sometimes she closed her eyes and tried to hear her memories above the silence. Lord knows, she had plenty of happy memories of this place, parties and picnics on the lawn and Christmas Eves with everyone gathered around the piano. Her mother would play and they would all sing: "Silent Night" and "Winter Wonderland" and a scrambled, laughing version of "The Twelve Days of Christmas." Once in a while she was able to hear a faint echo of their voices, but it was always a long way off, and eventually the silence muffled it entirely. The silence was always stronger.

With a sigh, she came away from the door and started up the stairs to her room. What on earth was she going to do about Jack? Allowing him to enlist was out of the question. Yet she refused to make the same mistake her father had made with her. And with Ted, she thought, feeling the throb of old wounds. No, she would have to be more subtle and persuade Jack to see things her way. Perhaps James . . .

She quickly dismissed the idea of involving James in this problem. He had an uncanny lack of paternal instinct. Maybe because he had never wanted to be a father. Correction—he had never wanted to be Jack's father.

From the start James had been bitterly opposed to the adoption. The only child he was interested in, he'd told her time after time, was one of their own flesh and blood. He certainly hadn't understood why she would want to "saddle" them with a toddler who had already had time to form too many bad habits to be undone. It wasn't true. Jack was, then and now, sweet and straightforward. Not to be confused with docile, thought Kay wryly. Only much later did she understand that what James wanted most from any child was to seal his place in the Delaney dynasty. Jack couldn't do that for him.

Kay had simply, and desperately, wanted children. Unable to conceive, she'd been convinced that in time an adopted child would draw her and James closer together and help ease the strain that plagued their marriage everywhere except the bedroom. She'd foolishly hoped a family might even change the leopard's spots and put an end to this philandering. And so she had allowed her parents to arrange the adoption and stood by while James was not so subtly strong-armed into accepting it.

Her parents had been as enthusiastic about the idea as James was opposed to it, perhaps because of losing Ted. She smiled, recalling the blessing Jack had been for them at the time, allowing them to put aside some of their grief and relive their son's childhood through another little boy. Her father had done for Jack everything that James should have, but refused to.

At one time she used to pray that James would realize what a wonderful young man Jack was and how lucky they were to have him for a son, and that he would want to spend more time with him. As Jack grew older and wiser, the lack of interest became mutual. Time after time her attempts to make them a close-knit family had failed. As recently as last year she had planned a Christmas ski trip that turned into a week-long cold war.

"You want us to behave like some fantasy you carry around in your head," Jack had lashed out in exasperation when he found her holed up in the bathroom, crying. "We're not, and we never will be, one big happy family. When are you going to accept that?"

"Never," she'd retorted.

How could she? To admit that would be to admit she had been wrong—about James, about so many things—and that was out of the question.

She had finally come to see James's lack of attention to Jack, and resulting lack of influence, as a blessing in disguise. James could be charming, but he could also be manipulative and ruthless, determined to get what he wanted when he wanted it, whatever the cost.

Suddenly, for the first time in years, she allowed herself to dwell on the elusive role he had played in Ted's decision to join the service. *Ted.* Even after all this time, thoughts of him still left Kay feeling unsettled, as if an important thread in the weave of her life had been dropped and left hanging.

Switching on a lamp by the bed, she shook off the melancholy mood before it could take hold of her. Ted was gone. It was Jack who concerned her now. Somehow she had to convince him to do the right thing, for him and for Delaney Silver. That was one more reason not to consult James about this. Although he'd never said so directly, she was certain James was not looking forward to the day he would have to make room at Delaney Silver for the grandson Charles Delaney had adored.

Her father's will had made it clear that while he tolerated James, he looked forward to a time when Jack would be at the helm of the company. He had further complicated Kay's life by naming her chairman of the board and leaving full control of Delaney Silver in her hands.

He had explained his reasoning to her a few days before he died. She recalled how she had sat on the edge of his hospital bed and tried to concentrate. It hadn't been easy to keep her mind on business when she was still struggling to come to grips with the sight of his once powerful body lying frail and doomed in that frightening white and sterile intensive-care bed.

"There has always been a Delaney at the helm of the company," he told her, speaking slowly, each word holding its own raspy echo. "I want to see it stay that way."

"But, Daddy, James has been doing a wonderful job of running things while you've been sick."

"Then let him keep it up. But it's your name on the will and in the end it will be your signature that counts. That's the way I want it."

"I understand that there's always been a Delaney in charge, but we have to face the fact that strictly speaking—"

He lifted his hand a few inches, then quickly let it drop to the mattress as if even that was too much effort for him now. "I know, I know, strictly speaking you're the end of the line, honey. My decision was easy compared to the one you'll have to make someday."

"You're talking about turning the company over to Jack."

His expression brightened noticeably. "I know he'll grow into the right man for the job. I know it as surely as I know . . . Bah." He shook his head. He didn't have to say that James was the wrong man in order for Kay to understand how he felt.

"The fact is," he continued, his voice growing weaker as he tired, "kids don't always do what we want them to do. I'd rather have you sell out than let the company be driven into the ground by mismanagement."

Kay was shocked. Sell Delaney Silver? It was unthinkable.

"Don't look at me that way," he said. "I mean it. I've seen it happen too many times. A man spends his life building something he can be proud of, something he can hand down to his own, and then some upstart with no regard for tradition comes along and takes and takes without putting anything back until there's nothing left. Don't let that happen, Kay. You sell out first, understand?"

"Do you know what you're asking?"

"Yes."

"Well, it's not fair."

"Not much in life is," he said, a hint of the old dryness in his voice.

Kay started to smile, then stopped short as he was racked by a violent cough. Watching him struggle for breath made her feel as if her own throat was closing up. He had smoked for over forty years and enjoyed every cigarette he ever lit. Now he was dying and all the silver in the Delaney vaults couldn't buy him an extra day, and as far as Kay was concerned that was the most unfair thing of all. The force of his coughing lifted his shoulders off the pillow. When he collapsed on it again she leaned over and stroked his forehead.

"Rest," she urged.

He wouldn't be distracted. "I want you to promise me, Kay."

"How can I promise a thing like that? I don't even know enough about the business to know if it's being mismanaged."

"Then learn."

She laughed nervously. It was too late to remind him that when she had desperately wanted to learn, he'd had other ideas. "It's a little late for that, don't you think?"

She didn't add that her stomach twisted just thinking about James's reaction should she decide to become involved in business matters. He would interpret it as a lack of confidence in him and he would be furious. No, their marriage was strained enough without that.

"Promise me," he said again. "Don't worry about what you know or don't know. You're a Delaney. When the time comes you'll know what to do."

Kay stared at him. His skin was wrinkled and thin, his expression weary, but his eyes were as blue and as wise and alert as when she'd been two or twelve or twenty and had looked into them to find answers.

"I promise," she said.

James had been outraged. Not by her promise. She'd kept that part to herself. But by the fact that she had been left full control of the company. "Twenty years. Twenty damn years and not so much as a thank-you from that old bastard."

Kay, bristling at his words, had wanted to lash out and remind him that he had been well compensated for every one of those years. But what was the use of stirring up more trouble? Her insistence that she was merely a figurehead, that he, as company president, was really in charge, helped very little.

Eventually time smoothed the conflict; James acted as if he was accountable to no one. Kay never told a soul that she understood why her father hadn't felt confident leaving the business he loved, the business that had been in the Delaney family for over one hundred years, in James's hands.

No one could deny that James was bright and ambitious and from the start determined to learn the silver business. And at least he'd learned all the facets of it that could be learned.

That was the problem. James was all graphs and flow charts and no instinct. He had no sense of what made one design work and not another, no emotional grasp of why some traditional patterns remained in the catalogue even when sales fell, and he had absolutely no gift for working with the sometimes temperamental designers whom her father knew were the backbone of the business.

Kay recalled the time she had arranged to meet James for lunch and had strolled into his office to find her father with both hands planted on James's desk, glaring at him.

"You fired who?" he demanded, his voice alarmingly soft considering that his face was nearly purple.

"Henri LaVeque," replied James, leaning back in his swivel chair to gaze at his father-in-law above the careless tepee of his fingertips. The tepee collapsed and he shot to attention when Charles Delaney pounded the desk hard enough to shake the Picasso and Matisse prints Kay had chosen for the walls of James's office.

"Have you lost your mind?"

"Hardly," snapped James. "It's no secret that LaVeque has been coasting for years. I can't think of the last profit producer he came up with."

"Try Alpine," her father shouted. "Or Venetian Rose."

James smirked. "Exactly. Those patterns are over twenty-five years old."

"Those patterns are part of our tradition." Her father shook his head, still bent over the desk peering at James as if he was something pinned in a petri dish. "You just don't get it, do you?"

In the end her father had ordered James to eat crow and re-hire Henri LaVeque that very afternoon. Kay had done her best to soothe her husband's ego, but then too, she had understood. Perhaps Jack would turn out to be no more attuned to Delaney tradition and style than James was, but she owed it to her father to find out.

A bath and a glass of wine didn't bring her any closer to a solution. What she needed was someone to talk this over with. Her thoughts quickly turned to Drew Goddard.

Too quickly, decided Kay, then chided herself. It was only natural that she think of Drew. Not only was he an old friend, but for the past several months they had been constantly thrown together on committees for one charity or another. Kay had always been fond of Drew, but at some point, without her being conscious of it, their casual friendship had jumped tracks, heading into new, uncharted territory.

When, she wondered, had she stopped thinking of Drew as merely a onetime friend of her younger brother and started thinking of him as a friend of hers? Maybe more than a friend.

It was one more question that these days left Kay, who'd once thought she had all the answers, feeling slightly bewildered.

She had been tempted to call Drew earlier this evening, when she needed an escort for the party, and she was tempted again now. Jack had come to her rescue then, but this time she was on her own, and her resistance was even lower than it had been hours ago.

"Oh, what the hell?" she drawled, perching on the edge of the ivory satin chaise by the window and reaching for the phone. The fact that it was midnight didn't deter her. Drew had always been a night owl.

She dialed his number from memory and listened to the ringing forty miles away, wondering if he was home. It was a weekend night, after all. Winding the phone cord around her finger, she told herself the reason her heart was racing was that she was still upset about Jack.

Just as she was about to hang up, Drew answered, his voice warmly masculine and familiar.

"Hello, Drew. It's Kay. I hope I'm not calling too late."

"You're not. Is everything all right?"

"Yes, of course. I was just thinking about driving up to Providence for that committee meeting on Tuesday and remembered that you mentioned something about getting together for lunch beforehand. I wondered if you were still interested?"

There was a pause. Kay pictured his thoughtful expression.

"I was under the distinct impression you weren't interested," he said.

It was said lightly, no pressure. The only pressure came from the air sealed inside her lungs. She exhaled, deciding not to mention the problem with Jack in case she changed her mind about telling him. "I was hoping I could run my ideas for the spring fund-raiser by you before I present them to the others. Sort of a dry run."

"A dry run," he echoed softly, with a characteristic undertone of humor. "Well, I suppose a dry run is better than none. Yes, Kay, I'm very interested in sharing lunch and a dry run with you."

"Good," she said, conscious of a ripple of excitement she hadn't felt in years. "The meeting is scheduled for two, how does twelve sound for lunch?"

"Not as good as eleven."

She laughed. "Drew, no one eats lunch at eleven."

"So we'll eat brunch. I know just the place. Meet me at the corner of Thayer and Meeting."

"At eleven?"

"Sharp. The food is great, so I know we're going to eat too much. This way we'll have time to go for a long walk afterward and work it off."

"The forecast is for rain."

"That's perfect. I'll be there waiting for you. Good night, Kay."

His last words were slow and heavy with an offer that prompted Kay to have second thoughts about calling. She hadn't called looking for brunch at some favorite haunt of his or a walk in the rain. She was forty-seven years old, for heaven's sake, although she could honestly say she didn't look it. Oh, there were a few lines and some gray hairs to color, but there were no extra pounds, no stretch marks from bearing children, and limited sagging thanks to tennis and great genes. Still, tennis could only do so much. Forty-seven years of gravity took its toll on a body.

Regardless, how old she *looked* didn't change how old she *was,* and she was old enough to understand exactly what Drew had on his mind. Unless this was all in her imagination. Or wishful thinking. No, not that. In her own way she was happy with James. It was pure silliness.

They were going to have lunch, period. She had known Drew forever. He was a friend and that was exactly what she needed right now. Someone to have lunch with, a familiar smile across the table, someone who would listen and look at her when she spoke without drumming his fingers or checking his watch. Someone she could talk with about Jack. A friend.

And if Drew was offering something more, or less, than that? She shook off the thought. She would worry about that when, and if, she had to.

SIXTEEN

When Lily left school on Monday afternoon, she noticed Jack's car parked directly across the street. She could hardly miss it, since he was leaning on the back fender, his gaze riveted on the front door of the school as if it might disappear if he looked away for even a second.

When he saw Lily he straightened and took off his sunglasses, his broad smile leaving no doubt that she was the one he was waiting to see.

Lily took her time crossing the street, savoring the moment. This was the first time she'd ever been met at school by a gorgeous guy driving a sports car. In hindsight she'd realized that the reason Andrea Evans had looked so dumbstruck at seeing Jack and Lily together last Friday was not simply that Lily was with a guy as impressive as Jack, but that she was with Jack Terrell, local legend.

Wealthy and with a reputation for being slightly wild, pictures of Jack were occasionally run on the society pages of the *Sun*, but those pictures were of the spit-shined, tuxedo-clad stranger Lily had encountered Friday night, not the carefree charmer who haunted her dreams.

She had spent the weekend telling herself that he was a jerk who only wanted to play games at her expense and that she didn't care if she ever saw him again. All the while, the hope that he might call or stop by offering some plausible explanation had been ticking inside her, a time bomb she could no longer deny. In fact, now that he was actually here, it threatened to explode.

Jack seemed unaware of the dozens of pairs of female eyes that were following his every move, cataloging each and every detail of his six feet, two inches. His gaze never strayed from Lily as he stepped forward to meet her. "Hi."

"Hello, Jack," she replied and continued walking toward the bus stop.

He fell into step beside her. "I've been waiting for you."

"How unfortunate."

"I take it you're still angry?"

"Not angry exactly. Wiser."

"Wise enough to let me drive you home?"

"Wise enough not to."

"Haven't we played this same scene before?"

"Same scene, different ending."

He grabbed her arm so that she had no choice but to stop walking and look at him. She hated cocky grins, she reminded herself, and his was the cockiest she'd ever encountered. It suggested that while she might be kidding herself, she wasn't fooling him.

The problem was, she was no longer even kidding herself. Deep down she knew that although she might protest and feign disinterest, in the end she was going to do what every fiber in her entire body was clamoring for her to do. She was going to get into that car with him.

"Come on, Lily," he said, his voice soft and beguiling. "I made a mistake. Haven't you ever made a mistake?"

"Sure, lots of them. If you had forgotten your name or mispronounced it, that would have been a mistake I could overlook. It's the reason you didn't tell me who you are, the very calculated reason, that bothers me most."

"And what is this supposed reason?"

She shrugged. "I don't know exactly..."

"Oh, but you know enough to condemn me for it?"

"I know it had something to do with the fact that you're a Delaney-slash-Terrell and I'm the gardener's daughter."

"Give me a break, Lily. This isn't feudal England."

"Don't kid yourself."

"You still haven't explained your reasoning. If I wanted to take advantage of you—which is what I think this is all about— wouldn't I have tried to impress you with my name instead of the opposite?"

Ignoring the logic in that, she said, "Unless you were afraid that if I knew who you were, *I* might try to take advantage of *you.*"

His eyes sparked and narrowed. "Now there's an interesting possibility."

"In your dreams, Terrell," she drawled.

His silent, wicked smile left Lily struggling not to look seventeen and flustered.

"Or maybe," she continued, "you knew that once my folks realized who you were they would forbid me to see you, spoiling all your fun."

"I've got to hand it to you, that's close." He stopped her from walking away. "But not in the way you're thinking. Did it ever occur to you that maybe I didn't tell you up front who I was, because I wanted you to see *me,* to get to know *me?* Not some packaged commodity named Delaney-slash-Terrell?"

"That's ridiculous."

"Don't kid yourself," he shot back. "Admit it, you thought differently of me the second you realized who I was."

"I admit it, but only because you lied about it in the first place."

"Sure. Think back to that afternoon when you let me walk you to work. If you had known I was Jack Terrell, instead of just some guy—"

"It wouldn't have changed anything," she interjected.

"Oh, no? Would you still have let down your guard and told me about applying to RISD? Would you have showed me your sketches? The truth, Lily."

The truth? She bit her lip, then shrugged. "Maybe not."

"Then it would have changed things. It would have changed everything for me," he added emphatically. "I liked listening to you talk about your plans. I liked listening to you talk to *me,* not a name from the social register."

"Don't you think you're exaggerating just a little?"

"No. Everybody thinks a famous name can open doors, and it can. But it can also build walls. I didn't want to take a chance on that happening with you."

Lily didn't know what to say. The sincerity in his deep-pitched voice was plucking new, pleasurable chords deep inside her.

"From what you said the other day," he continued, "I got the impression your folks might hassle you about seeing me. I guess I wanted to stack the deck in my favor beforehand."

"In what way?"

"You told me that when you want something badly enough, you always find a way to get it. That you fight for it. I guess I hoped that if you got to know me, you'd want me enough to fight.''

Lily's senses danced. Part of her cautioned that this was probably a well-practiced line. Part of her was beyond caring.

''You could have trusted my instincts,'' she told him. ''Being afraid to tell me your name sure doesn't say a heck of a lot for me.''

''I think it does,'' he said softly, then flashed that teasing, utterly distracting grin. ''It's not many girls I like enough to lie to, fewer still whom I chase after.''

''Lucky me,'' Lily retorted, managing a look she usually reserved for Joey at his most obnoxious.

Jack laughed. ''So am I forgiven?''

''I'll think about it.''

''Close enough. We'll start fresh, and I promise to behave like a Boy Scout.''

Lily smiled, her surrender complete. ''You, a Boy Scout? This I've got to see.''

It was a relief to settle into the front seat of the car. The verbal duel had left her weak-kneed and fluttery, feelings she'd heard other girls talk about and that she'd always dismissed as naive nonsense. Now it seemed as if *she* was the one who had been naive.

Jack slid behind the wheel and revved the engine. ''You know, I actually had an ulterior motive for picking you up today.''

''So much for the Boy Scout routine.''

''Nothing sinister. It has to do with what I said a minute ago, about how I liked listening to you talk about your plans. The fact is that listening to you inspired me to do something I should have done long ago.''

''What's that?''

''Tell my mother that I don't want any part of the career she has mapped out for me at Delaney Silver.''

Lily looked at him in surprise. ''She must have been very...''

''I think shocked is the word you're groping for,'' he offered wryly. ''Shocked, horrified, furious, take your pick. She's since spent every waking moment—and a few I wish I hadn't been awake for—trying to convince me that I'm making a huge mistake.''

''And?''

''I remain unconvinced.''

"So there are no silver spoons in your future?" teased Lily.

"I figure the one they stuck in my mouth when they took me in is enough to last me a lifetime."

"Have you given any thought to what you do want to do?"

"Lots. That's where my ulterior motive comes in. Do you have to go straight home?"

"I usually take the bus directly to the club, but I have an hour or so before I have to be there."

"Great."

"Not so fast. First, I want to hear more about this ulterior motive of yours."

"I'd rather show you. Feel like taking a ride?"

All Lily knew was that she felt like being with him. What harm could there be in going for a ride? She settled back against the soft leather seat. "Why not?"

They drove northeast. Lily suffered a fleeting stab of guilt over the fact that she hadn't told anyone where she was or who she was with. Of course, if she had called home and explained that she was going for a ride with Jack Terrell, her mother would have only one thing to say: *no.* Not that she could keep this—whatever *this* was—from them indefinitely. If Jack asked to see her again, she would tell them everything, she promised herself. *If* Jack asked to see her again.

It was a tantalizingly big if. Lily would have pinched herself to see if she was dreaming, except that she was afraid she might wake up. Dream or reality, she wanted it to go on and on. At the same time she was practical enough to acknowledge that Jack could prove to be a very big distraction if he wanted to be and if she wasn't careful. She'd worked so hard and looked forward for so long to graduating and moving on. The last thing she needed was extra baggage weighing her down.

It wasn't as if she hadn't been on dates. She had. A few. Usually with friends of her brothers and usually she was relieved when they were over. Her mother sometimes gave thanks that she wasn't boy-crazy like some girls her age. But that was because Lily's dreams were much bigger than any one boy, or man, or romance. She had to remember that.

At the sign for the Westerly Airport, Jack turned into the parking lot, heading for the section reserved for private planes.

"This is what you wanted to show me?" she asked. "The airport?"

"Actually we're just passing through the airport," he told her, parking the car. A sign on the building in front of them read Ocean State Flight Center. "Come on."

It still took a while, long enough for Jack to stroll inside, greet everyone by name, sign into the logbook open on the counter and pull her along with him to the tarmac outside, before Lily realized exactly what he intended. She chalked her slow reaction time up to inexperience. She'd never in her life been near an airplane, much less on one.

If this was, in fact, a plane that Jack was circling and scrutinizing so intently. She thought of airplanes as being big and silver, with solid names like Boeing, not something this small and with bright red stripes she deemed more appropriate for a sailboat.

"She's all ready," Jack said.

"Ready for what?" asked Lily, masking real fear.

"Us. I told you I was taking you for a ride."

"You're serious?" She stared at him, her short laugh uneasy.

"You're not afraid?"

"Ha! Afraid? Me? Afraid of climbing into this little red and white Tinkertoy with a guy who drives his car like a wild man, not to mention being given to strange and mysterious flights of fancy? Whatever makes you think I'd be afraid?"

He ducked under the wing so they were standing face-to-face, with only inches separating Lily's inwardly trembling body from the rock solidness of his.

"She's in tip-top condition, Lily," he said, patting the side of the plane as affectionately as if it was a thoroughbred race horse. "And I've had my pilot's license for years. I started going up with my grandfather when I was six and I've been handling the controls since I was nine. And I would never, ever let anything happen to you." He reached out and laid his palm against her cheek, lightly, devastatingly. "Trust me?"

Lily was scared to death to set foot in the plane. It was a basic and, as far as she was concerned, very healthy fear. The problem was that at the moment another basic and healthy instinct was short-circuiting it. This one was telling her that taking a chance on Jack was the right thing to do.

Trust me? he'd asked.

She met his eager gaze and realized her answer meant a great deal to him. Without fully knowing why, she nodded.

"Just one thing," she cautioned, grasping his arm as he moved to swing open the cockpit door. "Promise me you won't go to fast...or too high." She thought about it as he helped her climb in and added, "Or too low."

Lily would forever think of her first plane ride in terms of surprises. It was more exciting, more breathtaking and more all-around terrifying than she had anticipated.

Once Jack had completed his preflight checklist, she squeezed her eyes shut for a takeoff that was smooth and quick and still made her feel like she'd left her stomach behind. Before she'd caught her breath, she peeked to see treetops where the ground should be. Her spine tingled and her palms were sweaty. She was flying, she realized with fear and amazement, suspended in the air, held aloft only by some principle of physics she didn't understand and Jack's skill.

She had thought the sight of his hand working an automobile shift was fascinating, but it was child's play compared to this. That was another surprise. That such a small plane should require so complicated a dashboard, or rather, as Jack told her, instrument panel.

He pointed out to her the basic controls—the yoke, which reminded Lily of a ram's horns and was used to steer the plane, the hand throttle, which controlled engine power, much like the gas pedal in a car, and the rudder, operated by foot pedals, which stabilized the plane and reduced yaw.

Yaw?

Jack smiled and explained that yaw simply meant skidding left or right. He explained whatever she wanted to know, his patience and obvious depth of knowledge doing a lot to relax Lily. Soon she had released her death grip on the seat and was leaning forward as they flew low over her neighborhood, over her own house. Oh, Mom, if you could see me now, she thought. The houses and cars looked like pieces on a game board, the people like tiny dolls.

"I had no idea the streets were all so neatly arranged," she exclaimed at one point. "As if it had all been drawn out ahead of time."

"I think it probably was," Jack said dryly, and they both laughed.

"Everything looks so different from up here."

He nodded. "That's one reason I love it."

They were flying along the coast now, and suddenly Delaney Place came into view. Lily excitedly pointed it out to him before realizing that of course Jack knew exactly where they were, that he had probably flown this route dozens of times.

"My grandfather had an old Bentley that he loved," he said suddenly, flying a lazy circle over the Atlantic to approach Delaney Place from another angle.

"I remember it," Lily replied. "Your mother still uses it."

"Sometimes. But as much as he loved driving that car, he always said there was one thing you could get up here that you could never get down there. That's perspective."

For a moment the only sound was the whir of the engine, which was so steady it somehow made the silence more complete, enclosing the two of them in a private world that hung there between the clouds and reality.

"I think I know exactly what your grandfather meant," Lily told him.

Jack nodded at Delaney Place as it once more loomed ahead of them, elegant and imposing, surrounded by brick walls and the flawless green lawns that her father tended. "That's the only home I've ever known," he said, "and yet the only time I really feel at home there is when I'm up here, looking down. Weird, huh?"

Lily, who knew what it was like to feel like a stranger in your own family, even a family you loved, didn't think it was all that weird.

"What I think," she told him, "is that since you can't control how you feel about things like that, you shouldn't waste time worrying about whether or not anyone else considers it weird."

Lifting the plane's nose for another go-around, Jack glanced at her. "Down there, I always feel small. Insignificant."

"It's a big place."

He frowned and shook his head. "It's not about size. It's about...tradition. Heritage. Responsibility. Of course, strictly speaking, since I was adopted, it's not my heritage at all. But that only makes it more difficult. It's as if I've been given so much, I can never repay it no matter how hard I try."

"Oh, Jack, you don't really think it was given with the expectation that you would somehow repay it, do you?"

"Sometimes that's exactly what I think. Like they got me from adopt-an-heir. Oh, I know how lucky I am," he said quickly, as if wanting to beat her to the obvious punch line. "I know all about looking a gift horse in the mouth and that millions of guys would like to take my place." He paused.

"I guess maybe that's it. I wish there wasn't a place to take, a place that's there waiting for me to just step into it. Tailor-made, predetermined, one size fits all as long as you're a Delaney or, in my case, a reasonable facsimile. All my life there's been so much importance put on the Delaney name and Delaney heritage that it's hard to know what's really important to me. Except at times like this," he said, briefly meeting her gaze. "Up here I always know."

"What *is* really important to you, Jack?"

"This," he answered without hesitation. "Flying. This is what I wanted to show you. This is why my mother's threatening to disown me, what I'm giving up my future for, according to her. I guess I feel about flying the way you feel about painting. It was hearing you talk and seeing how determined you were to go after what you want that gave me the kick in the butt I needed to do the same."

Lily listened as he talked about his plans for the future, about joining the Air Force, about flying planes that hadn't even been built yet. The passion in his voice made it clear that if he was giving anything up in the process, it wasn't anything that mattered to him.

As she listened, Lily tried to block out the image of Jack flying over the same jungle where Cliff was fighting. Instead she concentrated on what he was saying about his love for planes and flying and on the unmistakable joy in his expression. He looked, she decided, the way she must look when she talked about painting. He talked the way a thirsty man gulps water, as if he would never stop. Lily, who knew how it felt to have so much bottled up inside and finally find someone who understood, listened.

She listened and she asked questions. Because she knew her interest would please Jack. Because she wanted to know as much as possible about the way he felt and thought and dreamed. She thought it ironic that Jack wanted out from under everything that she'd always dreamed of having. The conversation continued even after they landed and returned to the car, all the way to the door of the club.

"I must be boring you out of your mind," he said a couple of times.

But Lily wasn't bored. In fact, when he turned off the car's engine and stretched his arm along the back of his seat, his fingers idly catching and twisting a lock of her hair, all the physical signs indicated the opposite of boredom. It felt more like she'd just run a very long, very fast race. Her pulse thundered, and her breathing was shaky.

"Thanks for coming with me," Jack said.

"I'm the one who should thank you. It was wonderful."

"Wonderful enough to wipe the slate clean between us?"

"Yes," she said with a laugh.

"Good. When can I see you again?"

"I get a break around nine-thirty," she reminded him.

He shook his head. "I want more than fifteen minutes." Much more, suggested the dark, impatient look in his eyes. "What are you doing Friday night?"

"Working."

"Saturday?"

She regarded him ruefully. "The same thing."

He swore softly. "Don't you get a night off?"

"Monday, but that's a school night, and Sunday...unless there's a big party and they need extra help."

"Here's to small parties," he muttered. "All right, Sunday it is."

Lily suddenly formed a painful image of herself walking into the house and announcing that on the one night she reserved for homework, she planned to go out with Jack Terrell. Her mother would throw a fit. "I'm sorry, Jack. Sundays are bad for me. Homework backs up and..."

He ran his fingers through his hair, his expression black. "Look, are you trying to tell me something? Like get lost?"

"No, really. It's just that between school and work, I'm pretty busy."

"I want to see you," he said emphatically. "You name the time."

Lily shrugged uneasily, and repeated, "I get a break around nine-thirty."

He made a sound that was part laugh, part frustrated groan. "It took us all that time to come full circle?"

"Oh, no, the time." Lily exclaimed, glancing at her watch. "I really have to run or I'll be late."

"Uh-uh," he said, catching her arm. "I'll settle for this much for now, but I don't have forever. I plan to have you all to myself for an evening sometime very soon."

"I'll consider myself warned," Lily retorted, laughing with the sheer, all-new pleasure of being pursued so relentlessly.

"Good," he said, reaching across to open the door for her. "That leaves just one more thing."

She hurriedly gathered her purse and book bag. "What's that?"

"This."

His mouth was on hers before Lily saw him coming. Cupping her head, he gently angled her face to his. His lips were warm and slow-moving, and he knew how to kiss. Lily thanked heaven her hands were full of book bag. She had a sneaky suspicion that otherwise they would soon be reaching to pull Jack closer, and instinct warned that was not the way to keep this sort of thing under control.

This was control? jeered a small inner voice. If so, it was all Jack's. The insistent pressure of his lips clouded her brain and started a new and unfamiliar fluttering deep inside. Just when she thought she was going to die from the sweetness of it, his tongue moved to touch hers, hot and rough. An initiation. A promise.

Throughout the kiss he kept his hand on the door handle, so that only their lips touched. Still, when he finally lifted his head, Lily's entire body felt scorched, branded.

"See you at nine-thirty," he said.

SEVENTEEN

The corner of Thayer and Meeting streets was in the heart of Providence's college district, a place where the city's elite and Bohemian peacefully coexisted. Thayer Street, a one-lane thoroughfare lined with shops and casual eateries, cut a path through the city campuses of RISD and Brown University.

Tuesday morning Kay drove herself to the city, circling the congested area several times before finally finding a parking place a couple of blocks from where she was to meet Drew. She didn't mind the walk; she welcomed it. It had been a long time, too long, since she'd done more than drive past this neighborhood, which had once been as familiar to her as her own hometown.

Streams of students carrying books and bulky backpacks moved along the sidewalk in both directions. They looked so young and very different from when she'd walked this same path as a student at Pembroke College, Brown University's sister school. There were no penny loafers in sight, no plaid skirts and coordinating sweaters with Peter Pan collars. No coordinating anything, Kay observed wryly. Faded jeans and calf-length Army surplus coats seemed to be the preferred garb for girls and boys alike. *Women's Wear Daily* had predicted that 1971 would see a return to fashion classics and an end to costume-party dressing. Obviously no one on College Hill read *Women's Wear Daily*.

New boutiques with strange names and cluttered front windows had replaced most of the shops she remembered. The Headless Woman, Emporium India, Inside Out. She caught a strong drift of incense from the open door of one; at another she impulsively paused for a closer look at some silver and turquoise jewelry until a young man with a braid and an earring paused to take a closer look at her.

Kay bit back a giggle. Boys with braids. She supposed she ought to feel very old, but for some strange reason the opposite was true. Being here again, hurrying along with the flow of young people, the mild breeze lifting wisps of hair from her French twist, made her feel young and carefree.

Her clothes helped. On impulse she'd chosen to wear a sweater dress of soft apricot, accentuated with a gold chain belt at her waist, an outfit she ordinarily would have dismissed as far too casual for making a meeting presentation. Her camel hair coat, left unbuttoned, swung open as she walked, and the knee-high caramel leather boots were comfortable enough to make her feel like walking forever. She'd worn them just in case Drew had been serious about walking off the calories from brunch. Thinking of Drew quickened her steps and drew her gaze from the shop windows to the street corner a block away.

She saw him before he saw her. Something about the way he was leaning against his car, hands thrust deep in his coat pockets, his navy plaid scarf whipping in the breeze, made him look as young as she felt. Or was that just the way she always saw him? Forever a quiet young man with horn-rimmed glasses and an ever-ready smile, seen with her memory instead of her eyes?

How did it happen, she wondered, that you could know someone for so long that you stopped really seeing them? They came to exist as some freeze-frame memory the mind chose to preserve until one day something made you blink and take a real look and think, my God, he's gotten so tall or fat or old. She slowed, suddenly wanting to take advantage of this chance to look at Drew unobserved.

She saw a man with dark, slightly curly hair, neatly cut and combed back from what she knew to be a nice face. Not as compellingly masculine as James's, or as handsome as Jack's, but nice. He was tall with an easy, inherently aristocratic way of holding himself, and trim enough to wear any of the exaggerated new trends in men's wear. However, beneath the open Burberry coat, he was wearing—as he had for as long as she could remember—a conventional, two-button gray suit and Brooks Brothers blue and white pin-striped shirt.

She didn't have to get close enough to see the plain gold cuff links and trademark tie chain to know they were in place. Goddard's, the jewelry store responsible for his family fortune, was renowned for gems of rare quality mounted in intricately designed settings, but she could never recall Drew wearing anything other than those simple cuff links and the narrow gold chain that held his tie in place. They were, like the man himself, quiet and understated. Drew had always been quiet, but somewhere along the way, without her noticing, the shy uncertainty of a boy had become the calm self-assurance of a man totally at ease with himself. It was, Kay acknowledged, tremendously appealing.

He turned then and saw her and immediately straightened away from the parked Mercedes to meet her. Not a young man after all, thought Kay, returning his wave and smile. Not old by any means, but no longer boyish. He was seven years younger than she was, although probably no one could tell that from looking at them. Funny how the passing years blurred differences that seemed so significant to the young.

"Hello, Kay," he said, gathering her against him for the quick hug that had marked their greetings for years.

"Sorry I'm late," she said when he released her, aware that as he did his eyes moved over her and warmed slightly. Yes, she thought, not especially displeased, this dress obviously does cling as much as I suspected. "I had trouble finding a place to park. I don't remember there being so much traffic around here."

"I take it you haven't been around here for a while," Drew countered with a chuckle. "This happens to be *the* place to be in Providence."

He led her to the door of a small restaurant sandwiched between the pharmacy and the Avon Theater, which catered to the offbeat tastes of the college community. There were café curtains hung in the front windows. Above them Kay could see that there were already quite a few people inside.

She paused to read the sign above the door. "Andrea's?"

"Right. I remember you saying that you liked Greek food."

It was true enough, although Kay couldn't even recall the last time she'd tasted Greek food. "When did I say that?" she asked as they stepped inside and joined the line waiting to be seated. A rich, spicy aroma teased her empty stomach.

"The time we were both at that party on board that Greek yacht in Newport. The one owned by that little old man who smoked those green cigars you said smelled like garbage."

"Christos?" she asked, laughing.

"That's him."

"Drew, that had to be twelve years ago."

"Right."

"And you remembered what I said about liking Greek food? All this time?"

He shrugged. "Sure."

"That's amazing."

"Why?" They had been standing side by side. Now he turned so they were facing each other, almost but not quite touching in the narrow area cordoned off with a black velvet rope. "I like you, Kay. I care about you, so it matters to me what you like and what makes you happy. I don't consider that amazing, I consider it normal."

In that instant Kay knew that she shouldn't have come. It wasn't only that she had sensed a change in Drew's attitude toward her. If she were truthful she had to admit that her own feelings were changing, as well, edging toward something reckless. In recent months she found herself thinking about Drew for no reason at all, looking forward to seeing him and talking to him, wondering what his opinion would be on matters that didn't even remotely concern him. And laughing. Lately it seemed like the only time she really laughed was when she was with Drew.

And now this. Discovering that he remembered some inconsequential remark she'd made years ago that her own husband probably wouldn't remember. *I care about you,* he had said. Those words weren't going to make it any easier to keep from sliding into deeper water. All she could do was keep matters light, she told herself. The hostess's arrival to seat them saved her from having to respond.

Glancing around the small restaurant, Kay smiled with genuine pleasure. It wasn't what she'd expected or was accustomed to. It wasn't candlelight and starched linen tablecloths and somber waiters. It was small private booths and woven straw place mats and black turtleneck clad students waiting tables. It was perfect.

Over her laughing protests, Drew ordered some of almost everything, determined she should experience the full range of flavors and textures that had seduced her so long ago. To go with it he ordered a bottle of Mavrodaphne, the sweet dark wine she remembered drinking aboard Christos's yacht.

Belatedly Kay recalled that the wine probably had something to do with her unbridled enjoyment of everything that day, from the long tables laden with unfamiliar food to the cloudless summer sky. Then, too, twelve years ago pleasure seemed a more plentiful commodity than it did these days. She'd been sure of so many things back then and hopeful of so many more.

One thing hadn't changed. The wine still worked the same old magic. Kay felt herself slowly relaxing. By the time the platters of food began to arrive, so many of them that they overflowed the small table for two and had to be crowded onto a serving cart as well, she was in the mood to sample everything. Skewered lamb and moussaka and *Papoulsakia*, or "little shoes," hollowed-out eggplant baked with tomatoes and cheese delicately flavored with cinnamon and nutmeg.

Vaguely she acknowledged that there was something improperly intimate about the way she and Drew went about sharing tastes of this and that, nibbling off each other's forks and occasionally from each other's fingers, but it was only vaguely. Mostly she didn't care. She was having fun, another severely rationed commodity in her life of late, and she wasn't about to spoil everything by probing the right and wrong of it.

They talked while they ate, catching up on news of mutual friends, reminiscing. Kay couldn't help thinking how much deeper and richer the history she and Drew shared was than that which she shared with her own husband. There was the simple fact that it went back further, of course, their families having known each other even before Ted and Drew became friends. But it was more than that. They shared a subtle awareness, or maybe sensitivity was a better word, that allowed so many things to be left unsaid or conveyed with no more than a shrug, a raised eyebrow or a remark as offhand as, "Well, she's a Maxwell, what do you expect?"

Everything had been cleared away except for coffee and dessert—crisp, paper-thin sesame cookies and glacé fruit, an assortment of pears, apricots, nectarines and figs—when she finally told Drew about Jack and how worried she was about his plan to enlist. She had held back, stricken by second thoughts about asking his advice on a family matter, but now she decided to confide in him.

She longed for him to offer her unconditional support for her position, but she expected common sense. Drew didn't disappoint her. He let her finish, then quietly, firmly told her what she already knew, that ultimately it was Jack's decision to make.

"Yes, but..." She paused, willing away the tears that threatened. "I can't help thinking of Ted."

"I know," he said.

Even with tear-blurred vision, Kay could see her pain reflected in Drew's somber gray gaze. If he had touched her or gathered her in his arms, she couldn't have felt more comforted. "Oh, Drew, I don't want the same thing to happen all over again."

"Jack's not Ted," he said softly.

"Are you trying to tell me that lightning never strikes the same place twice?" countered Kay, her tone glum. "That the odds against Jack being killed in action the way Ted was are so small that I shouldn't even consider them?"

"No. I'm telling you that although there are risks involved, it's Jack who will be facing those risks and it's Jack's call to make. Just as it was Ted's."

"I know that." Briefly closing her eyes, she said what she hadn't said to Jack and certainly not to James. "I'm so scared, Drew. If anything happens to Jack, what will I have left?"

"What you've always had, Kay. You'll have yourself."

She gave a bleak laugh. "That's small consolation."

"It's whatever consolation you make it."

Kay gazed across the table at him, certain he was speaking from personal experience. Drew had never married, although Kay knew there had been a long line of beautiful, available women in his life. Why hadn't he ever married one of them? she wondered suddenly, inexplicably pleased by the fact that he hadn't.

"Don't you think it's time you told me about these great ideas of yours? Kay?"

"Hmm?"

"Your ideas," he repeated.

Kay shook her head to clear it. She couldn't possibly let him hear the ideas sliding around in there right now. She had been busy pondering his mouth, intrigued by the way it curved up at the corners and the fullness of his bottom lip. And she'd been wondering if it could possibly feel as soft as it looked. Dear Lord, what was wrong with her today?

"Your ideas for the museum fund-raiser," he prompted.

"Oh. Right, the fund-raiser." She took a sip of coffee while she gathered her thoughts, then quickly ran through both ideas that she'd come up with, neither of which thrilled her. When she'd finished, Drew looked so unimpressed and so uneasy about saying so that Kay had to laugh. "The problem is that the committee wants something innovative and attention-grabbing, but there are so many benefits every year that everything that was ever innovative has been done to death."

"In that case, why not just have a sedentary ball and be done with it?"

"A sedentary ball? Something of a contradiction in terms, wouldn't you say?"

"At least it's innovative. Here's how it works—you sell exorbitantly priced tickets to raise money and then on the night of the ball everyone stays home and goes to bed early."

"Sounds...different."

"Trust me, it would be a big hit with those of us who are sick of formal shirts with starched collars."

Kay's laughter trailed off and she straightened in her seat, her expression thoughtful. "The Sedentary Ball," she murmured experimentally. "The First Annual Sedentary Ball."

"Kay, it was a joke."

"I know, but I think it just might work. Listen, you're not the only man—or woman—who complains about having to drag out the tux every time some worthy cause beckons. A sedentary ball would give everybody a break from all that...and maybe raise even more money for the museum than a traditional ball."

"How do you figure that?" he asked, leaning forward, the interest in his eyes genuine.

"Simple. In addition to the usual cost of the tickets, we can suggest that everyone figure out what they would have spent on a new gown or costumes or before and after get-togethers. Baby-sitters, limos," she went on, warming to the idea more and more. "Then we request that they send a check for the total amount to the Museum Fund. What do you think?"

What did he think? Drew stared across the table at the way she was leaning forward in anticipation, taking in the excitement that made her remarkable eyes sparkle with more fire than any diamond he'd ever seen, and her smile that was at once eager and vulnerable, and thought what he had thought for over twenty-five years. That Kay Delaney Terrell was the most beautiful woman he had ever seen and that he would do and say anything to keep that look on her face while she was with him.

"I think it just might work," he told her.

"I can't wait for that meeting now." She looked morosely at her watch. "It's not even one o'clock."

"Good." Drew counted, and then placed enough money for the check and tip on the small tray left by the waitress. "You promised me a walk, lady."

She hesitated as he slid from the booth and extended his hand to her. Drew saw her smile waver and was pierced by the sort of sharp disappointment he ought to be immune to by now. He should have known this was too good to be true. But he'd gone ahead and let himself hope that maybe . . .

"I did promise we'd walk after lunch, didn't I?" she said, catching him in the middle of his emotional descent. "Then a walk it is."

She slipped from the booth so quickly she ended up standing closer to him than either of them expected. For an instant he grappled for words, as tongue-tied by her nearness as he'd ever been at fifteen. Then, with a steady smile that hid the feelings roiling inside, he took her hand to lead her out of the restaurant.

In the air outside the coming rain was a promise that could be smelled and tasted, though not yet felt. Only someone out of his mind would propose a walk in this weather, he told himself, and only someone out of her mind would agree.

"How about heading this way?" he suggested, turning left and reluctantly letting go of her hand. He had no right to touch her, casually or otherwise. "We could walk down to Roger Williams Terrace."

"I'd like that," said Kay. "We used to have picnics there when I was in school."

As they passed his car he paused to take an umbrella from the back seat. "Just in case," he said, his smile droll.

Kay nodded. As if either one of them believed that a downpour was only a possibility instead of a black certainty hovering overhead. This was madness, she told herself, easily matching her steps to his. Utter madness.

It took them less than ten minutes to walk to the small, tree-shaded park known simply as the Terrace. The long narrow grassy area carved into the hillside overlooking the city of Providence was bordered on three sides by a black wrought-iron fence. At the edge of the park, poised to watch over the city he'd founded, was a towering bronze statue of Roger Williams.

"So, here we are," she said as they came to a stop by the fence. For several moments they enjoyed in silence the view that swept all the way from the Providence River to the city's west side. There was more than a hint of rain in the air between them now, and Kay told herself she ought to suggest that they head back before the sky opened up, before they were late for the meeting, before something happened that shouldn't. But she didn't want to head back, not yet.

She wanted, for just a few minutes longer, to stand there feeling his arm pressed against hers, as aware of the contact as if it was flesh to flesh instead of buffered by the bulky layers of his clothing and hers. She wanted to go on being nourished by the warm strength of his body.

"So," she said again, uncomfortably aware that she seemed to be starting all her sentences that way, "have you read anything interesting lately?"

Drew turned, looked at her and burst out laughing.

For a few seconds Kay simply stared at him, wafting between feeling annoyed and accepting that it had been a ridiculous thing to say.

"Small talk, Kay?" he said at last. "Aren't we a little beyond that?"

"Are we?" she countered and immediately wished she hadn't. She wasn't sure she wanted to know where they were with each other.

"I am," he said emphatically. He let his gaze rove over the city once more, then brought it back to her. "I turned forty a while back."

"I know." And knowing suddenly flooded Kay with awareness of her own age. She thought about how much more obvious the lines around her eyes must be in the daylight and about the hint of softness beneath her chin and was filled with an almost painful desire to be thirty again. She pulled the edges of her coat together, doing her best to listen to what Drew was saying.

"I woke up the morning of my birthday and looked in the mirror and thought, you're halfway there, pal."

"Not a very cheery thought to start off a new year," she observed.

"But a more or less accurate one. Actually I think that in terms of the national average, eighty years is a generous prediction. At any rate, I suddenly realized that I was halfway *there* without any idea of where it was I wanted to go." He forced a smile. "How's that for not cheery?"

Kay reached out to touch his arm. "Drew, you have so much to be proud of. I—"

He shook his head. "Please, Kay, I'm not looking for a pep talk, just stating facts. I'm forty years old and I have no wife, no kids, two sisters who seem to have dedicated their lives to trying to run mine and a family business I find about as exciting and challenging as picking lint off a sweater."

Kay smiled, feeling the knot that had begun to form at the back of her neck ease. For a second she had been alarmed, but this was the Drew she knew so well, his expression relaxed, his humor dry and self-deprecating.

"Anyway, I made up my mind that while I might not have much say in where I was going, I was sure as hell going to decide how I went about getting there. I guess all this is a way of telling you why I don't do small talk anymore. In fact, I made myself three promises that morning."

"Would it be too nosy of me to ask what they were?"

"You could never be too nosy where I'm concerned," he said quietly. "First and foremost, I promised myself I would stop pretending I liked playing golf no matter how many big deals are said to be clinched on the golf course."

"You quit playing golf?" Kay asked, feigning horror.

"Cold turkey. Dropped the clubs off at the Salvation Army and felt like a free man for the first time in years."

She laughed, amused at the whimsical nature his revelations had taken, especially when she had been afraid he was turning melancholy on her. "I can hardly wait to hear your other promises."

"The second was that I would stop letting Anne and Elise push me over the edge."

"And have you?" she asked skeptically. She knew his sisters.

His mouth twisted into a resigned smile. "Let's say I try."

"And the third promise?"

He stuck his hand out straight and caught a large drop of water in his palm. "What do you know? Rain. We better get moving."

"Oh, no, you don't," Kay exclaimed, pulling him a few steps so that they were both afforded the dubious shelter of a nearby oak tree's bare branches. "I'm hooked. Rain or no rain, I want to hear that third promise."

Drew's smile flickered and faded. He drew a deep breath, studying her with somber gray eyes. At that moment Kay wanted more than anything to tell him to forget it, all of it. She opened her mouth to speak just as his hands lifted to her shoulders, holding her in place when some deeply rooted instinct was urging her to run.

"What the hell," he murmured, his gaze still riveted on her face. "The third promise I made to myself was that I would stop backing away from the truth. That when the time came, if it ever did, I would have the guts to tell you the truth. That I love you." He drew another breath and said it again, more slowly, as if she hadn't heard it so clearly the first time that the words were already carved somewhere deep inside her where they could never be erased. "I love you, Kay. I have loved you for as long as I can remember."

"God, Drew." She could feel herself trembling and knew he must feel it, too, from the way he held on to her even more tightly. "God, I . . . I don't know what you want me to say."

"I don't want you to say anything." He smiled at her. The tenseness that had gripped him just a few seconds ago seemed to have vanished. "I realize that our situations are very different, that I'm free to say what I please and you're not. I didn't tell you this expecting you to either sanction my feelings for you or return them."

"Then why? Why did you tell me? Why now?"

"Because what I feel for you is real. It exists. Because it's existed for so long and because the time was right. Not to proposition you." His expression, which had been introspective, suddenly darkened with concern. "I hope you know that, Kay. I hope you understand that I would never do or say anything to compromise you in any way. This was not a proposition."

"No, I suppose the time for that would have been years ago," she said softly, once again lost in her awareness of herself, of reality. "I still don't know what to say."

"Then don't say anything. It's enough for me to know that you know. At last. For so long, especially the last year or so, I've sensed . . ." He stopped and shook his head as if censoring himself. "For a while now I've wanted to tell you how I feel just so you would know that I'm here for you if you need me, and that I always will be."

Beyond words, Kay ran her hand over her hair, surprised to find that it was wet. She hadn't noticed that the single rain-drop Drew caught in his hand had been followed by thousands more. They were both getting soaked. Still she didn't move.

"Look at me, Kay," Drew urged, his voice smooth and low, his hand gently cupping her face. With one finger he traced the curve of her cheek. "Are these raindrops or tears?"

"I don't know," she whispered. "I don't know."

He bent his head, smiling. "Shh. It doesn't matter."

His lips touched hers, warm and cool at the same time and tasting of the rain. He kissed her lightly, leaving Kay shaking, confused, longing.

"I'm sorry," he said. "I couldn't resist."

"You're all wet. Your glasses, your hair."

He took off the glasses and wiped the lenses. "Come on, let's go," he said, pulling her by the hand as he glanced at the gray clouds swirling overhead. "Maybe we can find a doorway or someplace to wait it out."

"Drew, wait," Kay said, hurrying to keep up with him. "Your house isn't far. We could go there and dry off and . . . I think maybe we should talk about this."

"What about the meeting?"

"Forget the damn meeting."

He stopped and swung around to face her, wet black curls tumbling over his forehead. "I would love to take you home with me. But considering that any number of people might have seen us together and be more than willing to speculate on the reason when neither one of us shows up this afternoon, I don't think it's such a good idea. You have too much at stake, Kay."

"Let me worry about that."

"You don't have to—I'll worry for you. Besides, I've caught you by surprise with all this. You need time to think before you make any decision, if there's a decision to be made."

Belatedly he remembered the umbrella clamped beneath his arm. Still when they arrived at the meeting—separately and with what Kay hoped were plausible excuses to account for their condition—they were both quite damp. Her proposal for the First Annual Sedentary Ball was initially received with skepti-cism. Only after a long and spirited debate, which had her feeling part cheerleader and part defense attorney, was a majority of the committee won over to wholehearted enthusiasm. Once she was certain the idea was a hit, she made sure to publicly credit Drew with providing the inspiration for it.

It was a relief when the meeting finally ended. She needed to be alone so she could stop pretending that nothing earth-shattering had occurred since she awoke that morning, when in fact her life had been swept up tornado style, like Dorothy's in *The Wizard of Oz*. Only Kay still had no idea where she was going to land.

She wanted to say goodbye to Drew, but he was involved in conversation, so she waved on her way out and was surprised when he caught up with her as she slid behind the wheel of her car.

He leaned over the top of the door. "Congratulations, your idea was a success."

"Your idea," she reminded him.

He shook his head. "It was my cynicism talking. You turned it into an idea and ran with it."

Her smile widened. "I did, didn't I?"

"And brilliantly, I might add. How would you like to come to work for me? I could really use someone with your imagination and persuasive powers."

"Oh, please. I may be able to twist a few arms on a committee of volunteers, but in the cold hard world of business I'd be a washout." It was true. James had told her so dozens of times, whenever she broached the possibility of taking a more active role in the business.

Drew's expression suggested something quite different, however. "Don't sell yourself short," he urged quietly.

"I'm not. I'm just being realistic. Besides, I'm so busy with my volunteer work and with the family..." She paused. Who was she kidding? Jack hadn't needed active mothering for years now, and Drew, ever the good listener, the sympathetic shoulder to cry on, was in a position to know that. As for James needing her, well...

"Anyway," she said to Drew, her smile so wide it hurt, "for the time being I'm content to bask in the successful launching of the sedentary ball. Who says there's nothing new under the sun?"

"Someone who hadn't reckoned on you, obviously. The best part is that this is one ball I can safely invite you to."

"And I can safely accept," Kay countered, unable to suppress the small catch in her voice as she added, "and that's that."

"Maybe not. Here's a more risky invitation for you, Kay. Next Thursday I'm driving to Boston to check on some stones being offered by an Australian dealer. How would you like to come along for the ride?"

"I . . ." She hesitated. She would like it very much. Did she dare admit it, much less go? "I . . ."

Kay stared into his eyes. They were sympathetic and at the same time faintly, gently amused; familiar and yet suddenly harboring new possibilities. He smiled and made her feel lighthearted in a way she thought she'd forgotten how to feel.

He stepped away from the car, breaking the tension.

"Don't look so worried," he said. "It's not an invitation to the guillotine, and it's not until next week. Call me."

EIGHTEEN

The following Thursday morning dawned with the kind of sunny brilliance that lifts the spirits and makes anything seem possible. When the light filtered through the embroidered lace panels on Kay's bedroom windows, she knew that sleep was a thing of the past. She'd made her decision. Today was the day.

She showered and dressed. When she entered the dining room an hour later, James looked up and greeted her with raised eyebrows. "Good morning. To what do I owe this rare pleasure?"

Kay offered only a smile in response. Her appearance at the breakfast table was indeed a rare occurrence. For good reason. She found it humiliating to compete with the sports section of the morning paper for her husband's attention, especially since she invariably lost.

That wasn't going to happen this morning, however. She had a humdinger of a conversation ball to fire at him. Helping herself to toast and a spoonful of scrambled eggs from the sideboard, she took her place across from him at the dining room table.

"Thank you, Madge," she said to the maid who filled her coffee cup and placed the silver creamer and sugar bowl within reach.

Kay would prefer to eat at the small table in the sun-filled breakfast nook, but James insisted on the maximum pomp and circumstance for even the most ordinary events. A psychiatrist would probably say that it had to do with his working-class roots and feelings of insecurity and inferiority. She understood all that. It still didn't make it any more pleasant to share breakfast with eighteen empty chairs.

She spread a teaspoon of low-cal orange marmalade on her toast and took a bite. When the dining room was redecorated last year, she gave the decorator express orders to make the view the centerpiece. Hence the wall behind James had three sets of French doors opening onto the terrace and framing a spectacular view of the cliffs and the foamy blue ocean beyond. Kay wondered how anyone could walk into this room on a day like today and sit with his back to such a sight.

After the dining room, she'd decided to redo the living room, then their bedroom and the guest rooms. In the end, with the exception of the library and Jack's room, which he'd declared off-limits, she had overhauled the entire house. Now, she thought, with a resurgence of the steely resolve she'd forged in the shower, she was ready to do the same with her life.

"James, I'd like to speak with you about something."

James continued to hold the newspaper in front of his face for as long as it took him to rid it of the instinctive grimace. He knew it. As soon as she sashayed into the room all powdered and perfumed and dressed to do battle in a silk print dress he'd never seen before, he knew something was up. All he wanted was to eat breakfast and read about the Celtics in peace. Was that too much too ask? Evidently it was.

"Of course, sweetheart," he replied, lowering the paper, but not closing it on the article he'd been reading, not yet. "What do you want to talk about?"

"A job."

"For who?" His fingers tightened on the handle of his coffee cup. He didn't like Kay's forays into business matters, subtle and infrequent though they were.

"For me."

He sipped his coffee, chuckling with restraint. "Very funny."

"I'm not joking. I want to go to work."

"Doing what?"

"I'm not exactly sure of that yet," she explained, refusing to be upset by his expression of benign amusement or goaded into anything other than the calm, logical presentation she had rehearsed. "Something in the design department, I think, that's closest to the field of my degree. Or maybe marketing. I have so many ideas for—"

"Design? Marketing?" he interrupted, his tone and his sudden shift from looking tolerant to looking flabbergasted causing her to fall silent. At last he closed the newspaper completely. "You're talking about coming to work for me?"

"No, not *for* you, James. Have you forgotten that Delaney Silver is my company?"

"How could I? Either you or your parents found a way to remind me of that fact every day for as long as I can remember. So now you're bored with your tea parties and bridge games and you figure you'll entertain yourself playing boss lady for a while?"

"No, that's not it at all. I don't want to have anything to do with the actual running of the company. That will remain your responsibility."

"How generous of you. I get to go on sitting in Daddy's chair, only with you there looking over my shoulder every time I make a move."

"It wouldn't be like that. I would have my own responsibilities . . ."

"You already do," he told her. "All your committees and charities. Stick to them, Kay, and stay out of my business."

"It's my business, too. *Our* business," she added hurriedly.

"Fine. Any time you don't like the way I'm running it, just say the word. Until then, I'll handle it my way."

"Which doesn't include my participation?"

"That's right. Hell, Kay, you're my wife. I want you here when I come home from work, soft and sweet-smelling and waiting just for me." He saw the words strike their mark and wished it had occurred to him to take this stance from the start, but hell, she'd caught him as off guard as a bull moose the first day of hunting season. "I don't want you to be just one more person I have to butt heads with all day long. God, sweetheart, that would kill me."

"We wouldn't have to butt heads," she argued. "And as for my being here waiting for you, you usually come home so late and so tired you don't even know I'm around."

He leaned forward, fixing her with a narrow gaze. "Believe me, I know. And that's what keeps me going through all those long days and nights. I need you here for me, babe."

"And I need to do something with my life besides plan dinners and host tea parties."

"Okay," he said, nodding slowly, thinking fast. "Okay, I can certainly understand that, and we'll find something for you to do, something that's right for you, for both of us."

"Drew thinks this sort of work is right for me. He said Goddard's could use someone with my creativity and persuasiveness."

"Goddard offered you a job?" James didn't like that idea any better than he did the prospect of having her come to work at Delaney.

"As a matter of fact he did." She briefly explained about her success at the meeting on Monday and how it had led to Drew's offer. "But I don't want to work for Goddard's. I want to work for Delaney Silver. I want to work with you, my husband, not so I can interfere, but so I can be close to you. I can drop into your office. We can have lunch together. I can…" She stopped, defeated by the brick wall of his expression.

"That all sounds nice, Kay, but it won't work. Trust me on this one. We're not running a charity committee down there. That design department is a boiler room and marketing is worse—brutal, absolutely brutal. Sweetheart, you're not cut out for the nine-to-five, cutthroat, workaday world. Your old man knew that, I know it, and believe me, so does Drew Goddard. He was just flattering you the other day. Don't embarrass yourself by pressing the matter."

"Don't worry, I won't." She got to her feet and tossed her napkin onto the table. "I guess a job isn't what I need to fill my days, after all."

James reached for the paper, flipping it open to the story on last night's Celtics game. Where was he? He scanned, found his place, read a few lines.

He glanced up. What the hell did she mean, a job wasn't what she needed to fill her days after all? What was she thinking of filling them with? And where the hell did Goddard get off putting these ideas in her head in the first place?

Shoving the newspaper aside, he left the dining room and found Kay standing by the desk in the hallway, engagement book in hand, going over her schedule for the day. The book was crammed with appointment cards and invitations. What the hell more did the woman need to fill her day?

"There you are," he said, moving closer to her.

She let him cool his heels for a full minute before glancing up at him with the preoccupied look he hated. "Hm?"

"I'm off. I just wanted to say goodbye and make sure you aren't upset."

"Upset? Because my husband wants to save me from the cold, harsh business world...and from my own ambition? Not at all."

"I'm glad you understand." He leaned down to kiss her. Her lips were like the entrance to a crypt, cold and tightly sealed. He tried her cheek and meandered his way down to the side of her throat.

"C'mon, Kay, don't be mad." Her skin was warmer there, but she was still as stiff as a mummy. "Kat." His tongue teased her ear, and he let his tone turn husky. "My sweet Kat."

Wrapping his arms around her, he jerked her against him, pressing his hands to her backside. He nipped at her neck and made a low-pitched growling sound. "You know, if you're really that bored, maybe I ought to take you upstairs and keep you there for the rest of the day."

She grabbed his jacket lapels so quickly it took him by surprise.

"Yes," she whispered, "that's exactly what you ought to do. Oh, James. It's been years since we spent a morning in bed." She kissed his cheek and pressed herself against him, trying to find room between his thighs for one of hers, desperately willing the excitement to come and push everything else aside. Before it had a chance to begin, she sensed him lifting his wrist behind her to check his watch.

"Damn," he muttered.

Already she was stiffening, removing herself from his loosened arms.

"Kay, sweetheart, I really would love to stay home with you, but I have a killer meeting scheduled first thing this morning. Sales reps from Federated Department Stores."

"I understand."

"That's my girl. I'll tell you what," he added, bestowing a final quick peck on her lips, "you hold that thought and I'll see what I can do about getting home early tonight."

Kay smiled her most gracious smile and waited until he was gone to hurl the engagement book at the closed door. "Don't bother, sweetheart. I won't be here."

All the way to Providence and later, sitting beside Drew on the drive to Boston, Kay waited for the black cloud of second thoughts to descend on her. It never happened. Instead she kept

remembering the undisguised joy that had been in Drew's voice
when she called to tell him to wait for her and the look on his
face when she arrived at his house on Benefit Street, the look
that was still there.

It was a mixture of pleasure and amazement, as if he half-
believed she was a mirage he'd conjured up and might vanish
if he looked away for too long. He kept stealing glances at her
as he drove along the Southeast Expressway and later in the
hotel suite of the gem dealer and even now as they sat in the
splendidly ornate dining room of the Ritz Carlton and shared
late-afternoon tea. In a far corner of the room a string quartet
played chamber music, the perfect accompaniment for Kay's
relaxed state of mind. She'd left a message for James, saying
she was shopping in Boston with a friend and wasn't sure what
time she would be home. All true.

They had shopped, albeit on a grand scale, choosing the
gems that would be featured next season in Goddard's exclusive designs, emeralds and amethysts and gorgeous lilac-colored
crystals of kunzite. At first, conscious of what James had said
about Drew's job offer being no more than idle flattery, she
remained a silent observer. Drew would have none of it. He
solicited her opinion, calling upon her to choose between two
stones he favored, cajoling her into feeling them, cradling them
in her hands, showing her preliminary sketches and asking if
she would use sapphires or the pale bicolored elbaite tourmaline with the gold filigree chains his designers had created. In
the end, convinced his interest was sincere, Kay entered into the
selection enthusiastically, once or twice persuading Drew to
change his mind about a particular stone.

It was exhilarating, and long after they left the dealer's suite
she went on offering suggestions, flattered that he took them
seriously enough to make notes in the small notebook he kept
tucked inside his jacket pocket.

"This has been a wonderful day, Drew," she said, as she
lifted her teacup to take a sip of tea. "I'm so glad I decided to
come."

"Not half as glad as I am," he told her. "But as long as you
brought it up, what made you change your mind?"

"How do you know I changed my mind?"

"Because I watched your face when I first invited you to
come along, and I was sure you were going to say no."

"I wanted to come," she said quickly.

"I know that."

"I guess I just thought it was..." She shrugged. "The wrong thing to do."

"And now?"

"Now it feels right. I feel ... You've made me feel like this is where I belong." She tossed her hair. Today, for the first time in a long while, she'd worn it loose, and she realized how much she missed the feel of it brushing her neck. "Besides, I didn't have anything else to do today."

He grinned. "Didn't have anything to do? Aren't you hosting a major charity luncheon on Saturday?"

"That's all been planned for ages and... All right." She laughed. "So I have a hundred and one things I should be doing. But none that I wanted to do nearly as much as I wanted to spend the day with you."

"That's exactly what I wanted to hear you say. After I left you on Monday, I was sorry I'd put you on the spot by asking you to come... but not because I didn't want you here," he added quickly. His smile was rueful. "Actually, I want you with me all the time."

All day the matter of their feelings for each other had been like quicksilver, right there between them and yet not there. Now, drawing a deep breath, Kay grabbed hold of it with both hands. "I guess we should talk about all this."

Drew startled her by shaking his head. "No, that's exactly what we should not do. Oh, I could give you a blow-by-blow account of all these years that I've loved you from a distance, tell you about all the times I've held another woman in my arms and wished she was you, explain how no woman has ever quite measured up because no woman was ever you. That would flatter you and soften your feelings for me and put even more pressure on you than I already have. I want to make your life easier, Kay, not harder."

Impulsively Kay reached across the table and laid her hand on top of his, startled by the shivery feeling the contact produced. Oh, Lord, she thought, this is real. It's happening and I don't want it to stop. "Drew, I appreciate your concern, truly I do, but this is hardly something we can ignore or turn the clock back on."

"I have no intention of ignoring it. Whatever's going to happen will happen. I just won't do anything to press it. But," he continued, leaning toward her with a small smile that made

Kay's heart race like a schoolgirl's, "I should warn you that I also won't do anything to stop it."

His gaze was direct, his message clear. He loved her and he wanted her; the rest was up to Kay. She didn't need to examine her own feelings. She'd done little else all week. His announcement on Monday had simply forced her to confront the fact that she'd been falling in love with Drew for ages. This morning, with desire and honor all twisted into a knot inside her, James had unknowingly set her free. She had set out to meet Drew with her eyes open, her decisions made. Now she sat back in her chair with a heady feeling of contentment. Drew was right. Whatever was meant to happen would happen.

"I stayed here once," she told him, gazing around the dining room. "A long time ago, with my aunt Grace. She took me to England when I was around thirteen. We were flying out of Logan so we drove to Boston the night before we left and stayed here at the Ritz. I was quite full of myself to be traveling without my parents and baby brother and so determined to be a woman of the world, which at that age meant being not overly impressed with anything." She smiled, remembering.

"And so I went about registering and having dinner here in the dining room as casually as if I flew off to Europe weekly. Then that night, when I turned down the covers on my bed, I found rose petals on my pillow and that was it . . . goodbye woman of the world," she said with a wave of her hand. "I squealed and went running into Aunt Grace's room to tell her what a glorious hotel this was to put rose petals on the guests' pillows. It was years before I realized that they were put there courtesy of my aunt and not the hotel management, but it did the trick, the ice was broken, and I didn't have to spend three weeks pretending not to be impressed by Big Ben and Buckingham Palace."

They talked for a while longer before Drew excused himself. When he returned Kay had finished her tea and could think of no reason not to agree when he suggested it was time to leave. Walking to the elevator she felt a crushing sadness. The day was ending too soon. Though she understood Drew's resolve to let things happen naturally, she couldn't help but wonder how long it would take for anything to happen if neither of them pushed the matter even the slightest bit.

She had her answer as soon as the elevator doors closed behind them. They were alone and instead of pressing the button for the lobby, Drew uncurled his fingers to reveal the brass room key in his palm. The number 725 was engraved on it. Now she knew where he had gone while she sat finishing her tea.

Slowly she lifted her gaze from the key to meet his, knowing the question she would find reflected in his eyes as well as she knew her answer. Her sadness of a moment ago disappeared and the hum of desire she'd been feeling all day grew louder. She felt intoxicated and only a little apprehensive. The last time she'd gone to bed with a man for the first time she had been twenty-one years old. She was considerably older now. But, she reminded herself before a tidal wave of insecurities could rise up, so was the man involved. Even better, that man was Drew.

She smiled slowly, suddenly cognizant of the fact that there was uncertainty mingled with hope in his eyes. So she wasn't the only one with insecurities. The thought was soothing. Without saying a word she reached to push the button for the seventh floor.

As the elevator slowly made its way up, Drew took her hand in his and held it, the key pressed securely between their palms. All the way down the hall, Kay kept remembering how he had kissed her in the park and wondering what it would be like to taste his lips when they weren't so gentle and wet with rain.

The room was spacious, done in shades of pink and gold, all plush, cushioned elegance. The bed was wide and inviting and seemed to dominate the room just as it did Kay's thoughts. She half expected Drew to grab her the instant the door was shut behind them and almost regretted the opportunity for second thoughts he permitted while he went to hang their coats in the closet.

Restlessly she paced to the window, gazing out on a city already tinged with gray, and then Drew's hands touched her shoulders. Everything else inside her began to spin out of control.

She turned, wrapping her arms around him as he pulled her closer. When he bent his head she rose to meet him, responding to his gentle kiss with a sudden hunger that took her by surprise. She sought him with her tongue and he in turn reached out to her, stroking deeply, filling her mouth until she was moaning softly and lifting against him in her impatience. Too soon he pulled back, his hands once again coming to rest on her shoulders. Not until she looked into his eyes did he speak.

"No, Kay," he said softly. "Not like that. I've waited twenty-five years for this moment. I want it to last, I want you to know it's me making love to you, I want you to *remember* this."

Slowly he undressed her, the removal of each piece of clothing a separate adventure, each newly exposed piece of flesh a place of worship. With his fingers and his mouth he teased and tickled her, teaching her that passion could be a slow-moving river inside her and that she liked it that way. Oh, God, she liked it.

By the time he finally led her to the bed she was trembling with desire. He threw back the covers and through the sensual haze they had created the scent of flowers rose up sweet and strong. Kay couldn't believe her eyes. Rose petals, thousands of them, red and white and pink, covered the pillows and the sheets and tumbled onto her bare feet. She turned to Drew, all the things she wanted to say suddenly locked behind a painful lump in her throat.

"I love you, I love you," she managed as they moved onto the bed.

The petals were softer than anything she had ever felt against her skin. They rolled in them like children playing in the first snowfall of the season. Drew gathered handfuls of them to rub on her shoulders and breasts and between her legs, making her cry out loud through her laughter. They made love for hours, desire and fulfillment a single wheel that never stopped spinning, and after each time he stayed with her, their arms and legs entangled so that she didn't know where she ended and he began.

It was late when Drew finally glanced at his watch and with obvious reluctance suggested that they should think about heading home. The windows were tall rectangles of black glass. Outside drifted ghosts of pale, filmy light tossed up by the headlights of the cars below.

"Will anyone worry because you've been gone so long?" he asked.

He didn't get any more specific than that, and Kay was grateful. She wanted no one else in this room with them.

"No, I left word that I might be late." As soon as the words were out Kay realized how calculating they made her sound, as if she'd intended for this to happen from the time she brushed her teeth this morning, when that wasn't the case at all. She thought to explain, then realized it wasn't necessary. Far from embarrassing her, Drew's smile made her feel conspiratorial and protected.

"Good," he said. "I suppose I should have asked you about that hours ago, but the truth is that I didn't want to hear that you had to get back. I didn't want to let you go. I still don't. But I know I've been very selfish keeping you here so long."

"Oh, no." He was stretched out above her and Kay reached up to push her fingers through his hair, studying his face so she could remember the light in his eyes and that it was all for her. "Drew Goddard, you are the most unselfish person I know. I have always considered myself very lucky to have you for a friend, and now to have this, too... It's such a bonus. I don't deserve it."

He turned to kiss her wrist. "You deserve everything."

"No." She shook her head. "Besides, most people would say I already have everything. Why did it take me so long to realize that all I want is you?"

Drew shrugged, refusing to think along those lines. Yesterday and tomorrow were beyond his control. At least they had today. "Who knows why anything happens the way it does? Isn't it enough to know you have me now?"

He watched her think that over, saw her delicate jaw lift in a show of the blind stubbornness, which was one more thing he adored about her.

"No. It's not enough," she said bluntly. "I want this to last forever. Promise me forever, Drew."

He lay his hand against her cheek, loving her, wanting her with an ache that was every bit as raw now as it had been when they walked into this room, wondering if it would ever feel any other way. And wondering if Kay had any idea of how complicated and serious a business they had set in motion here today. He sighed and smiled at her. No, probably not. Kay saw only what she wanted to see. At the moment she was seeing only rose petals and asking him for forever. He supposed he was partly to blame for that, but when he'd heard the story of her aunt Grace he hadn't been able to resist.

"I'll do better than that," he said finally.

She eyed him skeptically. "What could be better than forever?"

"I promise that I'll be around for as long as you want me to be, and not a minute longer."

"Forever," she countered, her absolute certainty making his heart twist inside him. "That will be forever."

Would it? Drew was willing, he just wasn't so sure. Smiling, he bent and kissed her mouth. "Then forever it is."

NINETEEN

Getting together during her break became a nightly ritual for Lily and Jack. She looked forward to the meetings ahead of time and relived them afterward. With the cooperation of some of the other waitresses, she managed to stretch their time together from fifteen minutes to twenty, then thirty.

Sometimes Jack brought along a couple of cans of soda; sometimes she brought him an extra dessert from the kitchen. Once he gave her a single red rose. They sat on the steps overlooking the golf course, alone together in the warm dark spring night, and got to know each other a few minutes at a time.

Technically the meetings were not dates, at least not the sort of dates Jack envisioned and complained about not having. To Lily they were better. She was more at ease and open in those precious moments than she would have been on a hundred traditional dates, and something told her that, in spite of his grumbling, the same was true for Jack.

Free of other distractions, she learned that his favorite color was green and that his thumbs were double-jointed and that he'd twice pitched no-hitters for the Delaney Silver softball team. She learned what made him laugh and what made him furious and how one rainy night when he was driving home from school he'd given his coat to a hitchhiker who'd then pulled a knife and stolen his wallet with two tickets to a Rolling Stones concert.

And she learned to kiss like a woman. She learned the heart-stopping wonder of Jack's fingers stealing inside the neckline of her uniform, sliding along her collarbone to tease the soft flesh just below, in a way she felt in small, dangerous explosions all the way to her toes. She learned that falling in love was a lot like riding a roller coaster, scary and exhilarating, never knowing what waited around the next thrilling corner and with no way to stop.

Several times Jack picked her up at school and took her flying. Lily grew to love letting her feet leave the ground, in every sense of the phrase. Jack became her world, or at least the dominant force in it. A secret, private world. She still hadn't told another soul about him.

Sometimes she felt guilty about keeping secrets from her parents and worried they would find out, anyway. Sometimes she felt so happy she longed to tell the whole world. What held her back was an uneasy feeling that once she let go of the secret, once it was out of her control, something would happen to spoil everything. Maybe, subconsciously, all her mother's warnings about the folly of dreaming too big had hit their mark after all. There was no denying that even in her wildest dreams she'd never pictured herself with Jack Terrell. When it came to dreaming beyond your means, she supposed this qualified. And still she couldn't help dreaming, even as she fought off the niggling echo of one of her mother's favorite sayings—*if something seems too good to be true, it usually is.*

Finally, after a few weeks of settling for afternoons and hurried coffee breaks, Jack took the matter out of her hands.

"There's a party at my house a week from Saturday," he told her one night. "And you're coming."

"What's the occasion?" she asked, not really caring. Parties at Delaney Place were legendary. They were described in lavish detail in the society pages, and still Lily always bugged her father for behind-the-scenes tidbits. Now she was being invited to one of those parties.

"It's my mother's birthday," Jack replied. "It's an annual thing, more business than pleasure, actually. Usually I grab any excuse to get out of going, but this year I'm looking forward to it, because I figure this is one invitation you have to accept. It's not a school night, it's so sickeningly respectable your folks can't say no, and I've given you plenty of warning so you can ask for the night off. I'll even speak to Higgins for you if—"

"No," she interrupted. "I can handle it myself. Right now I better get back in there, or I'll end up with every night off when he fires me."

"Sounds good to me," said Jack, pulling her hard against him. "Then I can have you to myself every night."

He held her close for a slow, deep kiss.

"I have to go," Lily pleaded.

"Mmm." He nuzzled her throat and kissed her again. "You'll come to the party?"

"I'll try," Lily countered, wanting to go to that party at Delaney Place as much as she'd ever wanted anything.

"Not good enough," insisted Jack, tightening his hold so that Lily was exactly where she wanted to be, so close to him she couldn't tell the pounding of his heart from her own. "You have to say yes."

"Yes," she said without thinking, allowing herself to be lifted into one more kiss. She would think later.

Inside she did nothing *but* think about it, and what she thought was that one way or another she was going to that party with Jack. She devised a dozen different ways to broach the subject at home, but in the end, impatience ruled.

When she left the club her father was waiting, parked in his usual place. She ran to the car and even before she had pulled the door shut behind her, blurted out, "Daddy, you're not going to believe what happened tonight."

"Mrs. Wellington's wig fell into the lobster bisque again?"

She laughed. "Not quite. I've been invited to a party. And not just any party, the absolute biggest social event of the entire year. Do you believe it? I, Lily Marie Saville, am going to a party at Delaney Place."

"What did you say?" he asked, his sudden tenseness piercing Lily's euphoria. She fully expected to do battle with her mother over this, but she'd counted on her father to understand.

"I said I've been invited to a party at Delaney Place next Saturday night."

"Mrs. Terrell's birthday party," he muttered. No doubt he was already hard at work on special flower arrangements. "Who would invite you there?"

"Jack Terrell." She took a deep breath. "Do you remember the day I applied for the job at the club? I told you that someone put in a good word for me and then gave me a ride home? I didn't know it at the time, but that was Jack Terrell."

Her father stared at the road ahead. "And now he suddenly invites you to a party?"

"It's not suddenly. I've seen him around the club," she said, balancing on that fine line between the truth and everything else. "We've talked a few times, and tonight he stopped by to invite me to the party."

"I don't know, sweetheart."

"Daddy," she exclaimed. "What's not to know? It's the chance of a lifetime."

"I don't know," he said again. "That boy..." He shook his head. "I don't know what your mother will say about this."

"The same thing she always says." Lily expertly mimicked her mother's brisk tone. "Know your place, keep a sensible head on your shoulders, you've no business going there, and on and on and on." Twisting in the seat she reached out to touch his arm. "But I can go, can't I, Daddy? You won't let her say no?"

A tortured breath lifted Rusty Saville's broad chest. Lily's fingers curled over the sleeve of his old black and red plaid lumberman's jacket and he was suddenly fifteen years younger, walking along the beach with two-year-old Lily tugging at his sleeve, asking him to lift her up for a closer look at the sea gulls sweeping the sky overhead.

They would go to the beach early, just the two of them, in time to see the sun rise from the ocean like a ball of fire. After the first sunrise they watched together, Lily had clapped her hands in delight and said, "Do it again. Please, Daddy," and he'd felt like the king of the world. "I will, honey," he'd promised. "First thing tomorrow morning."

"Please, Dad?" she was saying now.

He shook his head to clear it, his voice gruff. "You can go to the party." He turned his head to look at her. "But just in case your mother is still awake when we get home, don't say anything about it tonight. Nothing at all. Time enough to tell her in the morning, after I have a chance to think of a way to smooth things over."

Lily agreed readily. The last thing she wanted was to end this wonderful night on a sour note. She had more important things to think about than the fact that her mother never wanted her to have any fun. Like what she was going to wear to the party.

It had to be something spectacular and sophisticated and classy beyond words, which eliminated everything hanging in her closet. In a way she would be making a first impression at the party on Jack, who had never seen her when she wasn't wearing a uniform of some sort, and on his family and friends. It was crucial to her that it be exactly the right impression.

That's when she remembered the white dress in the window of Derring Do. Tomorrow, she decided later as she drifted off to sleep, she would stop on the way to work and see if it was still there.

In spite of her and her father's combined efforts the next morning, there was nothing smooth about her mother's reaction to the news or about the way she eventually gave in and agreed to let Lily go to the party. Not that Lily wasted much time worrying about it. Anticipation consumed her for the next week and a half, making her more impossible to live with than usual, according to her brothers.

The night of the party she spent hours getting ready, then braced herself before venturing downstairs. She knew what to expect, a whistle and a wink of approval from Ben and some simpleminded, backhanded compliment from Joey. Her father would frown, thinking the strapless white dress that had been there waiting when she went to try it on—surely a good omen—was a little too strapless, but he wouldn't say anything to upset her. As usual it was her mother's reaction she most dreaded.

"Lily, a new dress," she exclaimed with more surprise than approval. "Did Chandra..." She took a closer look before shaking her head. "No, I can see it's not one of hers. But I thought..."

She had thought—Lily had *let* her think—that she would be wearing her old navy blue dress to the party. As soon as Lily revealed that she had bought the dress at Derring Do, a place her mother knew only by reputation, she pursed her lips and took yet another, longer look at it. "How much did it cost?"

No surprises so far, thought Lily. Shrugging, she replied, "Not much."

That, of course, was a lie. The dress, along with a coordinating satin cape, new shoes, satin drawstring evening purse and a tube of Mary Quant's Hot Stuff lip gloss, had cost Lily more than she wanted to think about, but they were worth it. This was the most important night of her life. Her resolve must have shown on her face, because with a heavy sigh her mother let the matter drop.

"I hope you won't be cold in that flimsy little cape," she commented after a minute.

"I won't be. I'll only be walking from the house to the car."

"Unless the car breaks down or gets a flat tire. How many times have I told you to always be prepared for an emergency? Do you have tissues? And a dime tucked away in your purse?"

"Yes, Mom." Lily checked the clock. Almost eight. *Come on, Jack,* she prayed silently. She was nervous enough without having to stand around fielding her mother's last-minute kernels of advice. She glanced around the kitchen critically. "Is it really necessary to have this trash container in the middle of the floor?"

Her mother looked at the brown plastic container standing where it always stood at the end of the counter, and then at her. "That's not the middle of the floor."

"No, not technically. But it is right there in plain view, the first thing Jack will see if he comes to the back door." Please don't let him come to the back door, she thought.

"I suppose they don't have garbage at Delaney Place."

"I'm sure they don't have it sitting in the middle of the kitchen floor. Why can't we keep it under the sink like normal people?"

"Because your brothers miss as often as they hit when they throw something away. Then it gets on the floor under the sink and doesn't get wiped up. Out of sight, out of mind, you know. Then it goes bad and starts to smell. Imagine how you'd like that, Miss Fancy Pants."

"Forget it, just forget it." Aside from the trash, everything was neat and clean, and for once Lily was thankful that her mother was such a meticulous housekeeper or, as she and her brothers more commonly put it, a nag. If only... She was suddenly flooded by if onlys.

If only the kitchen curtains weren't homemade, if only the linoleum wasn't worn right through in places, if only the furniture in the living room wasn't lumpy and threadbare. Oh, well, there was nothing she could do about any of that except keep the lights low and hurry Jack out of here as fast as possible. But she could do something about the way she looked, she thought, catching sight of her reflection in the toaster.

"I definitely need something on my neck," she decided. "It's so...so white. And my hair." She frowned into the toaster, fluffing the loose waves at the side of her face, then smoothing them, finally heading to her room for heavy-duty adjustments.

After some work with the brush, she deemed her hair perfect for the second time that night and began rummaging in her jewelry box for a necklace. In quick succession she pulled out a plain gold chain, the cross her parents had given her the day of her confirmation, a slightly tarnished locket with a broken clasp. None of them was right, which was why she'd originally decided it was better to wear nothing at all.

There was a soft knock on her bedroom door. "Lily?"

Her heart clenched. He was here, and she hadn't even heard the doorbell ring. Now he was marooned down there with her father and Ben and Joey. Probably with every light in the house blazing. Belatedly she remembered that she had intended to take the plastic covers off the lamp shades in the den. Groaning, she snatched her purse off her bed and flung the door open.

Mary took one look at the panic in Lily's eyes and shook her head. "It's only me, honey. Relax. He'll be here any minute."

That's what Lily was afraid of. She wanted to get to those plastic covers, but her mother was blocking her path. "At least I'm finally ready."

"I thought you wanted something to wear on your neck."

"I don't have anything. It's all right this way, don't you think?" She touched her bare throat uncertainly.

"I think you look lovely."

It was true, thought Mary. She had been dead set against this date from the start. Having Lily get involved with James Terrell's son was her worst nightmare come to life. As the twig is bent, and all that. That's why tonight was going to be the beginning and the end of this nonsense.

Once she made up her mind to that, she tried her hardest to put aside her fear and think of Lily. The poor thing was as nervous as a cat on a barbed wire fence. It was while trying to think of some way to calm her that Mary had remembered the locket. She held it out to Lily now.

"Maybe you'd like to wear this," she said.

Lily reached for the oval locket. A delicate floral design was etched on the front, and it was edged with a very fine, twisted band of gold. "Mom, it's beautiful. But where did it come from? I've never seen this before. I never even knew you owned a locket."

"Your father brought it back from overseas, and it's been in my dresser drawer all this time. I guess I was just saving it."

"For a special occasion," Lily said softly. She was always teasing her mother about saving things for a special occasion that never seemed to arrive.

Their eyes met.

Mary smiled at her. "That's what this is, isn't it?"

"Yes. It really is special to me, Mom."

"Then let's try it on you. Unless . . . I understand if its not right."

"No, it's perfect."

The locket was the finishing touch Lily had known was missing. Mary stared at the beautiful stranger before her and could hardly believe it was her Lily. All grown up and looking as glamorous as a movie star. She told her so.

"At first I thought maybe that dress was too old for you, being strapless and all, but I was wrong. You look like someone who stepped out of a fairy tale, honey. Beautiful."

They went downstairs to wait. Mary said nothing when Lily removed the plastic covers from her new lamp shades. She'd put them back on later. A few hours of cigar smoke wouldn't do too much damage. When the doorbell rang exactly at eight, Lily sprang to answer it.

If Lily was the princess from a fairy tale, thought Mary, Jack Terrell was Prince Charming. He was too handsome for anyone's good in that fancy white dinner jacket, and his easy smile reminded her of another man and another time. The urge to forbid Lily to go with him rose up like bile in her throat.

It was all she could do to smile through the introductions and handshakes. Jack already knew Rusty, of course. Grudgingly Mary acknowledged that she liked the way he addressed him as Mr. Saville. She also had to like the way he smiled at Lily when he told her she looked beautiful and the careful way he helped her with her cape. But then, she reminded herself, his type always knew just what to say and how to act.

All too soon they were ready to go. As they moved to leave, Rusty told them to hold on a minute, as if he'd suddenly remembered something, and he excused himself to go to the kitchen. When he came back he was carrying a wrist corsage of miniature iris and baby's breath.

"This is for you, honey," he said to Lily. "My own irises. I held it back because I didn't want to steal Jack's thunder, but seeing as . . ." He stopped, not wanting to make it sound as if Jack had somehow fallen short by not bringing Lily a corsage.

"I guess corsages are a little old-fashioned, like me, but I thought since it's a party and all . . ."

"I wish I had thought of it, sir," Jack said, taking the flowers and slipping them onto Lily's wrist. "Though I'm sure no florist could have come up with something this perfect."

Rusty beamed. Shooting Jack a grateful smile, Lily stretched to kiss her father's cheek. "Thank you, Daddy, and thanks for reminding me about the party. I almost walked out without my present for Jack's mother."

She picked up the carefully wrapped package lying on the table behind her. Inside was a watercolor she'd done of Delaney Place, mounted in a simple beechwood frame. Lily had anguished over her gift, discounting whatever suggestions Mary made. Finally she'd decided on the watercolor, and Mary had to agree that it was a very special present.

After they left, Mary busied herself replacing the lamp shade covers and turning off the parlor lamps. She went upstairs to see that the light in Lily's room was off, as well, and found herself drawn inside to peer in the mirror above the dresser. At first it was Lily's image she saw, as if she were still standing in front of her, head bent, holding her long hair aside for Mary to fasten the gold chain. Then Lily was gone and she saw her own reflection in the mirror.

Automatically she smoothed her hair and was startled by the amount of silver she saw mixed with the dark brown. She supposed she could get some sort of a rinse to cover it. She sighed. A rinse wouldn't hide the extra pounds that had thickened her waist and softened her chin. Suddenly nothing about her appearance pleased her, not her reddened hands or her flowered housedress or all those little and not so little lines next to her eyes.

She was forty-eight years old. Did she look older? Probably. Some days she felt it, too. Mostly, though, she didn't notice. She didn't notice the gray hairs or the scale creeping upward or the passing days of childhood, and now those days were all gone. Yet when she looked straight into the mirror, straight into her own eyes, nothing much had changed. She was still the girl with all the dreams, only now all those dreams centered on her children, especially on Lily.

"Mary, are you all right?"

She whirled away from the mirror. "Heavens, Rusty, you scared the life out of me. I didn't even hear you come up the stairs."

"I called to you, but you didn't answer. I thought maybe you were up here...." He shrugged. "Don't worry, Mary, she'll be fine."

"Will she?"

"Sure. It's only one date. The Terrell kid's not a bad sort. Besides, you know what Lily said, he's got plans and so does she. Once she starts meeting those college boys, she'll forget all about him."

"And if she doesn't?"

"Then we'll just have to drive off that bridge when we come to it," he told her. It was an old joke between them, and Mary smiled on cue. "Standing around up here brooding about it isn't going to help any."

"I wasn't brooding. At least not about that. I was counting my gray hairs."

He grinned. "Can I help?"

"You might have helped by saying you didn't see any gray hairs or bulges or crow's-feet."

"I don't." He came closer and lifted his good arm to frame her face with one big hand. His touch was warm and rough and as soothing as a tranquilizer to Mary's jangled nerves. "How could I see crow's-feet, Mary, when every time I look at your face I'm busy seeing my whole life? It's all there, you know, the failures and the hard times and the times I let you down. But the good times are all there, too." He rubbed his thumb across her lower lip. "More of them than anything else, huh, Mary?"

She nodded. "A lot of good times."

"Look at me," he ordered, tipping her head back a bit. "What do you see when you look at me?"

"Spaghetti sauce."

"No..."

Laughing, she stopped him as he went to rub his mouth. "No, I'm teasing. I see ... I see the man I love. The only man I ever loved."

He smiled with great satisfaction at that. "Know what else I see when I look at you, Mary? The future." He held up a finger. "Listen." There wasn't a sound to hear. "Hear how quiet it is? No music blaring, no squabbling. Soon it will be quiet like this all the time."

"Please. Don't remind me. I hate to think of the kids all grown and gone. I loved it when they were all here with us. Safe and sound. I wish..."

He stopped her. "I loved it when they were all here, too, Mary, but the day is bound to come when they're gone. You have to accept that and look on the bright side."

"What bright side? Cliff is fighting in some jungle halfway around the world. Greg is off God knows where. And Joey..." She shook her head.

"Joey will land on his feet, you'll see. And Ben is studying to be a state trooper, and Lily is one smart cookie. They'll all do okay. I'm thinking about us, Mary. You and me. I read this poem once, by Robert Browning I think, and it stayed with me. It goes something like this—'Grow old along with me, the best is yet to be.' That's my idea of looking on the bright side."

Mary softly echoed the words, a smile slowly lifting the corners of her mouth. "The best is yet to be. I like the sound of that."

"That's what's coming up for us, Mary, the best years of our lives. After all these years of doing for others, there'll finally be time for us."

"To do what?" she asked, looking at him as if to ask what crazy idea he'd gotten into his head this time. It made Rusty feel young and strong.

"Well, I was thinking we could start with some of this," he said, bending his head to kiss the side of her throat. He felt the goose bumps rise beneath his tongue, still, after all these years. He knew his Mary. "And a little of this." He pulled her close, rubbing her back, pressing her against him in a way that aroused both of them. "Make that a lot of this."

He kissed her for a long time before taking her hand and leading her downstairs to their bedroom. As long as they were both going to lie awake waiting for Lily to come home, they might as well enjoy themselves.

TWENTY

Spring fever. It was, decided Kay, a most apropos name for her mood this evening. Spring had arrived, with June and the long hot days of summer just around the corner. The air was sweet and warm, the rhododendrons were in bloom, and life was wonderful. *Her* life in particular.

She smiled at her reflection in the dressing table mirror and ran the soft, thick powder brush over her nose once more for good measure. Of course, the reason her life was so wonderful and she was so cat-that-got-the-cream contented had little to do with sunshine and flowers—and everything to do with Drew.

She was, after all these years, wildly in love with him. More in love than she had ever been with anyone in her life, and there was no denying that love, for all its glory, was something like a fever. A fever in the soul. Love made her feel joyful and energetic and blessedly young—in spite of the fact that today was her forty-eighth birthday—and brought back to her all the giddy, unrestrained emotions that go with being young and in love, including a certain sense of invulnerability. It was as if, as surely as the sun would set and rise again, absolutely nothing could go wrong for her or Drew as long as they were together.

If not for such complete and welcome suspension of logic, she would probably be dreading the evening ahead instead of looking forward to it. Tonight would be the first time since she began her affair with Drew that the two of them and James would be together at the same event. As much as she wanted Drew with her tonight, she knew it was going to be a chore to pretend they were merely friends, to watch what she said and keep her hands off him except for the expected and perfectly respectable dance or two.

As always, just thinking about Drew lifted her spirits. They usually managed to get together two or three times a week, and though she lived for those secret, romantic rendezvous, the rest of her life had also taken on a rosy patina. Everything from shopping to boring old committee meetings was more enjoyable these days. Life was once more the way it used to be so long ago, the way it ought to be, she mused, exciting and spontaneous and fun. She woke up happy each morning and went to bed content.

Kay supposed there were those who would say it was a fool's paradise, that she ought to feel worried rather than content. But she refused to worry. She and Drew were scrupulously discreet, both of them aware that any scandal would have an unsavory effect not only on them, but on those close to them, as well, on Jack and on Drew's oh-so-prim sisters and on both respected family names. Her divorcing James to be with Drew would definitely be classified as a scandal. Not to mention sticky business all the way around, fraught with legal and financial complications she couldn't even think about without getting a headache.

The business aspects aside, there were two major obstacles to her divorcing James. She was a Catholic, and she was a Delaney. The state of Rhode Island might be willing to acknowledge publicly that she had made a mistake by marrying James, but she was not.

For it had been a mistake. Kay was at last able to admit that to herself. She paused with hairbrush in hand and gazed sadly at the photograph of her parents on the corner of her dressing table, its silver frame engraved with the family crest. *If only...*

No. She put down the brush so hard it clattered against the glass. There was no room in life for regrets, especially not tonight. Drew had made her promise to take things one day at a time, and she intended to do just that.

It was rare that she got a chance to dress up for him, she thought, pulling her dress from its padded hanger and slipping it over her head. She could hardly wear chiffon and diamonds when she was supposedly off to play tennis or have lunch with an old school chum. Tonight she was pulling out all the stops.

The dress was a Valentino, made of raspberry silk chiffon as soft as a whisper. Fastened over one shoulder with a diamond-studded bow, it left the other shoulder bare and was short enough to reveal to anyone interested that her long legs had held up very well, thank you—not to mention how it made her feel like kicking up her heels. Kay shimmied her hips to get it to drop into place.

The rolling and thrusting motion set off an instant reaction inside James, who had walked into the bedroom a few moments earlier as his wife was bending to touch a perfume stopper to the back of her knees. He'd paused in the doorway to watch. He found himself doing that a lot lately, watching Kay, with a combination of suspicion and mounting interest.

Suspicion because at first he'd thought this change in her, the brightness and unflagging good mood, was a trick of some sort, one more of her little games to try to capture his attention and bind him as close to her as she could. But as the weeks passed, he realized that if it was a game, she didn't especially care if he played or not. If anything, she seemed less restless, less demanding, less driven to know where he'd been and what time he would be home, than ever before in their marriage.

It was as if she'd come to terms with life, hers, his, the way they lived it together, and was at peace. Serene, that was the word for her lately. For some reason he was finding all that serenity incredibly alluring.

He watched as she slipped her feet into ridiculously high heels then checked her reflection in the mirror. For a second he thought she'd caught sight of him standing there watching, but she hadn't. He could tell from the way she tossed her hair and twirled with complete and uninhibited delight. Her eyes were wide and bright. She looked exuberant and young and sexy—the way he remembered her being—and the need to put his hands on her and make her remember who she belonged to was suddenly like a steamroller at his back.

He crossed the room to stand behind her, reaching out to run his hands up and down her bare arms as he met her gaze in the mirror.

She jumped at his touch, then relaxed. "James. I didn't hear you come in."

"Just got here." He bent to kiss her shoulder. "You smell good."

"Chanel . . . same as always."

"No. It's different. You're different."

"You're imagining things," she said, turning to face him in such a way that she slipped from his embrace. "It was getting so late I began to think you had forgotten all about tonight."

"Forget your birthday?" he countered and was reminded by the arch of her brows that it wouldn't be the first time. He hurriedly added, "Even if I had forgotten, one look at you would remind me." He touched her dress. "Is this new?"

"Yes. I wanted something extra special."

"You found it. You look gorgeous, Kay."

"And you look positively rumpled. You'll have to hurry if you plan to change. Guests will be arriving any second."

He reined her in again. "Let them. I'm not in the mood to hurry. What I am in the mood for is spending a little time alone with my wife on her birthday."

She gazed up at him with a smile, *that* smile, barely there, elegant and secretive. God, he thought, groping for the zipper at the back of her dress, he had forgotten how magnificent she was.

"Ah. One of *those* nights," Kay murmured. "What a deliciously wicked idea."

He tipped her chin up and kissed her mouth. "Then you're game?"

Slipping from his arms as gracefully as if she'd rehearsed it, she said, "I think not." She paused at the bedroom door to glance over her shoulder at him. "But you take all the time you like. I can handle the early arrivals without you."

James suddenly had even less desire to shower and change than he had to let her walk out of there thinking she could handle things without him.

"Hold on," he said, retrieving his suit jacket from the bed where he'd tossed it. "I can't have my birthday girl greeting her guests alone."

A vague feeling of uneasiness clung to him as he followed her downstairs. It kept him close to her side, watching and wondering as she made last-minute checks on the arrangements and graciously welcomed the arriving guests. He didn't like feeling uneasy where his wife was concerned, especially when he couldn't figure out why the hell he should. Then, when James was three vodka tonics into the party, Drew Goddard arrived. James had stepped to the bar for another drink, so he was only able to see, not hear, the warm welcome Kay gave him.

It was enough.

Downing the drink in one throat-scorching gulp, he let the truth wash over him. He had been right to think Kay was playing games. She was; she just wasn't playing them with him.

For the next half hour he watched as she and Drew pretended to cross paths accidently. He watched them nonchalantly move from group to group, always managing to end up close to each other. He watched them dance. And even knowing what he would have to be an idiot not to know, he did nothing to interfere. Not tonight. Not yet.

The vodka and the realization that his wife was playing him for a fool combined to produce an ugly mood. It didn't help any when he passed by the front hall and saw Lily Saville. She was wearing a white dress that reminded him she was nearly eighteen and all grown up. What the hell was *she* doing here? James wondered, all the hairs on the back of his neck standing up at the sight of her, here, where she didn't belong.

He knew exactly who the girl was. He'd made it his business to find out what happened to Dolly Martin's brat. If he'd gotten his way, she'd have been palmed off on some family far from Watch Hill. Instead, the Savilles had stepped in, and she'd ended up living in the next village. To add insult to injury, Kay had unknowingly hired Rusty Saville to work right here at Delaney Place, although in the end he'd come to see that as an advantage. It made keeping track of things that much easier. And through the years the irony of it all had brought James more than one private little chuckle. Not tonight, however.

At that moment, the cluster of people in the hallway shifted so that he was able to see Jack standing by Lily's side, and suddenly he knew. Of course, if there was a way to screw his life up royally, Jack would find it. Incensed, James watched as his son stepped away, leaving the Saville girl alone at the edge of the ballroom. The vodka dulled his better judgment, and a morbid, uneasy curiosity propelled him toward her.

Lily gazed around the ballroom, mesmerized. She was in heaven, and had been ever since they'd turned onto the private drive lined with flickering gas lamps and thousands of tiny white lights strung deep within the hedges and shrubbery. Jack seemed to understand how special tonight was for her, and his usual cynicism toward this sort of affair was nowhere in sight. He was treating her gallantly, making her feel like the fairy-tale character her mother had compared her to.

Delaney Place was like a dear old friend, dressed in her finest, most glamorous outfit. Everything gleamed and sparkled, and the air was scented with the special-occasion blend of furniture wax, lemon oil and freshly cut flowers. Silver candlesticks and bowls adorned the tabletops, and the lights of the front hall chandelier twinkled like diamonds against the candlelit backdrop of the rest of the house.

Lily paid particular attention to the flowers arranged in dozens of crystal bowls. Some were vibrant rainbows of yellow chrysanthemums, deep grape irises and anemones the color of peaches and strawberries. Others held pure white gatherings of tea roses, mums and hyacinths. The contrast was spectacular, and knowing her father had designed the arrangements made her proud.

"Well, well, who have we here?"

Lily whirled to find Mr. Terrell lurking behind her, and her bright smile dissolved like sugar in the rain. James Terrell was the one person she'd hoped to avoid tonight. She'd gladly forfeit the drink Jack had gone to get her to have him by her side.

"Hello, Mr. Terrell," she said, forcing a polite smile. "You probably don't remember me. I'm Lily Saville."

"I remember," he said, studying her, his pointed gaze giving his words an importance Lily didn't fully understand.

The day she broke the ship, is that what he was remembering? Did he expect her to say something about it? Lily pressed her lips together. If he wanted to rehash an accident that was ancient history, he was going to have to be the one to bring it up.

He rocked slightly on his heels, looking as comfortable with the prolonged silence as Lily was ill at ease. Where was Jack? she wondered anxiously.

"So," he said at last, nodding at the gift in her hands, "what's that you've brought?"

"A present for Mrs. Terrell."

He cocked his head to the side, his expression bemused, as if she'd said she had a giraffe in the box. "A present?"

"A birthday present." Lily swallowed, her mouth dry. "For Mrs. Terrell's birthday."

"I see. That was very . . . thoughtful of you."

"Maybe I should go and put it with the other presents," Lily said, seizing the opportunity.

He stared at her, his small, bemused smile frozen in place.

"Where are the other gifts?" she asked.

"Actually, as far as I know, you're the only one who saw fit to bring a gift. Not that it wasn't a fine gesture. I'm sure Mrs.

Terrell will be very . . . surprised." He put an off-key emphasis on the last word.

"I hope so," Lily said weakly. It was so warm in there. She brushed the hair from her forehead and saw his eyes widen. What now?

"Why, Lily, you're full of surprises," he drawled. "I can't recall the last time I saw a woman wearing a wrist corsage." Lily had to fight the impulse to jerk her arm away before he could touch the flowers. "But then, not many women have a gardener for a father."

Lily stood there with the painstakingly wrapped birthday present in her hands, the corsage suddenly feeling like a hundred-pound weight strapped to her wrist, and wondered how she could have been so stupid. All week she'd worried about how to wear her hair and whether her dress would be right. Now she realized that she could be wearing a thousand-dollar designer original and still be all wrong. Wrong in a million small ways she didn't even know enough to worry about, ways like those James Terrell had subtly managed to bring to her attention.

She didn't belong here. He'd said exactly that years ago on the day she'd dropped his precious ship. Miserably she realized it had been true then, and it was true now. Now, like then, she suddenly felt alone and powerless, at the mercy of this man who looked at her with scorn in his eyes.

Instead of being a relief, as it would have been even a moment ago, the sight of Jack coming toward her only added to her embarrassment. Jack had to have known that you don't bring presents to this kind of party and that no one else here would be wearing a corsage, and he hadn't said a word. He was probably embarrassed for her. And by her, thought Lily, heat rushing to her face.

"I see you've met my father," he said, his wide mouth curving into a smile as he reached her side.

"Years ago," Terrell replied for her.

Concern clouded Jack's eyes as he glanced at Lily. "I'm sorry it took me so long. I had to wait for them to pop open fresh champagne, and it had to be champagne, because this is a special occasion."

"Yes, indeed," his father said. "It's not every day a young man brings home the gardener's daughter."

Lily flinched as if struck by a whip. It hurt that much.

Jack turned to him in disbelief. "What is wrong with you?" he demanded through clenched teeth, his face above the brilliant white formal shirt turning a dark, furious red.

"Wrong with *me?*" James Terrell chuckled harshly. "Seems to me I should be asking you that question. After all, you're the one who got his ass booted out of school . . . again. You're the one who shows up here at his own mother's birthday party with the hired help."

"Lily doesn't work for you."

"The question is, what does she do for you?" his father shot back as Lily stood, horrified.

Jack gave an animal-like growl and shoved the two champagne flutes he was still holding at a passing waiter, spilling most of the contents on the poor man in the process. He grabbed his father's shoulder. "You jerk."

They were the last words Lily heard as she spun away from them and ran.

Jack saw her go out of the corners of his eyes, but all he felt at that moment was hate, as thick and pungent as only something simmering for a very long time can be. And all directed at the man in front of him.

Jack tightened his hold on his father. He was breathing hard and he ached inside and he hadn't even thrown a punch yet. He was bigger and stronger and younger than his father, and still the bastard stood there looking supremely unconcerned. His chin was held high, his expression speculative, taunting even.

"You want me to hit you," Jack said, with sudden understanding. "You'd like it. It would ruin Mother's party and you could blame me...my temper, my lack of self-control, my poor judgment, all those things that make me unfit to run Delaney Silver." He shook his head. "I'm going to be gone in a few weeks, out of your way for good, but you couldn't even wait that long. You always have to rub my nose in it, don't you? Even if it means hurting a girl who never did anything to you."

His father's mouth twitched slightly, but his eyes remained cold and challenging.

"I'd really like to oblige you by wiping the floor with you," Jack whispered close to his face, before turning him loose with a small shove. "But you're not worth it."

From across the room Kay observed the scene in bits and pieces, glimpsed over Drew's shoulder as they danced. "I hope nothing's wrong," she said. "For a second it looked as if James and Jack were having an argument."

"Would that be so out of the ordinary?" asked Drew.

"Not really," she admitted. "But they do usually have the good sense to save their disagreements for a private moment."

"Then leave it to their good sense," Drew advised, though there was no mistaking the sarcasm in his voice.

"I just hope he doesn't do anything to spoil the night for Jack. This is the first time in years I haven't had to bribe and threaten Jack to attend a family party. He actually seemed to be looking forward to it. In fact he told me he was bringing a very special date."

"Lily," Drew confirmed. "Jack introduced her to me when they arrived a few moments ago. Judging by the way they were looking at each other, I'd say the 'very special' description works both ways."

"Lily Saville?"

"I think that was her name, yes."

"Oh."

"Why do I get the feeling that you don't think she's so special?"

"No, it's not that, not at all. I like Lily very much. I always have. As a matter of fact I think she's very special indeed. I'm just not sure she's right for Jack." She met his curious gaze with a sheepish smile. "Lily's father happens to be our gardener."

Behind the tortoiseshell glasses, a look of surprise flickered in Drew's eyes. "Therefore Lily isn't good enough for Jack?"

"I didn't say she's not good enough," protested Kay. "I said she may not be right for Jack, and he for her. It's just so much easier for two people if they have more in common than chemistry. God knows, I learned that the hard way."

"That's the only way there is to learn some things," he said quietly. The slightly increased pressure of his hand on her back was reassuring, but not enough to erase the regrets stirring inside Kay.

"Oh, to be young again," she murmured wistfully.

"I don't know," countered Drew, his tone teasing. "I definitely prefer right now to being twenty, when the closest I ever got to you was worshiping from afar."

"How could I have been so blind for so long?" Kay murmured, fighting the urge to curl both arms around his neck and bury her face against his chest just to drink in the comforting scent of him.

"It doesn't matter. All that matters is now, Kay. We're together, and to me you are more beautiful than any other woman in this room, young or old."

She tilted her head back, her eyes shining recklessly. "Really?"

"Really. And if you don't stop looking at me that way I might forget there are several hundred people, your husband among them, watching us, and do what I've been wanting to do all night." He bent his head, tickling her ear with soft words describing exactly what was on his mind.

"Oh, my," Kay countered demurely. "Do you suppose it's safe for me to be dancing with you?"

"Not at all. But it's probably expected since we've always danced at parties."

"Right. Tell me, do I always get goose bumps?"

"I'm usually too nervous to notice."

They exchanged smiles as the band stopped and started again. Neither of them had the strength of will to part. Drew's hand rested on the small of her back, his touch a siren's song to Kay's senses. Her fingers curved over his shoulder, strong solid terrain that had become intimately familiar to her in the whirlwind of the past few weeks.

After a while Drew sighed. "I suppose I ought give someone else a turn to dance with the guest of honor."

"I suppose."

Neither of them made a move to separate for several more minutes. Eventually Drew tipped his head to look at her. "I've decided I'll let you go on one condition. I want to see you again tomorrow."

"Tomorrow is Sunday."

"So?"

"So that means James will probably be home and maybe Jack as well. I don't know how I'll manage to get away."

As usual Drew didn't press, although Kay wanted to see him the next day as much, if not more, than he wanted to see her—and with a little extra urging, she knew she would have agreed. Sometimes she wished he would be more demanding and take matters out of her hands.

Decisions. When had she ever been forced to make so many tough ones, and all on her own? It was a constant battle between impulse and restraint, and she'd never been very good at restraint.

"Oh, never mind," she told him now, "I'll think of something. Yes, darling, tomorrow sounds wonderful."

TWENTY-ONE

Jack found Lily as far from the house as she could get without actually leaving the property. After his frantic search, the sight of her sitting on a wrought-iron bench overlooking the ocean was a relief. Reassured that she was all right and that she was still there, he slowed his steps a little to give his breathing time to do the same.

Tonight wasn't the first time he'd stood up to his father; it wasn't even their most vicious exchange. But as always, it had brought bad feelings roiling to the surface and left him shaken. For Lily's sake he did his best to hide his feelings.

He sat beside her, relieved to see that if she had been crying, she'd stopped. He had a feeling that seeing Lily cry would kindle his urge to kill the man responsible.

"What can I say?" he asked after a moment, very aware that she was avoiding his gaze. "He's an ass."

"He's your father."

"Adoptive father. He's still an ass, and at the moment a very drunk one."

"You always make that distinction, don't you? About being adopted."

Jack gave a bitter laugh. "Do you wonder why? Not that it makes any difference. When it comes to family, all you can do is play the hand you're dealt. The bad news is he's part of mine."

She hugged the gift-wrapped box to her chest, the defeated curve of her shoulders making Jack feel both sad and angry.

"What he said in there…" She trailed off, huddling deeper. "It was awful."

"Yeah, well, saying awful things is my father's specialty."

"It isn't like that. What I mean is, *I'm* not like that, what he implied . . . easy," she added bitterly. "And I guess I just wondered, you know . . ."

Jack squinted at her in the darkness, confused. Then he stiffened. "You mean you're wondering if I thought the same thing? If I thought you were easy?"

She flinched at the sudden harshness in his tone, glancing at him quickly before looking away again. "I don't know," she said. "I guess I wondered if you thought it, or if maybe you were thinking it now that he insinuated it. If maybe you were sorry you asked me here in the first place."

He grabbed her, forcing her to look at him. "I think about you all the time," he snapped. "And yeah, I think things that would probably make you blush. But that's not one of them." He dragged his fingers through his hair. "Sweetheart, if there's one thing you haven't been from the start, it's easy."

He released her and stood, and for a second Lily was afraid he was going to walk off and leave her there alone. But he stopped a few feet away, keeping his back to her as he tore at the tie knotted around his throat. When he finally turned back to her the tie was hanging loose, and the top two buttons on his shirt were undone. His chest rose and fell as if his anger was choking him.

"Once when I was about six or seven," he began abruptly, "I took the training wheels off my bike and rode it along the drive. I was pretty damn proud of myself until I hit a rough patch and fell, crashing right onto my old man's precious new car. I put a good dent in the side, I admit, but nothing he couldn't have had fixed in an afternoon and for less money than he spends on a pair of shoes."

He jammed his hands in his pants pockets, his square jaw stubborn, a distant expression in his eyes. "All afternoon I prayed my mother would get home before he did, but she didn't and I ended up having to face him alone and tell him what had happened. I can still remember walking into his room. I was shaking like a leaf, so scared it's a wonder I didn't wet my pants. But somehow I got up the nerve to tell him what I'd done and to say I was sorry. And you know what he said?"

His mouth twisted into a smile so bitter it tore at Lily's heartstrings. She shook her head.

"He said, 'Sorry's not good enough,' and for the rest of the day or at least until my mother came home and tore it off me, he made me wear a sign around my neck that said, 'I'm sorry for being stupid.' "

"That's horrible," gasped Lily.

"No," Jack countered, "it's typical. And it was a lesson I didn't need to be taught twice. I figured that if saying 'I'm sorry' isn't good enough, then I wouldn't waste time saying it ever again, not to him or anyone else. And I haven't. The only reason I'm telling you this is so that you'll understand how it is between my father and me, how it's always been. I don't share his attitude toward women in general, and I sure as hell won't let anything he has to say influence how I feel about you. Understood?"

Lily nodded. "Understood."

"Good. Then what do you say we go back inside? We ought to find my mother and give her that present before you squeeze it into oblivion."

"No," she countered, shaking her head emphatically as she got to her feet. "I want to go home, Jack."

"No way." He looked exasperated. "Lily, don't let that jerk spoil tonight for us."

"It's already spoiled. I can't go back in there," she said softly. "I definitely can't give your mother this stupid gift. I was wrong to bring it in the first place."

"Says who? Him?" demanded Jack, hitching his thumb toward the house.

"What difference does it make? He was right. No one else in there was dumb enough to bring a present . . . and no one else is wearing a corsage, and there are probably a dozen other things about me that are different and wrong that I still don't even know about, but that everyone else will have no trouble spotting."

"Let them," he said sharply. Curling his fingers over her shoulders, he drew her closer. "Lily, the last thing I want, ever, is for you to be like everyone else in there. I just want you to be you."

A few minutes ago James Terrell had succeeded in filling Lily with doubts and insecurities. Now, as Jack pulled her against him, his mouth lowering to hers, those doubts began to drift away, overwhelmed by the strength of his approval. Belatedly she recalled the way he had stood up to his father and defended her, and she didn't feel so powerless or alone.

Jack made her feel wonderful. He made being different feel special. And he made her feel wanted by wanting her. The heat and urgency in his kiss left no doubt of that. As his mouth took command of hers, excitement shot through Lily, making her aware that she wanted him, too. For weeks she had been falling in love with him, without really understanding why or how it could happen so fast. Now she knew.

She trembled as Jack slid his hand down her back, pressing her closer to him. She felt him tremble, heard his soft groan. He kissed the corner of her mouth and the sensitive place beneath her ear, then cupped her face in his hands and looked at her.

"Are you sure you don't want to go back inside?" he asked softly.

In his glittering gaze, Lily read her alternative and understood what he was really asking her. She nodded, her eyes wide.

"But you looked forward to the party," he argued, his thumbs gently stroking her chin, sending a very different message. "I wanted tonight to be special."

"It is. All I need for it to be special is you."

He kissed her again, long and hard, then reached for her hand, clamping the present beneath his arm.

"Come on," he said.

He led her farther away from the house, along a path and down wooden stairs to the beach below. They were alone. After walking a few steps in the soft sand, Lily stopped and pulled off her high-heeled shoes. Jack stuck them in his jacket pockets, and something about the intimacy of that sent warmth spreading through Lily, making her whole body feel numb and highly sensitized at the same time.

They walked with their arms around each other's waists, their thighs brushing with each step. Conversation was limited and nervous, both of them thinking of the moment just ahead, when the bargain struck at the top of the cliff would be fulfilled.

When they rounded a bend so that there were only sand dunes at their back and the ocean before them, Jack pulled her into his arms without hesitation. He had already asked; Lily had already said yes. Neither of them wanted to turn back.

Gathering her against him, he lifted her into his kiss, squandering no time on preliminaries. He kissed her with his lips and tongue and teeth, roughly and completely, as if any instant she might evaporate in his arms and he would never get another chance. Lily clung tightly, conscious only of him, his strength, the luxuriant heat of his mouth, the fresh subtle scent that was his alone.

When he began tugging at her zipper, she tensed but didn't protest. He took his time, his hands caressing and soothing as they dragged the zipper downward, dispelling her instinctive fear. Letting her dress fall in a heap of soft white ripples at her feet, he slid his hands over her hips and bottom and along her legs, touching her in ways and places no one had ever before touched her, making her feel a yearning she'd never before felt.

His mouth roamed across her throat. Lily thrilled to the rough scrape of his teeth, the hot, wet sensation of his breath on her skin. Her senses were reeling.

When he ran his hand between her legs, her knees buckled so that she had to lean against him to stay standing. His fingers repeated the caress more slowly, sending desire shooting through her, making her gasp softly against his chest.

"Oh, God, Lily," he whispered, burying his face in her hair, "you feel so good. So good."

Tearing off his jacket, he dropped it to the sand, then reached for her, lifting her effortlessly and laying her on top of it.

As she gazed at him, he pulled off his shirt and tossed it away. His skin was golden in the moonlight, his eyes as black as the sky overhead. They locked with Lily's as he lowered his hands to his belt buckle and opened it.

In spite of the fact that her house sometimes resembled a locker room, Lily half expected to be shocked. She wasn't. Maybe because passion had glazed her senses; maybe simply because it was Jack standing there, shedding his clothes with the same nonchalant grace with which he did everything else.

The sight of his body made her breath come fast and hard. He was lean and strong, with muscular hollows and angles she longed to explore. The dark hair on his chest was a reminder that he was more man than boy, and a woman's desire to please and satisfy him rose up inside her. Naked, he dropped to the ground by her side, and Lily opened her arms and heart to him.

He studied her with eyes that smoldered as his fingers trailed down her chest, tracing the lace edge of her strapless bra, slipping inside.

Trembling in response, Lily bit her bottom lip to keep from whimpering.

"Don't," he ordered. "Don't hold back. Don't ever hold anything back from me."

He cupped her breast, kneading the soft flesh, sliding his thumb across her nipple. She did whimper then, from the sheer pleasure of it.

Jack smiled and bent his head, tugging her bra lower as his mouth closed over the peak of her breast. The contact was wet and shocking and electrifying. Lily crossed into a world of pure sensation, barely aware of him stripping off the rest of her underwear.

He moved over her, the roughness of his chest against her smooth skin incredibly arousing. Nudging her legs apart, he caressed the inside of her thighs, teasing higher and higher until she throbbed with longing. Finally, when she couldn't stand another second of not knowing what it would be like to be touched by him, his fingers claimed the soft, damp heat at her core.

Lily cried out loud and clutched his shoulders.

"It's okay, it's okay," he murmured.

It was better than okay, but Lily didn't have breath to tell him so. It was pleasure almost too pure to bear.

She was on fire to discover where it would lead, what it would be like to go all the way with him, and at the same time she was scared to death. When she felt the hard, masculine part of him pressing against her, every muscle in her body tensed.

"Jack," she gasped. "Please . . ."

"Please what?" His voice was strained, the skin of his back damp with sweat. "I won't do anything you don't want me to do, Lily, but if you plan to stop me, you better do it now. Right now."

Lily took a deep breath. "I don't want you to stop."

With a shudder of relief, he took her hand and slowly drew it down between their bodies until she was touching him. He overflowed her palm, hard and smooth and hot.

The heat, like satin melting in her hand, was one more awakening. He urged her to grip him tighter, coaching her in a sliding motion, slowly, up and down. Her thumb slid across the tip where he was damp. When he groaned against her throat Lily knew he must be feeling what she felt when his fingers had stroked her intimately.

"I can't wait," he muttered suddenly. "I can't wait. . . ."

"Please," Lily begged, arching into him.

He spread her legs with his and brushed the hair from her forehead.

"Hold on tight," he said as he laced his fingers with hers. "I might hurt you, but just this once, I promise."

It did hurt. But sharp, brief pain was nothing compared to the thrill of having him inside her and the excitement that gripped her as his thrusts grew faster and deeper. Lily was stunned by the physical closeness and the way it spilled over into her heart and soul.

She felt full, complete, powerful. Joy lifted her heart, instinct guided her hips, and the heat built and built until everything inside her melted and she lost her innocence in a wild explosion of ecstasy. Above the thunder-and-lightning pounding of her heartbeat, she heard Jack's hoarse voice echo what was in her own heart.

"I love you," he whispered. "I love you."

TWENTY-TWO

"Who can explain the significance of the fog in Sandburg's poem?"

Lily slid lower in her seat as Sister Raphael's stern gaze swept like a vulture over the senior English class. Her habit, long and black, with a point at the crown of her head and a stiff white band across the forehead, only enhanced the impression.

"Are you with me, girls?"

Lily definitely was not. She was miles away from the brick school building, on a beach, reliving last Saturday night. She had done nothing since but think about Jack and how loving him had changed things. There was no room in her head today for Sister Raphael or Carl Sandburg.

"Let's see," said the nun in the deceptively musing tone she used when she was about to pounce. "Who can help us out with this?" Her sharp gaze honed in on Lily only to shift to the left in a last-second surprise attack. "Rene Sharpiro, let me hear your thoughts on the matter."

Breathing a silent sigh of relief, Lily scanned her open book so she would at least know what poem they were discussing. Beside her Rene sputtered incoherently for a few seconds until the hiss of the ancient intercom speaker hanging on the wall beside the crucifix brought her a reprieve.

"Sister Raphael?" came a tiny, mutilated voice from the speaker. It was Sister Marie, who taught chemistry and served as the school secretary. "Will you please send Lily Saville to the office?"

"Yes, Sister, right away." Sister Raphael nodded at Lily, who escaped gratefully.

She hurried down the stairs to the office, anticipating that the summons had something to do with the Kettering scholarship. She was afraid to jinx matters by being too sure of herself, but the school rumor mill and the little smile Sister Assumption gave her whenever they passed in the corridor made her think the scholarship was hers. She still hadn't heard from RISD and hoped this might be a good omen. Her mother always said that good things came in threes. The scholarship, her acceptance letter and Jack. That was three and it was everything she wanted.

Sister Marie waved her directly into the principal's office and, after her initial surprise, the sight of her father seated across from Sister Assumption, his back to the door, reassured Lily that her hunch was right. Naturally Sister would invite him to be here when she informed Lily that she'd won the scholarship. The formal presentation, of course, would take place on graduation night.

"Lily, please close the door behind you," instructed Sister Assumption.

Her father still hadn't turned around or greeted her. As she slipped into the empty chair by his side she noticed that he had on his work pants and thought of what her mother would say about him coming to school with grass-stained knees. Then for the first time she noticed that she was the only one smiling. Maybe she hadn't won. But would they call her father here in the middle of the day to announce that? No. Then what? Something about the family? Her mother? Cliff?

"Dad . . . ?" Instinctively she touched the sleeve of his navy blue Windbreaker. He barely glanced at her, confusing her even more. She knew her father. If her father had come here bearing bad news, he would look her in the eye when he told her.

Sister Assumption cleared her throat. "Lily, I've asked your father to be here this morning because I have a very serious and, ah, quite awkward matter to discuss with you. I felt obligated, as principal, to make him aware of it."

Lily's hands clenched in her lap.

"I had a phone call a while ago from a most irate alumnus, who also happens to be the aunt of one of the other contenders for the Kettering scholarship. She made a very serious accusation against you. Now it may—and I hope and pray that this is the case—prove to be much ado about nothing. But only you can tell us that."

Lily nodded, bewildered. An accusation? Who would accuse her of anything?

"It seems," Sister Assumption continued, "that this woman was driving home after attending a party at Delaney Place on Saturday night. She took a wrong turn on that old dirt road that runs above the private beach there. Do you know the one?"

Lily nodded, her mouth suddenly going dry. An uneasy feeling stirred inside her as she recalled Saturday night and the moments just before she and Jack left the beach. He was helping with her clothes, being very little help, actually, when the sound of a car engine drew their attention to the top of the dunes and the seldom-used road Sister referred to. A dark sedan pulled to a stop, so far over to the side of the road that the overgrown bushes pressed against the passenger side door. At the time she'd had an icy suspicion that whoever was in the car was simply trying to get a better look.

Without thinking she had reached for Jack's hand. "How long do you think they've been up there?"

"It doesn't matter," he'd told her. "They can't see anything in the shadows down here."

Maybe not, thought Lily. Still, she'd been able to get a clear look at the car as it pulled away, and a glimpse of a pale, pinched-face woman she'd never seen before staring at her through the window.

Sister Assumption cleared her throat self-consciously. "She says that she saw a couple on the beach, a young man and woman, and they were, well, I cannot think of any delicate way to say this. They were both naked."

She continued, but from that point on Lily heard only fragments of what Sister had to say. She sat gripping the edges of her chair, her face as hot as if she'd spent all day in the sun, something sharp and sour grinding away in the pit of her stomach.

"Pulled over... Afraid something wrong... Shocking... Naturally distressed... Preposterous... That's what I told her," the nun repeated, and Lily finally recovered enough to force herself to listen attentively. "That it was preposterous to think that you could be the girl she saw. Why, the very idea that you could be involved in such a thing." Her veil scraped stiffly across her shoulders as she shook her head. "The woman admits it was quite dark, and that she's never so much as met you. But she insisted she was right, claimed she saw you earlier that night with the Terrell boy and that yesterday, when her niece happened to stop by with her yearbook, she recognized you right away.

"Still," Sister continued, the first hint of an encouraging smile on her face, "everyone makes mistakes. We need you to tell us that that's what this was, Lily, a mistake, that it wasn't you on that beach that night."

Sister Assumption leaned toward her. Lily could feel her father's tension.

"Well, Lily?" Sister prompted.

One word from her would end the nightmare and turn the clock back an hour, making everything the way it had been. One word. No. All she had to do was say it. All she had to do was lie. But even as she struggled to bring that word up through the ashes clogging her throat, she knew it was too late. She'd hesitated too long. Already she saw doubt in Sister Assumption's steady gaze. Even if she were to sink to lying, she would never pull it off now.

"It was me," she said softly.

There was no reaction from the seat beside her, but the sound of her father's heart breaking filled the small room, *filled* her. She couldn't bear to look at him. It was Sister who pulled herself together first.

She drew herself up, her face going white with disapproval, then pity. Her tone was crisp. "I see, Lily. Then I have no choice but to ask you to withdraw from scholarship consideration."

"Excuse me, Sister," her father said, his fingers twisting his old tan cap into a ball. "But there must be something else you can do, some way Lily can be punished for what she did without losing out on that scholarship. Without it, well, without it things will be tough."

"I'm sorry, Mr. Saville, but the requirements are quite specific. If I were to award the scholarship to Lily now, the woman who phoned me with these allegations would stir up a public outcry that would embarrass everyone involved, Lily most of all. Believe me, it will be easier this way."

"Begging your pardon, Sister," her father said, "but this isn't easy at all. Let's go, Lily."

He didn't look at her, not then or as they walked to the car. There was no question of her returning to class. He kept his eyes lowered, as if looking inside himself, as if, thought Lily, someone he loved had just died. In a way she supposed some-one had.

She spoke to him once in the car. "I'm sorry."

Even as she said the words all she could think of was the story Jack had told her. It seemed his father was right; sorry wasn't good enough.

Placing her hand briefly on his arm, she added the only ex-planation she had. "I love him, Daddy."

For a second his gaze left the road and met hers. His blue eyes were filled with sorrow. "You're only seventeen, for God's sake. You have your whole life ahead of you. I thought...I hoped—" His voice caught. "I should have..." Again, the same broken sound, as if he was going to cry. He shook his head and gave up trying to find words. "It's too late now."

At home Lily went straight to her room and listened as her father backed the car out of the driveway, returning to work the same as he did everyday, hot, cold, rain, shine, happy or tear-ing up inside, to sweep walks and weed gardens that weren't his. She paced across the room and picked up the silver house from her nightstand. She sat on the corner of the bed for a long time, looking at it and remembering the promises she'd made to her-self on the day Kay Terrell had given it to her. At the time she'd thought she would never let anything or anyone get in the way of those promises. How could she have known that Jack would come into her life?

She threw herself face down on her bed. The inky darkness behind her closed eyelids shifted and swirled, gradually be-coming a starlit beach. She remembered everything, every kiss, every touch, every word. "It wasn't the night I had planned," Jack had said later, when he walked her to the door, "but I'm not sorry."

She had smiled at him. "I'm not sorry, either."

Lily groaned into her pillow. She was sorry now, all right. Sorry about a lot of things, but not about loving Jack. Mak-ing love with him made her want to share more, made her want to share everything. All her hopes and plans for the future had expanded to include him at their center. She wasn't sure how yet, but she wasn't going to let this ruin things. She wasn't go-ing to give up her plans *or* Jack.

Around four o'clock, she heard her father return, having swung by the hospital to pick up her mother at the end of her shift. She didn't go downstairs and wasn't surprised when her mother—who had no doubt heard a brief summary of the situation on the drive home—didn't come upstairs to her room. This was, in Ben's words, a big-ticket offense. Family tradition had it that her mother handled day-to-day infractions— messy rooms, broken curfews—and her father dealt with the biggies. Only this time he didn't seem to know how to deal with it.

She had to go down for supper. It was strangely, painfully silent once Ben ran out of chatter, and it finally dawned on him that something was very wrong. He met Lily's eyes across the table. She gave a small shake of her head, and then there was only the clatter of forks against plates. Finally her father got up, his food untouched, and left the house without a word. The door slammed behind him. It was so extraordinarily out of character that even Joey paused with a meatball halfway to his mouth to ask, "What's with him?"

"Never mind," her mother quickly replied. "Just never mind."

Lily helped with the dishes, drying as her mother washed, without either of them saying a word about anything. When Ben and Joey cornered her in her room she gave them a brief, sanitized version of what had happened.

Around six-thirty Jack phoned, immediately sensing the strain in her voice. The only telephone was in the den where her mother was watching the news and working on the afghan she was crocheting. Lily carried the receiver as far into the hallway as the cord allowed and kept her voice low as she told him what had happened.

He was furious, with whoever had reported them, with the school for eliminating her from consideration for the scholarship, and he was determined to right matters, to single-handedly put her world back on course. Lily loved him for it, even as she realized that this time he couldn't rescue her.

"Who?" he demanded gruffly. "Who was it who called the school?"

"It doesn't matter," replied Lily wearily. "Whoever it was saw us. I admitted it was me. It's finished."

"It's not finished. I'm worried about you, Lily. I've never heard you like this before."

She tried to laugh. "Yeah, well, I've never felt like this before."

"I'll be right over."

"No," she shot back, forgetting to keep her voice down. She didn't want him there when her father got home. "Don't, Jack. Please. It will only make things worse."

"How could they be worse?"

"Just don't. Look, I have to go."

"No, Lily, please . . ."

"If you want to talk, meet me at work tomorrow tonight."

"No. I—"

"I mean it, Jack, please. If you really care about me, you'll wait till then."

Ben and Joey had found reasons to escape the house, leaving Lily alone with her mother. They sat in the den. Lily stared at the television without knowing what show was on. Outside the streetlights came on, and still her father didn't come home.

Where could he be? She knew her mother was worried from the way she kept checking the clock. Every time a car approached her crochet hook stilled as she listened to hear if it was going to turn into the driveway. Around eight-thirty she got up and went around closing all the windows.

"That night air goes right through me," she said.

Lily, thankful the silence had at last been broken, agreed, though with the windows shut she found it even harder to draw a full breath. Sadness, like a sea sponge, had swelled to fill every bit of space inside her.

She wet her lips, waiting for her mother to sit down. "I guess Daddy told you about the other night. About what happened. And about me losing the scholarship."

"He told me."

"Mom, I'm so sorry," she said, tears erupting at last. "I wish none of this had happened."

Her mother pushed her crocheting aside. "Oh, Lily, how could you do this? After all we've taught you? The way you've been raised? I'm so ashamed. And your father—"

"I know. I know," interrupted Lily. "It was such a stupid thing to do, but Jack . . . I love him, Mom, and somehow that was the only thing that seemed to matter at the time."

"I was afraid something like this would happen. That boy is—"

"I knew you'd think that and blame it all on him, but it wasn't Jack's fault. He didn't make me do anything."

"You're sure?" her mother asked sharply.

"Yes, I'm sure." She got to her feet, pacing across the small room. "I don't know. Maybe I should have just gone ahead and lied, said it wasn't me. Then Daddy would be home, and everybody would be happy."

"Everybody except you."

Surprised, Lily turned and met her mother's gaze. "Right. Then I would be even more ashamed of myself than I am now."

"Then you did the right thing. A lie..." She trailed off, shaking her head with a distant look in her eyes. She blinked, back with Lily again. "A lie is like a hole deep down inside you, always there no matter what you do, no matter how hard you try to cover it up. It's always there waiting for you to forget and fall in. I don't want that for you, Lily." She wrung her hands together. "God, I don't want that for you. Whatever happened with the scholarship, it's better that you owned up to what you did."

"Losing the scholarship doesn't hurt half as much as knowing that I let you and Daddy down, that I made you ashamed of me when all I wanted was to make you proud."

"Oh, Lily," her mother said, crossing the room and hugging her. "I'm ashamed because that's the way I was raised, to think you don't do...*that* until you're married. But deep down, I'm proud, too, proud of the way you handled it. So is your father."

"No, he's not. He can't even bear to look at me."

"Because he can't bear to see you so hurt."

"That's why he walked out and hasn't come back? Or even called to tell you where he is?"

"He just needed some time alone, that's all."

"Where do you think he could have gone?"

"Oh, back to Delaney Place, most likely. You know how he likes to fuss with his flowers when he's got something on his mind. Just like me and my crocheting."

"Maybe we should call. Just to see."

Her mother shook her head, smiling as she smoothed Lily's hair away from her face. "Nine-thirty at night is no time to be calling anyone. No, we'll just wait. He'll be home any minute now, you'll see. In the meantime, how about if I make us both a cup of tea?"

Lily nodded, but inside she knew this wasn't something that could be made okay with tea and cookies. Time would probably heal the wounds in her family, but it wouldn't put her plans for college back together. And Jack . . . She hadn't even begun to think about what this would mean for the two of them. Her parents were still in shock, but once they recovered there was no way they were going to blithely go along with her seeing him. The fact that she would soon be eighteen, a bona fide adult, wouldn't matter. She'd heard the famous as-long-as-you-live-under-this-roof lecture often enough to know that.

The eleven o'clock news came on and ended. Her mother stayed right where she was and—maybe for the first time in her life, Lily thought—watched Johnny Carson. He joked about the smog in LA and about a radical plot to kidnap Henry Kissinger, but neither of them laughed. It was a while later, sometime after Ben and Joey came home, that the doorbell rang.

For a second nobody moved. Then, even as her brothers started toward the door, her mother said, "No. I'll get it. That's your father for you, always misplacing his house key."

When she swung open the front door there was a young policeman, not her father, waiting on the porch.

"Are you Mrs. Clifford Saville?" he asked.

She nodded.

"I'm sorry, Mrs. Saville, but I'm afraid your husband has been in an accident."

They all immediately huddled around her in the doorway, their questions spilling over one another. But the officer steadfastly maintained that they would have to learn the details at the hospital.

The four of them went to the hospital together, refusing the policeman's offer of a ride and instead all piling into Joey's noisy heap. All the way there they took turns assuring each other that he was probably fine, that the official notification was just a formality, that he would laugh when he heard how they had all come rushing down to the emergency room because of a few scratches or maybe a little bump on his head.

But all the time Lily suspected, as she thought the others must as well—especially her mother who'd worked in a hospital her whole life—that the truth was far worse. The fact that the somber, overly polite officer wouldn't tell them anything about her father's condition meant that the news was very bad.

In spite of that understanding, her mind balked at defining "very bad" as anything beyond some sort of emergency surgery or maybe, at the absolute worst, a coma, where they would all take turns keeping vigil by his bedside until he finally woke up. She'd read that people in comas can sometimes hear and understand what's going on around them even when they can't respond, and Lily knew already what she would whisper to her father when it was her turn to keep watch, the same thing she was praying for right this minute. She would tell him how sorry she was for everything and how she would give anything, *anything*, she reiterated, feeling only the faintest twinge of regret for the loss of all her foolhardy dreams of a future with Jack, if only her father would be all right.

Inside the emergency room, some of her mother's friends from the hospital were already gathered, waiting. Word travels fast in a hospital. They hugged her and Lily and patted her brothers on the back, their forced smiles grim and frightening.

"Where's Rusty?" her mother kept asking over and over, even as they were all shepherded to a private waiting area. "I want to see him. Please, I just want to see him."

The clock on the wall registered the passing of only three minutes, but to Lily it felt like forever until a doctor wearing a rumpled green scrub suit arrived to talk to them. The instant she saw his face she knew that it was worse than very bad. The unthinkable, the worst thing possible, had happened.

The doctor's face expressed sorrow as he held out his hands to her mother. "Mary," he said, "I'm so sorry. We did all we could."

"Oh, no," she said, in a long raspy whisper that reverberated like a scream inside Lily's head. "I should have been with him. Oh, no, if only I had been here."

Lily reached for her mother's hand as the doctor looped his arm awkwardly around Mary's bent shoulders.

"There was nothing you could have done, Mary," he told her. "Nothing any of us could have done. At least you can rest assured that he didn't suffer, that it was instantaneous."

"But how?" Mary whispered dazedly. "Oh, God, how could this happen? Where was he? How did it happen?"

"The police can give you the full accident report," he replied. "If you want to know the medical details . . ."

"I do," she said when he hesitated. "I want to know everything."

The doctor nodded. "Your husband suffered massive head trauma compounded by loss of blood due to extensive internal injuries. All of his injuries were consistent with the police statement that the car he was driving struck a tree head on."

"A tree?" echoed Joey, speaking for the first time. "He hit a tree? How?"

"As I said," the doctor replied, "you'll have to get the details relating to the accident itself from the police. I believe the first officer to arrive on the scene is still outside. I could send him in."

"Yes, please," said Mary. "I'd like very much to talk to him."

Patrolman Jerry Reed was a solid, red-faced young man who looked like he'd be more at home facing an armed assailant than a grieving family. He shifted from foot to foot awkwardly as he greeted Mary and nodded at the others, then kept his eyes cast downward on the notebook in his hand as he raced through the accident report he had prepared.

It started off innocuously enough, relating the time and place the accident had occurred. Her mother had been right about her father being at Delaney Place. It had happened at the end of their drive.

Did Jack know? Lily wondered, briefly losing track of the policeman's words. No, he couldn't possibly, she decided. If he knew, he would be here with her. It had been hard enough to convince him not to come storming over to her house earlier. Nothing would keep him from her side if he knew what she was going through now. Nothing. That, she thought with bitter irony, is what love was all about.

Reed had reached the crux of his report, and even delivered in his rapid monotone the words had the power to conjure up a visual nightmare. Lily winced as if to ward them off. Shattered glass . . . victim unconscious . . . bleeding profusely . . . lacerations . . . unable to remove from vehicle. Reed's report went on to say that he had called for backup assistance as well as an ambulance. It ended with his summoning a tow truck to haul away her father's beloved old station wagon and his concluding observations of the accident.

"What?" Joey interrupted him suddenly, just as Lily herself was wondering if she'd heard correctly.

"It says here," Reed replied without looking up, "that there were numerous empty beer cans sighted in and around the vehicle."

"It doesn't just say it there," Ben countered loudly. "*You're* saying it. You're the one who wrote that damn report, aren't you?"

"Ben, please," interjected Mary.

Ben jerked away from the restraining hand she laid on his arm. "No. I want to hear what he has to say about this."

"I stand by the report," said Reed, finally looking up, his gaze rapidly slipping from one of them to the next. "I did observe a number of beer cans in the car and some that had obviously fallen out in the process of removing the victim from the vehicle."

"Don't call him a victim," Ben shouted. "He had a name, damn it. He's not just some victim in some damn accident report."

Mary shook her head. "Ben—"

"And he damn well wasn't drunk, if that's what you're implying."

"I'm not implying anything," Reed countered, snapping the notepad shut. "I write down the facts as I observe them. That's what I just read to you. I'm real sorry for your loss, Mrs. Saville, but if you have no more questions . . ."

"I *do* have questions," Ben broke in.

Joey nodded, his arms folded across his chest. "Yeah, me, too. There's just no way Dad had beer in his car. He didn't even drink, for God's sake."

"I'm sure you're right," Officer Reed said tightly. "But I did in fact see the cans there. Any other questions?"

Hundreds of them, thought Lily, feeling as if the hard ball of pain inside her would drive her right through the linoleum floor of the lounge. And almost wishing it would, wishing there was some way to just check out from what was happening, to wake up in her own bed and have it be yesterday, or last week, anything as long as her father was alive again.

Ben and Joey were right. He never drank, not a beer in the summer or champagne on New Year's Eve, not a drop, ever. Lily recalled that once, when the subject of drinking had somehow come up, her mother had said that a long time ago her father drank a lot. Lily got the impression that by a lot she meant too much. And she told Lily that he had quit, just like that.

He had been, Lily knew, a man of tremendous self-control. So if Reed was right and there were empty beer cans in his car and he had been drinking tonight, it would have taken something really horrible to drive him to it. It didn't take a genius to figure out what that had been, and guilt rose up to mingle with the pain lodged in Lily's gut.

This was her fault, all her fault. My God, her father was dead, and it was her fault. *If only*... The words formed a vortex in her head, swirling around a suddenly obscene image of her and Jack making love on the beach. *If only*...

"He's wrong," Ben was saying, and she became aware that they were still debating the matter of the beer cans. "There's no way that Dad could have been drinking. I mean, even if he did drink, what did he do? Get loaded in the greenhouse and then hide all the empties in the car and try to drive home?"

The words had a sickeningly possible ring to them in the silent room.

"No way," Joey said a little too emphatically. "There's just no way he'd tie one on like that unless . . ."

He stopped suddenly and although no one actually turned toward her, Lily felt the heat of unspoken accusation settle on her, joining forces with all the accusations bubbling within.

For a moment, no one said anything. Then her mother suddenly drew herself up to dominate the center of the small family group, her strength something Lily could almost feel.

"You're right. Your father did not drink. I have no idea how those beer cans got there. Maybe he left the car unlocked and someone tossed them in. But they were not your father's. He did not drink, at all, for any reason. Period. Now I think we should all go home. There'll be a lot to do tomorrow."

TWENTY-THREE

"Where the hell have you been?"

Kay stiffened. She hadn't expected to run into James. Ordinarily he wasn't around to greet her when she returned home. But then, ordinarily she didn't return home this late. She and Drew had driven across the state line to have dinner at a small inn outside Mystic, Connecticut. Afterward they sat and talked, not noticing the evening racing away from them.

Slowly she closed the front door behind her and made a project out of placing her purse on the small table to her right. Finally she replied. "Out."

"Out?" James nodded, his lips thinning into a smile that really wasn't one at all. He had come out of the darkness to confront her. "Just out?"

Kay met his gaze directly, startled by how old and pale he looked. "Just out."

"All right," he said in a tone that said it wasn't all right, but that he would allow it to pass for now. "It's just a shame that you weren't around for your husband when he needed you."

"I was under the impression you had stopped needing me years ago."

He grabbed her arms as she tried to pass him. "Going somewhere, dear?"

"I'm tired. I'm going to bed."

"Fine." He dropped his hand to his side. "You can read about it in the morning paper."

"Read about what?"

"Ah, not quite so aloof now, are we? That's right, Kay, something happened tonight while you were off God knows where. What was it this time? Tennis? Dinner with another old college friend? You know, until recently I had no idea you were so popular in school."

"Just tell me what happened."

"The picture of wifely concern," he drawled, his expression cold and mocking.

"Please, James, let's not start. Just tell me whatever it is you have to tell me."

"There was a car accident tonight. A bad one."

He might have been reporting the weather, he was so off-hand.

"Jack?" she cried, pressing fingers to her heart as if to slow its thundering beat. "Is he hurt? Where is he?"

"Jack had nothing to do with it. He's been out all evening. But I'm fine, thanks for your concern."

"You were in an accident?" She ran her gaze over him quickly, breaking into a worried frown. "Were you drinking?"

"Not according to the official police report. Can't say the same for the other poor bastard."

An uneasy feeling claimed Kay. "You hit another car?"

"More or less. Happened right there at the top of the drive." He gestured in that general direction, his exuberance leaving Kay no doubt that he was drunk, regardless of the official police report. "Seems good old Rusty was here working late on his damn flowers. He must have left just as I was pulling in. I tried to avoid him, but it was too late."

"You're telling me Rusty Saville was driving the other car? Oh, no," she cried as he nodded. "How badly was he hurt?"

"He's dead."

"Oh, no," Kay said again, cupping her hands to her mouth, her eyes filling with tears as sorrow crashed over her, ripping her in a dozen different directions. She thought about Rusty dead, his wife and children, Lily. "Does Jack know?"

James laughed derisively. "Jack, always Jack. A man is dead, I could have been killed, or worse, arrested and charged with God knows what," he said, gesturing wildly. "And all you can do is ask whether Jack knows."

"What do you mean, arrested?"

"I thought that would get your attention. Imagine, one of the high and mighty Delaneys arrested... Well, more or less one of them. Now that would be a scandal, wouldn't it?"

"For God's sake, James, you said it yourself, a man is dead. A kind and decent man, with a family that depended on him."

"Yes." He nodded solemnly. "A family. Quite a family."

"And you're responsible. Doesn't that mean anything to you?"

"A more interesting question is, what does it mean to you? What would you deem a fitting punishment for me for killing this good man?"

Shuddering, Kay backed away from him a few steps. "How can you talk this way?"

"Because I have no class, remember? And because when I want to know something, I ask. C'mon, Kay. What would be fair recompense? Five years? Ten? The electric chair?" He laughed at her stricken expression. "Don't worry, Kay. I won't be going to prison. I took care of everything. Same as I always do. I took care of everything so you wouldn't have to get your hands dirty. Just like I always do."

She looked at him, suddenly cold inside and out. "What do you mean, you took care of it?"

Still wearing that same smug smile, he glanced around as if someone might be behind him or just around a corner somewhere, listening. "Come with me."

Kay followed him into the study and collapsed into the leather swivel chair behind her father's desk. James poured her a brandy and sat across from her.

"What did you mean when you said you took care of everything?" she asked again.

"Exactly that. The first cop on the scene was an acquaintance of mine, a fellow who owes me a favor or two. Saville was already dead, died instantly, the hospital said. I simply convinced my police officer friend that screwing up my life wasn't going to bring Saville back. Like I said, he owed me one. He even helped me with the rest before he radioed in."

"The rest?"

"Just to be on the safe side, I arranged to have my car towed across the state line for repairs—if the damn thing can even be repaired. Then we tossed a few empty beer cans in the back of Saville's car, spilled a little beer on him, scraped some silver paint off his fender and presto, a simple case of a guy who drank too much and drove his car into a tree."

"You mean you..." Kay paused, unable to think of words to describe the sleazy thing James had done. "You made it look as if he was the one who'd been drinking? As if the accident was all his fault?"

"Better his than mine," countered James, shrugging. "Wouldn't you agree?"

"No, I certainly would not agree."

His brows lifted. "No? Think, Kay. Think of the alternative. Think of the headlines. The repercussions. The gossip."

Kay swallowed hard, not wanting to think of any of that. Suddenly it was hard to think straight at all.

James snickered. "Yeah, that's what I figured."

"What you did was wrong," she snapped.

"Fine. I thought I was doing what you would want me to do if you had been around. But seeing as you disapprove, I'll just call my friend and undo what's been done." He reached for the phone.

Kay managed to sit still only long enough for him to dial the first four numbers. "Stop. I . . . As you said, it's already done. Rusty's family has probably been told everything by now and . . ." She drew a deep breath in order to go on. "Maybe we should just . . . leave things as they are."

"But what about right and wrong?"

"It is wrong. I meant that."

She looked away and was brought up short by the small watercolor of Delaney Place that Lily had painted. Jack had been so proud when he gave it to her this morning. Only this morning?

She closed her eyes. This would only deepen the rift with Jack, destroying any chance that he might change his mind about working for Delaney Silver. Oh, God, why did this have to happen? Why now, when she was so happy? Oh, Drew, she thought, need for him an ache at her core.

"So what's it going to be?" inquired James, with a smugness he didn't bother to hide.

She stared at him over her neatly folded hands. "The damage has been done, and it will only look worse now that you've tried to cover it up. I can't see any sense in jeopardizing the future and the family name for no reason. Of course, if it would bring Rusty back or lessen the heartache for his poor family... Oh, I absolutely cannot bear to think of the Savilles right now."

"Then it's settled."

She nodded grimly. "You're sure you can trust this policeman?"

"I'm sure. He'll do whatever I say."

"Thank heavens for that, at least."

"Isn't it me you should be thanking?"

"You? You're the cause of all this. If I had been here, I never, ever would have let things get this far."

"Then it's a damn good thing you weren't here," he commented. "Which brings us to the next item on this evening's agenda."

Kay stood and placed her glass on the desk. "If you don't mind, I'm really quite worn out from all this and—"

"Don't panic, Kay, I'm not going to ask again where you were tonight and with who...whom." He smiled.

Kay did her best to hide her relief.

He continued. "Why should I, when I already know?"

"Know what?"

"That you're getting some on the side from Drew Goddard."

"Really, James..."

"Don't bother to deny it, Kay. I know exactly what's been going on. But, as we've agreed already, what's done is done. What matters is what happens next."

"Assuming you're right about this, what would you have us do next?"

"Not us, *you*. End it, Kay."

She made a laughing noise, her fingers gripping the edge of the desk. "As I said, assuming—"

He cut in. "End it. *Now*. Or I'll see that the truth comes out about what happened tonight, and believe me, I'll do it in such a way that you end up smelling like garbage."

"What on earth does tonight have to do with me? Until a few minutes ago I didn't even know there had been an accident, never mind that you'd lied to cover up the truth."

"But no one will believe that, Kay. They'll believe what they want to believe, that the high-and-mighty Kay Delaney Terrell bought off a police officer to avoid a blot on the family name. Especially when that police officer steps forward to say so."

"But how could he? I never even—" She broke off as James shook his head with a twisted smile of pity.

"Kay, Kay, wake up. He lied once. If the price is right, he'll lie again."

"So I'd get to pay for my own public lynching, is that it?"

He grinned. "Perfect, isn't it?"

"Except for one small detail. To implicate me in this, you'll have to first incriminate yourself."

"Do you really think I give a damn?" he snapped. "I like this life I'm living, Kay. If I'm going to lose it, it might as well be in a criminal court as a divorce court."

"Is that what this is all about? You're afraid that I'm going to leave you for Drew?"

"I'm sure you won't. Not now that the ball's back in my court. This thing with Goddard..." He paused, smiling and shaking his head as if he was scolding an errant toddler. "It's just plain against the rules, Kay."

"Since when?" she demanded, more shrilly than she would have liked. "Shall I drag up all your past transgressions?"

"Why bother? None of them mattered a damn to me or were ever any threat to you. I'm yours, sweetheart, for better or worse, richer or—God forbid—poorer. I don't plan on leaving our happy home or standing by while you slowly ease me out of it." He smiled and sipped his drink. "The bottom line is that none of my transgressions, as you so nicely put it—and incidentally, that's what I love about you, Kay, all that class, and still, underneath you're no better than any other whore—none of mine were ever serious. I've got a hunch this thing of yours just might be. That's why I have to put a stop to it."

Kay, feeling battered, had to sit down. James sensed her bewildered panic.

"Don't worry," he said, his soothing tone sending shivers along her spine. "You don't have to give me your answer tonight."

Kay took a deep breath. A reprieve. Time to talk to Drew. He would help her find some way to handle all this.

"First thing in the morning will be just fine," James concluded, setting his glass directly on the priceless cherry desk as he turned to go. At the study door, he paused. "One more thing. Chalk it up to curiosity, but I was wondering...was your four-eyed lover as good as me?"

Kay heard him laughing as he climbed the stairs. Then she ran to the small bathroom off the kitchen and vomited. She bent over the sink to splash water on her face and as she straightened caught a glimpse of herself she usually avoided— at the end of a long day, her hair flat, her makeup faded and streaked.

In the harsh fluorescent light there was no hiding from the wrinkles at the corners of her eyes and mouth. And why should she? she thought suddenly. Maybe, when she came right down to it, they were all she had to show for her years.

The desire to call Drew and cry on his shoulder was overwhelming, but she didn't dare, not while James might listen in and gather more ammunition.

She remained in her room when she heard Jack come in, not ready to face him with the truth, or with whatever portion of the truth she decided to tell him. Sleep was out of the question. Finally she returned to the study and her father's chair, to do the only thing she could do, take a long hard look at the horrible mess she had let her life become and decide what she was going to do about it.

When James came downstairs in the morning, dressed for battle in a new hand-tailored suit that had been delivered just that week, his whistling was interrupted at the bottom of the stairs by Madge.

"Good morning, Mr. Terrell," she said. "Mrs. Terrell asked me to tell you that she's waiting for you in the breakfast nook."

"The breakfast nook?" James frowned, then shrugged. He supposed Kay was entitled to choose the site for her surrender. He joined her there, bending to kiss her cheek because he knew that under the circumstances it would irritate her and throw her a little further off center. She smelled good, arousing his interest. Not today, he thought resignedly, but soon. Very soon. It would be good to have her back in line again.

As he settled into the chair across from her, he smiled, noticing how carefully she had dressed for this meeting. Her upswept hair and her makeup were impeccable. No one but him would ever notice the shadows beneath her eyes, evidence of a night spent tossing and turning. Personally, he'd slept better than he had for weeks. The sleep of a confident man.

"You look very nice this morning, Kay," he said. "Is that a new outfit?" The pale gray linen suit and white silk blouse were crisp and tailored, a marked change from the loose, colorful things she'd been wearing lately.

"As a matter of fact it is. I haven't had an occasion to wear it. Until today."

"Well, you look very serious and in control," he said, figuring that's what she intended and indulging her. He was rewarded with a bright smile.

"Good. This is, after all, a very serious matter."

"I agree." He pushed his cup toward Madge, waiting for her to pour his coffee and leave the room before continuing. "I hope you have an answer for me."

She nodded. "I've decided to do as you ask and stop seeing Drew. As a matter of fact I spoke with him first thing this morning and made the situation clear to him." The memory of that call, of Drew's silence as she spoke the hardest words she would ever have to speak, made her feel weak. But only for a few seconds.

"Good," James said, nodding approvingly and reaching for his fork. "Enough said."

"Not quite."

"Kay, I'm not looking for an apology."

"You're not getting one." She watched surprise flare in his eyes at the unfamiliar sharpness in her tone and watched as he quickly masked it. "If I slept with every man in Watch Hill it would probably only even the score between us."

"You give me too much credit," he murmured.

"What I gave you is too much rope. And you nearly used it to hang me." She leaned forward, staring directly into his eyes. "Never again."

He was still smiling faintly, but he put his fork down as he waited to hear where this was headed. Kay let him wait. She sipped her coffee and patted her lips with her napkin before folding it and laying it beside her plate. Finally she spoke, never shifting her gaze from his.

"Last night you forced me to make a choice between the man I love and the Delaney name. I made the only choice I could. As you knew I would. In a way I'm grateful to you. I never understood how important some things were to me until they were threatened by you. Things like pride and heritage. Oh, I talked a good game about Delaney traditions and passing them on to the next generation, but I never truly comprehended all of it. Now that I do, I intend to do something about it."

"That's good, Kay," James said, his relief notable, almost comical. "You always were good with all that heritage stuff. I like to see you have something to do with your spare time. Especially now." He dropped his voice to a sympathetic level. "Believe me, sweetheart, I know these next few weeks will be tough for you, and I want you to know I'm here for you."

"Thank you, James, that's very generous of you. You're right, the next few weeks will be tough. Because with all my newfound spare time, I've decided to run Delaney Silver."

His expression was priceless, slack-jawed and stunned and nearly worth all that it had cost her. "What the . . . ? I run Delaney Silver."

"You *did*. I've decided it's time for a change. Starting today I'm the new company president. You will be kept on as vice-president . . . Unless, of course, the situation becomes unworkable. It will be a week or so before I can give you further details about what your new responsibilities and limitations will be. To help me with that I'd like you to arrange for me to have a complete financial report and rundown of day-to-day operations by the end of the week. I'm particularly interested in the company's current silver reserve," she added, lifting her brows ever so slightly.

"You bitch. You self-centered bitch."

"Thank you. The new me will accept that as a compliment. I think that about covers everything for the moment. Of course I won't expect you to be out of my father's office immediately. I'm sure I can find some empty corner in which to hang my hat for a day or two." She stood. "I'm off. I don't want to be late my first day on the job. Enjoy your breakfast."

James came after her, catching her by the arm. "Hold on a minute. You can't do this to me."

"I already have. After I called Drew I phoned my attorney and got him out of bed. He'll handle the formalities."

"Do you know how this is going to make me look?" he asked, his voice a whisper.

"Do you really think I give a damn?"

"I won't take it, do you hear me? If you go ahead with this I'll . . . I'll file for divorce and end this sham. I can prove adultery, Kay. Think about how that will drag your precious name through the mud."

"I already have. I don't want a divorce and all the scandal that goes along with it, but if it happens, I'll somehow find a way to survive with my head up."

Kay made the declaration with utter conviction. It was one of the resolutions she'd made the night before.

She smiled to herself, uncaring of the antagonizing effect her good mood was having on her husband. She was at long last completely and finally detached from him. She'd thought that had happened months ago, when she fell in love with Drew, but she was wrong. Her love for Drew had only made her more vulnerable to James's blackmail, just as her love and concern for her family and for Jack had. She had done as much as she could to change that, to minimize the risk to her past and her future.

"I'm gambling that you won't do anything stupid," she told James, "because if you do you'll lose everything. Without me, you're nothing, and you know it. I'm trusting that you'll do what you always do, look out for your own best interests. In this case, that means going along with my plan."

"Some plan," he scoffed, releasing her. "I give you two weeks. You don't know anything about running a business."

"Which probably makes us even on that score, too," she replied wryly. "With one important difference that I would really like you to keep in mind in the future—we're playing with *my* ball."

Kay retrieved her purse and the hat she'd decided to wear today because it added a touch of importance and self-assurance, and that was how she felt. Last night she had faced herself alone for the first time in too many years. She'd turned back the clock and taken a good look at all her old dreams of happiness, holding them one last time before putting them aside, like a favorite old dress that no longer fit. It was time for something new, and she felt good about that.

Good. It was a solid way to feel. Not hollow and aimless as she had for so long, or deliriously happy as she had been with Drew, but at peace and as certain of what she wanted to do as she was of her ability to do it.

She stopped at the front door, turning to find James still watching her.

"One more thing," she said. "Just to satisfy your curiosity... he was better."

TWENTY-FOUR

The upholstery in the limousine was steel gray and as plush as fine carpeting. The windows were tinted a bluish color, and that took some getting used to. It was odd, but Mary kept getting this urge to turn to Rusty and say, "Will you get a load of us? Riding in a limousine."

But Rusty wasn't there. He had ridden to the cemetery in the hearse directly ahead of them and now he would be staying here, in the bronze-tone casket with the pale blue sateen lining and stainless steel hinges, while Mary and the others went home.

The casket, like the limousine, was part of the Grand Deluxe Funeral Package. That was how they did it nowadays, she had discovered. A package deal, to spare the bereaved having to make dozens of petty decisions in their hour of grief. Grand Deluxe sounded, well, grand, unless you happened to know about the Supreme Elegance Package and the Presidential, which included a replica of the casket President Kennedy had been buried in, and all the other higher-priced packages. Actually, in spite of its name, the Grand Deluxe was one of the DeBellis Funeral Home's most modest offerings. But then, Mary supposed they could hardly call it the Minimum Life Insurance Special.

The package deal was another thing she longed to tell Rusty about. He would get such a kick out of the whole business. Personally she wasn't so thrilled with the idea. She would have preferred making decisions, no matter how petty. Anything would be better than thinking of all the things she could no longer share with Rusty.

Maybe the worst part was knowing that now she was alone with the secret. Not that she and Rusty ever talked about it much. Hardly ever, really. But just knowing that someone else knew what had happened, knew about Lily and Dr. Lagasse and the letter, and that he was there if she ever did need to talk, had made her feel better.

The limousine was parked by the side of the narrow road that curled through the cemetery, its powerful engine idling quietly while they waited for Lily, who was standing halfway between there and the grave site, talking with Jack Terrell. Jack had also come to the wake last night, which Mary thought took a lot of gumption under the circumstances. He and Lily had talked then, too, alone in the back room where smoking was permitted, for so long that Mary couldn't imagine what they had left to say.

With the palm of her hand she wiped the window so she could see them more clearly, but naturally the tint didn't rub away and she couldn't find any handle anywhere to roll the window down. She thought about asking the driver to lower it—it would be nice to have a breath of fresh air—but just then Lily began edging her way toward the car, so she didn't bother.

"Here she comes," said Cliff, who had been shipped home from Vietnam three weeks before his stint was over in order to attend the funeral.

Joey, sitting in the front seat beside the uniformed driver, muttered, "About time."

"Please, Joey," Mary pleaded.

At the moment, she felt a great need for harmony. She, the two boys and Lily would be riding in the limousine. Ben had decided to drive his own car so he could ride with Carol. Mary had sent word of what had happened to Greg at his last address somewhere in Canada, but there was no telling when he would get the message.

At least Cliff was here. Mary prayed he would be allowed to serve out the little time he had left right here in the States. With Rusty upstairs pulling for him, she figured he stood a good chance. There was no way to know for sure, but coming home early might even have saved Cliff's life. It was possible. She liked to think of some good coming out of all this. It was like she told the kids last night, God never closed one door without opening another.

She believed that. Somehow or other they would manage on their own. The boys were all grown up, men really, and Mary was confident they would find their way. Even Joey. And though they were as different from one another as night from day, they were all survivors, made of the same sturdy stuff as she and Rusty. Look at all they had endured to make a good life for themselves and the kids.

It was Lily who worried her. What was Lily made of? For the first time in years she imagined Dolly, so pretty and so young. Back then Dolly hadn't been all that much older than Lily was right now. More and more lately Mary saw traces in Lily of her real mother. They were there in her smile and the way she held her head sometimes. Fleeting, but definitely there. It was the traces of Dolly she couldn't see, however, that worried Mary the most.

"Here you go, honey, take the window," she said, sliding over to make room for Lily as she climbed into the back seat.

"Are you sure you wouldn't rather sit by the window?" Lily asked.

"I'm sure. There's nothing out there I want to see."

As they pulled away only Lily turned her head to look back. Mary, not sure whether she was looking for her father or Jack, took her hand.

"I have to give that boy credit for one thing," she told Lily. "It was decent of him to come today, considering."

"Considering what?" demanded Joey. "That he was the cause of this whole thing? If not for him being with Lily that night . . ."

"No one was the cause of this," Mary snapped with a worried glance in Lily's direction. She'd felt how Lily tensed at Joey's words. "It was an accident. Period."

"An accident that Dad was drinking? My whole life I never even saw him with a can of beer and all of a sudden for no reason at all he—"

"That's enough, Joey. I never want to hear you say a word about this again."

"What am I supposed to do? Forget it happened the way it did? Smile and slap Terrell on the back when he comes around wanting to see my sister?"

"I said, that's enough," Mary told him.

Cliff, who had been silently staring out the window, turned and shot his younger brother a warning look. "Cut it out, Joey."

"Who made you boss?" Joey retorted. "I'll say whatever—"

"Will you stop?" Lily shouted. "All of you. You don't have to say anything, you don't have to do anything, because Jack isn't going to be coming around anymore. It's over and done with, so just drop it."

Mary's heart ached for Lily, and at the same time a giant wave of relief passed through her. Had Lily broken things off with him? Or was it the other way around? It didn't matter, she told herself. It only mattered that it was over. She had been so worried, so afraid that Lily would get caught in the same trap Dolly had.

She squeezed Lily's hand. "I know it hurts, honey, but it's for the best. You'll see. Just let it go. Don't be bitter. Don't go looking for someone to blame—"

"I don't blame Jack," Lily cried out. Then, as if startled by her own vehemence, she quickly turned to stare out the window again, resting her forehead on the glass. "I don't blame him for anything."

In the silence of the limousine, Lily thought about the scene that had just played out between her and Jack.

"You blame me for what happened, don't you? That's really what this is all about."

Lily shook her head wearily, folding her arms across her chest as if huddling from a cold wind, although there wasn't enough breeze in the cemetery to stir the leaves on the rows of pink and white dogwoods along the roadside. She had been trying for days now, every time she saw him, and in long, awkward phone conversations, to make Jack understand. She wasn't getting anywhere. Which wasn't all that surprising when she considered that she really didn't have such a good grasp on things herself.

She knew only two things for sure: that she definitely did not blame him for her father's death, and that whatever had been— or might have been—between them was over forever.

"I don't blame you," she told him yet again. She didn't tell him that she blamed herself, that guilt ran like poison through her veins. She didn't acknowledge that to anyone else, because she didn't want to hear them protest or try to comfort her. She didn't deserve comforting. "If nothing else, please, please believe that I don't blame you for what happened."

"Then why are you doing this?"

"Because it wouldn't work. Not now."

"Because you blame me."

"No, because I could never forget that it was because of what happened the other night on the beach that my father is dead. Admitting that doesn't mean I blame you for it. It's just the way things are."

"Kissing me off isn't going to change the way things are."

"I know that. But I would never feel right about us being together. It would be a constant reminder of how I gave in, how I let him down."

"Gave in?" he countered tightly. "You mean to me?"

"No. To me. To... feelings."

"Listen, Lily, we didn't do anything wrong."

"Don't you understand? I broke his heart, Jack. That was wrong."

"And now you're breaking mine."

She wanted to cry out, "What do you think I'm doing to myself?" But she couldn't. Wouldn't. No matter how bad it got inside, she would pay the price for what she'd done.

Jack went to touch her and when she leaned away, jammed his hands into his pockets instead. "Don't do this, Lily."

"I have no choice. It would only be worse later. I would never be able to forget what happened. Sooner or later I would end up blaming you. It's nobody's fault. It's just the way it is."

"You have to put it behind you and get on with your life. There'll be other boys who are right for you. You'll see. No matter what he said to you, when push came to shove, he'd go looking for his own kind."

Lily turned to her mother, her eyes blank slates. "You don't have to convince me, Mom. And you don't have to worry about it anymore. Jack is leaving."

"Leaving on a trip?"

Lily shook her head. "No. Leaving for good. He's going to enlist in the Air Force. He wants to be a pilot."

Cliff chewed on his knuckles and gazed out the window.

"What about school?" Mary asked. "What about graduation?"

Lily shrugged. "This comes first. Flying is the most important thing in Jack's life."

"You think I care more about flying a damn airplane than about you?"

"I think you should. This is what you've always wanted."

"It can wait." His jaw was rigid, his expression blacker than she'd ever seen it. It wasn't his anger, however, but the entreaty blazing in his eyes that made her keep looking away as if she were staring into a hot sun. *"Just say the word, and I'll stay."*

"You can't do that. You've made plans, you've told your folks…"

"Forget all that," he said. *"This is just between you and me. I love you, Lily."*

When she didn't respond, he shook his head and stared over her shoulder, his broad chest lifting with a roughly drawn breath. Lily had seen him in jeans and in a tux, but never before in a suit and tie. Typical of the mood swings afflicting her these days, she suddenly longed to touch him, to smooth his collar and tell him how wonderful he looked.

"The other night you told me that you loved me, too," he said at last. *"Was that a lie?"*

"No, no," she insisted, shaking her head. *"I did love you."*

"Did?" His short laugh was riddled with disbelief. *"But not now?"*

She shook her head again, slowly, and stared at the dirt.

"Then you say it. I want to hear you say that you don't love me. Look me in the eye and say it, Lily."

Lily lifted her gaze to meet his. *"I don't love you."*

Now there was a lie, she thought. Big enough and black enough to blot out the sun forever.

Jack exhaled slowly, as if just breathing was painful. It made the hollows beneath his high cheekbones even more pronounced.

As he turned away she instinctively clutched his sleeve. *"Jack, listen…"*

He shook her off. *"Go to hell."*

Now her mother was talking about the get-together at the house, about who might come and whether or not she had ordered enough food from the caterer. They had finally managed to talk her out of trying to prepare it all herself. Now she was worrying that something wouldn't be right.

"I hope enough people come that we don't have too many sandwiches left over. They get soggy when you don't make them yourselves. It's that mayonnaise they use."

Lily turned to her, forcing a smile. "I don't think leftovers will be a problem, not with Joey, Ben *and* Cliff around."

The corners of her mother's mouth lifted briefly, then tightened into a thin line again. "I only wish I could have gotten in touch with Greg. It would have been nice to have the family all together."

The only sound inside the limo was the quiet hum of the air-conditioner. No one said what Lily knew they all must be thinking. That even if Greg had come home, they would never be all together again.

The expected assortment of relatives, friends and neighbors returned to the house. It was strange, like a party and yet not. Sometimes the buzz of conversation and laughter grew strong and then, as if everyone remembered at once the reason they were there, the room fell into an awkward silence until someone finally cleared his throat and broke it. Lily wished they would all go home and at the same time dreaded their leaving, afraid that alone, they wouldn't know how to break the silence.

Finally the last of her father's war buddies and distant cousins had departed. They were left alone, but scattered. Silent. Out of careful things to say.

When the doorbell rang, Lily went to answer it, expecting another neighbor bearing another casserole or homemade pie. Instead she opened the door to find Kay Terrell standing on the front porch.

"Hello, Lily," she said, her smile gentle. "How are you holding up?"

"Fine, thank you, Mrs. Terrell." She gave up her attempt to smile back. "I guess."

"I know how difficult this is for you. Both my parents passed away within the past several years and it's a loss you don't adjust to easily, even at my age. I was hoping I might speak with your mother for a moment if she's not busy or resting."

"Of course, please come in. She's in the kitchen. I'll get her," she added quickly, not wanting Mrs. Terrell to follow her into the cluttered kitchen. "Please, sit down."

She hurriedly snatched the sports section from the morning newspaper and a sweater belonging to Joey off the sofa and by the time she turned around her mother was already there, wiping her hands on a red-checked dish towel as she came to see who was at the door.

"Lily, who... Oh, Mrs. Terrell. I didn't know it was you."

"Hello, Mary. I hope I'm not catching you at a bad time."

"No, no. We were just picking up a little. Would you like a sandwich? A cup of coffee? There are some brownies left, too."

Mrs. Terrell was shaking her head. "No, thank you. My driver is waiting out front. I'm on my way to a business dinner. I just wanted to stop by to tell you that if there's anything I can do, anything you need, anything at all, I want you to let me know."

"That's very kind of you, Mrs. Terrell."

"No, it's not kind," she replied, her gaze shifting uneasily. "It's the least I can do. Rusty was a wonderful man. We'll miss him very much."

"Yes. Yes." Her mother's voice cracked. Lily stepped closer, lightly touching her arm. "We'll all miss him."

"I know this can't possibly lessen your pain," Mrs. Terrell said, opening the cream leather handbag that exactly matched her cream and white spectator pumps and the nubby cream linen of her tailored suit. She looked fresh and shiny against the worn rumpled backdrop of the Saville living room. "But maybe," she continued, as she unfolded a check and held it out to Mary, "it will make things a little easier."

Mary took the check and glanced at it for a moment, her eyes wide. "Ten thousand dollars? Mrs. Terrell, I thank you, but I couldn't possibly take money for nothing."

"Of course you can," Kay Terrell interrupted. "I want you to have it."

Mary shook her head firmly as she held the check out to Kay. "No. Rusty wouldn't want me to take charity, not even from you, Mrs. Terrell."

"But it's not charity, Mary. Really it isn't. It's..." She hesitated only a split second before saying. "It's payment for the iris Rusty was developing. I've been so excited about the prospect of an entirely new flower being created in my own greenhouse that I just can't bear to think of the project being abandoned now. Of course, by rights, all his notes and work belong to you, but I'm not sure you have the space or the capital to devote to continuing the development process."

"Oh, heavens, no," agreed Mary. "And even if we did, none of us would know where to begin."

"Then why not let me see to it that Rusty's dream is carried on? I'm sure that's what he would want, and I'm sure he'd want you to be compensated for all the work he's already done on it." She pressed the check into Mary's hand.

"I still don't know. This seems like an unbelievable amount of money to pay for a flower."

"I've paid more for less," Kay said softly, then flicked her smile into place. "I'm just glad there's something I can do to help you and at the same time see the work on the iris go forward. If there's anything else, ever . . ." She hesitated and took Mary's hand in hers. The two women's eyes met.

Looking on, Lily felt excluded, as if there were questions and messages being transmitted with that touch and look that she couldn't begin to understand.

"Ever," Kay Terrell said again. "Just call."

"Thank you." Mary placed the folded check in her apron pocket. "Let me get that screen door for you," she said as Kay turned to go. "It sticks a little."

Lily couldn't decide which of the two women looked more relieved that their little meeting was over. She stood beside her mother and watched Kay Terrell's car pull away. Heads turned as it passed. Even the kids playing jump rope across the street stopped to gawk. It wasn't every day a chauffer-driven Mercedes made its way down Hazel Street. When it was out of sight, Mary shut the front door, pulled the check from her pocket and stared at it.

"Can you believe this, Lily? Ten thousand whole dollars."

"And you always said dreams don't come cheap."

Her mother stared at her. "What's that?"

"Ten thousand dollars doesn't seem like much to pay for a man's dream."

Mary's face reddened. "That's not it at all."

"Isn't it? Developing that iris meant everything to Daddy. His baby, he called it, you heard him. You know it…and what have we got to show for it? A check for ten thousand dollars. It just doesn't seem right."

"Lily, I know you're upset right now, and hurt. But you heard what Mrs. Terrell said. She has the means to go ahead with this and we don't."

"I heard," Lily agreed, wrapping her arms around herself. "But somehow that just makes it feel worse. Like we didn't even have a say in it."

"Lily, think of what we can do with this much money. I was worried about how we'd make ends meet, and now we won't have to. We can pay off the house, and you'll be able to go to school after all. It's a godsend, is what it is."

For a second, no longer, Lily thought of the acceptance letter from RISD that had arrived only yesterday and now lay crumpled in the wastebasket in her room. She shook her head. "No, Mom, that money is yours. Pay off the house and put the rest in the bank for a rainy day."

"Your father would want me to use it to send you to college, and that's what I'm going to do."

"No," said Lily, a sudden sour taste in her throat. After all that had happened it didn't seem right that the money earned from selling her father's dream ought to be used to make hers come true. "I'm not even sure I want to go. At least not right now. I need to sort things out."

"But..." Mary stopped, the wrinkles in her brow smoothing to faint indelible lines. "All right. We don't have to decide right this minute. We'll talk later, after we've all had a chance to pull ourselves together." She gave Lily a hug. "Now I better go finish up in the kitchen."

Alone in the living room Lily listened to the sound of a Red Sox game coming from the den. From behind the closed door of Cliff's room filtered the music of Led Zeppelin. He seemed to have developed a passion for hard rock in Vietnam. On the windowsill behind the sofa was a tray of iris seedlings her father had planted a few weeks ago. They were no more than fragile green stems that no one had remembered to water. She went for the watering can.

As she gently poured the water over them, she had to close her eyes to hold back the tears. She suddenly felt the way she'd felt years ago when she'd watched her father kneel to pick up the pieces of broken glass from the floor of Delaney Place. Frustrated and helpless and seething with resentment at the injustice of it all.

And she had the same burning desire to do something about it. Only now she was wiser. This time she wouldn't let anything or anybody get in her way. Not her mother, not losing some damn scholarship. Not even Jack, she thought, with a wrenching feeling of loss she was certain she would carry with her forever.

PART THREE

TWENTY-FIVE

Providence, 1978

Lily pushed her safety goggles to the top of her head and glanced around the classroom, surprised to see that it was full-blown afternoon sunlight that slanted through the towering windows behind her and warmed her back. It must be nearly three o'clock. She'd been working for hours.

She wasn't nearly as surprised to find the surrounding workbenches deserted. On a beautiful spring day like today the others in her advanced jewelry design class were eager to get outside and toss a Frisbee around or just bask in the sun. It was another reminder of how different she was from most RISD students. It wasn't just that she was older; there was a certain carefree irreverence the other students had that Lily just didn't share.

With graduation only weeks away there were more impromptu parties than ever and she found herself constantly making excuses.

"Don't you ever want to have fun?" a friend from class had asked her only a few days ago. "Cut loose? Go crazy?"

The answer was no. Fun, along with most other things that mattered so much to her contemporaries, were not on Lily's agenda at all. In one brutal stroke, her father's death had forged her dreams into goals and she was single-minded in her pursuit of them. What she wanted was to succeed, to prove herself and to prove that her father's faith in her had not been misplaced.

She didn't bother trying to explain all that to her friend. Instead she replied that for her, the time spent in the metal workshop was fun—and she was met with an exasperated look. It was the truth, but Lily understood why that was difficult to understand for someone who had gone straight from high school to college, without doing a four-year stint on the assembly line at Delaney Place as she had.

With a final stretch of her tired shoulder muscles, she slid the safety goggles into place and reached for the soldering torch. To anyone else the bits and pieces of unpolished metal scattered on the table might appear confusing, but to Lily they were a puzzle waiting to be solved, a story waiting to be told, and she was eager to get back to it.

The intricate silver and marcasite brooch was one of several pieces that would comprise her senior project. Graduating students in all fine arts departments, from glassworks, sculpture and apparel design to jewelry and light metals, displayed their projects in a gala showing attended by prospective employers in every field as well as artists and critics from around the world. Among seniors the show generated both great excitement and mass anxiety. Years of hopes and dreams culminated in a single showing that could generate either exciting opportunities or yawns.

Lily had spent days deciding what to do for her project. The current trend was to be shocking and avant garde, and she made several false starts in that direction, discarding everything she attempted. Inspiration had finally come from an unexpected source, the small silver house Kay Terrell had given her years ago, which now sat on a corner of her desk in the cluttered third-floor apartment she shared with a trio of architecture students.

Lily, although skilled in all facets of the craft, when left to her own devices returned to the past, to jewelry that was delicate and glamorous and ornate, to the jewel-encrusted brooches and engraved lockets and lacy silver filigree that adorned the pieces she studied at flea markets and antique shops. Jewelry with the same timeless elegance as Delaney Place. That was what she sought to capture in the pieces she was creating, sacrificing whole nights of sleep on occasion as she struggled to make the past her own.

With the preliminary work of casting, chasing and repoussé completed, all that remained was to solder several curved bands into place then set the hundreds of tiny marcasites. Many considered soldering even more difficult than casting, but not Lily. Her experience soldering knives at Delaney Silver enabled her to wield a soldering torch as surely and precisely as a brain surgeon did a scalpel.

She worked boldly, using a high flame that quickly heated the pieces to a temperature hot enough to melt the paillons, the tiny snippets of silver solder she'd prepared earlier. The old-timers on the assembly line had taught her to plan her work and then get on with it, breaking her of the novice's tendency to heat slowly, with a gentle flame, in the mistaken belief that that was the way to avoid boiling the flux used to protect the surfaces not being soldered.

It was while working at Delaney Silver that she'd discovered she liked using her hands, being able to touch and shape and hold her creations, much better than she did applying a brush to canvas. After two years of employment she had become eligible for the company's tuition reimbursement for work-related courses and had immediately enrolled in the evening metalworking program at RISD.

Jewelry design was part of the program, and the first time she set foot in a jewelry design class, Lily knew this was what she wanted to do forever. Not only did she have a natural aptitude for it, but to those lucky few who succeeded, the field promised all the fame, glamor and wealth of her childhood dreams.

Her hands-on experience quickly caused her to stand out in the class of beginners, and the instructor, Maggie Pearson, a designer for a large costume jewelry maker, had taken a personal interest in her. Maggie encouraged her, insisting that the wall that had for years kept jewelry design a male-dominated industry was cracking. She clipped articles from trade magazines about the work Elsa Peretti and Angela Cummings were doing for Tiffany's and impressed upon Lily how crucial it was to develop her own style the way they had.

Most important, she prodded Lily to tackle a financial-aid maze Lily hadn't even known existed. Maggie explained that the college offered a variety of scholarships, some for students studying in a particular field, like jewelry design, others awarded strictly on the basis of financial need. It took another year, but Lily was finally granted enough money to enroll full time. Goodbye assembly line, hello heaven. Others might complain about the long workshops and tedious, repetitive assignments required to master the craft, but not Lily. Nothing was as tedious as an eight-hour shift in a hot, airless factory, performing the same task over and over.

The soldering complete, Lily switched off the torch and automatically began scraping together the unused solder shavings to save for future use. Her grant money covered tuition and room and board in approved housing. That still left books and incidentals and supplies, which were monstrously expensive, even at the school store. Gold, silver, stones . . . it was a joke to call any of them semiprecious.

At one time or another she had waited tables, baby-sat for a professor's spoiled children and worked at a car wash to earn money. For years she refused her mother's offers to help, knowing the money came from the sale of her father's prized iris. Eventually she had relented, bowing to her mother's insistence that it was what her father would have wanted done with the money. She still insisted on paying her own way as much as possible, however, working summers and during school breaks as a waitress at the club.

She never saw Jack there, although sometimes when she passed the place where they used to meet, she felt a strange shivery sensation and turned away quickly, as if he might really be there waiting for her. He never was, of course, and the hollow feeling that resulted would linger for hours.

Soon after that final bitter meeting by her father's grave, she'd heard that Jack had enlisted in the Air Force, and about a year ago there had been a picture of him in the local paper, along with the announcement that he'd been promoted to lieutenant colonel and assigned to an elite flight unit for special training.

His success hadn't come as a surprise to Lily, but the razorlike pain that slid between her ribs when she flipped open the paper to find him staring back at her had shocked her. For a few seconds it had been impossible to breathe, and her fingers had gone to the grainy reproduction of the familiar lines and angles of his face. The smoothness of the paper had been another jolt, as if she'd truly expected to feel the warmth of his skin or see the somber line of his mouth curve into a smile at her touch.

If Jack ever returned home to visit, Lily didn't know about it. He never called her or stopped by, and she'd long ago given up dreading and hoping that he might. She'd also given up daydreaming about what might have been for the two of them.

There had been no one else in her life since Jack, and she couldn't foresee when there might be. She had no time for romance or for the elaborate games it entailed. Eventually, when she was an established and successful designer, she might consider a relationship with the right man—someone she admired and enjoyed being with and who didn't threaten her self-control.

Her work was her life, and Lily liked it that way. To succeed the way she was determined to took planning and dedication and self-control. She had succumbed wholeheartedly to passion once, with Jack. She had risked everything—more than she could even know at the time—for a dream, and she had lost. Never again. She'd learned to play it safe, to save her passion and her impulsiveness for her work.

In the case of her senior project, following her instincts paid off. Her graceful, romantic jewelry stood alone in a sea of bold, angular pieces, winning honors and earning her a mention in nearly every major review of the event. "Vintage with a fresh twist," proclaimed one critic. Most thrilling to Lily, however, was the praise she received from Drew Goddard. She did her best to appear composed, amazed to discover that he remembered her from their brief meeting years earlier at Kay Delaney's birthday party.

"Beauty and originality," he said, after an unhurried study of her display, "An all-too-rare combination."

He may have been referring to the pendant alone, but something in the intent, thoughtful gaze he allowed to linger on her, almost as if he couldn't help himself, made Lily wonder. It left her feeling unsettled, though not in a disturbing way. There was nothing in his smile or in their brief exchange to suggest the sort of ulterior-motivated attention older men sometimes paid attractive young women. Lily savored the warmth of his praise long after he'd wished her good luck and walked away.

Graduation took place on a brilliant Thursday morning in May. The entire family turned out to beam with pride as Lily did what no Saville had done before her. She searched the crowd for them as the procession of graduates made its way along historic Benefit Street. Finally she spotted them, clustered in the shade of an old maple tree, an assortment of adults and children dressed in their very best.

Cliff was there with his wife, Jackie, four-year-old Cliffie on his shoulders and Lori, two, in the stroller. Beside them stood

Ben and Carol, a navy blue dress with a sailor collar doing little to disguise the fact that she was eight months pregnant with
their first baby, and of course Joey. Greg had sent her a graduation present from Bolivia, a set of three carved wood masks,
exotic, useless, typical. Lily had chuckled affectionately over
the accompanying card. Congratulations on your marriage, it
read, with the word marriage crossed out and graduation written in, and a hasty postscript explaining that the selection of
cards wasn't all that great in Bolivia.

Perched on the edge of the curb was her mother, looking
older and grayer to Lily, all of a sudden. Well, she wasn't getting any younger. Caught up in her own life, Lily seldom took
time to pay much attention to her mother. Now she noticed that
the new blue and white flowered dress her mother had bought
for the occasion looked pretty on her, hiding the extra pounds
she tried so hard to control. Lily vowed to remember to tell her
so later.

After the ceremony there was a party at home, a typical Saville celebration with an abundance of food and laughter and
a six-foot-banner reading Congratulations, Lily strung above
the front door. Amidst the familiar noise and confusion, her
mother found a quiet moment alone with Lily to give her a
small box wrapped in foil.

"Congratulations, honey," she said, her eyes shimmering
with tears the same way they had when Lily passed by her in the
procession. "This is for making us all so proud."

Inside was the locket she had once lent to Lily. It had been
freshly polished, and the simple gold chain Lily remembered
had been replaced with a more elaborate one of braided gold.

"Mom it's beautiful," she said. "I love it."

"I could have bought something new," her mother replied,
her tone at once worried and eager. "A watch, maybe, but I
thought it was from both your dad and me. You
know, he was the one who gave that locket to me years and
years ago and now it's being passed on to our little girl." She
stopped and wiped her eyes with the back of her hand. "I know
he'd like that. Oh, Lily, he would be so proud of you if he was
here."

No words could have made Lily happier, or brought on tears
more quickly. She, too, felt certain her father would be proud
of how far she had come, but it wasn't far enough. Not yet, not
nearly.

TWENTY-SIX

Two weeks after graduation Lily went to work for Bonatelli Creations in Providence, putting her mother's "starving artist" worries to rest once and for all. The job wasn't her first choice. Working as a jeweler's bench man at a costume jewelry factory wasn't what she would have chosen at all, but Maggie Pearson had convinced her it was the wisest move she could make.

"Take time to learn the underside of the business," she warned Lily over lunch one afternoon, "or you'll wish you had."

Lily sighed impatiently. "Whatever happened to the woman who was always telling me to take risks? Be daring? Develop my own style?"

"She's sitting right here," Maggie replied, chuckling. She was tall and slender, with close-cropped salt-and-pepper hair and an uninhibited laugh, and Lily valued the friendship that had grown between them over the years. "But I was talking about being daring with your *work,* about taking *artistic* risks. With your future, you need to be a little more pragmatic."

"Sometimes I get tired of being pragmatic," Lily countered, feeling the rumblings of the adventuresome soul she kept so deeply buried. "I want to get going, strike out on my own. How else will I ever find out if I've got what it takes as a designer?"

"Lily, what do you know about overhead?" Maggie inquired calmly. "About pricing a piece to insure a profit? About how much to pay an assistant? And I haven't even gotten around to the pitfalls involved in dealing with the more unscrupulous wholesalers out there."

"I took professional practices last year. I know there are risks involved."

"Professional practices?" Maggie scoffed. "Honey, that's pie-in-the-sky stuff. Jewelry looks so shiny and elegant on the pages of a catalogue, but behind those glossy pages there's a lot of backstabbing and thievery and heartache. I know. I've worked in the business for almost thirty years."

Lily shrugged. "You're right. I *do* need to get some experience before I try to start my own business, but why get it at a joint like Bonatelli's? I'd rather work as an assistant designer at a small jewelry shop, either around here or in Boston, maybe even in New York. Look at the way Angela Cummings just walked into Tiffany's with her portfolio and was hired on the spot."

"You might pull that off, if you had a European pedigree like Angela Cummings or family connections to get your foot in the door. Besides, strip away the fancy assistant designer title, and you'd still be a glorified bench man, making pieces of someone else's design."

"Yes, but at least I'd be doing quality work."

"You already know all about quality; what you need now is to learn what's practical. You need to learn about designing a piece that can be efficiently manufactured and marketed. You need to find out how to work the shows where the big buying and selling goes on, you need to see what works and what doesn't, and where you want to position yourself in the market—and how the hell to do it." Maggie leaned forward, her dark eyes flashing. "Honey, you need a Vic Bonatelli to pay for your mistakes so you don't have to."

As always, Maggie made sense, and so Lily reluctantly joined the Bonatelli *team,* as Vic Bonatelli, founder, owner and slave driver in residence, liked to refer to his three hundred or so employees.

"What do you say, *team?*" he would ask in his booming voice. "Is this spring line gonna be a hit or is this spring line gonna be a hit?" Or when he sprang for a round of drinks— beer or wine only, please—at the company Christmas party, "How about it, *team?* Is Vic Bonatelli a class act or is Vic Bonatelli a class act?"

A class act Vic Bonatelli was not. He was tall and muscular with slicked-back black hair. His wardrobe consisted of black pants, spread collar shirts and an assortment of neck chains that weighed in with more gold than his entire spring line. For the first year she worked for him, he called Lily "kid."

"Let the kid take care of it," he would instruct Rick Pacheco, the head of the design department and a man who—when it came to jewelry—Lily could conceive, design and execute circles around. "So how's the kid working out?" Vic would ask him without ever breaking stride to hear the answer.

At least she was learning. She kept her eyes and ears open and her mouth shut and dreamed of the day when she would leave Bonatelli's. Unfortunately that day didn't arrive as soon as Lily hoped.

She had planned to stay there for a year, two at the most. But two turned into three and she still dragged her feet, giving Bonatelli's their forty hours a week and pouring most of her energy and talent into the designs she worked on at home in the evenings. She kept telling herself she stayed put to build her own collection, but deep down she wondered if the real reason was that she was afraid. Afraid to fail.

One night as she was leaving work, Lily ran into Vic in the hall outside his office.

"Good night, Mr. Bonatelli," she said, as he passed her with barely a glance.

"'Night, kid." He was a few steps past her when he called out, "Hey, hold up a minute." As Lily stopped and turned, he hurried to her side. "You're just the person I was looking for."

Right, thought Lily. "Really?" she said.

"Sure . . ." She could tell he was grappling for something to call her besides kid. "Rose, right? No? But it's a flower, right? Daisy? No."

"Lily," she supplied before he had a chance to call her Pansy or Petunia. Ragweed.

"Right. That's it, right on the tip of my tongue. Lily, how'd you like to help out the *team?* I was going to bring Claudette along to the show tonight to help me out, but she went and got her foot caught in a damn door. She's at the emergency room right now."

"How awful. Is it broken?"

"Nah, just a little crushed, maybe a few toes is all." He made an impatient gesture. "Anyway, she won't be making the show, so how'd you like to stand in for her?"

The show he referred to was the United Jewelry Show being held at the Biltmore Hotel. A very big deal. "I'd love it," Lily replied.

"Great. I've got a business dinner to do first. You run home and change. Doll yourself up a little, if you get my drift. And meet me in the Biltmore lobby at seven."

Although she had no desire to work her way up the Bonatelli ladder to Vic's inner circle, Lily couldn't help being excited by the invitation. Since the eighteenth century, when local silversmiths developed techniques for making jewelry more cheaply, Providence had been the undisputed costume jewelry capital of the country. So it was fitting that the twice-yearly show that gave jewelry makers the opportunity to unveil their new lines to buyers and wholesalers should be held locally. Vic always attended the shows, of course, along with the sales staff and Rick Pacheco, or one of the other designers who had been there for so long there were cobwebs on their workbenches—and their designs.

In the small apartment she rented on the city's east side, Lily quickly showered and changed. She surmised that Vic's idea of dolled up was not the high-neck teal suede dress that had cost her more than a week's salary, but she wasn't dressing for Vic. The dress was classy, cut close enough to turn heads in a subtle way and, most important to Lily, it provided the perfect backdrop for a new silver necklace she'd made combining pink and green watermelon tourmaline and a trio of magnificent heart-shaped lockets she'd come across in an antique shop.

She would dutifully tout the Bonatelli spring line at the show tonight, but if anyone should happen to ask where she got the jewelry she was wearing, she would certainly tell. This was her first real opportunity to do what Maggie was always exhorting her to do, make contacts. She was eager to talk with buyers and wholesalers and hear firsthand what they were looking for.

When she met Vic, his gaze shot from her neck to the hem of her dress, which was well below her knees.

"Hell, don't you own anything, you know, more... Never mind. I guess beggars can't be choosers. Come with me."

He led her to a quiet corner of the lobby, away from the steady stream of men and women in business suits arriving for the show's evening session.

"All right, here's the scoop," he said, fishing in the pocket of his canary yellow sport coat for a small notepad, which he handed to Lily. "The show is on the eighth, ninth and tenth floors. Every maker has got his own room, see? And no one except buyers are allowed inside the showrooms. That's where you come in. No one here knows you or that you work for me, so you just kind of blend with the crowd as they move from room to room and check out what's what. The goods will be spread out, on tables, on the bed, everywhere. You know the kind of stuff I do. When you see something they've got that we don't, you slip into the john and get it down here for me." He tapped the notepad. "Got it?"

Lily shook her head. "No. You mean you want me to steal other makers' designs?"

"What steal?" He glanced around uneasily. "Keep your voice down, would you? In six months all this stuff will be on the counter at Sears for the world to see. I just want a little advance preview, is all. What's the matter? You look like you bit into something rotten. It's all part of the business, honey. Everybody does it."

"Then why not do it yourself?"

"I told you, technically no one but buyers are allowed into the competition's rooms. Everybody here knows me. Besides, you're a woman. You can just smile at the security guards and breeze right in. Of course, it would have helped if you'd worn something a little more . . ." He gestured in the direction of her dress. "Forget it. You all set?"

"I'm not sure I want to do this."

"What are you? Some sort of saint? When you work for Vic Bonatelli, you do what's best for the *team*. Right? Right. Now let's get up there. You go first."

Vic was right about the security. There were only a handful of blue-blazered guards and hundreds of people milling between the bedrooms turned showrooms. Lily tagged along with one group and nobody seemed to notice she was the only one not wearing one of the green name tags that distinguished buyers from exhibitors.

Inside the rooms, the lights were bright and the tables were stacked with padded cards of jewelry samples, priced by the dozen. A necklace tagged forty-eight dollars would cost four dollars wholesale. Lily knew that by the time it reached the store, the price tag on the same necklace could be ten or twelve times that.

She wandered through the first few showrooms, telling herself that even if she intended to go along with Vic's sleazy request, none of what she saw was what he was looking for. Actually a whole lot of it looked like the same stuff already on display in the Bonatelli Creations showroom on the ninth floor. She certainly didn't see anything worth copying.

In one showroom she stopped by a display of earrings made of twisted gold-plated threads studded with rhinestones and dangling from a post. Eye-catching, but hideous.

"This just doesn't work for me," the woman standing next to Lily was saying to the company representative on the other side of the table. A glance at her name tag told Lily that the woman was a wholesaler from Atlanta. Unlike buyers for a specific store or chain, wholesalers put together seasonal collections of jewelry to resell to small shops and boutiques.

"Maybe if I catered to a clientele of hookers or teenyboppers who don't know any better," she continued, "but otherwise, no go. You see, the attitude in the south is that a dangle or a drop earring is sleazy. And none of this pavé stuff, either. I'm looking for serious jewelry, but not dead. Colors, show me colors."

Lily wandered off as the rep produced a padded card covered with bright enameled shapes similar to a line Bontaelli was pushing for spring. She found that the few intriguing pieces of jewelry she *did* see were not pinned on display cards, but being worn by the more chicly dressed buyers.

In the showroom of Coronet Manufacturers, Bonatelli's biggest competitor, she idly perused a display of rings and continued to worry about how she was going to explain the blank notebook to Vic. There were a few designs here worth copying, but even they were part of Coronet's line of fine jewelry, which had no counterpart at Bonatelli's. Feeling a sneeze coming on, she turned away and hastily rummaged in her purse for a tissue, pulling out everything in her way in the process, including the notepad. Suddenly a strong hand clamped onto her shoulder.

She jumped, nearly spilling the collection of clutter onto the floor.

"I beg your pardon," she snapped, gazing up at a tall young man with sandy hair and an angry expression.

"Won't do you any good to beg," he said with a sneer. "Not if you're up to what I think you are."

Lily cursed the guilty flush that instantly heated her cheeks. "What I'm up to," she told him in as haughty a tone as she could manage, "is looking for a tissue. Now would you mind taking your hand off me?"

He reluctantly let her go, but when she stepped back to put some breathing room between them, he moved forward, cornering her in the crowded room.

"How come you're not wearing a name tag?" he demanded. The lapel of his polyester sports coat was adorned with a tag announcing that he was Chuck Santucci, a Coronet salesman.

Lily quickly patted the area of her left shoulder. "Oh, my goodness, it must have fallen off."

Chuck didn't look convinced. "Yeah? Or maybe you're not wearing it because it's the wrong color. Didn't I see you downstairs a while ago, jawing with Vic Bonatelli?"

"Bonatelli?" she repeated, trying her best to look blank.

"That's right, Bonatelli. Maybe you're up here on a little spy mission for him...or do you always carry a notebook to a trade show?"

"Spying?" she gasped, her throat going dry. "That's ridiculous."

"Okay, then, who do you work for?"

Lily thought quickly. "The Langton Group."

"Never heard of them."

"We're new," she said, shrugging as she attempted to move past him.

"Yeah? Well, why don't we just check with security and find out how new?"

This time he grabbed her by the elbow, and as Lily tried to pull free they drew curious glances from those in the immediate vicinity. Great. Once security verified that there was no Langton Group and that she was wandering around under false pretenses, she would be branded a design thief before she even marketed her first design. With real fear uncoiling inside, she stopped struggling and glared at him.

"Look," she said hotly, "just because I—"

"Lily, there you are."

She turned to find Drew Goddard standing beside them. He was smiling as if she was an old friend of his, instead of a woman being held prisoner by an irate man and about to be exposed as a thief.

"Mr. Goddard," she said weakly.

"We must have gotten separated in the crowd outside," he continued before she could say more. "I'm lucky to have caught up with you so quickly." Still smiling, he dropped his gaze to Chuck's death grip on her elbow. "Is there some problem?"

Lily's embarrassment reached new heights. "Yes, I . . ."

"She doesn't have a name tag," Chuck stated bluntly. "That's against the rules, so I'm going to call security to have her checked out."

"I see," Drew replied. His smile disappearing, he peeled the Goddard's name tag from his pin-striped lapel and gently patted it into place below Lily's shoulder. "Now she does have one." He met Chuck's suddenly uncertain gaze. "Would you like to call security to have me checked out?"

"No, sir, Mr. Goddard," the younger man answered without hesitation. "Everyone knows who you are, sir."

"Good. Then there's no longer a problem. Lily?" he said, extending his arm for her to proceed him out of the overcrowded room. His manner was the quiet, confident one of a man who doesn't have to shout to have his words heard or heeded.

Lily gratefully allowed him to escort her to the hallway outside, where it felt at least twenty degrees cooler. She stopped in an out-of-the-way spot a short distance from the Coronet showroom.

"I don't know how to thank you, Mr. Goddard," she said, relief spreading slowly through her still trembling limbs.

"Call me Drew," he replied. "And no thanks are necessary."

"You just rescued me from what could have been a very embarrassing situation." Her mouth curved in a nervous smile. "Actually, it was already plenty embarrassing."

"Forget about it. We all make mistakes."

"But I didn't . . . make a mistake, that is. I certainly wasn't stealing designs, which is what he accused me of doing. This is my first show, you see, and I was just sort of wandering around," she continued, searching for a way to convince him she wasn't a thief without implicating Vic. "I was just . . ." She stopped and shook her head. "Just acting like an idiot. I can't imagine what you must be thinking."

"You don't have to," Drew said, smiling at her. "I'll tell you. I'm thinking that you're even lovelier than I remembered."

"Thank you."

"And I'm thinking that I'm very glad I was around to help you."

There was nothing heart-stopping about Drew Goddard, yet at that instant Lily thought he might be the most attractive man she'd ever encountered. His face was long and narrow, his mouth too generous and framed with laugh lines, his dark, wavy hair short and threaded with gray. But what attracted Lily wasn't the way he looked, but the way he made her feel. Safe.

"Why did you?" she asked. "I mean, you hardly know me. I can't believe you even remembered my name."

"Why not? You remembered mine."

"Yes, but that's different."

He laughed, his gray eyes warm and gently amused behind the tortoiseshell glasses.

"Not only did you remember who I was," continued Lily, "but you stopped to find out what was happening when most people would have looked the other way and kept walking."

Drew was still laughing softly, one shoulder resting lightly against the wall as if he was in no hurry to get rid of her, even though she knew there were many more important people around for him to talk with.

Lily persisted. "For all you knew I might have been guilty, and yet you went out of your way to help me. I guess I was just wondering why."

"Because of your eyes," he said matter-of-factly.

"My eyes?" she encountered as they narrowed in confusion.

"Right. I looked into your eyes, and I knew you weren't guilty of anything."

"Oh."

"And I suppose maybe also because they're green. I once loved a woman with green eyes very much," he explained when Lily looked at him quizzically. "You remind me of her in a way. Maybe I wanted to help you because I was never able to help her."

TWENTY-SEVEN

Lily met Vic as planned, about a half hour before the show closed.

"Any problems?" he asked her. They were standing in the same out-of-the-way spot as earlier.

Lily shook her head. "Not really. A Coronet salesman asked why I wasn't wearing a name tag, but it worked out all right."

She had already stuck Drew's name tag in her purse, reluctant to share the details, because they were embarrassing, because they were confusing and because she still hadn't sorted it out in her own mind.

"Good girl," said Vic, rubbing his hands together. "Let's see what you got for me."

With a worried frown she fished the notepad from her purse. "Vic, I think . . ."

He snatched it from her fingers before she could explain. Lily stood by silently as he thumbed through it, forward, then, eyes widening with disbelief, back again.

"What the . . . ? It's empty. What've you been doing for the last three hours?"

"Exactly what you told me to do. Going from one showroom to the next looking for something interesting enough for Bonatelli's to knock off, and you know what, Vic?"

"What?" he asked suspiciously.

"There wasn't anything. I mean it," she went on hurriedly when his suspicious expression looked as if it might turn angry. "Why copy what you already do better than anyone else? Vic, you are without question the king of low-level costume jewelry."

"What's that supposed to mean?"

"I guess it means that I think it's time the Bonatelli team moved ahead and set its sights a little higher. It occurred to me tonight that there's a new customer out there who is being totally ignored."

"Who's that?"

"The working woman. Almost nothing I saw tonight is right for the woman who is serious about her career and wants her appearance to reflect that. She's young, smart, ambitious. She might be married, but she's put kids on hold until she establishes herself professionally. She can't afford to shop at Goddard's or Tiffany's—yet—but she knows the right accessories are important and she's willing to splurge a little to get them. What she doesn't want is her mother's single strand of pearls or her kid sister's zodiac pendant."

"What does she want?" asked Vic, looking a little bewildered by her fervent sales pitch.

"She wants something classy and simple, but not so simple or understated that she blends into the woodwork. She wants to add a touch of freshness and femininity to her business suits. She wants quality and comfort. No gold-tone chains studded with rhinestones. No three-inch hoops. No slogan bracelets."

"What's left?" he asked wryly.

Lily chuckled. "A whole new world of designs, Vic. A very *profitable* world," she added and saw his eyes brighten. "A woman working her way up the corporate ladder has more money to spend on jewelry than a high-school kid looking for earrings shaped like umbrellas."

"Hey, I made a killing on those umbrella earrings."

"Somebody's going to make a killing on this, too, Vic. Why not you?"

"How come marketing doesn't know about this new woman out there?"

"They know, but they're still trying to sell her the same old stuff while they jump on every fad they catch scent of. How much of a killing did we make on the knife and fork earrings?"

He shrugged. "You got to expect a few dogs. At least when we take a bath on junk like that we don't go all the way under. What you're talking about sounds expensive."

"Without a doubt, but the profit margin will be higher, too. And you'll be tapping a whole new market. In fact I think you should create a separate division of Bonatelli's to produce this new line, to keep it distinctive from your traditional product."

"Whoa. What new line? If anything, I was thinking maybe a piece or two, test the waters a little."

Lily was shaking her head. "A piece or two will get lost in the shuffle. Besides, this woman I'm talking about isn't a traditional Bonatelli customer. You have to make a splash, convince her to take a look at us, win her over."

"I don't know," he said, rubbing his thumb against his finger the way she'd seen him do when he was worried.

"I saw a lot of buyers tonight, Vic, and I listened in while they talked to each other. They might not have put it all together in quite the same way I did, but this is the product they'll be looking for in the eighties."

"You think you could put something on paper for me to show marketing?" he asked her.

"Yes, of course." Lily was stunned. Even if she managed to convince Vic, she'd expected him to go to Rick with the idea. "I haven't got anything specific in mind yet, but I know the look. And I know I can do it."

"Good. Have it to me by Monday."

"Monday?" This was Friday. Even if she worked all weekend . . .

Vic was already walking away. After a few steps he turned to her and smiled. "You're a smart kid, Lily. Who knows? This thing just might fly."

Lily worked nonstop through the weekend, catnapping when she absolutely had to, going through stacks of paper. On Monday morning she dressed more carefully than usual for work, wanting to look as polished and professional as the set of finished sketches tucked into her briefcase.

After taking off in a hundred different directions she'd decided to limit herself to one central idea. Sketching free-form, she produced a series of loose fluid shapes that, when eyed together, resembled falling leaves. Instantly Lily felt the visceral jolt that comes when you know you've found what you've been looking for. *Falling leaves.* It was perfect, simple and yet allowing for a variety of textures and designs. The design was timely, as well, since they were now planning next fall's line.

Vic called for her at ten o'clock. She sat in the chair across from his desk as he examined the sketches one by one.

"I made notes on each sketch regarding specific techniques and materials," she said.

"I see."

"I planned almost entirely for fourteen-carat-gold-filled, with touches of copper incorporated into some of them for depth and added interest."

Vic blanched and grunted at the mention of fourteen-carat-gold plating, but he didn't ask her if she'd lost her mind, which was the reaction she expected.

"That's one of the ones using copper," she said, as he studied a sketch of earrings and matching lapel pin in a graceful swirling pattern. The rough-textured gold surface washed away in places to reveal pools of burnished copper.

"Mixing metals," Vic muttered. "We don't usually do that."

"Exactly. We're working on something new here. It's different and unexpected."

"It's a pain in the ass."

Lily bit her lip.

A second later he nodded with approval at the clean lines of an open-worked design loosely based on an oak leaf, gently curling in a way that made it seem to be floating on a soft breeze.

"What's this?" he asked, stopping at one of the more elaborate designs, a necklace, bracelet and earrings of hammered gold, cut in almost circular leaf shapes so thin they would lie flat against the skin. He squinted to read her notes. "Repoussé? Have you lost your mind? This ain't Goddard's, kid. We don't have the people to handle that."

"We could hire them."

He flicked her an impatient look.

"All right," Lily said. "We could compromise and settle for roller embossing. It won't produce the same richness of texture, but it will do."

"Thank you for that, Miss Art School Graduate."

He shook his head as he looked at the final drawings, occasionally muttering, "I don't know, I don't know." He was rubbing his thumb on his finger again, too. Lily wished she knew him well enough to know if that was a good or bad sign.

Finally he looked at her, leaning back in his chair. "I got to hand it to you, kid, this looks better than I thought. Falling Leaves. It's just like you said, simple, but eye-catching." He picked up one of the sketches and looked at it again. "They got a certain style, a classiness. Sorta like you, kid."

Lily was so excited she got to her feet. "So you're going to do it?"

"Hold on a minute. First I have to show these to the guys in production to see if we can handle them."

"Vic, I know our equipment and personnel, and I considered all that when I was working them up."

"Well, we'll just see. Then I have to check with marketing. Maybe make up a few samples, and I mean a few, to see if there's any interest out there. This is a big step."

"Very big," agreed Lily. "But you won't be sorry."

"Maybe. Just in case, I did some thinking over the weekend about what you said about starting a new division to handle this. Me and Anna tossed it around a little. I'll tell you," he said, reaching for a cigar, "she likes the idea. Says maybe she'll finally be able to wear something I make. Classy broad, my Anna. Wants only the best. Anyway, we came up with a name for this new line. Tellis," he said, gesturing with spread figures as if framing the word in the air between them. "See, I dropped the Bona from the front and added an S. Bonatelli. Tellis. Get it?"

Lily tried it out. "Tellis."

"You know, just in case we do decide to run with this." He grinned and said it again. "Tellis. So what do you think?"

Lily thought that very soon now she was going to like working at Bonatelli Creations a whole lot better.

Over the course of the next week the production and marketing experts whittled Falling Leaves down to four designs, but no one was willing to sit beside her in the hot seat by giving the idea wholehearted support. Luckily, time was on Lily's side. If her designs were to be included in the spring preview of next fall's line, they had to move now. Vic, with his wife like a strong wind at his back, finally decided to pull out all the stops and make Tellis a reality, stunning everyone by naming Lily the chief designer.

Falling Leaves was unveiled at the spring show to great advance interest, thanks to a mention in *Women's Wear Daily*. It described the pieces as "fascinatingly simple" and went on to say they were "motion captured in a surprising mix of metals from an even more surprising source. Tellis is a new division of costume jewelry firm Bonatelli Creations, whose biggest claim to fame until now has been chain belts and umbrella earrings. The new line is aimed at the working woman on her way up, a customer whom, according to Lily Saville, the line's creator, has been ignored. Sounds like an idea whose time has come."

Orders were healthy enough for Vic to expand the line to six designs for the spring. Feathers, a collection of curling and etched shapes that forced Vic to invest in new electroplating equipment, broke all previous sales records. The following fall they presented Ribbons, narrow slivers and ripples of gold and brass, some inlaid with chips of opal and mother-of-pearl. Tellis designs became a hot new status symbol. Demand increased when the sales director decided to hold back orders through the fall then flood the market just before Christmas. Again sales nearly doubled.

Lily was invited to be a guest lecturer at RISD and was interviewed for trade journals. She'd been given a generous raise when she was put in charge of the new division and again with the launch of each new line. When Vic offered her the choice of another raise or profit sharing, Lily jumped at the profit sharing and soon had a rapidly growing nest egg for the day she left Bonatelli's.

The only problem was that rather than coming closer, that day seemed further away than ever. Ironically, part of the reason was the money she was making. Unbelievable, liberating, secure sums of money. Enough to buy a condo on the East Side, enough to make interest-free loans to her brothers for down payments on homes of their own and set up college funds for all her nieces and nephews.

"I hate to give it up," she confided to Maggie one night when they managed to get together for dinner, a rare occurrence these days. "I would risk everything by going out on my own. I have a job other designers would kill for. The money is great. I have profit-sharing, IRAs...." She dropped her head to her hands with a soft wail. "Oh, my God, stop me. I sound like my mother."

Maggie chuckled. "It happens to us all sooner or later. I think it has something to do with hormones."

"I want to try it on my own. Hell, that used to be all that I wanted," she recalled wistfully. "But now..." She shrugged. "Growing up without money sure makes you cautious with the stuff." Her mouth twisted into a wry smile. "I guess maybe that's why my mother is the way she is."

"Look," said Maggie, "I won't tell you what to do, only that taking risks doesn't get any easier. I know."

Lily nodded, understanding that Maggie was referring to her own career. With a disabled husband to support and two kids to put through college she'd never had the option of giving up the security of a full-time job.

"I don't want to sound preachy," she continued, "but for a woman in your position—no kids, no responsibilities—there might be things more important than making piles of money."

Lily arched an eyebrow. "Name one."

"Satisfaction. Are you satisfied doing what you're doing, Lily?"

Was she? Lily wrestled with the question on and off for weeks after her dinner with Maggie. She wouldn't describe herself as unsatisfied, exactly. Restless was a better word. True, Vic gave her a pretty free rein with Tellis, and she had carved her own respected niche in the male-dominated company. No one called her kid anymore, and when she talked, people listened. All in all it was better than she ever expected.

Still, whenever she sat down to work there were built-in limitations. A piece couldn't cost too much to produce or take too long to demand any special skills. And chief designer or not, she was still producing costume jewelry rather than the glamorous one-of-a-kind pieces she yearned to create. So why didn't she do something to change things?

Deep down, Lily knew it was because she was afraid. Afraid to fail.

On Tellis's sixth anniversary, Vic took her to lunch at Camille's, a venerated Italian restaurant on nearby Federal Hill. They had pasta primavera and champagne, and Lily returned to work to find a surprise among her messages. She walked to the reception area.

"Pam, did you take this call from Drew Goddard?"

The receptionist nodded.

"Did he give you any hint of what he wanted?"

"None. Just left that number and said for you to call him when you had time. Dreamy telephone voice, don't you think?"

"I don't know. I've never spoken to him on the phone."

Lily closed the door of her office-workroom before placing the call. Drew's secretary said he was away from his office, then quickly asked her to hold when she learned Lily's name. A few minutes later Drew came on the line. Pam was right about his voice.

"Lily, thanks for returning my call. When I heard you were off having a celebration lunch I was afraid you might be gone for the day."

"I wish," she said with a laugh. "At this time of year I'm too busy for all-afternoon lunches, no matter how special the occasion."

"But not too busy to join me for dinner, I hope?"

Lily could hear her breath rushing against the mouthpiece. The last thing she expected Drew Goddard to be calling her for was a date.

"I've caught you off guard," he said after a minute.

"No. No, you didn't, really."

He chuckled and Lily could picture his smile and the way his eyes crinkled at the corners. "Are you always speechless when a man invites you to have dinner with him?"

"All right, I guess I am a little surprised."

"Would it help if I admitted up front that I have ulterior motives?"

"No, but it would certainly make me curious."

"Curious enough to say yes, you'll have dinner with me at Cappricio's tonight?"

Now Lily chuckled. "Yes, Drew, I'd love to have dinner with you."

Lily spent a wasted afternoon trying to keep her mind on work, finally giving up and leaving early for the first time in years to go home and take a long bath before slipping into the taupe silk dress she'd decided to wear.

They met at the restaurant. Lily had seen Drew a number of times since that awful night he rescued her from her own stupidity, usually at some business-related function. He always greeted her warmly. Sometimes they talked for a few minutes. Gradually Lily's awe of him had faded while her fondness and respect grew stronger. They were what she'd call friendly acquaintances. And now this. Dinner and ulterior motives.

In Providence, Cappricio's was regarded as the place to go when you wanted to impress your date. The decor was opulent, with high-back leather captain's chairs and an abundance of starched white linen. The menu was northern Italian, the waiters vigilant and discreet. Dishes arrived and disappeared from the table almost without Lily's noticing, partly due to their waiter's expertise and partly to Drew's.

He was a wonderful dinner companion, relaxed and charming, with a dry wit she hadn't been treated to before now. They discussed books and music and all the exciting places Drew had been and Lily dreamed of going. Except for a toast at the start of the evening, they didn't talk business.

"To your success," Drew said, lifting his wineglass. "Which did not come as a surprise to anyone who knows you."

It was the first time they had ever talked for any length of time and Lily found herself wishing the evening could go on and on. Over salad she wondered exactly how much older than her he was. Over dinner she decided she really didn't give a damn. By dessert she was ready to admit she was having more fun than she could remember having in a long time.

"You haven't asked me about my ulterior motives," he said as she sipped her coffee.

"Not because I haven't been wondering about them, believe me."

"Then let me satisfy your curiosity. Lily, are you happy working at Bonatelli's?"

She responded with a rueful laugh. "Funny you should ask. I've been grappling with that question myself."

"Why, Lily? What's wrong?"

She found herself telling him about her growing frustration with the built-in limitations at Bonatelli's, about her desire to strike out on her own and about her fears. He was the first person aside from Maggie to whom she'd spoken in detail about the kind of work she dreamed of doing.

Drew listened attentively, his thoughtful expression encouraging her to say whatever was on her mind. When she finished, he nodded and smiled.

"That's about what I expected, and to be truthful, I would have been disappointed to hear anything else, to hear that you were satisfied with your success—impressive as it is. I think I can offer you the perfect solution to your dilemma." His clear gray gaze held hers across the candlelit table. "Come and work for me, Lily."

Five years ago Lily would have revealed herself by dropping her jaw or gaping at him in surprise. Now she managed an intelligently thoughtful expression and reached for her coffee cup.

So, she thought as she took a sip, it wasn't a real date after all. His ulterior motives were professional rather than romantic. She might have been disappointed if his motives weren't also so intriguing.

"I won't waste your time talking salary," he went on. "Just know that I'll top whatever Bonatelli offers. But I can also give you what he can't, a showcase for your own designs and total freedom to pursue them. We can work out the details to your satisfaction," he promised, the wave of his hand indicating that it was a minor point. "At Goddard's at least half of your time would be exclusively devoted to your own work...probably more as time goes on."

"And the other half?" she asked, hooked.

"John Lancing will be retiring in six months. Everyone assumes I'll be selecting a new design director from in-house, but I won't. I want you, Lily."

So much for appearing sophisticated, she thought, openly astonished. The design director was responsible for overseeing every detail of a store's image, from the window displays to the color of the wrapping paper. "Are you serious?"

"Absolutely serious."

"Drew, I'm stunned...and very flattered, and I have to confess I'm also feeling a sense of déjà vu. Here I am crying on your shoulder about my problems, and the next thing I know you're charging to the rescue. Just like last time."

"Not exactly." He straightened his glasses. It was the first time Lily had ever seen him look the least bit awkward, almost sheepish. "You see, Lily, the last time you were the one who needed my help. Now I need yours."

TWENTY-EIGHT

Shock waves rippled through the local business community when it was announced that Lily would be Goddard's new design director. In spite of her achievements at Tellis, the facts that she was a woman, not quite thirty-five years old and from outside the closed world of fine jewelry design made her a surprising and therefore newsworthy choice. The public reaction, however, was nothing compared to the seismic quake that resulted within the Goddard family.

Drew's older sisters, Anne and Elise, did not share his conviction that Lily was the person to lead Goddard's in a new direction, mainly because they saw nothing wrong with its current direction, the same tried and true route that had been followed since Goddards had been founded.

Drew arranged a small dinner party so that Lily and his sisters could meet and exchange ideas. In spite of Lily's best efforts to win them over, disaster was in the air from the start. Both women were considerably older than Drew, whom Lily had discovered was in his mid-fifties. Clad in look-alike silk brocade and pearls. Anne and Elise were a walking advertisement for the Goddard's of yesterday, the Goddard's Lily was going to help take apart and put back together.

Over a dinner of grilled salmon and wild rice, which she hardly tasted, Lily turned on the charm to convince them that she understood the Goddard mystique and wanted only to enhance it. Her efforts were met with sugar-coated disdain as solid as the cornerstone of the family's flagship store downtown.

"Goddard's," Anne announced, patting her lips with a napkin and accompanied by her sister's vigorous nod of agreement, "is perfectly fine just as it is."

"The recent sales figures Drew showed me suggest otherwise," Lily pointed out as gently as possible.

Both older women shot Drew a look of daggers, as if he'd shared with Lily the family's dirty linen.

"Lily is right," he said simply, relaxed and confident as always. "Things are not fine. Things are sliding downhill and getting worse every quarter. We need help to turn that around. We need Lily."

The sisters huffed and looked indignant, but the fact that Drew wasn't in the least intimidated by them bolstered Lily's courage.

"What we have to realize," she continued, "is that Goddard's traditional customers are aging. To put it bluntly, they're dying off, and dead people don't buy jewelry."

"People die, people are born," snapped Anne. "Goddard's goes on."

"Not for long, unless it begins to attract a new breed of buyer. Like it or not, that will require substantial changes in both the look of the stores and merchandising strategy."

"Goddard's has survived quite nicely without your help for nearly a hundred years," Elise told her.

"Times have changed," Lily insisted quietly. "Women no longer sit on the sidelines and wait for men to buy them jewelry. They buy it and pay for it themselves. We have to make Goddard's a place where those women feel comfortable."

"Women like you, you mean?" inquired Anne, her thin smile doing nothing to dilute the undertone of contempt in her voice.

Lily felt Drew tense for the first time that evening. He leaned forward, but before he had a chance to speak in her defense, she locked gazes with Anne Goddard. "Exactly like me," she said.

The sisters, as Lily had come to think of them, as if they were a two-headed monster, left abruptly, before dessert was even served. Lily accepted that they would probably never approve of her and were only going along with her appointment out of deference to the younger brother they adored. The fact remained that Drew had brought her aboard to make dramatic changes, not to preserve the status quo.

Still, as she took the microphone at the press conference announcing her new position, she knew that what she had to say was tantamount to waving a red flag in front of the two women who legally controlled two-thirds of the business.

Anne and Elise sat in the front row. For the sake of her own nerves, Lily sent a warm smile their way then steadfastly ignored their icy, disapproving expressions. Instead she played to the assemblage of press and Goddard employees, a mixture of supporters and skeptics.

She told of how she had grown up peering wistfully into the windows of Goddard's, first standing on tiptoes and eventually being old enough to be taken inside without getting fingerprints all over the glass display cases. Goddard's was the grand dame of downtown Providence, she declared, but then acknowledged that in recent years it had earned a reputation for being stodgy, expensive and intimidating.

"So you want to make it more middle of the road? More accessible?" asked a young reporter, playing right into Lily's hands.

"Oh, no," she retorted with a mixture of reverence and humor. "I want to make Goddard's what it used to be...*exciting* and expensive and intimidating!"

Lily officially joined the Goddard ranks in January 1988 and over the next several years she did exactly what she said she would do—with Drew's full cooperation. He not only welcomed but expected Lily's input in every phase of Goddard's overhaul. They worked well together, the twenty-two year difference in their ages more of a help than a hindrance. Drew's experience and her freshness and creativity made a winning combination, and from the start their contrasting styles meshed in a way that made working together fun.

Drew was naturally thoughtful and analytical, a trusty anchor who made it safe for Lily to unleash the impulsive nature she'd had to keep so tightly reined for so long. At least professionally. There was no such trusty safety net in her personal life—what personal life she had time for, that is—and Lily proceeded accordingly. The long, hard hours she worked these days made her tough schedule at Tellis seem like a vacation.

Early on she suggested that Drew consider paring down the number of stores in the Goddard group. He studied the financial impact and overrode strong family opposition to reduce the number of stores from nine to four, keeping open those in downtown Providence and on the city's East Side, along with the branches in Newport and Watch Hill.

The surviving stores were then completely redesigned, one at a time, each on a six-month schedule Lily was adamant about sticking to. She ate, slept and breathed Goddard's, coordinating the work of in-house designers, buyers and architects to achieve the perfect balance of old and new. The original mahogany and brass display cases remained, but within a new, meticulously crafted world of glass and light, where everything from the crystal chandeliers to the trademark fragrance in the air was chosen to enhance the atmosphere of elegance and splendor.

She was even more painstaking in deciding what would go into those time-honored cases, going through the entire inventory piece by piece, weeding out the misconceived and unremarkable and just plain tacky. What remained in every department, from precious gems to the bridal registry, were designs that were truly timeless, traditional pieces and one-of-a-kind masterpieces, along with the very best work of contemporary designers, both local and struggling and internationally famous.

Although Lily had been behind the scenes to see the magical transformation unfold, when she stepped into the downtown store each morning her reaction was the same as when she'd been a little girl entering Goddard's for the very first time. Her eyes widened and her pulse raced in anticipation at the sight of the treasures nestled in the sparkling glass cases. She wasn't the only one who felt that way. These days Goddard's was once again known as *the* place to shop for the absolutely perfect gift.

Drew had given Lily her choice of territory, and she'd commandeered an unused corner storeroom on the top floor of the downtown store. Bright and airy, it was part office, part workshop and all comfortable clutter of the sort that inspired her best work. Today she was holed up there with photos and copy for the Christmas catalogue.

A knock sounded on the closed door a second before Drew pushed it open.

"Hi, how's it going?" he asked.

"It's not. I don't think I'm ever going to get used to thinking Christmas in May. Cover shot," she said, holding up two photographs, the first of a diamond and ruby necklace and ear clips that were an exclusive Goddard's design, the other a close-up of a royal blue satin bow, the store's trademark for over half a century, laced with a single strand of perfect, blue-white diamonds. "What do you think?"

Drew glanced from one to the other. "The diamonds," he said, pointing to the second photo.

Lily looked at it closely. "You're right. Only fifty pages to go."

"Does that mean you will or will not be able to have lunch with me?"

Lily chuckled. "Sorry, Drew. I swore on my life that I'd have all this back to advertising before I left this afternoon. I'll be lucky if I have time to grab a sandwich at my desk."

"How did I know you were going to say that?" he asked teasingly as he stepped into the room. Lily saw that in the hand that had been hidden by the door, he was holding a bag from the deli down the street. "Turkey on whole wheat for you," he said, placing a sandwich on the desk before her. "Roast beef on rye for me."

"Thanks, you're a lifesaver," she said, opening and taking a sip of the soda he'd brought her and nibbling at a corner of her sandwich while Drew bit wholeheartedly into his.

He peered at her quizzically and swallowed. "Nervous about this afternoon?"

"Why should I be? We've been through this three times already."

"Yes, but this is the first time the opening of one of the stores will feature a showing of your designs."

Lily managed a shrug and another small bite. In the past, if she'd had one complaint about her work at Goddard's it was that with all her other responsibilities, the time promised for her own designs never materialized. It wasn't Drew's fault—only so many hours could be squeezed out of a day, and besides, Lily loved her work as design director. She never complained.

As it turned out, she didn't have to. One morning about six months ago, Drew strode into her office and decreed that he didn't care who she had to hire, promote or bully to take up the slack, but from that day on she was to give top priority to her own work. When Lily protested that he was asking the impossible, he explained that it wasn't a request. He intended to make her work the centerpiece of the Watch Hill opening, and he expected her to be ready. She continued to protest, but secretly she was excited and very grateful for the intuitive link that enabled Drew to deduce the secrets of her heart.

She had obediently hired, promoted and bullied, and for the first time in her life enjoyed total freedom to turn the glittering, sparkling fantasies in her head into reality. This time Lily had free rein in design, execution and materials. The premiere Saville collection offered no compromises, no cut corners and no excuses. Later this afternoon it would be seen for the first time at an invitation-only champagne reception at the Goddard's store just a few miles from where she'd grown up. For Lily, it would be a personal moment of truth. And Drew was right; she *was* nervous.

"Are you going to eat your pickle?"

She shook her head. "Too salty."

"You sound like Anne," he observed, popping it into his mouth.

"I do not. Anne would have reminded you that salt is bad for your blood pressure. And is that mayonnaise I see?" she continued, slipping into a nasal, disapproving tone reminiscent of his sister's. "Tch, tch. You know that's bad for your heart. And so is the caffeine in the cola. Then there's me," she concluded, dropping the impression. "Just plain all-round bad for you."

Drew's warm gray gaze caressed her. "You are the best thing that's happened to me, and my heart, in a very long time."

"That's not what your sisters say."

He shrugged. "Let me worry about them."

The fact was, he didn't worry about them, or their opinions, at all. From the start Lily had been impressed by his air of utter self-confidence. She'd attributed it to wealth or maturity, but the longer she knew him, the more she realized it was simply his nature.

He'd told her of being sick with a rheumatic heart for most of his childhood, of how he'd waited day after day, summer after summer, to be able to swim and fish and run with the other kids. Maybe that's where he developed such serene acceptance of things he couldn't change. If a crucial delivery was late or an important order botched up, Lily might fume and fret. Drew simply shrugged and directed whoever was responsible to handle it.

It was the same with his sisters. As far as he was concerned their opinions were just that, their opinions. His attitude took a lot of heat off Lily, since Anne and Elise's opinion of her only seemed to get worse. They had tolerated her as a purely professional threat. But as she and Drew worked closely together, their relationship had gradually shifted.

During late nights and long lunches spent poring over blueprints or design sketches, the line between business and pleasure had steadily blurred. They'd become friends. Close friends. And the closer they became, the less the sisters liked her.

Speculation over exactly how close they were existed outside the Goddard family, as well. Lily's co-workers wondered, her family wondered, and though he never pressed her, she knew that at times Drew wondered, as well, and that he grew restless for more than the gentle kisses and caresses they'd shared so far. Only she was content to let things roll along as they were, undemanding and undefined.

"I've been thinking about your idea," Drew said, drawing Lily from her own thoughts. "About the museum piece reproductions."

"And?" Lily countered. Several weeks ago she'd suggested the possibility of designing a line of dressing table items to coincide with an exhibit of Victorian silver planned by the RISD museum.

"And I definitely think we should give it a shot."

"We'll have to move fast. The exhibit is scheduled for early spring. I think the publicity we stand to get out of it will make it well worth the rush. Besides, I can free up some more time after today."

Drew shook his head. "Your work comes first."

"This was my idea, remember? I want to be involved. I already have sketches for some possible pieces—old-fashioned powder pots and hand mirrors. And Maggie Pearson gave me the names of a couple of free-lancers in New York City I think will be perfect for a project like this."

"Great, why don't we go down there and check them out personally?"

"Just let me know when you're free."

"How about this weekend?" Drew countered, getting to his feet. He stood with his hip resting against her desk, his hands in the pockets of his pleated trousers. "I have to meet with a wholesaler there anyway, and you mentioned that you'd like to see the new Neil Simon play."

"You mean stay overnight?" asked Lily, an ominous thumping starting up in her chest.

"Would that be so bad, Lily?"

For a second, no longer, he let the full weight of the question in his eyes rest on her. Then he straightened, his easy smile in place. "Think about it. And think about where you'd like to have dinner later tonight," he said, leaning down to brush a quick kiss across her lips. "I have a feeling you're going to be very hungry," he added, slanting a wry look at the sandwich she'd barely touched.

As the door closed behind him, Lily sank more deeply into her chair, her head thrown back as she studied the plain white ceiling. Just her luck. Two moments of truth in the same day.

For some time now she'd been aware that Drew was waiting for a signal from her to move their relationship to the next level. Patient as he was, had she really expected him to wait forever? Of course, Lily knew that if she declined his invitation, or if she went along and requested separate rooms, Drew would accept her decision like a gentleman. She also knew that he deserved better.

Kneading the knot that had formed between her eyebrows, Lily tried unsuccessfully to return her attention to the photos strewn across her desk. Instead, the same question kept flashing before her, as relentless as a caution light warning of trouble ahead. What was she going to do?

Her relationship with Drew was one of tenderness and humor and honesty. With Drew as her escort she did all the things she'd always dreamed of doing. She attended the theater and the ballet, accompanied him to parties at houses on the historical register and private dinners for senators. At the same time, Drew's wry insight made her aware of flaws and pitfalls in that glamorous world that weren't obvious to an outsider looking in. He introduced Lily to a new way of looking at life, and of living it. He made her think and laugh and feel alive in unexpected ways. With Drew she felt cherished and safe.

The one thing she never felt was passion, that raw, overwhelming rush toward pleasure she had experienced only once, that long-ago night when she gave herself to Jack Terrell. Lily told herself she didn't miss it, that she preferred the milder, controllable brand of pleasure she felt when Drew took her into his arms. Being in control was very important to her.

And if longings that were sleeping deep inside her ever did threaten to quiver to life, she simply reminded herself of what that one night with Jack had cost her. The heartache, the sacrifice, the guilt. As far as Lily was concerned, the only safe surrender to passion took place within the pages of a novel, where a happy ending was guaranteed. She wanted no part of it in her own life.

Now all she had to worry about was what Drew wanted.

TWENTY-NINE

Kay's plan was to go directly from the airport to the office, but a quick glance at her watch told her that was out of the question if she wanted to make it to Lily's reception. For once, business would have to wait.

Not that she was in the mood for socializing, she thought, as she instructed the driver to go directly to Goddard's in Watch Hill. Throughout the long flight from Japan she had volleyed between restless naps and seething anger. Now she was operating in an agitated state somewhere beyond exhaustion, and her temper was growing shorter the closer she got to its target. James. Again.

She would be content to have him draw his salary and stay away from Delaney Silver, but not James. Oh, no. He enjoyed being the fly in her ointment. This time, however, he'd gone too far.

She had taken control of the company at the threshold of the most difficult period in its history. Inflated silver price and lifestyle changes begun in the sixties combined to give sterling silver a bad name. Sales to new brides, historically the core of Delaney's profits, plummeted as silver gained a reputation for being only for the fabulously wealthy or hopelessly old-fashioned.

To succeed, she'd had to develop into a smart, hardheaded businesswoman in a hurry, cutting costs and demanding efficiency. Kay doubted anyone would still describe her as they once had, as warm and easygoing, and she didn't particularly care. Sure, she'd lost friends along the way, but she had managed to hold Delaney Silver's head above water. That's what counted.

Holding the line had been a challenge, to say the least, but the price of silver had finally stabilized, and the social pendulum was slowly but surely swinging toward more elegance and formality. Even so, to flourish as it had in the past, Delaney Silver needed to develop new markets and new products. The most promising of those new markets was Japan, and now, because of James's petty one-upmanship, she was forced to choose between expansion she desperately needed and the dignity of the Delaney name.

Just thinking about it fired Kay's anger until she felt that if she had to wait until after the reception to confront James she would explode. Reaching for the car phone, she punched out the office number and waited for the call to go through.

"Janet," she said when his secretary answered, "let me speak with my husband, please."

"I'm sorry, Mrs. Terrell," she replied. "Mr. Terrell has left for the day. May I take a—"

"No." Kay cut her off. "Thank you."

She slammed down the receiver, still fuming. It wasn't even five o'clock, she was away from the office on business, and the company's top vice president, at least in title, had already left for the day. Kay knew that if she really wanted him, she could find James at the club bar. But it had been years since she'd wanted him.

As they drew closer to Watch Hill, she pulled her compact from her purse and freshened her makeup, forcing herself to calm down. After all, this was a big day for Lily, and Kay didn't want to spoil it.

Through the years, Kay had done all she could to help the Saville family. Subtly, of course, so that no one would suspect the truth—that every cent she gave them was blood money. But Lily had never needed help, Kay's or anyone else's, Kay thought with admiration. Lily had done it on her own, and the least Kay could do was acknowledge her triumph. That was her reason for rushing back especially to attend the reception, to show support for Lily.

Really? probed a small inner voice. Was she really going to support Lily? Or to see Drew?

Drew. Closing her eyes, Kay snapped the cover on her lipstick and inhaled deeply. It didn't help. Fresh air was no better than time had been at washing away the ache inside. As the car drew to a halt in front of Goddard's dark blue canopied entrance, she ran her hand over her hair, wishing it was as easy to smooth her emotions.

One of these days, she promised herself, she was going to be able to walk into a room and see Drew and feel nothing more than affection for a dear old friend. The driver hurried to help her out and she entered the store, which was already crowded with dozens of well-wishers. It could have been thousands, and still, like sand driven through a funnel, her gaze would have been drawn directly to Drew.

He was across the room, talking to a woman Kay didn't recognize. When he happened to glance over and see her, his eyes ignited and she knew he momentarily lost his train of thought. She knew because it had happened so often to her in just the same way.

Yes, Kay promised herself, one of these days she would get over all this for good. She would grow too old for a racing heart and impossible desires. One of these days. But not today.

As soon as she saw Kay walk in, Lily began making her way toward her. She'd hoped Kay would come. After all these years, Kay Terrell was still her role model. As far as Lily was concerned, she had it all, family, career and friends, as well as style and grace. Lily envied her.

Her own life looked happy and successful enough, and it was, in a way. But she didn't need her mother's frequent reminders to know there was a black hole at the heart of it. There was a time when she'd blithely assumed that someday she would have the loving husband and perfect children her mother nagged about.

That was followed by a time when, to avoid painful memories, she'd lumped all those aspirations under the heading Future Plans and avoided thinking about them. She was too busy getting ahead, making a name for herself, proving what she had to prove. The more settled her career became, however, the harder it was to ignore what was missing in her personal life.

There was no denying that Drew was the perfect man for her. He was attractive and intelligent and more fun to be with than most men she'd dated who were closer to her age. The two of them had everything in common. In fact, being with Drew was as comfortable as being alone. And he was a great catch—no less an authority on the subject than her mother had said so. Where Drew was concerned, Mary seemed to lose her fear that Lily was going to be chewed up and spit out by the upper class. He was perfect. So why wasn't she jumping at the chance to seal their relationship? What was wrong with her?

Each time Lily took a few steps in Kay's direction, someone in the exuberant crowd stopped her to offer congratulations. If this small sampling was any indication, her earlier jitters had been for nothing. Her designs were a success. Now, as the champagne began to hit its mark, she regretted not eating more at lunch.

It was probably the champagne that made her blink and question her own eyesight when she saw her mother, wearing a hesitant expression as she stood in the raised foyer that overlooked the store. Lily felt a rush of excitement, followed quickly by another feeling, one she was ashamed to acknowledge and that kept her momentarily rooted where she was.

She had sent her mother a formal invitation to the reception, entertaining Drew with the story of how she had immediately displayed it beside a half dozen of her grandchildren's drawings, in the family's traditional place of honor, the refrigerator door.

"That's terrific," he'd said, leaning back in the big swivel chair in his office. Lily stood with her hip resting on the corner of his desk. "So she's coming?" he asked her.

Lily shook her head. "She said 'We'll see,' but that usually means no."

"Doesn't she realize that the reception is in your honor?"

"Yes, and she ran through her usual litany of excuses. She won't fit in, she won't know anyone there, she doesn't have anything to wear."

"She'll know us, and I'll buy her a new dress—hell, I'll buy her the whole damn store so she'll have her pick."

"I already offered. She refused. She said the last time she let me take her shopping she ended up with a fur-trimmed cashmere coat, and Lord knows she has no place to wear a thing like that."

"Well, now she does," Drew had countered, grinning and reaching for the telephone. "I'm going to call and tell her so."

"No," Lily said, surprising herself with her sudden vehemence. Drew cocked an eyebrow. "I mean, I'll call her myself. Later. I think she's more likely to agree if I talk to her."

"Whatever you say," Drew replied.

He'd smiled at her as he replaced the receiver, but something in his eyes told Lily that he saw what she was trying so hard to hide even from herself. As much as she wanted her mother to come, she was also afraid. Afraid that Mary would show up wearing a housedress beneath the new cashmere coat or that she would say or do something wrong, something that would call attention to herself and expose the fact that she didn't really belong there. And that maybe Lily didn't, either.

Sometimes Lily's chest tightened with fear that maybe the designer clothes and all the other trappings of success were just an elaborate facade; that the years of hard work and sacrifice didn't count the way she wanted them to. Fear that it could all end tomorrow, disappear, and she'd be right back where she started. Nothing proved, nothing resolved.

God, what a moment to be standing there worrying about that. Struggling to put her own feelings aside, she hurried to greet her mother. In spite of what she always told Lily about not being able to make a silk purse from a sow's ear, it was obvious how hard Mary had tried today. She'd had her hair done and was wearing a new red silk print dress and clutching a red leather purse as if it was a lifeline. Even her shoes matched, Lily noted happily.

Suddenly she saw her mother's nervous expression erupt into a smile of genuine pleasure as Drew appeared at her side. He kissed her cheek and leaned closer to whisper in her ear, something charming, Lily could tell by the way her levelheaded mother blushed and turned her head away like a schoolgirl. For an instant she looked as young and pretty as she did in old photos, and a rush of affection for Drew added to the emotions churning inside Lily.

"Mom, why didn't you tell me you were coming?" she exclaimed, joining them and gathering her mother in a quick hug.

"Well, it was a last-minute sort of thing, really," Mary explained. "When Drew called and told me how much it would mean to you and how important a day this was, well, I just knew I had to be here."

Lily's smile to Drew was grateful. "I'm so happy you are," she told her mother. "And you look absolutely beautiful."

"You really think so?" Mary asked, fussing with the way the softly pleated skirt fell over her hips. "I didn't have the first idea about what to wear to a thing like this, but Drew told me where his sisters shop and the woman there was real nice. She said this dress was me."

"She was right. You look great in red."

"But red shoes, too?" her mother countered with a flustered shake of her head that couldn't disguise her pleasure in them. "At my age?"

"Age is a state of mind," Drew said. "Come on and I'll prove it to you." He took her mother's hand and folded it over his bent arm. "I want you to meet a very, very old friend of mine."

She hung back. "Oh, I don't know. Maybe I'll just stand here and chat with Lily for a bit."

"Lily's the guest of honor," he countered. "She has to circulate. And so do you. You two can chat to your heart's content later, when you join us for dinner. Now come with me."

With a helpless glance at Lily, Mary allowed Drew to lead her away.

As she watched them go, Lily's anxiety quieted. Her mother was in good hands, she thought. Maybe they both were. Content, she rejoined the fray, circulating as Drew had instructed. The invitations had specified three to six, and as six o'clock approached, the crowd began to thin. Eventually Lily found herself beside Kay Terrell, who was admiring some of her designs that combined silver with the bright pink and soft bluegray tourmaline mined in New England.

"Hello, Kay," she said. "I'm so glad you could make it."

Kay looked up and smiled. "Lily. I wouldn't have missed it for the world."

"Someone mentioned that you were in Japan on business."

"I was. As a matter of fact I came straight here from the airport. Which explains the wrinkles," she added with a rueful glance at her coral linen suit.

"Wrinkles add character," Lily teased. "You look terrific, as always . . . just a little tired." In spite of Kay's meticulously upswept blond hair and the narrow-fitting skirt that made it clear she still had an enviable figure, Lily was conscious for the first time that Kay was the same age as her mother.

"I am a little tired," Kay confessed. "It was a trying trip."

"But a successful one, I hope?"

She grimaced. "Don't even ask."

For a split second her expression softened and Lily saw that Kay was beyond tired. Once, on her way to work, she had seen an elderly bag lady chasing a piece of newspaper. She'd almost caught up to it when a gust of wind carried it up and over the interstate on ramp, out of reach. Lily would never forget the old woman's face as she stood and watched until it was out of sight. Her expression had been as bleak and disappointed as if the wind had stolen from her a million-dollar check instead of yesterday's newspaper. Everything was relative, of course, but that was how Kay looked now.

Instinctively Lily reached out to touch her hand. "Kay, is everything all right?"

"Of course," Kay replied, smiling, herself once again. "Just the usual business worries. Oh, Lily, I do envy Drew. He was a wise man to choose you for Goddard's, and you are a brilliantly talented lady. Which is why we should be talking about you, instead of me and my problems. Your work is exquisite, Lily. Congratulations... once again. Tell me, do you ever get tired of hearing that?"

"Truthfully? Never."

"Everything you've done is gorgeous, but I have to confess I especially love your silver pieces."

As Kay pointed out several of her favorites, Lily couldn't help noticing the heavy silver bracelet she was wearing. "What a great bracelet," she exclaimed. "Other people's charms have always fascinated me. Like photo albums. May I take a closer look?"

Chuckling, Kay obligingly lifted her wrist so Lily could examine the dozen or so sterling silver charms dangling from it.

One glance told Lily that these were no mass-produced costume pieces. There was a tiny, perfect Statue of Liberty, a jewel-encrusted camel and a delicate rococo magnifying eyeglass, its frame made of intertwined gold and silver wires threaded with pearls.

"I know charm bracelets are out of style," Kay said, "but this has great sentimental value. I always find myself reaching for it on days when I think I'm going to need an emotional lift."

Lily nodded, thinking that each of the charms probably represented a story worth hearing. "They're beautifully cast," she said, "and so unusual."

"Some of them were my mother's. That one is my favorite," she added as Lily fingered a nickel-sized medallion, stamped with the image of a ship between two castles.

"It looks like a crest of some sort."

"Actually it's a town mark dating back to 1631."

"Really?" Lily countered, even more fascinated. She recalled that at one time silversmiths throughout Europe had used a town mark, along with their own initials, to identify where and by whom a piece was made.

"It's from Cork, in Ireland," Kay explained, "The Delaneys were silversmiths there for generations before coming to this country. In America it was customary to use only a marker's mark and so it was dropped along the way, but it's lovely, don't you think?"

"Beautiful."

"Originally the charm was one of a pair of cuff links belonging to my great-grandfather and handed down from father to son. That seemed quite unfair to me," she told Lily with a smile, "so to please me, my father had the links made into medallions so my brother and I could each have one. Ted always wore his on a chain around his neck," she said, her smile fading into a faraway look.

Lily knew little about Ted Delaney other than that he had been Drew's best friend and that he had been killed years ago, in the Korean War. "I can see why the bracelet is so special to you," she told Kay gently. "My favorite piece of jewelry is a locket that..."

The sound of raised voices interrupted, drawing their attention to the entrance where the security guard was evidently having a bit of difficulty.

"The store is closed to the public," he said firmly to someone standing just out of their vision. Someone who was obviously moving forward as quickly as the uniformed guard was backing up. "Since you don't have an invitation, I'm sorry, but—"

"No need to be sorry, pal," Lily heard the intruder reply. "It's not your fault I wasn't invited."

Glancing around, Lily saw Drew moving toward the entrance, but she was closer and got there first.

She hurried up several carpeted steps to the foyer. "What seems to be the problem?"

"Me. I'm the problem."

Lily gasped as the very last person in the world she expected to see stepped from the shadows. He smiled at her, and the floor beneath her shook.

"Hello, Lily."

THIRTY

Lily heard herself whisper, "Jack."

"In the flesh. Such as it is," he added, executing the sardonic shrug she hadn't seen in almost twenty years. "You want to do me a favor and tell my friend here that I don't need an invitation?"

"Of course . . ."

But she didn't have to tell anyone anything. Time hadn't stopped around them. It had only felt that way for a few seconds as every nerve ending in her body flashed the message that Jack was standing right there, close enough to touch. Right on cue, Lily's pulse raced, and tingles that she was too old and too damn smart to feel spread from her spine all the way to her fingertips and toes. Snap out of it, she told herself, this was 1991, not 1971, and she was thirty-seven, not seventeen. It didn't help.

His presence was palpable, charging the air around her like an impending storm. She was sure she must be gaping at him like a kid encountering Santa Claus for the first time. No one seemed to notice. Numbly, she became aware that Drew was busy explaining matters to the guard and that Kay was laughing and crying as she hugged Jack.

Over Kay's shoulder, Jack's gaze kept sliding to Lily. *He looks the way I feel,* she thought shakily, *like he's dreaming and afraid he might wake up.*

Most of the handful of remaining guests were locals who knew Jack. They shared Kay's joy, grinning and laughing as they gathered around to clap Jack on the back and welcome him home. Lily stayed on the fringes of the group, unable to move. She'd finally figured out that the floor wasn't trembling, her legs were. It seemed safer to simply stay put.

As each guest left, however, a little bit of the human safety barrier between her and Jack was chipped away. Get a grip, she told herself over and over, her thoughts a dangerous jumble. She wasn't aware her mother was beside her until she squeezed her arm.

"Are you all right, honey? You look so pale."

"I'm fine," Lily said, struggling to smile. "It's just a surprise to see Jack after all this time."

"Yes," her mother agreed, worry lines fanning across her forehead. "A big surprise. I'm happy for his mother."

"Me, too. Very happy."

"You're sure there's nothing else bothering you?" she persisted.

Lily shook her head. "Not a thing. I'm just a little tired. It's been a long day, with the excitement and all."

"But if there was something, you'd tell me?"

"Of course," Lily lied.

Her mother eyed her dubiously. "I hope so. Well, as long as you say you're all right, I'm going to slip out now."

"But Drew's expecting you to join us for dinner," Lily reminded her. "I know he'll be disappointed."

"And I know the poor man would much rather spend time alone with you. Don't argue. Mothers know these things. You have a good time, and don't stay out too late. And..." She hesitated, clutching Lily's arm. "Just be careful, honey."

Outside Goddard's, Mary gulped the crisp evening air and pressed her hand to her lungs as if she could deflate the balloon of fear lodged there. She'd had to get out of there before someone noticed how upset she was and asked why. There was no way she could tell anyone. Just as there was no way she could have managed dinner with Lily and Drew. Her chest felt so tight that if she tried to eat, she'd choke. Since her heart attack the doctor had told her to avoid stressful situations and thoughts, but that was impossible tonight. All she could think about right now was Jack Terrell and how easily he had turned Lily's head years ago.

But Lily was older now, Mary reassured herself a little desperately, and a whole lot smarter. And she had Drew Goddard. It had been obvious for months now that Drew was interested in Lily for more than business reasons. At first Mary had been worried because he was Lily's boss and so much older, but the two of them had stopped by a time or two recently, just to visit when they were down here working on the Watch Hill store, and she'd changed her mind about him. There was something about Drew that Mary liked and trusted.

Definitely in this case he was the lesser of two evils. So what if Jack Terrell wasn't a Terrell by blood? If he tried to pick up things where they broke off nearly twenty years ago, it could mean big trouble for Lily. For all of them.

Kay had finally released Jack, stepping back to look him over with a mother's watchful adoration, as if she couldn't believe he was really here. That made two of them, thought Lily, studying him just as intently, but with very different points of reference.

In some ways he was the same. The same single dimple slashed his right cheek, and his eyes were still the same unbelievable blue. But there were changes, too. His shoulders were broader inside the tweed jacket he wore over black jeans, his build more solid, a man's build; his dark hair was cut shorter. And there was something else. Something not so easy to decipher, but that nagged at Lily's senses like a crooked picture on a crooked wall.

"You should have told me you were coming home," Kay admonished him.

"I thought you liked surprises," he replied, his chuckle drifting through the cluster of people, stirring more memories than Lily could handle.

"But I see now that I should have warned you," he continued. "I've been sitting in a hospital in Germany, hearing stories about the yellow ribbons and red-carpet welcome Gulf vets get when they make it home. Nobody mentioned that you needed an invitation."

"Hospital?" Kay echoed, ignoring his teasing. "What hosp— Jack, is that a cane you're holding? What happened? Why were you in a hospital in the first place? And why on earth wasn't I informed?"

"It's a cane, all right," he answered, tossing it up and catching it, turning it as he would turn a diamond to reveal its hidden facets. "A beauty, too, don't you think? Hand-carved black hickory. I need it because my rehabilitation wasn't quite finished when I decided I had to get out of that place or go crazy. As for why you weren't told..."

Gazing over the crowd from her vantage point on the steps, Lily bit her lip at the tenderness in the sheepish smile he directed at his mother.

"I warned them not to," he confessed.

"But why?"

"Because of that look that's on your face right this minute." He touched her cheek lightly. "I didn't want to worry you."

Kay shook her head. "Worrying is a mother's prerogative. Don't you know that?"

"Sure. I also knew that no matter what anyone said, you'd have to see for yourself that I was still alive and kicking. You'd have been over there on the next flight, taking charge, turning the place upside down and inside out, probably wanting to move me back here."

"Without a doubt."

"I'd already made up my mind I wasn't coming back until I could walk in under my own power."

"Walk?" Kay pressed her fingers to her throat. "My God, Jack, how badly were you hurt?"

He flashed a negligent grin. "I've got a few nuts and bolts holding me together, but at least the pieces are all there." He sobered, looking directly at Kay. "Really. I'm fine. Now is this a party or not?"

"It *was* a party," Kay said, glancing around the nearly empty room. "Your timing was just a little off."

"Not at all," corrected Drew, stepping forward to shake Jack's hand. "We might not have any yellow ribbons or red carpets, but there's plenty of food and champagne. The party can go on in your honor... All night, if you're up to it. Welcome home, Jack."

"Thanks, Drew. It's good to be here, even though I do seem to have chased away most of the guests." Even as he said it the last of them said goodbye and departed, leaving the four of them alone with the catering staff and employees already swinging into action to clean things up.

"It's just as well," Kay said. "We have a lot of catching up to do. You don't really think I'm going to be satisfied with that half-baked explanation of what happened to you, do you?"

"No," said Jack, "but I had sort of hoped maybe you'd feed me before the inquisition. The flight meal was something called Chicken Surprise. I abstained."

"Sounds like one of the club's steaks is in order," Kay said with a laugh. "No, on second thought someplace quieter would be better; someplace where I won't have to share you. Why don't the four of us go to the Inn?" she suggested, naming a quiet place only a short distance away.

"Sounds good to me," Jack replied.

Drew glanced questioningly at Lily.

"I'm sorry," she said, with an awkward laugh. She wasn't sure how she was going to get out of going to dinner with Jack, or why, only that she had to. "I'm really pretty tired. It's been a long day. Besides, this should be a time for family."

"But we want you to come along," Kay insisted. "Don't we, Jack?"

"Very much," he said, his gaze riveted on Lily, as unblinking as a kid's in the front row of a magic show.

"Thank you, but I really do have to beg off." She turned to Drew. "You go along, if you like. I can grab a cab to my mother's and spend the night there."

"Nonsense. You're right all the way around; it has been a long day, and family reunions are for family."

Beneath her thin smile, Kay looked disappointed, forlorn even, it seemed to Lily. Jack, on the other hand, looked as smug as the man who'd guessed the correct number of jelly beans in the five-gallon jug. *Coward,* his unblinking gaze taunted. Lily felt the heat of it on her back as she and Drew walked toward his car.

The look was intentional. And it was only the beginning, Jack thought with anticipation. Not until they were safely out of earshot did he speak. Without taking his eyes off them, he said, "So, that's the way it is."

"What way?"

He glanced briefly at his mother's quizzical frown, wondering if she was purposely playing dumb. "Lily and Drew. They seem pretty chummy."

"Don't be ridiculous," she chided with a brittle laugh. "Drew is Lily's mentor, and old enough to be her father, I might add."

"Yeah, well, maybe that's the attraction."

"What's that supposed to mean?"

Jack shook his head. He felt wasted, like he'd just run the longest race of his life only to discover it wasn't a race at all, that there was no finish line, no victory, no prize. Had he really run all this way for nothing?

His leg throbbed, and his back felt like it was on fire. He wanted to lie down, preferably with a quart of Scotch. A small part of him, a part that he'd spent years trying to destroy, wanted to cry.

He was about to say that he wasn't as hungry as he'd thought when he noticed that, for some reason he couldn't fathom, his mother seemed to be fighting her own battle to hold back tears. Maybe because his father hadn't shown up? He quickly dismissed the idea. True, his visits home were sporadic, but they were enough to clue him in to how that scene had played out. On the home front and at Delaney Silver, the balance of power had shifted to his mother. He'd venture it had been a long time since she'd wasted tears on James Terrell.

Then why her sad expression? He had no idea. He only knew that going home and tumbling into bed was out of the question. What the hell, he thought resignedly. He might not be able to cheer himself up tonight, but he'd bet the cane holding him upright that he could make her smile.

"Hey," he said, "how about that steak?"

"Hm?" She seemed obsessed with the disappearing taillights of Drew's Mercedes.

"My steak," he repeated. "That was our deal, right? You buy me a steak, and I tell you everything you want to know about the two years since I last saw you." As the corners of her mouth began to curl in anticipation, he added, "Within reason, that is."

The interior of the Mercedes was dark and well-insulated, no squeaks and rattles, no road turbulence. No distractions at all. Lily closed her eyes and surrendered to the smooth, steady drone of the engine, hoping it would put her to sleep.

No such luck. She could will her body to be still, but her mind was ignited and flashing like the Las Vegas strip. Thoughts blinking on and off, memories coming out of nowhere, insistent, Technicolor, dangerous memories.

Overshadowing them all, as feathery and dense as a down comforter, was the knowledge that Jack had returned. It hung over her mind, a question, a promise, a threat. Maybe it was whatever she wanted it to be, she thought frantically. So what did she want it to be? What did she really want?

The miserable truth was that she wasn't sure. After all this time she'd assumed she had put Jack, and all that had happened, behind her. She had given him up, paid her debt, lived with the heartache, accepted it, survived. Hell, she'd done better than survive. She'd made it. Proved what she had set out to prove. She was successful and respected and on the verge of seeing her ultimate dream become reality; very soon her jewelry would be featured in all four Goddard's stores, in private boutiques bearing her name.

And now, just by sauntering into a room, this man from her past had reduced her to adolescent-like jitters. The boneless, airy way she felt when Jack trapped her with his gaze was something she should have outgrown, but had not.

She didn't want to feel this way, damn it. Breathless and tingly and out of control. Not for anyone or anything, but especially not for Jack Terrell. On some purely instinctive level, she knew that Jack was the real price she'd had to pay for letting her father down. And she had paid it. It was a no-exchanges-no-returns deal. Jack was forbidden, off limits. It was right. Some things you just knew were right.

Knowing them evidently didn't mean the battle was over. Jack got to her. He always had. It was like he emitted some primal scent for which she possessed all the right genetic receptors. He walked into a room, and she got goose bumps. He stared; she trembled. He Tarzan; she Jane. It was ridiculous and frightening as hell.

If seeing Jack so briefly had this affect on her, she was scared to think what would happen if she had to sit next to him at dinner or make small talk or—heaven forbid—be alone with him.

She would avoid him, she decided. That was the easiest and safest solution. She would avoid him for however long his leave lasted.

It wouldn't be easy, she acknowledged, shifting restlessly in the contoured leather seat. She and Drew often ran into Kay socially. They were bound to run into Jack, as well, while he was here. There would probably be parties thrown in his honor. They would be invited. Next time it wouldn't be as easy for her to squirm off the hook as it had been tonight.

In fact, she thought anxiously, if Jack was feeling even a fraction of what she was, he wouldn't make it easy for her at all. She recalled the hard glint in his eyes, and how the cane had in no way detracted from his air of lethal power, sort of like a big cat asleep in its cage at the zoo. You still didn't go poking sticks through the bars. No, nothing about the way Jack had matured suggested he would be any more docile about taking no for an answer now than he had been twenty years ago. Like it or not, that thought triggered others that made Lily's heart skitter.

She folded her arms across her chest. She couldn't let this happen. She couldn't let Jack breeze into her life and scramble all her well-ordered emotions. That was precisely why she liked Drew so much. He fit into her life with the easiness of a stream flowing downhill, tumbling over and through the landscape, but leaving it basically undisturbed. Jack was more like rushing rapids, tearing things up, leaving a mark on everything in its path.

Once she had found the chaos he caused inside her tremendously exciting, but no longer. Things had changed. *She'd* changed. Drew was the right man for her now, she told herself once again, with the tenacity of a child trying to learn the multiplication tables. Say it over and over and it would eventually become second nature.

She turned her head and studied Drew's profile, etched in the dim glow from the highway lights, the solid line of his jaw, the way his hair would curl in the back if he ever permitted it to grow long enough. He visited his barber every other Wednesday afternoon at two. He was that predictable. And if he didn't set off fireworks for her, that only meant he would never let anything blow up in her face.

As if feeling the affectionate caress of her gaze, Drew turned his head to glance at her. "I thought you were sleeping."

"No, just thinking."

"Want a penny?"

Lily shook her head. "No, what I really want is to go home."

"What about dinner? Since you were resting I thought I'd drive straight to the city and we'd eat there."

"I'd rather skip dinner."

"You must be hungry."

"Not for dinner," she said with sudden vehemence.

Drew shot her a look that rapidly went from startled to incredulous to happy.

"I have some cheese and crackers at my place," she told him, "and a terrific chardonnay. Interested?"

"I haven't made any secret of how interested I am," he said, reaching for her hand. "But, Lily, I wasn't trying to push you into anything by asking you to come to New York with me. You know—"

"Shh," she said, gently pressing his lips to silence with her fingertips. "You never push. This has nothing to do with this afternoon."

"You're sure?" he asked in a voice laced with hope. "You're sure this is what you want?"

Lily took a deep breath. "Absolutely sure. It has nothing at all to do with this afternoon."

THIRTY-ONE

Lily let her hand remain tucked inside Drew's as he steered toward a downtown exit, taking side streets that soon brought them to her condo overlooking Providence's revitalized waterfront.

They parked the car and went into the condo in silence. Lily tossed their coats onto the brass hall tree and opened the wine. They clinked glasses and sipped, Drew watchful and reserved, Lily resolved.

For a few minutes they exchanged thoughts about the reception, what a success it had been, how good it felt to finally have all four stores once again up and running. They stood leaning on the wide marble bar that separated a state-of-the-art kitchen from a flawless cream and taupe living room that reflected much more of her interior decorator's personality than it did Lily's. She didn't have time to do everything, and besides, she told herself whenever all that blandness brought on a fleeting urge to tear it apart and start from scratch, she was hardly ever here. When she finally remembered the cheese and crackers and moved to get them, Drew caught her hand from behind.

"Suddenly I'm not very hungry, either," he said quietly.

Slowly, his gaze holding hers, he pulled her into his arms, and Lily went to him willingly, going up on her toes to meet his kiss. She didn't want to waste any time tonight. Time was nothing but a porthole for doubts and second thoughts.

Closing her eyes, she tried to concentrate on the sensation of his warm, soft lips coasting over hers. Instead she was distractingly aware that it was too bright in the room and of the ticking of the small crystal clock on her writing desk. Was it always that loud? She squeezed her eyes shut tighter, and instantly there appeared on the back of her lids a cascade of colored dots that floated to the edges and evaporated, leaving behind only a pattern of black. Black tweed. Black denim.

No.

Her eyes shot open. Drew was the only one she wanted to see or touch or remember tonight. He was the only one she wanted. Only him.

Winding her arms around his neck, she pressed closer to his body. At fifty-nine, he was still lean and strong, his chest reassuringly solid. She ran her hand over it, curling her fingers around a clump of his shirtfront. His lips flirted with hers, the pressure as mild as rainfall. The pace steady and slow. Too slow. Lily arched her neck and pushed her tongue against his.

Drew retaliated with a low laugh. His hands slid over her shoulders, worshiping, caressing, down her back, rubbing her skin beneath the teal blue silk of her dress.

Reaching for his tie, Lily tugged it loose and opened the buttons until his shirt hung open, revealing a mat of dark hair tinged with gray. She traced through it with her fingertips and raked a path across his hidden nipples.

"Ouch," he said, his quiet tone mildly amused.

Pulling his mouth to hers, Lily felt his hand lift to the back of her head and his fingers sifting through her hair as if it was as fragile as butterfly wings, drawing it aside so he could kiss the side of her neck and gently nibble the sensitive spot beneath her ear.

"Oh, yes," she murmured, rolling her shoulders to shed some of the tension there, willing herself to feel more...to feel *something*.

Straining against him, she sought to deepen their kiss. She clutched at his shoulders and shoved her hips against his.

"Hold on," Drew laughed, carefully disentangling himself enough to ease back and look at her with a blend of desire and concern. "We're not in any hurry."

"Yes, we are," countered Lily. "I want you, Drew. I want you now."

Several plodding heartbeats elapsed before he nodded. "All right," he said, catching her off guard as he bent and lifted her into his arms. "This is your night. Whatever the lady really wants, she gets."

He found the bedroom without delay and fell with her to the mattress. Suddenly his kisses were no longer slow and coaxing, his hands not so patient. This was better, thought Lily, much better. He lifted her to lower her zipper, then quickly peeled her dress and slip to her waist. He kissed her breasts through the sheer fabric of her bra, scraping her nipples with his tongue, eliciting a rapid, visible, purely physiological response.

Lily ran her fingers through his wavy hair and tried to expand upon it. It was as if he'd suddenly caught the urgency she wanted to feel. Instead of urging him on, now she was the one struggling to catch up and falling further behind with every labored breath and each inch his hand advanced up the soft terrain of her thigh beneath her dress.

She tossed her head, gazing at the white ceiling overhead, and was aghast at the dark-haired, blue-eyed image smiling back at her from there, the same one she'd already discovered waiting behind her closed eyelids and at the edges of whichever path her mind chose to wander.

No, her mind screamed. This wasn't working.

Drew was braced above her, absolutely still, his palms planted on the mattress, his gray gaze solemn. How long ago had he stopped kissing her breasts? Lily wondered frantically. She tried for a coy smile and failed.

"Now," he said, when it became clear he had her full attention. "Before this goes any further, don't you think we both deserve to know what's really going on here?"

"What's going on?" she echoed. Her laughter was feeble, disoriented. "We're making love."

"Are we? Really?"

"Yes, of course."

"All right, then, tell me, are we enjoying it?"

Was he asking for reassurance? Lily wondered, her uneasiness skyrocketing under his watchful gaze. If so, she'd give it to him. It wasn't Drew's fault she was an idiot. None of this was his fault. And whatever it took, she was going to treat him the way he deserved to be treated.

She touched his cheek gently. "Can't you tell I'm enjoying it?"

"No. Only you can tell me that, Lily."

"Well, I am. You're a wonderful lover."

"Thanks," he said, his mouth twisting into a wry smile. "It's nice to know that you noticed. But I'm not talking about technique. If you want to make love, we'll make love. If you want me to satisfy you, I'll do my best. But I think you're after something else.''

Lily's throat went dry. "You're confusing me, Drew."

He rolled away from her to lie on his side, his head propped up by his bent elbow. There was no animosity in his expression or his tone. "You're using me, Lily."

"No..."

"Yes. You are, but it's all right. You see, in a way, I've been using you, too."

"How?" she asked, self-consciously dragging her dress up to cover her breasts.

"By reliving happy memories. You touch something inside me, Lily. I can't explain it, because I don't really understand it— I'm not sure I want to. It's like some strange, personal form of déjà vu, and it happens over and over. Sometimes it's just the way you turn your head or an undercurrent in your laugh. All I know is that when I'm with you, some of the best, happiest times of my life seem very close."

"Is that wrong?"

"Not at all. It's wonderful. For me. I'm nearly sixty, Lily. Old enough to relive a few memories from the past. But you should be making memories of your own."

"I thought I was," she said, touching his shoulder lightly. "I thought we both were."

"No. My guess is that you're avoiding them, or trying to. Sex is a powerful distraction, Lily. That's what I think you were trying to do, distract yourself from something—or someone—you'd rather not think about."

"Oh, God," she moaned, pulling her knees up as she sat and buried her face in her hands. "You must think I'm awful."

"I think you're human. And I'd be more than happy to provide you with the diversion you're looking for if I didn't know you so well. I'm pretty sure that if we finish this, you'll be sorry and blaming yourself in the morning. Especially if the memory you're running from is what I think it is."

She turned her head a fraction, her eyes wary, her bottom lip clamped between her teeth.

"It's Jack Terrell, isn't it?" he asked gently.

Lily winced. "Am I that transparent?"

"Not at all," he said soothingly. "Having a vested interest in all this, I simply couldn't help noting the fact that Jack's unexpected appearance coincided with your sudden overwhelming desire to go to bed with me.''

Groaning at her own stupidity, Lily buried her head again. The feel of Drew's fingers kneading the steel cables running along the back of her neck helped ease her tension. Her conscience was another matter.

''I seem to remember you two were an item at one point a while back,'' he commented.

''A long, long while back. Ancient history.''

''Even ancient history has an effect on the way we live today.''

Lily sighed. ''I suppose I do owe you some sort of explanation.''

''You don't owe me anything. If you want to talk, I'll listen, period.''

There was a lengthy pause while Lily searched for the right words and as painless a way to string them together as possible.

''You're right,'' she said at last. ''I was using you. Seeing Jack tonight really threw me. I guess I was trying to use you to wipe him from my mind, looking for someplace to hide. That's no excuse for what I did, and I'm sorry.''

''Forget it. That's what friends are for.''

Friends. With that single word he eased Lily's discomfort and solved at least one of her problems, the matter of how to define the feelings between them. Drew was her friend, and that was a great deal. Right now she needed a friend a lot more than she needed a lover.

''You were right about the rest, too. I did love Jack once,'' she confessed. ''If it's possible for a teenager to be in love.''

''Never doubt it,'' he said instantly. ''That's when love is at its purest and least complicated. At eighteen, we know what we want and we're free to go after it . . . if we have the sense to, without letting extraneous things get in the way.''

''But that's wrong,'' she cried, shoving her arms into her dress and twisting to wrench the zipper up. Drew intervened before she ruined the dress.

''Why is it wrong?'' he asked.

''We can't just go after what we want and do whatever we want to do, because other people are always affected. Other people get hurt.''

''Is that what happened with you and Jack?''

Lily nodded, feeling the sting of tears. "Yes. A lot of people got hurt."

"Especially you. Am I right?"

"No, it doesn't matter what happened to me. I was the one who was wrong. It was all my fault."

"Tell me," he urged, pulling her into his arms as tears slowly started down her face. "Tell me about it, Lily."

Haltingly, fitting words together between sobs, Lily talked for the first time in years about Jack and losing the scholarship and about how it had all led to her father's death. And about how she was to blame for all of it.

Drew listened, horrified, his heart feeling like shattered glass being ground beneath a relentless boot heel. Lily's pain was so intense, and so senseless, it made him furious. He wished he could reach back through the years and rip it out by the root, freeing her from a prison of her own making. But that was impossible, so he just listened, knowing that was the first step of whatever meager help he might be able to provide her.

Heartbroken, and convinced she had been the cause of her father's drinking and his accident, Lily had blamed herself for his death. Drew couldn't imagine being burdened with that kind of guilt at any age. At eighteen it must have been devastating. It was no surprise Lily had reacted the way she had, driving herself to succeed in order to justify her father's faith in her, and shutting Jack out of her life in the process.

Drew didn't have to try to imagine Jack's reaction. He well remembered that time in his life. Once his heart had been broken by Lily, Jack turned around and did the same to Kay by withdrawing into a shell of his own. He refused to finish school and eventually made good on his threat to join the service. And it was sometime right around then, Drew recalled, registering an inescapable echo of pain, that Kay decided that her first loyalty was to some abstract notion of family honor, and she had broken his heart once and for all.

Now all that pain and heartache had come full circle, he thought, stroking Lily's hair as she finally fell silent in his arms. He didn't know how he was going to convince Lily to let go of the past, only that he had to try to stop her from making the same mistake Kay had made.

Lily was too young, too loving, too damn special to choose some mistaken self-ordained burden of guilt and responsibil-

Love Child

ity over living her life the way it should be lived. Whatever that turned out to be.

As carefully as he could, he told her exactly that. When he finished, she shook her head stubbornly.

"No," she protested, as she'd protested throughout. "Don't you see? There's no way that Jack and I could ever be together again. Ever. I owe that much to my father's memory."

"Lily, this isn't about what you owe his memory. It isn't even about your father anymore. It's about guilt, and about what you're letting it do to your life."

"Whatever you call it, the result is the same," she insisted, not wanting to explore her reasoning too deeply. As far as she was concerned, guilt was an acceptable category in which to place all the complex and confusing feelings she had for Jack. She didn't want to admit to Drew that one of those feelings was fear...fear of getting caught in an old dream, fear of losing all over again. "The fact is that Jack Terrell is off-limits to me. That was decided when my father drove his car into that tree."

"No, Lily, you're the one who decided it. And now you're the one—the only one—who can decide to change things."

She got up and paced across the room. "You're wrong. It's not my decision to make. In fact, there isn't even any decision to be made," she added, throwing her hands in the air. "It's crazy to even sit here discussing it. I overreacted tonight, pure and simple. Jack probably isn't the slightest bit interested in seeing me after all this time. In fact I'm sure he isn't. Maybe he's even married."

"Maybe."

She whipped around to face him, her eyes widening as the possibility landed in her stomach with a sickening thud. "Do you really think so?"

"No," Drew said, chuckling. "Judging from Kay's occasional complaints about not having grandchildren, I'm ninety-nine percent certain Jack has never married. That's not the point."

He moved to stand before her, cupping her chin in his hand to gently direct her gaze to meet his. "Maybe he's not interested, or maybe once you spend some time with him, you won't be. That's not important. What matters is that you face the past and put it behind you once and for all. Forget about family honor, forget about guilt. You have to forgive Jack, Lily, so that you can forgive yourself."

Stepping away from him, Lily folded her arms stiffly across her chest and lifted her chin, looking as determined and implacable as he'd ever seen her when fighting for one of her ideas at work.

"I appreciate you trying to help, Drew, truly I do. But this is something you can't understand. I don't think anyone can except me. I don't have to forgive Jack, because I don't blame him. I blame myself. And before I could even think about letting him back into my life, I would have to let myself off the hook for what I did. And I have no intention of doing that. Ever."

THIRTY-TWO

"I think a gold bracelet is a wonderful idea," Lily told her mother, scanning her appointment calendar as she spoke. They had been on the phone for nearly twenty minutes, ostensibly discussing the perfect gift for her niece Lori's high school graduation.

She had a lunch date with a Rolex sales rep at noon and about a hundred things she ought to catch up on beforehand. Between plans to expand her own line and preliminary work on the museum reproduction project, she was busier than ever. She liked being busy, especially these days, when the alternative— her own thoughts—was so fraught with tension and confusion. She also usually liked talking to her mother. This morning she simply wished her mother would cut to the chase.

"I'm planning on driving down to see you on Saturday," Lily told her. "Why don't I pick out a few bracelets here and bring them along? You can choose whichever one you think Lori would like."

"That would be a real help. But remember, Lily, nothing too—"

"I know, nothing too expensive."

"Don't you laugh, Miss Fancy Pants. Some people still have to watch their pennies. And no finagling with the price, either. I know what things cost these days, so don't try to fool me."

"I wouldn't dream of it. Will you at least let me buy it with my store discount?"

"I suppose that would be all right."

"Fine, then I'll see you on Saturday."

"You'll stay for dinner?"

"Sure, why not? Maybe I'll spend the night," she added on impulse. "If it's warm, I might even hit the beach for a while on Sunday."

"By yourself?"

"Unless you want to come along."

"I just wondered . . ."

"Drew's busy this weekend," Lily said, anticipating her question.

"I just wondered, that's all."

That little white lie was for her mother's sake. One of them might as well have peace of mind. Although she and Drew usually spent time together on the weekends, nothing had been said about the upcoming weekend by either of them. They were still friends, but after the other night that friendship had changed, and it was going to take a while for them to learn its new pattern.

At work this week they had been as close and in tune as ever, but that's where it ended. Part of Lily missed Drew miserably; another part understood there were some things she had to face alone. Jack Terrell was one of those things.

He was also the dark, unspoken thread running through this phone conversation, winding tighter and tighter the longer it dragged on.

"Well, then, I guess that's it," her mother said. "It will be wonderful to have you here all weekend."

"I'll see you around noon on Saturday," said Lily, thinking maybe she was going to escape the inevitable, after all.

"There's just one more thing."

The inevitable wins again, she thought, careful not to sigh into the phone. "What's that, Mom?"

"Lily, is everything all right with you?"

"Yes, Mom. Everything is fine."

Actually she was balancing on the nearly invisible line between all right and emotional overload. No matter where she went or what she did, she couldn't escape the oppressive feeling of anticipation brought on by Jack's return. That wasn't something she would confide to a born worrier like her mother. Or anyone else, for that matter.

She smiled as her mother tried another tack. "Have you . . . That is, did you . . . Oh, heck," she said, surrendering. "Have you seen Jack Terrell since the other night?"

"No." Lily decided not to mention that he'd called twice and left bland messages on her answering machine at home and that she'd dodged another call from him here at the store just yesterday afternoon. She might not be able to avoid him forever, but she could try.

"Good." Her mother's relief poured through forty miles of telephone lines. "It's for the best, really, Lily. Let sleeping dogs lie, I always say. Besides . . ."

A short buzz signaled a call waiting on another line. A reprieve. Lily put her mother on hold and listened as Jill, her secretary, explained that there was a customer downstairs interested in commissioning something very special and that he'd specifically requested to meet with Lily about it. She emphasized the "very special."

"They told him that you would probably be too busy to handle it personally," she added, "but that perhaps you could recommend one of the staff designers to—"

"No," Lily interrupted. "I'll see him myself. Have someone bring him upstairs to the salon. I'll be there as soon as I can."

Duty called. Thank heaven. Although she rarely had time to get personally involved in the lucrative custom jewelry aspect of the store's business, she loved working with people directly, and today she could use the diversion.

Ten minutes later, carrying a sample case, catalogue and sketch pad, she approached the door of the private sales salon on the third floor. It had been the first room overhauled after she arrived, much to the distress of the Goddard sisters. Out had gone the heavy drapes, burgundy leather furnishings left over from their grandfather's reign, and the musty smell Lily suspected had been ripening nearly as long.

She had replaced the old furniture with a table big enough to scatter sketches and samples across, comfortable high-back chairs upholstered in woven silk of gold, melon and jade, and plenty of sunshine. Who wanted to buy diamonds in the dark? The typical custom jewelry client was a man buying for a woman. More often than not he wanted something spectacular and unique and was willing to pay for it. The salon's new design was intended to enhance the mood of generosity.

Summoning a professional smile, Lily opened the salon door and stepped inside. Her smile dissolved into a bewildered frown when she realized the room was empty. Puzzled, she took another step. Immediately the door clicked shut behind her.

Lily whirled, visions of being trapped by a psychopath bringing a scream close to the surface, and found Jack standing behind her, his shoulders resting against the closed door.

"Morning, Ms. Saville," he drawled.

"It's you," she said, struggling to breathe normally. "What kind of stunt is this?"

The brief movement of his lips could hardly be called a smile. "The kind that guarantees you can't ignore me."

"Of all the . . ." She trailed off in exasperation. "All right. Now that you've *captured* my attention, what do you want?"

He was wearing black jeans again, this time topped with a battered leather jacket too reminiscent of the one he had worn the first day they met for Lily's peace of mind. The lazy, speculative gaze he sent over her made her skin prickle. Her initial fear gave way to a different, deeper uneasiness.

"What do I want?" he repeated. "No Hello, Jack, sorry I missed your calls and haven't had a single free minute to return them? No, How have you been? Not even a lousy Welcome home, Jack, it's good to see you?"

"I've been busy," she said with an uneasy shrug. "And I said welcome home the other night."

"No, you didn't. *That* I definitely would have remembered."

"In that case, hello, Jack, welcome home. It's so nice to see you again. Now what do you want?"

He came away from the door and pulled out his wallet. "About a half hour of your time. How much do I have to spend to get it?"

"Price isn't an issue at Goddard's," she recited. "The customer always comes first. If you're serious about buying something, I'll stay and help you. If you only want to hassle me, I'm leaving."

"Not unless you're strong enough to move me out of the way."

Lily shot a pointed glance at the telephone on the desk to her right. "I could phone security and have you out of here so fast your head would spin."

"I'm sure you could. But you won't, because you're smart enough to know how that would look to people, and dumb enough to give a damn."

"Perhaps. But I'm not dumb enough to stand here wasting valuable time being insulted."

"You won't be wasting time. I'll make this your biggest sale of the day, of the whole week. I promise," he said, making a cross over his heart, even as his darkly gleaming eyes promised things of a different sort.

"Look, Jack, you don't have to pay to talk with me—"

"Really?" he interrupted. "I didn't seem to be having much luck any other way. Why are you avoiding me, Lily?"

"I'm not." She saw his dark brows arch. "All right, maybe I have been avoiding you. Why stir up a lot of old memories?"

"Maybe because some of those old memories were pretty good," he said softly.

"And some were pretty painful. And there are a few I'm not all that proud of and would rather forget entirely."

He stiffened, the brash, cavalier expression back in place. "Right, I gathered that."

"I'm sorry. I didn't mean to hurt you."

"No problem. I got calluses on all the parts that hurt a long time ago." He came away from the door, walking toward her until he was close enough to affect her breathing. "So we'll keep this strictly business, right?"

Lily studied his face. His expression was closed and inscrutable. "You're really interested in buying jewelry?"

"Very interested."

"Is that why you've been calling me?"

"Why else?"

Why else, indeed? And why did that leave her feeling hollow instead of relieved?

"All right," she said, placing the sample case and books on the table. "What would you like to see?"

His eyes glittered. "What are you willing to show me?" He held up his hand. "Sorry, reflex mouth action. Actually I'm open to suggestions."

"Then why don't we sit down? Maybe looking through the catalogue will help narrow things down a bit."

He waited for her to sit, then claimed the chair beside hers, shrugging out of his jacket and leaning close in order to see the catalogue.

"Is this a gift?" she asked.

"Yes. A surprise."

"I see. For a woman?"

He flashed her a sardonic look. "What do you think?"

"I think it would help to know if I should be pointing out pieces designed for a woman or a man."

"A woman," he replied, his gaze moving over her face, making her feel suddenly warm. "Most definitely a woman."

"Young or old?"

"Younger than I am."

"I see," she said.

Dozens of questions she had no right to ask crackled in Lily's head as she watched him thumb through the catalogue. How young a woman was she? And how beautiful? And how special was she to Jack that he was going to so much trouble to buy her a gift?

"Have you given any thought to the sort of jewelry she favors?" she asked him. "Bracelets, earrings, rings? Or perhaps you're interested in a particular stone?"

"You mean like a diamond?"

She turned and confronted the solid, impenetrable blue of his gaze. "That's one possibility."

He smiled wryly. "No, a diamond would definitely be premature. Actually, I think she's more of a necklace-type woman," he said, lowering his gaze to the silver chain circling her throat. "I like what you're wearing."

"This?" she asked, touching it. "This is one of my own designs, a one-of-a-kind piece."

"That's what I want," he said, bringing his gaze to hers. "One of a kind."

"All right, let's start by looking at some different types of chains. Later we can discuss the actual design and whether or not you want to incorporate gems."

"Whatever you say," he said quietly. Too damn quietly for Lily's peace of mind. Why hadn't she taken the quick easy route and simply maneuvered him into selecting something from the catalogue? But it was too late now.

"There are different weights and textures of chains," she explained. "Some are rolled, like this," she said, indicating one, "some flat. The advantage to the flat type is that it reflects light better, so it has more sparkle, and it rests smoothly against your skin, which a lot of women prefer. See?"

She took the sample necklace and draped it around her throat, holding the ends together at the back of her neck to give him an idea of how it looked on. The gold chain lay against her skin above the rounded neckline of her ivory silk blouse. Jack stared at it in fascination, as if she was doing something phenomenal before his eyes.

Without warning, he lifted his hand to touch it, caressing both the gold and her skin. Lily's pulse fluttered. His fingertips were rough, his touch warm and gentle and thoroughly inappropriate. If he was any other customer she would have quickly put him in his place, but he wasn't anyone else, and as much as the contact unnerved her, part of her welcomed it like a long-lost friend.

"I like this one," he said at last, dropping his hand with a look of reluctance, as if relinquishing a prized possession.

"Fine." Hoping he didn't notice her hands shaking, she replaced the chain on the black velvet tray before her. "Do you want to use gold or silver?"

"What's the difference?"

"Price-wise, about three hundred dollars an ounce."

"Forget price."

"This woman must be very special to you."

"She is."

"So?"

He was staring into her eyes as if he hoped to find something there. "So?"

"So do you prefer gold or silver?"

"Which do you prefer?"

"Silver, but you should consider the woman's own taste and what flatters her most. What tone is her skin?"

"Soft. Beautiful."

Lily cleared her throat and tucked a piece of hair behind her ear. "Jack, soft is not a skin tone."

"Her skin is pale," he said, "like ivory, but with a hint of color that always makes me think of peaches."

"Peaches. I see. Well, it sounds as if she could wear either. What color does she look best in?"

Her tenuous composure shattered when his eyes met hers.

"Beach sand," he said, watching her reaction with frank interest. "She looks beautiful in beach sand."

Lily's breath caught in her throat. "This isn't going to work," she muttered, haphazardly grabbing papers and samples and slamming them into the case. "I'll send someone else to help you if you want."

"I want you."

Their gazes locked, fire and ice.

"Sorry, that's out of the question."

He clapped his hand on her shoulder to keep her in her chair. "What happened to the customer always comes first?"

Lily stilled, professional pride boiling to the surface. She would not let him rattle her. "You're right. Why don't I just work up several designs on my own and send them to you for approval?"

"No way. I want to be in on this every step of the way. It's very important to me."

"Then I want you to remember that this is business. And," she added, shrugging from his touch, "keep your hands to yourself."

"Deal."

After taking her time rearranging the hastily gathered materials, she leaned back in her chair, pencil poised over her open sketchbook, determined to remain outwardly composed in spite of the storm within. "So then, exactly what color beach sand were you referring to a moment ago? Tan? Gray?"

"Wet," he replied, looking straight at her. "Warm, wet sand."

She swallowed hard. "Fine, we'll go with the gold."

She bent over the pad, grateful she'd resisted the occasional urge to cut her shoulder-length hair. It came in handy to veil her face, while enabling her to glance surreptitiously at Jack. Right now she'd rank him about a nine on the smug amusement scale, which annoyed her and didn't help get the job done.

She forced her attention to the blank page in front of her. It might as well have been a television screen, playing reruns from her past. All she could see were hazy images of beach sand and Jack's broad tanned shoulders blocking out the moon overhead. Several times she began scribbling to eradicate the pictures, only to crumble the page in a fit of frustration.

"Problems?" Jack inquired.

She smiled at him. "Not at all."

Finally, by chance, a few of her scribbled lines came together, and something she couldn't command or will into motion clicked into place inside her head. She expanded on it, adding curves and angles, erasing them, her mind beginning to outrace her fingers as her excitement grew. As always when she got caught up in her work, everything else receded. The finished sketch was rougher than she would have liked, but it clearly showed her vision of a foxtail chain joined in the center with a spectacular starburst of sapphires and pearls.

Startled to discover she'd been working—and he'd been watching—for nearly an hour, she passed the sketch to Jack.

"Yes," he said. "This is perfect for her. It looks like a small explosion. Like fireworks you can hold in your hand."

Lily grinned at him, her anger having been burned off while she worked. "Very expensive fireworks."

"Don't worry, I've been saving my pennies. There's not a lot to spend money on in a military hospital."

"I guess not," she agreed, sobering. "It must have been awful for you being there all that time, alone."

He shrugged. "Gives a man time to think."

"Were you badly hurt?"

"Yeah, it hurt enough."

"How did it happen?"

"By accident. I don't mean to sound facetious. It's just that as far as I'm concerned that's what it was. After nearly twenty years of lucky breaks and close calls, my number came up. End of story."

"You were flying when it happened?"

He nodded. "I've been working with this special unit for a while now. You know," he said with a grin, "the sort of group that thrives on machismo and self-delusion. What's that saying? The difficult is all in a day's work, and the impossible just takes a little longer. That was us."

"Your mother told Drew and me a little about it once. Very little, actually. But I remember she was very worried."

"Very little is all she knew, all any of us were allowed to say about it. Even now," he added bluntly.

"I understand. Can you at least tell me about the accident? I don't mean what you were doing or anything like that. Just about you. How you got hurt."

"I was dropping another special forces operative behind the lines in Iraq. The smoke from all those burning oil wells had me flying low. Too damn low. It screwed up the radar, everything. I ended up getting a little too close to a hot spot and blew an engine.

"We bailed out," he continued, "something I can do blind-folded in my sleep, only this time I landed wrong side down in the wrong place, right inside a cranking cement mixer, it felt like. I broke my back, along with a lot of other things."

"My God, Jack, I can't imagine how horrible that must have been."

He grinned and gave a philosophical shrug. If the accident disturbed him still, he was good at hiding it. "Landing wasn't half as bad as lying there for two days waiting for them to get a Jolly Green Giant to us."

"A Jolly..."

"Rescue chopper," he explained. "Big ugly bastards, and the sweetest sight you ever want to see."

"From there you went to a hospital in Germany?"

He nodded. "Great place. They repair and reprogram, replace all the broken parts, supply any needed props." He indicated the cane leaning on the table nearby.

"Did the doctors say how long you'll have to use it?"

"Maybe forever," he replied flatly.

"Jack, I'm so sorry," she said, searching his eyes for some trace of the anguish a man as active as he'd been must feel over being restricted in any way. She might as well have been staring into twin black mirrors. The only emotion she saw was a reflection of the pain she was feeling on his behalf. "I wish I'd known."

"Why?"

"Why?" she echoed, startled by his directness. "I don't know. So I could do something for you."

"Like what?"

"I don't know," she said again. "Send flowers. Write, maybe."

"Would you have written to me, Lily?"

She bit her bottom lip. "I don't know."

"At least you're honest," he said dryly. "What would you say if I offered you a chance to make up for all those unwritten letters?"

Her eyes narrowed. "What sort of chance?"

"Have dinner with me."

Lily's emotions declared war. At that instant, dinner alone with Jack was the most enticing and frightening proposition she could imagine. "When?"

"Tonight. Tomorrow. Name it. I'm at your disposal." His sly grin told her that the open-ended invitation was intended to rule out any extraneous excuse she might come up with.

"All right," she said with misgivings. "How about tomorrow night? I leave work around seven on Fridays."

"I'll be here." He stood and reached for the cane. "How about this?" he asked, nodding at the sketch. "Should I leave a deposit?"

Lily shook her head. "That's not necessary. We can bill you if you like and have the finished necklace sent to you on approval."

"Fine."

"It will be a few weeks before it's ready, though."

"No rush."

"How long will you be home on leave?"

He glanced at her quizzically. "Leave? I thought you knew. I'm home for good, Lily."

"Home for. . . ? But I thought it was just because of your injuries?" she said, wondering what he must think of the dismay in her voice. "I thought you came home to finish recuperating."

Jack shook his head. "As far as the doctors are concerned, they've done all they can. Time might make a difference, it might not. It doesn't really matter. I didn't come home to recuperate." Not until he reached the door and pulled it open did he pause and add, "I came home for you, Lily."

THIRTY-THREE

The next day, Lily devised at least a dozen excuses to break her dinner date with Jack, and an equal number of reasons not to. The most basic was her fear that he would challenge, none too graciously, any excuse she threw at him.

Besides, she thought in an effort to bolster her confidence, there was really no reason she shouldn't have dinner with him. They weren't enemies, she reminded herself. Far from it. Certainly she could control her emotions for one evening. They would have dinner, for old times' sake, and that would be that. Over. Finis. Once and for all. If Jack had something else in mind, that was his problem.

A week of soul-searching hadn't changed her conviction that it was too late for her and Jack. It was very easy to look back from the vantage point of thirty-eight and second guess emotional decisions made nearly twenty years ago, but Lily refused to get caught up in that. She'd done what she thought was right at the time, and she was prepared to live with the results. It was pointless to go poking through the tatters of some old dream and wonder what might have been if she'd reacted differently.

Instead she forced herself to focus on where she'd ended up, and to consider the fact that whether it had been inspired by grief or guilt, the burning desire to live up to her father's pride in her had been instrumental in getting her where she was today, which was not at all a bad place to be. Now all she had to worry about was getting through tonight without giving Jack the wrong signals about the future.

While her head assured her she could handle it, every fiber of her body was telling her that agreeing to see him alone was as foolhardy as a drunk walking a high wire. Where Jack was concerned, and only where he was concerned, she still had an unruly urge to act first and think later. If she grew more shaky and apprehensive as the time to meet him drew closer, Lily figured it was with good reason. Part of her was afraid that if she went searching through the deepest regions of her heart, she might find that far from being in tatters, her old dreams of him were as shiny and alluring—and *dangerous*—as ever.

When she left the store a few minutes before seven, Jack was already outside waiting, leaning up against a dark gray Landrover. It was men like him, she decided at first glance, who gave navy blue blazers and starched white shirts their classy reputation. Although she suspected he still loathed wearing a coat and tie, he looked wonderful.

His face was even more appealing to her now, with laugh lines and lifelines etched across it, than it had been at twenty-two, and in spite of the slight limp, his tall, lean body was the best advertisement for military discipline that she'd ever seen. When she appeared, he straightened and stepped to meet her.

Dark glasses hid his eyes, but body language alone told Lily that he was taking a long, slow look at her and that he liked what he saw. She was foolishly glad she'd given in to vanity this morning, fussing with her clothes and hair as if headed for a coronation—her own—instead of simply dinner with an old friend.

Her role at Goddard's demanded a look that was at the same time professional, glamorous and as up to the minute as the store itself. She achieved it with a rainbow of what was currently her trademark suit, comprised of a short, narrow skirt with a long, loose-fitting jacket, a style that made the most of her slender, leggy, five-foot-eight frame. The bright turquoise version she'd chosen today was her favorite. By buttoning the double-breasted jacket she had eliminated the need for a blouse and, judging from his unabashed gaze, managed to capture Jack's undivided attention.

They exchanged polite greetings, then he asked where her car was parked.

"I took a taxi this morning so we wouldn't have to worry about it," she explained.

"You always were good at planning every move ahead of time."

"Maybe because I learned how disastrous it can be to act on impulse."

He glanced around as if perplexed. "Did I miss something here? Like maybe the bell to start the first round?"

"What's that supposed to mean?"

"Just that I hoped we could at least get to the restaurant and maybe even order before we came out fighting."

Lily stared at him for a second before succumbing to laughter. "I'm sorry for being so defensive."

"I'm sorry for making you feel you have to be defensive around me."

She gazed at him with narrowed eyes. "What happened to the guy who never said I'm sorry to anyone for anything?"

"I like to think he grew up a little," Jack replied with a self-effacing shrug. "You can decide for yourself."

"Fair enough. So we've agreed to eat first and fight later?"

"Unless we think of something more interesting to do in the meantime," he added, his smile wolfish as he helped her into the Landrover.

At Lily's suggestion they went to Cheshire's, an intimate downtown restaurant that elevated pasta and vegetables to the level of art. The decor was stark, with white linen-clad tables and dark green walls. All creativity was reserved for the food, and even Jack eventually admitted that the complex subtlety of herbs and spices compensated for the fact that there was no steak on the menu.

Once the waiter had taken their order, poured the wine and left them alone, they indulged in a predictable game of catch-up that lasted throughout dinner and continued over coffee. Jack was curious about how she'd ended up designing jewelry.

"I thought you wanted to paint," he said.

"I did and sometimes I still do," she confided. "I'll see something or someone and the desire to capture it on canvas is almost a physical ache." Like right now, she thought, watching the candlelight play across the compelling lines of his face.

"So why did you give it up?"

"Because as much as I loved it, I discovered that I loved what I'm doing more."

She gave him an encapsulated version of her introduction to silversmithing at Delaney Silver and how it led to her studying jewelry design at RISD. She filled him in on her days at Bonatelli's, unreasonably pleased by the interest and admiration in his eyes as he listened and asked questions.

"That's enough about me," she said finally, after bringing him up to date on her work as design director at Goddard's. "How about you? What are you going to do now that you're a civilian again?"

"Fly," he replied without hesitation. "I'm already in the process of starting my own charter flight service. We'll be based in Westerly, and strictly local at first—New England, New York, the islands, but eventually . . . who knows?"

Lily's surprise showed on her face. "But . . ."

"But what? Just because I can't run marathons doesn't mean I can't fly."

"I'm sorry. It's just that when you said you were leaving the service I assumed . . ."

"That they gave me the gate because I'm washed up? You're right. They did. You see, flying was just a part of what I did for the military. It was the other part, what I did after I landed in whatever hellhole they needed someone to fly into, that I can't handle anymore."

"I'm not sure I understand."

"Even if I explained in detail, I'm sure you would never understand," he said matter-of-factly. "Let's just say that sometimes the things this country needs to have done are things nobody in his right mind wants to do. That's where my unit came in.

"Don't look so shocked," he said with a chuckle, as she attempted to hide her reaction behind her wineglass. "I wasn't a paid assassin or anything like that. Antiterrorist strikes or saving the butt of some flea-brained diplomat who wandered in over his head in a not-so-friendly third-world country was more in our line."

"It sounds dangerous."

"For most of the guys I flew with, danger wasn't considered a drawback. It was a way to remind yourself you were alive."

Lily shivered. "I have about a million questions I want to ask you."

"You can ask," replied Jack, smiling. "It's just that most of them I can't answer."

"How can you be so loyal after the way they treated you? Dropping you just because you'd been injured . . . and in the line of duty, no less."

"I knew the rules when I decided to play the game," he replied placidly. "Besides, just because I can no longer do what they wanted me for doesn't mean I can't do what I want to do. You might call that the silver lining in all this. I finally realized that it's way past time I started doing what I want with my life."

"I thought flying was what you wanted to do?"

"It was. It still is. It's just no longer *all* that I want to do."

Suddenly, all Lily's sensible resolutions to be prudent and circumspect gave way to rampant curiosity.

"Does this have anything to do with what you said yesterday?" Prompted by his quizzical look, she added, "When you said you'd come home for me."

He looked bemused. "Did I say I came home *for* you?"

"Yes. You did."

"I suppose I should have said it was because of you."

"All right, then, why did you come home because of me?"

"It's hard to explain," he said, gazing directly into her eyes. "I told you I had time to think after the accident. A great deal of that time I spent thinking about you."

Startled, Lily twisted her fingers around the stem of her wineglass. "Me? Why on earth would you think about me?"

A slight smile flickered across his lips. "It doesn't matter why. It doesn't even matter what I was thinking. The thing is," he said, leaning forward, "that no matter what I thought, or how long I thought, I always ended up in the same place, knowing that what's between you and me is unfinished business."

"I'm sure," Lily said with a nervous laugh, "that most people feel the same way about old..." She halted, unwilling to say the word "lovers."

His eyes glittered darkly.

"Relationships," she finished. "I'm sure there's always an element of uncertainty over what might have been."

"This is something more. Maybe it's because I devoted nearly the last twenty years of my life to risking it, and you've obviously devoted yours to your work. For whatever reason, I see us as two people who have grown older, but haven't progressed much at all in one very important facet of life." Pinning her with his gaze, he said it again. "Unfinished business."

"I see," Lily said, managing a breath that didn't deliver nearly as much oxygen as her suddenly spinning head was calling for. She didn't even pretend not to understand what he meant by unfinished business. She understood all too well. Even while knowing she should change the subject, she recklessly plunged deeper. "So, just how do we go about changing that?"

"I beg your pardon?"

Cursing the heat that flooded her cheeks, she said, "I mean how do you propose we finish what's between us?"

He watched her over his wineglass as he took a swallow. "I wasn't even sure you'd want to. I mean, with Drew in the picture."

"Is that your subtle way of asking me about Drew?"

"Evidently not," he said with a rueful smile. "So I'll just be unsubtle and ask outright. What about Drew?"

"Drew and I are friends."

"That's all?"

"Yes. For a while I thought we might be more, but . . ." She paused and pushed the hair from her face, conscious that he was watching her more intently than a moment ago. "We just weren't, that's all. I'm grateful to Drew for many things, and I love him as a friend."

"And how does Drew feel about you?"

She smiled. "The same, I'm sure. As flattering as it would be to have a man like Drew fall hopelessly in love with me, it's not the case. The fact is, I think Drew is still passionately in love with someone else."

"Who?" Jack inquired, looking unconvinced.

Her shoulders lifted in a shrug. "Some mystery woman from his past. He's never mentioned her by name, but I know she was the one great love of his life. No one else could ever measure up."

"So why aren't they together? Did she cut him loose for another guy?"?

"He never said, but I don't think it was that. Drew is much too sensible to go on loving someone who didn't want him. I think maybe she's dead." She'd been staring into the candle flame. Now she glanced at Jack. "You've known Drew all your life. Can you think of any woman from his past?"

He shook his head. "I haven't been around in a long time," he reminded her. "And when I was home, I was more interested in my own love affairs than those of my parents' friends."

The reference to his youthful love affairs seemed to hang in the air between them, like smoke on a windless day.

Resting his elbows on the table, Jack leaned closer. "Getting back to *our* unfinished business, I would say that dealing

Drew out of the picture definitely increases the range of possibilities.''

"Not necessarily. Besides, you said this dinner would settle the score between us," she reminded him.

"Not quite. What I said was that dinner would compensate for all those letters you never wrote."

"Seriously, Jack," she said, in spite of the fact that he looked very serious indeed, "I know there's a lot of..." She searched for the right word, feeling as if she was venturing onto thin ice emotionally. Who could tell where the danger points were? "A lot of misunderstandings between us," she said finally.

"I didn't misunderstand anything. You made yourself pretty damn clear."

"I know, I know," she said, avoiding his gaze. "That was a very bad time for me."

"Don't you think I knew that?" he shot back in a voice that slashed the air like a knife. "Damn it, Lily, I thought— Well, forget what I thought. I knew what you were going through. I didn't care that you blamed me... Hell, I blamed myself for being stupid enough to let us get caught the way we did. I understood how much you were hurting. But I was stupid enough to think that when the chips were down, you'd turn to me, not push me away."

"I had to. I didn't know what else to do."

"You could have tried trusting me. That was the worst part, Lily. I trusted you enough to tell you everything...things I didn't tell anybody else, things I didn't even like thinking about. After that night on the beach, I thought you trusted me the same way."

"I did."

"You did like hell. If you had maybe we wouldn't be sitting here catching up on the last twenty years of each other's lives."

"And maybe we would. Maybe we would have broken up over something else or just outgrown each other."

"I would have liked a chance to find out."

"I can't turn back the clock and change things."

"Would you if you could? Change things, I mean?"

"Yes," she said, her gaze deliberate. "If I could, I would go back and wipe out everything that caused my father's accident."

"Do you hear yourself?" asked Jack. "Lily, you can't wipe out what caused that accident. Accidents happen—that's why they're called accidents."

"I don't believe that. Not in this case. If not for me, my father wouldn't have been drinking that night, and he wouldn't have lost control and wrapped his car around a tree, and he would probably be alive today."

Jack drew back, his dark eyes narrowed in disbelief. "You can't possibly still blame yourself for what happened? Not after all this time?"

"Time has nothing to do with it."

"It has everything to do with it," he said, the anger in his words no less potent for the quiet tone he used to deliver them. "After twenty years I thought you'd have come to your senses. And that maybe we'd have another chance."

"That's out of the question."

"Just like that?" he ground out.

"Just like that," Lily countered, fighting for control. "So if that's what this was all about, I'm afraid you've wasted your time."

"No," he said, dragging his fingers through his hair. "I don't believe that. I can't."

"It really doesn't make any difference what you believe. That's the way it is." Her bravado faltered in the face of his ferocious expression. "Look, Jack, it's not that I'm not sorry, because I am. I'm sorry things happened the way they did. And in a way I'm glad I finally had the chance to say that to you. But it doesn't change the way things are." She forced a smile, hoping to return things to at least the semblance of civility. "I guess that takes care of our unfinished business."

"You really think this settles anything?" he demanded.

"I hope so. There's no reason we can't be friends."

The corners of his mouth turned stiffly upward. "Friends? Sort of like you and Drew?"

"More or less. Now that you're back, our paths are bound to cross from time to time. I'd much rather be friends than be constantly sparring."

For what felt like the longest moment of Lily's life, he stared across the table at her, his expression fixed and unreadable. Then, without warning, he flung his napkin onto the table.

"Let's get out of here," he said.

Lily quickly gathered her purse while he dealt twenty-dollar bills onto the table as if he were discarding playing cards. Outside they walked in silence toward the parking lot several blocks away. The financial district where Cheshire's was located was nearly deserted at this hour. The warm, still night served to magnify the tension she felt radiating from Jack in waves that seemed to shimmer in the air around her, like heat rising from the pavement on a steamy summer day.

Lily bit her tongue for as long as she could stand it.

"So," she said finally, "was our rapid exit your eloquent response to my suggestion that we be friends, or did you suddenly have a craving for fresh air?"

Jack stopped and turned on her.

"Actually," he said, bracketing her shoulders as he maneuvered her back against the solid brick wall of the Fidelity Trust Company, "I had a sudden craving for this."

Before Lily fully realized his intent, he'd wound his hand through her hair, coiling it tightly enough to discourage her from pulling free. With a crisp tug, he tipped her face up to his and lowered his head.

Her strangled sound of protest was broken by the pressure of his mouth as it opened over hers. He held her still for a long, hard kiss that Lily suspected was intended to punish rather than excite. It failed miserably.

"Stop," she said, when he lifted his head without releasing her. His body was a steely pressure she knew it was useless to struggle against. Her heart was pounding, her breathing choppy. When she dragged her tongue across her bruised lips, she tasted him. It was the taste of the past. It scared the hell out of her.

"Why should I?" he demanded on a raspy breath she felt against her lips. "I don't want to stop, and you don't really want me to."

"Oh, really?" Lily managed a feeble laugh. "Are you such an expert on women that you know when stop means stop and when it doesn't?"

"Nope. My vast experience with women didn't involve semantics at all. I just happen to be an expert on you."

"Were," she corrected. "Almost twenty years have passed since then."

"I don't care if it's been twenty years or twenty thousand," he declared, dragging his fingertips slowly across her cheek and down her throat to the top button of her jacket. "You haven't changed, Lily. You're just as beautiful. Just as soft. Just as desirable."

"I have changed, Jack," she said, resisting the treacherous impulses of her own body.

"Not in the ways that count."

"In all the ways that count."

"Fine." He bent and rained kisses along the side of her throat as he spoke. "You've changed in all the ways that count. One thing is still the same." He straightened, pinning her with a knowing gaze as he made her tremble by sliding his hand slowly along her spine and back up again. "You still get turned on when I touch you."

"You're right," she agreed softly. "I do. What's changed is what I'm going to do about it."

"What's that?" he asked, caressing the back of her neck.

"Nothing."

He gave a surprised chuckle. "Nothing?"

"That's right. You see, I never, ever get involved with men who turn me on."

"What kind of stupid thing is that to say?"

"The absolutely carved-in-stone kind of stupid."

This time his surprise caused him to straighten up enough to enable Lily to step from between him and the building. To his credit, Jack made no move to pull her back to him.

"You're serious about this," he observed incredulously.

"Very. So you see, even if what happened to my father wasn't still between us, I wouldn't be interested in anything more than friendship."

"Because I turn you on?" When she nodded, he muttered something obscene. "Tell me, what kind of man does interest you sexually these days? One who makes your skin crawl?"

"Not at all. I date men whom I consider attractive and intelligent and sensitive and . . ."

"Manageable," he drawled when she hesitated. "Right?"

"Men who don't threaten my self-control, yes, that's right."

"Why, Lily?" he asked, his eyes narrowed suggestively. "What are you so afraid of?"

"I'm not afraid of anything. I simply like being in control. I don't like thinking with my heart instead of my head. And I definitely don't like letting my libido make decisions for me."

"Your libido, huh? That's funny, I'm not convinced you still have one." He reached for her. "Convince me, Lily."

Lily refused to struggle and give him the dubious satisfaction of besting her a second time. She decided to use passive resistance instead.

Big mistake, she realized almost immediately. This time Jack sought to conquer with finesse rather than strength, and the impact on her senses was a thousand times more devastating. The tenderness of his embrace left her weak. Her hands clung to his shoulders as she helplessly savored the delicious, tingling sensations that built and splintered inside her.

At last he released her, reluctantly putting space between them. In a tone that was rough and grudging, he said, "Okay, Lily, you win."

She blinked rapidly in the darkness. "I do?"

He nodded, his mouth a grim line. "If you want to be friends, we'll be friends. And like a good friend I promise I won't do anything to turn you on. I won't even touch you if you don't want me to."

Jack watched with great satisfaction as suspicion kindled to life in her eyes. It was working already, he thought. Maybe he was no longer an expert where Lily was concerned, but his instincts were still damn good.

He had felt the way she tensed up and resisted the first time he took her in his arms and how she melted the second time. The only thing different had been his approach. He was willing to bet he could push that one step further. He was willing to bet everything that the surest way to get what he wanted from Lily was by not touching her at all.

THIRTY-FOUR

Lily was glad she'd planned to spend the weekend at Mary's. After the emotional upheaval caused by Jack's return and the change in her relationship with Drew, she needed time to think things through. Her mother had cooked her favorite meal for dinner; afterward they watched an old movie and went to bed. With her old lumpy pillow tucked beneath her head and the familiar water stain above, she'd slept more soundly than if she'd been in a five-star hotel.

She woke to an annoyingly persistent noise at her window. Rain? she wondered sleepily, snuggling more deeply into her pillow. No, too loud. Ping. Ping. Ping. Hail, that was it, she decided as she pulled the pillow over her head. Ping. Ping. Ping. Just her luck on the one morning she wanted to sleep. When was the last time they had a hailstorm? Unearthing her head, she forced her eyes open. When was the last time they had a hailstorm in May?

Dragging her hands through her hair, Lily climbed out of bed, her white cotton nightgown swirling around her legs as she crossed to the window to peer outside with blurry eyes. She recognized the gray Landrover before she saw Jack.

"It's about time," he said. "I was just about to go looking for a ladder."

He was standing about ten feet from the house, staring at her window, a pile of pebbles in one cupped hand.

"Jack. What are you doing here?"

"Delivering your wake-up call. You said you wanted to go to the beach today, remember?"

Lily vaguely recalled mentioning to him that she was coming home for the weekend. Had she also said something about the beach? Apparently so.

"I was thinking that *maybe* I would go to the beach for a while later this afternoon. *If* it warmed up," she added, hugging herself with arms left bare by the sheer nightgown and wondering how well he could see through the screen.

"This afternoon? That's too late. If you want to get a good spot you have to be there early."

"Jack, it's seven o'clock in the morning."

"I know. Hurry up, will you?"

"No one goes to the beach at seven o'clock in the morning at this time of year."

"I do. Get dressed. Don't worry about lunch. I've already taken care of all that."

"Jack, I really..."

"Come on, Lily," he urged softly. "You know you want to."

He was right. It was a gorgeous morning, the sort created for walking along the shore, bundled in a thick sweatshirt and sipping a cup of hot coffee.

Reading her mind, he said, "I've got two cups of coffee waiting in the car." When she wavered, he added, "And a bag of jelly doughnuts."

"I'll be right down."

Predictably, when they arrived at the town beach, the parking lot was deserted except for a few cars.

"See?" grumbled Jack, pointing at a rusty blue Nova parked opposite the ramp to the boardwalk. "My favorite spot is taken."

"I'm sure we can find another spot," she said dryly.

"That's not the point."

Lily chuckled. "The point is that you're crazy."

"Be thankful. Having crazy friends around you is a sure way to feel sane."

It seemed a throwaway remark, tossed over one broad shoulder as he climbed from the car. Watching him pull a small cooler, blanket and other beach requisites from the back, Lily couldn't help wondering if his use of the word "friend" had been spontaneous or calculated to remind her of the limits she had set. And that he had willingly agreed to.

They spread the blanket in a spot close to the water, then walked a mile along the hard-packed sand before Jack suggested turning back.

"Is your leg bothering you?" asked Lily, seeing signs of strain on his face.

"Nah, my back. Using the cane in this sand is a pain. You can keep on going if you feel like it."

She did feel like walking some more. Conversation had been comfortably minimal, and she found the combination of quiet and exercise was having a revitalizing effect on all of her, body and soul.

"You really don't mind?"

"Why should I? I want you to feel comfortable enough with me to do whatever you want to do."

"I wanted to sleep," she reminded him.

"Nah, you just thought you did," he said, turning away with a laugh.

When Lily returned an hour later, he was dozing on the blanket. Sticky situation. Wanting nothing more herself than to stretch out and fall asleep beneath the warm sun, she settled for sitting cross-legged on the opposite corner of the blanket.

She couldn't recall the last time she'd spent a day so aimlessly and was surprised by how good it felt. No plans, no commitments, no work waiting at home. Suddenly she was glad Jack had come throwing pebbles at her window this morning. Not that she trusted his motives for a second, of course.

Ever since Friday night, when he had suddenly capitulated to her suggestion that they be friends, Lily had been braced for the punch line, some remark about the thin line between friends and lovers, something that would convey exactly how ludicrous he considered the notion that they could ever be merely friends. There had been nothing.

Friday night, on the drive to her place, he steered the conversation to a different path with the agility of a veteran engineer switching train tracks, as if the matter was truly settled. Just like that. They talked some more about his plans for the charter service and about Kay's grudging acceptance of the fact that he was never going to join her at Delaney Silver. They had even discussed the damn weather. It was all very... *friendly*. Throughout, Lily had remained poised, waiting for the other, more lethal shoe to drop. She was still waiting.

When Jack woke up, they played cards and ate the sandwiches he'd brought, washing them down with a thermos of homemade lemonade. Lily had worn her bathing suit with the intention of sunbathing, not getting wet, but somehow she let Jack goad her into the icy water.

"Last one in carries the cooler back to the car," he shouted when he was too close to lose.

After letting her pride push her in chest deep, Lily ran shrieking to shore, convinced it had to be ice chips, not drops of water, clinging to her body.

Jack produced a thick towel, and in spite of the goose bumps that revealed he was as cold as she was, wrapped it around Lily, pulling her close enough to rub some heat into her shivering arms and shoulders. They stood facing each other, his closeness and the proximity of his smoothly muscled chest warming her more than the towel.

"You know," she said, panting from the shock to her system, "you're in pretty good shape for a guy who just spent over a year recuperating from major injuries."

He shrugged. "I worked out."

"With a broken back?"

"Eventually. Where there's a will. I can be a pretty stubborn son of a gun when I want something."

Wondering if she was imagining the cryptic edge to his tone, she lifted her chin to meet his gaze. Jack's hands fell still. "And what did you want so badly that staying in shape could get you?"

"To beat you into the water first chance I got."

Now, Lily thought, as he continued to stare into her eyes. She'd known his abrupt change of heart the other night had to be a ploy of some sort. Now he would make his move. Although he was holding the ends of the towel in such a way that it felt like an embrace, he wasn't actually touching her at all. But he would, any second now. Every part of Lily's body was alive with anticipation.

"You know what I wish?"

"What?" she prompted, her voice a soft breathy sound.

He released his hold on the towel. "That I brought coffee in that thermos instead of lemonade. Feel like packing up and driving into town to get a cup?"

Lily nodded, even though what she really felt like doing was screaming in frustration. Not because she had wanted anything to happen. She definitely had not wanted him to bend his head and kiss her the way she'd been so certain he was about to. She simply wanted everything out in the open so she could deal with it.

For there was a disturbing undercurrent here, a hazy sensual awareness that hovered just beneath the surface, bathing every word he spoke with heightened significance, making even the careless brush of his arm against hers cause for a small sensory explosion inside her. It was unsettling and relentless, and her only consolation was that sooner or later Jack had to slip up, and then . . .

Lily wasn't sure what would happen then. Only what wouldn't, she told herself firmly, sort of like a trainer urging a boxer to stay in the ring. . . .

Monday morning, Lily was doing her best to put the distractions of the weekend behind her and get to work when Jack phoned to ask if she could recommend a graphic artist. He explained that he wanted to consult someone about a logo and some advance advertising for his new company.

"You're really moving on this," she remarked.

"Full steam ahead," he agreed. "Can you help me out?"

Lily flipped the Rolodex on her desk and gave him the name of a local guy whom she considered top-notch.

"Thanks," he said, and hung up, as if that was the only reason he had picked up the phone and called her.

She didn't hear from him again until Wednesday, when he phoned to say he was in the city and asked if she wanted to get together for lunch. She did. They had lunch, period. When she picked up the check afterward and offhandedly suggested they split it, Jack just as offhandedly agreed.

Lily returned to work feeling restless.

"Is everything all right?" Jill inquired cautiously, when Lily stopped at the secretary's desk to check her messages.

"Why wouldn't it be?" snapped Lily.

The pretty young blonde gave a shrug. "No reason, I suppose. You just seem a little tense lately. That," she added, her lightly freckled face twitching as she struggled not to chuckle, "and the fact that you've flipped through the same three phone messages about six times."

"What?" Lily glanced at the pink slips in her hand and smiled ruefully. "I have, haven't I? I am a little . . . distracted. Sorry if I've been tough to be around lately."

"No problem."

Easy for her to say, Lily thought, as she carried the messages to her desk to look at a seventh time. Personally, *she* had a big problem. Jack.

Her usual method of dealing with a problem was to confront it head on, logically and methodically, and keep at it until she came up with a solution. That wasn't possible in this case. First of all it was tough to attack a problem that was virtually invisible, and any reasonably sane person observing her and Jack together would no doubt conclude that this problem was all in her mind. The question of reasonable sanity led directly to her second difficulty: where Jack was concerned she was never at her most logical.

He called again on Friday. Aha, thought Lily triumphantly. There was no denying that three calls in one week was a bit more than friendly. He told her he had been given a couple of tickets to the Pawtucket Red Sox game that night. Did she feel like coming alone? The Pawtucket Red Sox were the minor league team for the Boston club of the same name, and in all the years she'd lived in Rhode Island Lily had never even had the slightest desire to attend one of their games.

She told him she'd love to go.

The baseball game was more of the same. Jack sat beside her in the crowded bleachers, neither pressing his jean-clad thigh to hers or making any particular effort to avoid it. He was behaving perfectly, exasperatingly normally. Lily was still watching for a slip, some insight into what he was really thinking, proof that he was thinking something besides what a great pal she was to bring along to a ball game. Instead, all she got was enough baseball to last her a lifetime, hot dogs oozing with catsup and ice cream served in a souvenir bowl shaped like a baseball cap.

Alone, after Jack had dropped her off, she slammed doors, hurled clothes across the room as fast as she peeled them off and tried to come to grips with the irony of the situation. Talk about being hoisted with your own petard.

Jack's behavior was everything she could ask for in a friend, she reminded herself glumly. She couldn't help thinking of that old proverb that warned to be very careful what you ask for, because you just might get it.

THIRTY-FIVE

No matter how much Drew enjoyed seeing the downtown store full of shoppers and bustling with activity, there were times when he preferred it as it was now, silent, darkened and deserted.

He used the excuse that he had paperwork to catch up on, but really he just liked wandering through the store alone, maybe stopping to exchange a little sports talk with Sam, the night watchman who had been here almost as long as he had. Goddard's was not only Drew's life, but his legacy, and he visited each floor in turn, noting potential problems, admiring unique qualities, like a loving father tucking in his children for the night.

He felt more at home here than he did anywhere else, and more at peace. Usually. Tonight something kept niggling at the back of his mind, just out of reach. Was it something he had done or failed to do? Drew wondered. Just to be sure, he double-checked the sales floors, then the private salon on three. Lily's room, he thought, that's what he always thought when he gazed on the simple bright place of beauty she had created there. He thought that maybe someone had left some samples lying around but, as it was throughout the store, all was as it should be in the room.

Still vaguely unsettled, he climbed the private back stairs to his own office. Maybe, he thought, this feeling had nothing to do with the store, but was something else entirely. Maybe it was connected to the recent changes in his relationship with Lily. At the top of the stairs he paused and pressed his hand to his chest, feeling an odd bubbling sensation somewhere deep inside. Not terribly painful, just there. He'd felt it before. Maybe he should have taken the elevator instead of the stairs. It had been a long day.

Something inside him immediately stiffened in rebellion. *No!* He would not give up climbing stairs or his occasional cigar or a roast beef sandwich now and then. When it came to living he'd made his choice long ago. He'd rather live whatever life he had, his way, than a long, supposedly healthy life doing exactly what he was told. Not that he wasn't prudent—he was. But enough was enough. Besides, he had no desire to live to be a doddering old man, propped up at family gatherings and always talking about his gout or his gall bladder.

It never occurred to him to connect the pain near his heart with his thoughts of Lily. As much as he loved her, and he did, it hadn't been that hard to let her go. He'd pondered that, and he realized the reason for his peace of mind was twofold. First, the fact was that while his love for Lily was real, it was measured and not the wild, out-of-control mixture of madness and joy that is written about in books and, as he knew firsthand, existed. Quite simply, he didn't love Lily the way he had loved—would always love—Kay.

Giving up Kay... Now that had been something to make his heart break, he thought, remembering with an ache that was just as strong now, twenty years later. It had been so sudden, so out of the blue and so inadequately explained. And though he'd finally given in to her wish that they never see each other again, he had never given up hope that it wouldn't really be that way, that something would happen to change her mind and they would someday be together again. That hadn't happened, of course, and even he had to admit it was beginning to look like it never would. At least not in this life.

The second reason he felt so right about Lily's future was that her situation was so different from Kay's. He supposed that could be summed up by saying that he had all the confidence and respect in the world for Jack Terrell, and none at all for his father. He knew both Jack and Lily, but he knew Lily better, so well he could read her emotions and her desires in her eyes even when something quite contrary was coming from her mouth. No matter what she said, Lily and Jack belonged together. Drew knew in his heart it would work out for them, and that brought him only happiness.

And... that niggling feeling again. What is it? he thought, growing irritable with himself. What is it I want to remember and can't? He had even less chance of recalling it now than he had had a few minutes ago, he thought wryly. As always, when

Kay came into his thoughts, memories of her crowded everything else aside. Tonight he was hooked on recalling those difficult days nearly twenty years ago, after she had called him at the crack of dawn to say they couldn't go on the way they were.

He recalled discussing the matter endlessly, on the phone and in that last meeting they ever had alone. They were in the study at Delaney Place, and for just an instant before Jack burst in and interrupted her, he was certain Kay was about to tell him the real reason they could no longer be together.

That her decision had been in some way orchestrated by James, he had no doubt, then or now. Kay had been overwrought and emotional enough to let slip things that she clearly would have preferred to conceal, determined as she was to bear the burden of whatever it was alone. He understood that James was involved, that he'd done something—or something had happened that James was somehow using as leverage against Kay. That afternoon in the study she had at one point referred to "the accident," her green eyes suddenly filling with tears of unquestionable anguish, but as far as Drew knew none of the Terrells had been involved in an accident of any sort, and it became just one more confusing element of a situation he had never fully understood.

He turned that over in his mind again now and suddenly, like the tumblers on a vault lock clicking into position, it all fell into place in his head—the accident and Kay's anguish and the niggling feeling that had been haunting him. It was as if that vault door had swung open on the truth, and he suddenly knew, beyond doubt, beyond all the hows and whys and bits and pieces of facts he couldn't yet enumerate, that somehow James Terrell had been responsible for the accident that killed Lily's father.

Poor Lily. Did she have any inkling of this? No, no, of course not, he chided himself, thinking of all the heartache and guilt she'd had to bear unnecessarily, and of the wasted years for her and Jack. His chest heaved, and he pressed his hand there in a distracted effort to quiet the mounting pressure.

And Kay? She had to know the truth about the accident, but did she know the rest of it? About how it had devastated Lily and destroyed the future for her and Jack?

No, he decided instantly. Kay had her faults, but she adored her son. There was no way she would stand by and watch him be hurt that way, and no way she would allow an innocent girl to bear that guilt if she'd known the whole story. He was convinced of that, and just as convinced that James would have no such reservations. He was a snake, always looking out for himself first, regardless of who else might suffer. In this case they had all suffered, Kay and Jack, Lily and Drew. Lily most of all.

But this was one time James wasn't going to get away with it. And Drew would be the one to do something, he thought, filled with such rage it was hard to breathe. He tugged loose his shirt collar, trying to focus his thoughts.

Obviously he was the only one who had all the pieces of the puzzle. And he knew and loved both Kay and Lily. He was the only possible one to bring them together and forge some sort of understanding. Without him . . .

The pain in his chest suddenly became unbearable, so bad the room around him faded to black. He pushed himself from his chair, scared now, and found he couldn't stand. No, he thought, even as his knees hit the floor and his face fell against something soft . . . The carpet, he realized distantly. This couldn't happen now. Not now, when he'd finally found a way to save Kay from herself.

Heading downstairs for breakfast, Jack was surprised to hear his mother summoned to the phone. She was usually gone by this time, and his father was more often than not still sleeping off what Jack had observed to be a staggering nightly amount of vodka.

Not that Jack had any complaints about eating breakfast alone. On those few occasions since his return when the three of them had been forced to dine together, the undercurrents of hostility reminded him why his visits home had been so infrequent in the past. In fact, what he was really looking forward to was eating breakfast in his own house.

Even as a kid, Delaney Place had seemed to him more like a place to visit between boarding school and summer camp than a real home. Home was something different, something he'd never really experienced. He hoped to learn about it firsthand in the house he'd bought a short distance from Delaney Place.

As an investment, the old bungalow was overpriced and undermaintained, but it met the only two hard and fast requirements he'd set for the real estate agent: an oceanfront location and plenty of room to expand. Except for some critical plumbing and electrical repairs that had to be done before he could move in, Jack was in no hurry to tackle the renovations. He wasn't sure exactly what or how extensive they would be. He couldn't be sure for a while yet.

He would have just grabbed a cup of coffee and a muffin for the road, but as he was passing the open door of the study he heard a wrenching note of distress in his mother's voice and paused to see if she was all right.

Kay, already dressed for the office in a summery white dress, was standing with her back to him.

"When did it happen?" he heard her ask. There was a long pause while whoever she was talking to replied. "Oh, my God," she said then, with such pain in her voice that Jack knew he was right to stick around. "I'm just so stunned, Anne, and so... so very sorry... Yes, I'm sure you do... If there's anything I can do, anything at all... Yes... Thank you so much for thinking to call to let me know."

Jack watched her slide the receiver into place, then grip the edge of the desk, her shoulders swaying slightly.

He quickly stepped forward. "Mom, are you all right?" he asked, grasping her arm. "What is it?"

She turned to him, her face grayish-white. "Oh, Jack, something terrible has happened."

"Trouble at the plant?" Except for his grandparents' deaths and the day he left to enlist, a crisis at Delaney Silver was the only thing he'd ever seen her get this worked up about.

She shook her head, her gaze clinging to his as if seeking support there as well as from his strong grip. "No, it's Drew. He's dead, Jack. That was Anne Goddard who called to tell me he had a heart attack last night... He's gone. He's really gone."

As she said it her voice dropped and her face softened in a way that reminded Jack of a sand castle crumbling from within. The morning sun slanting through the window behind him accentuated the hollows beneath her eyes where tears were slowly forming a puddle swirled with black mascara. Her eyes were glazed, as if reflecting a loss the proportions of which she couldn't yet comprehend. Jack was startled, thinking she looked more vulnerable than he'd imagined possible for his strong, self-assured mother.

Reaching out, he pulled her into his arms and stroked his hand along her back, feeling the motion of her silent sobs. "It's all right, Mom," he whispered. "It's all right."

For just an instant, his thoughts shifted to Lily and he wondered how she would take the news of Drew's death. Calling on a core of self-control the years alone had honed to steel, he banked down on the urge to go to her and find out if she needed comforting, too. Not this time, he thought. He had to stick to his plan. This time, she had to come to him.

He held Kay until she grew still and he felt the muscles along her back relax.

"Come on," he said, releasing her gently as he used one arm to steer her toward the door. "You need to get off your feet and have a cup of coffee . . . maybe with a shot of brandy."

"No, no," she protested, but she sounded distracted and she let him lead her into the dining room where they were both surprised to see his father seated at the table, a plate of eggs and a pile of packing material before him.

He greeted them with, "Well, well, a family reunion. I ought to get up early more often."

Jack felt his mother stiffen, and he shot his father a warning look as he seated her and reached to pour her a cup of coffee. "Mom just got some bad news," he said. James's brows lifted with interest. "Drew Goddard died of a heart attack last night."

"So what's the bad news?" James shot back.

Kay gasped and lowered her head.

"For God's sake," cried Jack, jerking the coffeepot so that coffee splashed across the table. "Don't you even have the common decency to lay off her at a time like this?"

"Why should I?"

"Why? Because she—"

"Jack, please," interjected Kay, leaving her hand on his arm, "don't bother trying to reason with him." She turned to James. "I suppose I really shouldn't be surprised by your reaction."

"No, you shouldn't," James retorted, pausing with his coffee cup at his lips to add, "so why the hell are you?"

"I suppose I hoped that maybe, just this once, you might put someone else's feelings before your own."

"You thought maybe I would have tried to comfort you, is that it, Kay?"

Kay simply stared at him.

"Maybe if I had the right words and the right pedigree, I could live up to your lofty expectations," he said, his tone unemotional, amused even. "Maybe if I was more like the inimitable Drew Goddard. Of course there is one little thing I've got that old Drew didn't," James continued. "Longevity. I guess there's something to be said for peasant blood after all, since, when all is said and done, I'm here and he's not."

Kay lunged from her seat and swung out as if to slap him across the face. Instead of drawing back, James picked up something from the table and twisted so that it was out of her reach.

"Oh, no, you don't," he said with a harsh laugh.

"You bastard," she cried. "Look what you're doing to me." She covered her face with her hands. "Oh, God, I just can't believe it. I can't believe he's really gone."

"What's not to believe?" snapped James. "The guy's had a bum heart since he was a kid."

Kay slowly lowered her hands to reveal an expression of revulsion. "True," she said, "but at least he had one."

James shook his head as she hurried from the room. "Women. Take it from me, except for my mother and yours, they're all whores."

"She *is* my mother," Jack reminded him through gritted teeth.

"I meant the real one."

"As far as I'm concerned, she is the real one."

"Well, fine then, you're welcome to her. Now tell me, what do you think?"

"I think you owe her an apology," Jack said.

"What the...? I wasn't talking about her," his father replied impatiently. "I meant what do you think of this beauty?"

For the first time Jack paid attention to what all the packing material was for, the glass-encased model ship framed in James's outstretched hands. That's what he had moved so quickly to protect a few moments ago, Jack realized, and that's what was on his mind right now. A damn ship in a bottle.

He'd been collecting them for years, going to auctions and hiring acquisition agents to hunt down rare finds, doing whatever he had to do, legally and otherwise, to get his hands on the ones he wanted. The most prized and valuable ships in his collection ended up in a specially built display case in his office at

Delaney Silver. Judging from the way he was nearly salivating, that's where this one was headed.

"What do I think?" Jack countered. "The same thing I always thought. She's right. You *are* a bastard."

Jack caught up to his mother in the front hallway, standing in front of the oval mirror as she arranged a hat pin in a broad-brimmed straw hat that matched the dark blue dots on her white dress. She'd already retouched her makeup and combed her hair, and that seemed to pull her back together.

"Are you going to be all right?" he asked, feeling at a loss now that she was no longer so obviously in need of comforting.

She turned to face him. "Of course. It was a shock, but I'm—" She breathed in sharply. "I'm better now."

"Why do you stay here?" he asked suddenly.

"Why do I stay?" she echoed, the fine lines in her forehead deepening in bewilderment. "I stay because Delaney Place is my home, of course."

"I mean why do you stay with him? Why the hell don't you throw him out?"

"Oh, that." She shrugged wearily. "I stay in this marriage because that's what Delaneys do, what we have always done. We stay, we endure, we succeed."

"That's crap."

"Perhaps," she agreed with more placidity than Jack expected after impugning the Delaney tradition. "But it's what I've built my life on, what I've worked for and fought for and sacrificed—" She broke off, pressing her lips together. For just an instant, she visibly struggled for control. "I have sacrificed more than you can ever know, maybe more than I should have. But it's done. I did it because I'm a Delaney, and because I believe that counts for something, and because I'm too old to stop believing it now."

"You? Too old?" he teased, but it sounded flat even to him, and for once she didn't smile. "Look, why don't you take the day off? You're in no shape to work."

She shook her head. "I'll be better off with something to keep me busy."

"Then how about if I drive you?"

"No." She squeezed his hand. "I appreciate your concern, sweetheart, but I'd like to be alone for a while."

She turned away quickly, but not quickly enough to hide from Jack the tears that once again filled her eyes. No matter what she said, she was really broken up about this, he thought. It was understandable; she and Drew Goddard had been friends for years. In a way, Drew was a last link to her brother, Ted.

Jack thought about that, about all they must have shared and about the thousands of memories that had bound them. And he thought about another time he'd walked in on his mother in the middle of a heated discussion.

That time she had been closeted in the study and the man with her had been Drew Goddard. When Jack showed up they both struggled to recover from what had obviously been a very emotional exchange. They had passed it off as a disagreement about a mutual friend. It was around the time of Rusty Saville's death and Lily's brush-off, and he, wallowing in his own misery, had bought it. He wasn't buying it now.

Standing in the open door watching her go, Jack suddenly knew the answer to the question Lily had asked that night over dinner. The mystery woman from Drew Goddard's past was his own mother.

Returning to work for the first time after Drew's funeral was one of the hardest things Lily had ever done. For her, Drew *was* Goddard's, and she couldn't imagine being there without him. She didn't even want to imagine whom his sisters would tap to take his place or what sort of changes they would make in the day-to-day running of the store.

She wasn't overly worried, however. Figures didn't lie, and she knew that any financial analyst they consulted would tell them the same thing, that she and her ideas had been good for the bottom line, too good for anyone who wasn't totally ignorant and bitter to tamper with. The sisters were plenty bitter, that had been obvious in their treatment of her at the funeral, but they weren't stupid.

Lily had to steel herself to walk by the closed door of Drew's office. Once inside her own, she struggled to raise the one window she'd insisted remain unsealed. Air-conditioning was fine most of the time, but today she needed fresh air and plenty of it.

As soon as she sat at her desk, memories came tumbling at her from all directions; Drew stopping by to share an impromptu lunch or simply to watch her at her workbench. The time he'd stood right in this very office badgering her to volunteer herself for a celebrity auction to benefit a local charity, then had embarrassed her and his sisters by shamelessly outbidding everyone to win an evening with her.

He'd taught her more about business and beauty than she would have learned in a lifetime at Bonatelli's. And he taught her other, more subtle lessons. By opening her up to the world of privilege and elegance she had once so desperately wanted to be part of, he'd let her discover for herself what all her mother's dire warnings couldn't teach—that it paid to keep your eyes open, because nothing was ever exactly what it seemed on the surface.

The world of the very rich had its share of hidden ugliness, just as even the most modest, shabby places—like the home she was once ashamed to call her own—offered things of real, lasting value. Distance, and Drew, had taught her to appreciate those things.

Enough, Lily told herself, trying to shake off her melancholy mood as she turned her attention to the stack of papers and notes on her desk. She managed to get through a few before freezing at the sight of a reminder to herself to check with Drew about using a single motif for the entire reproduction line.

Crumbling it, she tossed it into the wastebasket, aware of a gnawing emptiness inside. She would just have to decide that, and a great many other things, on her own. It wasn't a happy prospect, but if she was honest, she had to admit that if she was able to check with Drew, he would listen and draw out all the subtle shades and angles of her idea, then say, "Go with your instincts."

It was, she recalled sadly, one of the last things he had said to her. She was grateful all the way to her soul that in the days before his heart attack, the two of them had recaptured the easy affection they used to share. One day last week he had playfully commandeered her from her office for what had become a private tradition on the first day of the year that the thermometer topped eighty degrees, a walk to the sidewalk stand a few blocks away for frozen lemonade.

They had taken their time, talking about everything from a book he had just finished reading to a problem he was having with his beloved sailboat. Eventually the conversation had gotten around to the subject of her and Jack, which wasn't surprising, considering how her thoughts lately seemed to be locked in that pattern, like a jetliner endlessly circling a cloud-covered airport.

It was a relief to argue the matter with someone besides herself, and Lily found herself telling him about her fears and suspicions and about how she seemed to be the only one aware of the physical attraction whenever they were together.

"A physical attraction?" Drew queried. "Are you sure that's all you're feeling?"

"Of course. I mean, it's not like I'm still in love with him or anything," she concluded a little desperately. "How could I be after all this time?"

Drew smiled, a little sadly, Lily thought, but he didn't comment.

"I'd just like to know what he's up to," she grumbled.

"Then why don't you ask him?"

"Ask him?"

"Sure. If you really want to know."

"Then it would look like I'm the one who has more than friendship on her mind, which is probably exactly what he wants." She glanced at his bemused expression. "I get it, you think maybe I'm enjoying his little game?"

"I didn't say that. Although I do think romance can be very enjoyable."

"Romance? Ha!" Lily shot back, uneasily aware that it sounded as if she was complaining. "He treats me like one of his flying buddies."

Drew chuckled. "Take it from me, Lily, romance comes in a variety of flavors."

"Well, I don't like this flavor."

"Maybe it will grow on you. Like pistachio."

"More like fungus." She drained the last drop of lemonade from the paper cup and crumpled it. "Maybe you're right, maybe I should force it out into the open by asking him. Not that he would tell me the truth, anyway."

"What makes you so sure?"

"Because I've narrowed it down to two possible motives on his part, and neither one is something he's likely to confess. Either he's softening me up for the kill," she explained, "or he's after revenge."

Drew clapped her on the back. "Either one promises to make your life very interesting for the foreseeable future."

"You're not taking this very seriously."

"I think you're taking it seriously enough for the entire western world. Besides, I trust Jack. Cheer up, Lily," he urged, offering her a hand up. "Having a man like Jack pursue you—regardless of his unorthodox approach—isn't the worst thing that could happen to you. In fact, I think it's exactly what you need."

"Jack isn't just any man," she reminded him grimly.

"That's right, I'd forgotten. He's the ghost of mistakes past."

"Don't laugh at me," she chided.

"I would never laugh at you, Lily."

"You're certainly not helping me decide what to do about him."

"I told you the night Jack arrived home what I thought you should do. You just didn't like hearing it. My advice is still the same. Think it over," Drew urged. "Then go with your instincts."

Lily smiled now at the recollection. The problem was that where Jack was concerned, her instincts went so haywire they couldn't be trusted. The boundaries, between what she wanted and what was smart became confused, and she was stricken with all sorts of strange, exciting, forbidden feelings.

Deep down, she knew she'd felt it all before, and that Jack had been the cause then, too. But it was so long ago, she'd managed to convince herself that she imagined most of it, that time and fantasies had enhanced what she'd only thought she felt, that desire so intense, pleasure so pure, just didn't exist.

Certainly on those few dismal occasions when she had tried to recapture it, she had failed miserably. Her statement to Jack that she never got involved with men who turned her on had been totally spontaneous, the fastest way out of a tight spot. Only in thinking it over later did she realize how much truth it contained. The only men she ever allowed herself to date were those who met some subconscious definition of "safe." Men who were *manageable*, as Jack had put it. Any man who didn't meet that criterion received the cool hands-off signal she'd perfected years ago. It was a foolproof method of self-control . . . and a perfect formula for disastrous sex.

Now, it all threatened to backfire with a vengeance. Jack was rousing feelings she'd kept too tightly reined for too long. And for all her success and sophistication in other areas of life, Lily felt nearly as ill-equipped to handle an explosion of them now as she had at eighteen.

With a sigh, she reached to answer the intercom, which she realized had been buzzing for several seconds.

"Yes, Jill," she said.

"Lily, you just had a call from Bernard Shields."

Lily recognized the name of the Goddard family attorney. "Fine, I'll take it."

"Uh, he didn't stay on the line. He just asked me to tell you that he'd like to meet with you right away."

"What?" Frowning, Lily glanced at her appointment calendar. "I can't possibly get away this morning. Did he say what he wanted?"

"Not exactly."

"Never mind, just ring him back, please."

"Lily, I think you ought to know that he's here."

"Here?"

"In Mr. Goddard's office, I mean. That's where he said he wants to meet with you."

Puzzled and a little annoyed, Lily made the short walk down one flight to Drew's office. Drew's secretary was still at her post. The woman's nervous smile as she ushered Lily directly to the inner office was Lily's first warning that something was amiss. The sight of Anne and Elise Goddard, seated like bookends in the chairs in front of Drew's antique mahogany desk, was her second.

THIRTY-SIX

Lily nodded at the two older women, trying not to think about how eerie it felt to be in that room without Drew present, and they nodded back. Bernard Shields sat in Drew's place behind the desk, looking trim, successful and very ill at ease. Warning number three.

An empty straight-backed chair waited for Lily.

Bernard half stood and motioned her toward it.

"Thanks," Lily said, "I have a feeling I'd rather stand for this."

Bernard frowned. "Really, Lily, I'd like to make this as—"

"Let her suit herself," Anne interjected. "This won't take long."

Lily braced herself for the worst and listened as Bernard stiffly explained that since Anne and Elise were now entirely in control of Goddard's, they would be making some sweeping changes. The first thing to be swept out the door was her.

The news was like a knife twisting inside her, driving home to Lily just how much Goddard's had come to mean to her. It was as if she'd taken in an ailing child and nursed it back to health, loving it and watching it grow strong and healthy, only to be suddenly told that its parents wanted it back. The fact their name was Goddard and hers wasn't didn't change the way she felt. Some truths were written in the heart, not on a legal pad.

She listened as Bernard talked about severance pay and continued benefits, all very generous, he assured her, and as numb as she was, Lily knew it was true. Evidently it was worth any price to Drew's sisters to get rid of her. Lily bit the inside of her cheeks and kept her hands loosely folded atop the chair back, determined they shouldn't have the added bonus of seeing how much they had succeeded in hurting her.

"Do you have any questions, Lily?" Bernard asked when his rehearsed spiel was finished. Obviously this was a move that had been in the works for some time. Probably within minutes of their learning that Drew's heart attack was fatal.

"Just one," she said. "What about the Saville boutiques that were planned to feature my designs?"

"As for the boutique idea," he began, "I've been told that there is no interest in going ahead with it."

"None at all," Anne reiterated.

"Now concerning that jewelry itself," Bernard hurriedly continued, "I've looked into the matter very closely." He paused to shuffle papers, squirming in his seat. "Since none of the work you did on behalf of Goddard's was ever copyrighted separately or in your own name, it is considered part of the store's inventory. A very profitable part, I might add, so you can understand why—"

"Those designs are mine," Lily snapped, finally having a legitimate reason to spew some of the venom building up inside. "There was never any question of that."

"No one is questioning it now," Bernard replied stiffly. "But the law is the law. You are, of course, free to consult your own attorney for an interpretation."

"Maybe I'll do just that," Lily replied, but it was a hollow threat. Profitable or not, the Goddard sisters wouldn't have launched a battle over the designs if they thought there was even a slight chance they might lose. They weren't half as interested in profits as they were in revenge. As far as they were concerned, she had stolen their influence over Drew and the Goddard stores, and now they were returning the favor.

She stared at them, their thin, smug, red-lipstick-coated smiles looking formed and baked, like something from a beginner's ceramics class. They stared back. Bernard had to clear his throat twice to get everyone's attention.

"The good news for you, Lily," he said, "is that because Saville is your own name, you are free to use it any way you choose in future work, and of course you will share in whatever profits your designs earn for Goddard's, per the terms of your original contract."

"Fine. Is that all?"

"I believe so." He glanced at the two older women. "Unless either of you have anything to add?"

"Not I," said Anne. "Elise, dear?"

Elise shook her head.

"Well, I do," Lily said. "I have a question for you. Have either of you given any consideration to the effect it will have on Goddard's to lose both Drew and myself at the same time?"

"I'm sure we'll manage," Anne retorted.

"How? The way you were managing before Drew had the guts and foresight to turn things around? My God, these stores have been in your family for nearly a hundred years. Your father and grandfather and Drew spent their entire lives working to make them a success. Doesn't that mean anything to you?"

"It did," Anne said. "Once."

Elise nodded, a quick, birdlike motion of her head. "Everything's changed now. Why, just walking into the downtown store makes me want to cry. So many changes."

"But they were changes for the better," Lily exclaimed. "They worked."

"In your opinion, perhaps," countered Anne, her pinched expression revealing how much value she put on that.

"We've felt this way all along," Anne reminded her, "but of course Drew wouldn't hear of going against you and your notions."

"But now Drew is gone," said Lily, gripping the chair for support. "And you can finally have your way."

"Yes," agreed Anne, the curve of her lips a restrained display of pleasure, "now he's gone. My poor brother, run ragged, the stress of knowing he betrayed all that his father and grandfather struggled—"

"Betrayed?" Lily exclaimed. "He saved it."

"Oh, no, those stores with all their glass and escalators aren't the real Goddard's. Anyone who used to shop at Goddard's knows that. Why, people stop me on the street all the time to tell me so. Don't think they didn't tell Drew, as well, or that it didn't eat away at him no matter how he tried to cover up for your sake. Everything he did was for your sake, the pace he kept. It's no wonder his poor heart gave out."

"Drew was happy with my work at Goddard's."

Anne's eyes were small black beads, bullets aimed directly at Lily. "Yes, well, perhaps if he'd been a little less *happy*, he would be alive."

The sly insinuation was more than Lily could deal with right then. The solid wood door crashed against the wall as she threw it open. Bernard caught up with her in the reception area outside.

"Lily, please, wait. Let me finish up with them and then we can talk. Perhaps I can explain why—"

"I've heard enough. And as for explanations, I know better than anyone why they're doing this."

"I didn't want to handle it this way, believe me. Drew and I went back a long way, and he would not have wanted this. You were absolutely right in there. I can't count the times Drew sang your praises to me."

"You don't have to tell me that," Lily said bluntly. "Those old bitches can think and say whatever they like. I know where I stood with Drew."

"I'm glad to hear that. I was afraid you might blame me for—"

"I don't," she interrupted. "This is between them and me, and it's been a long time coming. In a way, I'm glad it's over."

In another way, a big part of her was dying, but Lily couldn't allow herself to think about that until she had packed a few personal items in her office and gotten away from there. Bernard had made it clear that the terms of her dismissal were immediate.

Tossing photographs and her favorite sketching supplies into a canvas tote, she gave a tearful Jill instructions for packing the rest of her belongings. Lily's brother Joey used a truck in the landscaping business that was his career of the month; she would ask him to pick up the boxes for her in a few days.

The last thing she did was clear off her desk, tossing some papers into the trash, putting aside others that she knew her replacement would have to deal with immediately. She paused when she picked up the folder containing material on the museum reproduction project.

This wasn't copyrighted in her name, either. In fact it hadn't yet been copyrighted at all. Only she, Drew and Maggie had been aware of the project's scope and theme. It was the last thing she and Drew had worked on together, and he had been as excited about it as she was. If she left it behind, Lily was certain it would be ignored, or worse, horribly mishandled.

Damn it, she didn't want that to happen. She'd worked too hard. The research was all hers, the sketches were hers, even the inspiration for them was hers alone. Go with your instincts, Drew would tell her if he were there. Without a shred of remorse, Lily dropped the folder into her tote bag and walked out.

It felt odd to be outside in the middle of a weekday morning and not be on her way to a business appointment or to handle some crisis at one of the branches. At the adjacent garage, Lily tossed the tote bag onto the back seat of her white Saab and took off with absolutely no idea where she was going. Home held little appeal. She didn't want to be alone and wasn't ready to talk. Plugging in a classical music cassette that Drew had taped especially for her, she drove aimlessly, with no conscious thought of visiting the cemetery until she found herself outside its gates.

The winding, tree-shaded road through the private cemetery curved and crisscrossed, and it took Lily a few minutes to locate the black marble monument that marked the Goddard family plot. She parked and started up the grassy knoll to the place where Drew was buried. Not until she reached the top did she notice that someone was already there. Her heart skipped a beat, as she thought that maybe Anne or Elise had decided to share their victory. Then she realized that the tall, slender woman in a sleeveless, black-and-white checked dress was Kay Terrell.

Coming to a halt a discreet distance away, Lily saw that Kay was holding a bouquet of roses. A rainbow of petals covered the soft ground at her feet, as if she had purposely shaken them loose.

After a moment, she lifted her head and noticed Lily.

"Hello, Lily," she said. "I passed a street vendor selling roses on my way to work today, and it suddenly occurred to me that Drew deserved some flowers that weren't all perfectly arranged in those hideous funeral baskets."

Lily looked on as Kay stooped and carefully placed the bundle of flowers on the ground. "I'm sure Drew would prefer these."

"Yes," agreed Kay, her smile tremulous, "I think he would."

"I didn't mean to intrude," Lily said. "I didn't see your car when I pulled up."

"I asked my driver to give me a few moments alone. Funerals are always so crowded and formal. I wanted a chance to say goodbye in my own way."

"I'm sorry, I should leave..."

"No, please don't go. Standing here, I finally realized that Drew and I said the goodbyes that counted a long time ago." She shrugged a little awkwardly. "There's a line from a song I heard the other day…'Who taught time to fly?' Trite, but true, I'm afraid."

She lowered her gaze to the fresh emerald green sod covering Drew's grave. "Sometimes we throw something away, but deep down we cling to the belief that it isn't really gone, that someday, if we want to, we can get it all back. Then the day comes along when we have to face the fact that it really is gone forever."

Her oversize sunglasses couldn't hide the sorrow etched on Kay's face. Lily wasn't sure how to comfort her. Clearly, whatever regrets Kay was suffering had to do with Drew, but as far as Lily knew the two had never had a falling out or even a serious disagreement. Drew always spoke of Kay in the most flattering, affectionate terms.

"Maybe the best we can do," Lily offered, "is to accept that there are some things we can't change, and just let go of the bad feelings they bring and go on with our lives. Actually," she added, "it was Drew who helped me to understand that."

Kay smiled. "Yes, that sounds like Drew. Always so accepting. Always so understanding. Perhaps if he hadn't been quite so understanding—" She broke off abruptly, a single tear sliding from beneath her sunglasses. "Will you listen to me?" she said with an attempt at laughter. "Now I'm intruding on your privacy."

"Not at all," Lily assured her.

"Well, I'm sure you didn't come all the way out here to listen to my morose ramblings."

Removing her sunglasses, she dabbed at the corners of her eyes with an embroidered handkerchief. When she lifted her head, her smile was brittle and Lily found herself staring into eyes as green as her own.

Funny, she had never before paid much attention to the color of Kay's eyes. Now she did. As surely as if Drew was standing beside her, she heard him telling her what he had the night of the jewelry show at Biltmore, that he had once loved a woman with green eyes. He'd told Lily he had come to her rescue because he had never been able to do so for the woman he loved.

In that instant, a number of things that had puzzled Lily became clear, including why Kay was standing at Drew's grave

with her eyes full of sorrow and regrets. At the same time new
puzzles took shape. Those would have to remain, Lily told
herself firmly. If neither Kay nor Drew had ever chosen to reveal what was between them, it wasn't her place to start asking
questions now.

"Actually, I'm not sure exactly why I came here," she told
Kay in an attempt to make this easier for Kay by turning the
focus of their conversation elsewhere. "Maybe for moral support." She briefly explained what had happened that morning.

"Those bitches," Kay snapped, stabbing her sunglasses into
place.

"My words exactly."

"I'm sure this is a terrible shock, Lily, but you have to tell
yourself it was for the best. I can't imagine what it would be like
to work for those two and to have to kowtow to their petty de-
mands on a daily basis."

"I know you're right, but it's going to take me a while to see
the bright side. Goddard's was my whole world."

"Well, the benefits of your association work both ways,
don't ever forget that. At least you won't have any trouble
finding another position. Your success at Goddard's hasn't
gone unnoticed. I know for a fact that there are any number of
firms that would... What is wrong with me?" she demanded
suddenly. "I must be so caught up in feeling sorry for myself,
I'm not thinking straight. Why else would I stand here, plugging the competition, when for years I've fantasized about how
wonderful it would be to steal you away from Goddard's myself?"

"You mean to work for Delaney Silver?"

"Of course. I can't promise you the lofty title of design director—at least not right away—but you would be guaranteed
a virtually free rein. Think of it, Lily, while Delaney might not
offer the product diversity of Goddard's, everything we do is
of our own design... and unless I miss my guess, designing is
still your first love."

"That's true," Lily admitted. "But I've only been unem-
ployed a few hours. I hadn't even thought about finding another job. Maybe I'll just take some time off. I haven't had a
real vacation in years."

"Then you deserve a nice long one. Just promise me you'll
think about my offer. I need you, Lily." She pressed one of Li-

ly's hands between both of hers. "And I'm not being overly dramatic when I say that Delaney Silver needs you. Promise me you'll think about it?"

Lily promised she would.

Alone, after Kay had gone, she clasped her hands together and said a quiet prayer for Drew. She had come here still fuming after her morning ordeal, hoping for what, she wasn't sure, some sort of cosmic comfort, perhaps? Instead she'd ended up pouring her heart out to Kay, and with much more concrete results, a job offer. Fate, Lily wondered, glancing at the rose-covered grass, or something else.

As tempting as the offer was, however, she couldn't work up much joy or enthusiasm at the moment. Seeing Kay's bleak, hollow expression as she alluded to mistakes she had made—mistakes that perhaps cost her a lifetime of happiness with a man she obviously loved very much—certainly put losing a job, any job, in perspective.

It also left Lily with a chilling sense of foreboding. It didn't always take psychic powers to see into the future. And it didn't take much imagination to picture herself where Kay was today, standing at a point of no return looking back on a life that looked so perfect and felt so wrong.

THIRTY-SEVEN

For several weeks after her encounter with Kay, Lily did just as she'd suggested she might—she treated herself to a long-overdue vacation. With no reason to stay in the city, she packed the essentials and moved home. She'd forgotten the benefits of spending the summer just a bike ride away from the beach. June melted into July and with no time constraints, she got to know her hometown all over again.

In the years since she'd moved away, the distinctions between Watch Hill and Misquamicut had blurred. An influx of yuppie money in the early eighties had polished some of the honky-tonk off the waterfront close to home, and several miles farther along the coast, a few of Delaney Place's stately neighbors had succumbed to the sudden economic downswing and been converted to luxury condos.

A few things remained exactly the same—the flying ponies on the Watch Hill carousel and the tearoom in the village; the clam shacks along Misquamicut Beach and the shouts and laughter pouring from the oceanfront roller rink on hot summer nights. But that solid, unbreachable line of demarcation had paled, or perhaps, thought Lily, she'd just become better at straddling it.

She spent her days in lazy splendor, watching soap operas and eating junk food and catching up on all the books she'd been wanting to read. She went to the beach and made her mother happy by learning to cook and she saw more of Jack than either she or her mother thought wise. She didn't come any closer to forcing his hand, but there was something about the long, hot days of freedom that took the edge off her need to have every last detail of her life neatly resolved right that very minute.

He still made her crazy, but it was a more mellow kind of crazy. She accepted Jack as part of the moment, one more fleeting pleasure to be savored, like the smell of summer rain or the warmth of the sun that was gradually turning her pale skin to golden brown. Dangerous, she knew, but since this was the first—and probably last—summer she would ever have to indulge herself, she refused to worry about it.

She also kept her promise to think about Kay's offer. It was hard not to think about it. Lily found the prospect of working at Delaney Silver intriguing on several levels, much more intriguing than any of the other offers that had come her way thanks to Maggie for spreading word of her availability on the industry grapevine that stretched all the way to New York City.

For one thing, joining Delaney Silver as a top designer would be a triumphant return to the place where she'd gotten her start on the assembly line. A homecoming of sorts, and she was discovering a new affection for things connected with home. It would also provide new creative challenges and the chance to apply her designs to something beyond jewelry. Then, too, the business side of her couldn't resist noting that Delaney Silver would be the perfect place to bring her idea for the museum reproductions.

Since her mother was in her glory having her around, Lily expected her to be in favor of anything that would keep her close by on a more permanent basis. Instead, Mary was vehemently opposed to the idea of Lily working at Delaney Silver.

"I just don't understand why you would want to go back to that place," Mary said one afternoon when she and Lily were sitting on the front porch, sipping iced coffee with cream and sugar, one more delectable ritual they'd established.

Since they had been over the more artistic reasons a dozen times, Lily decided to try a more practical form of persuasion. "Did I mention the salary Kay Terrell offered the last time she called?"

Her mother shrugged. "Money isn't everything."

"Oh, my God, quick, the smelling salts."

"Be quiet," Mary said, chuckling in spite of herself. "It's the truth."

"Of course, money isn't everything," Lily agreed. "There are also pension plans to consider, stock options—"

"All right, go on," her mother interrupted. "I'm only thinking of your happiness."

"Mom, why are you so convinced I won't be happy at Delaney Silver?"

Mary gripped the arms of the old metal porch chair and set it rocking gently. Maybe Lily would be happy working there, for a while. But she had plenty of other people calling here and wanting her to go to work for them, and Lily was the type who'd make good anywhere. And none of those other jobs would put her right under James Terrell's nose, day in and day out. It was just too risky.

"I don't *know* for sure you won't be happy there," she said. "It just seems to me to be the opposite of what you always said you wanted to do. I remember how you were always talking about striking out on your own."

"I guess I got a lot of that out of my system at Goddard's. Drew gave me total freedom with my own work, and at the same time he made me see a bigger picture." Her expression introspective, Lily idly traced a gouge in the wooden floor with her bare toe. "I'm not sure I want to go back to the limitations of working on a small scale. Besides," she added, looking askance at Mary. "I remember how you were always lecturing me about security. Nothing is more risky than trying to make it as a free-lancer."

"Some risks are worth taking," Mary told her. "Some aren't."

"I get it," said Lily. "It's not Delaney Silver, but a particular member of the Delaney family that you consider a risk not worth taking. Am I right?"

Fear lodged in Mary's throat. How on earth . . .

"Obviously I am," Lily continued. "You look like you're about to pop a blood vessel. Mom, how many times do I have to tell you not to worry about me getting involved with Jack? Whether I decide to stay around and take the job at Delaney or not, that's not going to happen."

Jack, Mary thought with a surge of relief. She was talking about Jack. She didn't know anything about James and the rest of it. She couldn't possibly.

"Seems to me you're already too involved," Mary said, mopping a sudden excess of perspiration from her face with a napkin.

"We're friends. I explained all that to you."

"Friends, humph."

"It's the truth," Lily insisted, draining the last of her iced coffee. "And since he's going to be here in a while, I better run upstairs and change."

"What sort of *friendly* excursion has he planned for the two of you this time?"

"Shopping," Lily replied, pausing at the front door. "He wants some help choosing furniture for his new house."

"Yup," Mary said after she'd disappeared inside. "That sounds friendly, all right."

It wasn't like she had anything against Jack Terrell, other than the fact that he *was* a Terrell. For years she'd been nagging Lily to find a nice man and settle down. Now it looked like she might have done just that—and he turned out to be the one man who was a sure path to heartbreak.

Lily could say what she pleased about this "just friends" nonsense. All it took was one look at her eyes—which finally had their sparkle back after the sorrow of losing Drew and all that bad blood with his sisters—for Mary to know what was what. It was hard enough to face the prospect of Lily working side by side with James Terrell, but to have to marry right into his family... just thinking about it made her insides shudder.

Mary lurched to her feet so quickly the metal runners of the chair clanked against the floor. She couldn't stand to sit there brooding over this for another minute, knowing that it was leading where it always led lately.

Besides, she had work to do. The whole gang was coming for dinner on Sunday. She planned to make lasagna ahead of time, then all she'd have to do was heat it in the microwave oven that Lily had insisted on buying for her. The things that girl couldn't live without. That thought quickly led Mary back to Jack Terrell. There was just no escaping it.

She filled a pot with water and put it on to boil, then poured oil into a deep frying pan. If she concentrated hard enough on what her hands were doing, maybe the question that was haunting her would go away. Stooping, she fished inside the corner cupboard for the right pot cover, silently reciting the ingredients for a recipe she knew by heart. One package of wide noodles, one pound of mozzarella cheese, two chopped onions...

It was no use. The truth wound itself through her thoughts like a weed snaking its way thought a garden of daintier blooms, choking them. The truth was that Lily was no longer a child in need of constant protection, and Mary had to ask herself what she was really trying so hard to protect. Lily's future? Or the secrets of her own past?

Lost in the unhappy maze of her own thoughts, she slammed the cover onto the frying pan, leaving the water uncovered, and went to find two onions. She'd been chopping for a few minutes before she glanced over and realized that she'd covered the wrong pan. Wiping her hands on her apron, she automatically reached to make the switch.

As soon as she lifted the cover and the air reached the overheated oil inside, there was a loud whoosh, and the pan exploded into flames that shot all the way to the ceiling.

"Oh, no," Mary cried, as she saw a fiery offshoot ignite the window curtain she'd hitched back to let the breeze in. Flinging the cover aside, she began batting at the curtain with her hand. When that didn't work, she grabbed the iced coffeepot she had left soaking in the sink.

"No!"

She hadn't realized Jack was there until he shouted and snatched the pitcher of water from her.

"Is that grease in the pan?" he demanded.

She nodded frantically. "Oil."

He glanced around, then lunged for the cover she'd tossed onto the floor and brought it down over the flaming pot, sealing the fire inside.

"Oh, thank God," she murmured, looking on gratefully as he quickly wet down the smoldering curtain with a dish towel. "Thank God. I don't know what I was thinking of, throwing water on a grease fire. I ought to know better."

Jack turned and smiled at her. "We all get flustered at times like that."

"You didn't," Mary felt obliged to point out.

He shrugged. "They're not my curtains."

She had to smile. "I guess I owe you one."

"I guess you hate that. Feeling they way you do about me."

"I don't feel any particular way about you," she said, busying herself sweeping bits of charred fabric off the counter.

"You don't especially like me hanging around Lily."

"What's the harm in it? Since you're only interested in being her friend," she added, with a pointed look his way. "At least that's what she told me."

"That's because that's what I told her. But I lied." He flashed that smile again, and it was easy for Mary to see how he could have turned Lily's head. Not once, but twice.

"You lied?"

"That's right."

"Aren't you afraid to admit that to me?"

"No. I figure you already know I lied."

"I mean, aren't you afraid I'll tell Lily?"

"No, she already knows, too."

"Then why lie in the first place?"

"Because I was on the spot," he admitted ruefully, "and it was the only thing I could think of at the time that wouldn't scare Lily away. It still is." He rested his hips against the counter, balancing the cane by his side. "If you can do better, I'm open to suggestions."

Mary shook her head, incredulous. "Why would you ask me for help thinking up something to tell Lily?"

"Because I love her," he said simply.

His guilelessness caught Mary off guard, chipping away at her resistance where his smile had left off. She crossed the room and lowered herself into a chair, thinking about how to respond.

"Not that she isn't bright and beautiful and you wouldn't be darn lucky to have her," she said finally, "but why have you settled so hard on my Lily?"

"Because she's bright and beautiful and I'll be darn lucky to have her."

"Why her and not one of your own kind? Don't laugh," she admonished him. "You know what I mean."

"I know exactly what you mean, Mrs. Saville. I'm just not sure how to answer that."

"Not with another lie," she warned.

"Deal." He reached for the cane and crossed to stand in front of the refrigerator, staring at the photos of her grandchildren in the their Little League uniforms and ballerina outfits and at the ever present gallery of their drawings.

"When I was younger," he said, still without looking at her, "I used to wonder what it was like to live in a house like this, with a real family, brothers and sisters who picked on each other and had nicknames for each other. With a mother who cooked and a father who knew how to do things with his hands." His broad shoulders lifted awkwardly inside the dark blue cotton shirt. "Sometimes, when I was real young, I'd see your husband working around and I even wondered what it would be like to have him for a father. I wondered if he ever took his kids fishing."

"He did," said Mary quietly.

"I never told Lily any of this," he said with a quick glance over his shoulder at her.

"I understand."

"Anyway, I've lived most of my life alone, more or less. It took coming close to dying for me to realize I don't want to spend the rest of it that way." He turned and faced her. "I want that family I used to think about having, Mrs. Saville. Only I don't have the slightest idea how to go about it. I don't know what kinds of things go on in houses like this, what families say to each other or do for each other. I couldn't know," he continued, "because the place where I grew up was nothing like this. I want a woman who does know."

"A woman like Lily."

He nodded. "It won't be easy." Breaking into a grin, he added, "Not much that I decide to do ever is."

"You've got spunk, I'll say that much."

"There's a lot of leftover baggage between Lily and me. That's why I decided to give her time to come around in her own way, all the time she needs."

"And what if she doesn't come around, Jack?"

"She will." He took the seat across from her. "Do you believe in God, Mrs. Saville?"

"Of course."

"Well, for a long time I wasn't sure I did. Then when I was in the hospital, out of my head with pain half the time and from the painkillers they fed me the other half, I opened my eyes one day to find a priest standing in my room. He asked me my name, and when I told him, he smiled and said I was the one who had asked for him. I just laughed and said, 'Sorry, Father, but not even if I were delirious would I ask for a priest.'"

Mary sat silently as Jack stretched his long legs out in front of him and crossed them at the ankle before going on.

"He was decent about it, said no problem and left behind a pamphlet on the nightstand for me. It was days before I even felt like looking at it. I remember it was bright yellow, and in big black letters on the front, it said, 'Is there something missing in your life?'"

"Faith," Mary said.

"I'm sure that's what the good father had in mind for my answer," Jack countered with amusement, "but after thinking about it for a long time, I came up with my own answer. If I could name one thing I wanted that my life was missing, it would be Lily."

Goose bumps spread across Mary's skin the way they always did when a movie had a happy ending. But this wasn't a happy ending, she reminded herself.

"That's when I made up my mind that when I got back here, I was going to do whatever it took to get her back," he explained. "And that's why I know she's going to come around."

"And you're telling me all this because you want me to help?"

"I wouldn't argue if you wanted to put in a good word for me," he admitted. "Mostly, though, I just wanted you to understand. I know you have your own reservations about me, and I've been waiting for an opportunity to tell you that one thing you don't have to worry about is Lily getting hurt. Because I will never let that happen. No matter what."

"We can't always keep people from being hurt, no matter how much we love them. Sometimes it's out of our control," she told him.

And sometimes, she thought, absently twisting her wedding ring, *we just have to accept that fact and let things run their course.* How many times had poor Rusty tried to get her to see that? Maybe it wasn't too late for an old dog to learn new tricks.

As she fumbled in her pocket for a used napkin, she heard Lily's footsteps on the stairs. Jumping up, she hurried over to the cutting board and picked up the knife.

"Hi, Jack," Lily said as she entered the kitchen. "Have you been waiting long?"

"Long enough to put out a fire and save your mother's life," Mary replied before he had a chance to, her eyes on the cutting board.

"What fire?" Catching sight of the charred curtain, Lily exclaimed, "Mom, what happened? Are you all right?"

"I'm fine, thanks to Jack."

"That's an exaggeration," he told Lily. "It was a little grease fire. All I did was put a cover on a pan."

Lily came to stand beside Mary. "Are you crying?" she asked quietly.

Mary wiped her eye with the back of the hand holding the knife. "Don't I always cry when I chop onions? And at the rate I'm going I'll be here crying all night. One interruption after another... I swear, some things never change."

"I can take a hint," Lily said, with a smile that didn't quite conceal her concern. She brushed a kiss across Mary's cheek. "We're going. I won't be late."

"All right," Mary replied. As the screen door squeaked open, she suddenly turned and called out, "Lily..."

Lily stopped and looked at her. "Yes?"

"Have a good time, okay?"

She didn't usually wait up for Lily; their notions of "late" were very different. Tonight she did. All through the eleven o'clock news she debated the best way to say what she had to say, and finally decided that sometimes the least said the better.

They shared a quiet cup of tea, and Mary waited until Lily was headed up the stairs to say, almost as if it was an afterthought, "You know, I've been thinking some more about that job Kay Terrell offered you."

Lily groaned and yawned. "And?"

"And I think you ought to take it."

THIRTY-EIGHT

Lily decided she would take the position at Delaney Silver with the stipulation that it was a package deal—either the company took her and her idea for the museum reproduction project, or nothing.

Over the summer she'd researched and refined her original concept with the Delaney tradition in mind. Still, it was an innovative venture, being proposed by a designer who didn't even have her foot in the door yet, and Lily anticipated a hard sell.

She was pleasantly surprised to instead find Kay instantly receptive to the idea, agreeing wholeheartedly with Lily's assessment that the current trend among rival silversmiths to offer products that were starkly modern was all wrong.

"It's a wonderful idea," she told Lily when they met in her office to discuss it. "I've been saying for years now that all those aging baby boomers out there can be prodded into buying silver. All we have to do is find the perfect prod, and unless I miss my guess, you've done just that. What's that saying...everything old is new again?"

"That's what I intended," Lily responded, "to come up with a fresh twist on the old, and the tie-in with the museum pieces helps to underscore that."

Kay turned to the color sketches Lily had brought along, studying the detailed renderings of silver powder pots and treasure boxes and silver-handled sable brushes reminiscent of Victorian originals. There were tiny oval frames, perfect for holding a lover's photograph, purse-size compacts no woman could resist and silver-topped perfume decanters that any man would love to buy for the woman in his life. Each piece was beautiful and extravagant and irresistible, and yet all bore a variation on a single motif. The fleur-de-lis.

Lily had derived the motif from a retired Delaney silverware pattern of the same name. It had been one of the company's top sellers from the turn of the century to the fifties. Only later, when she was researching the name for her presentation to Kay, did she discover that traditionally the fleur-de-lis was an iris, most often a white one.

Curiosity had prompted her to ask Kay what had ever happened to her father's effort to produce a new iris, but Kay's response had been vague, almost evasive. Lily attributed it to her uneasiness at having to admit that, with Rusty gone, the project had eventually been abandoned. Still, the fact that she'd happened upon the name fleur-de-lis seemed to be fate, and it made the project even more important to her. It was almost as if, symbolically at least, she was reclaiming his dream. Only this time the dream was going to come true.

During her presentation, Kay concurred with Lily's conviction that timing was crucial.

"Not only because of the museum exhibit," she said, "although I can see where that could be advantageous for publicity and advertising photos." She peered through the black half glasses she wore only in the office at a sketch of a potpourri jar. "We'll be missing out if we don't hit the wedding market hard with this. I'm thinking of shower and bridesmaids gifts and the like."

Impressed by Kay's marketing savvy, Lily asked, "Can we move that quickly?"

"We sure can," Kay shot back, her eyes flashing with excitement above a full grin. "And I intend to stand this place on its ear if I have to, in order to do it."

Lily leaned forward excitedly. "Does that mean you're interested in going ahead with my idea?"

"More than interested, Lily. I'm thrilled that you brought it to me. This is precisely what Delaney needs to jump start sales."

"And the copyright stipulations I mentioned?"

"I think you're very wise to insist on them. I'll have the legal department draw up an agreement satisfactory to both of us."

"I'll understand if you also want to check with your production staff before you commit yourself."

Kay laughed. "You'll find that around here, people check with me, not the other way around. Take my word for it, Delaney Silver is going to put everything it has behind this, and when the time comes," she continued, with a broad smile of anticipation, "We're going to unveil the Fleur-de-lis line with more fanfare than this industry has seen in a long time." She stretched her hand across the desk. "Welcome aboard, Lily."

September seemed an appropriate time for Lily to be making a fresh start. Maybe it was the crisp air or simply an overdose of summer, but she was eager to get back to work. And, as much as she'd enjoyed the weeks at home, she was looking forward to finding a place of her own nearby. She settled on a spacious, white-walled apartment with an ocean view, and moved in all her belongings.

With wall hangings and furniture in place, it was startlingly similar to her condo in Providence, with one major difference. This time the minimalistic theme irked her more than ever. One of these days, Lily promised herself, she was going to go shopping for color.

During her first weeks at Delaney, she learned that Kay's management style resembled Drew's, with lots of listening, a few valuable insights, then a tendency to stand back and let whoever had the ball run with it. In the case of the Fleur-de-lis project, Kay made it clear to everyone involved that the ball was indisputably Lily's. That elicited a little grumbling from some of the senior designers and a great deal of resentment from Kay's husband.

It didn't take Lily long to realize that James Terrell's role in the company bore little relation to the lofty title on his door. Along with the title, he had a premium parking space and a corner office second only to Kay's—in short, all the trappings of power and none of the substance. File clerks and low-level management snapped to attention when he was around, but to anyone with any insight it was obvious that he was professionally impotent. Kay wasn't kidding; she called the shots, and her disregard for the strain it caused between them only bolstered Lily's certainty that Drew was the man Kay had really loved.

Under the circumstances, Lily couldn't blame James for being bitter, only for being weak. What she couldn't understand now any more than she ever had was why he seemed to single her out as the target of his resentment. He was openly contemptuous of her ideas, several times challenging her during meetings, only to back down with a smugness that left Lily feeling battered regardless of the outcome. He made it very clear he'd rather she wasn't around, and Lily responded by ignoring him as much as possible.

That's why she ground to a sudden halt when she rushed into Kay's office late one afternoon to find James seated at her desk instead. In the short time Lily had been there, she and Kay had developed a warm working relationship. If Kay's door was ajar, even if her secretary was away from her desk or gone for the day as she was at this hour, Lily usually gave a perfunctory knock and walked in. Now she silently cursed her lack of formality.

"I'm sorry," she said automatically. "I was looking for Kay."

"And instead you found the big bad wolf," James drawled in response. He beckoned with his finger. "Come a little closer. Let's see what you've got there that's so urgent."

"It's nothing," she said, loosely folding the papers in her hand and slipping them into her jacket pocket. First thing tomorrow morning they would unveil product prototypes of the Fleur-de-lis line at a meeting of in-house VIPs, and she'd wanted to run past Kay a few of the references to the company's history she had included in her remarks.

"Ahh." He nodded with that sly twisted smile she hated. "Top secret. Well, you brought it to the right place. This is the house of secrets, you know."

She turned to go. "I'll come back later."

"Why not sit down?" he urged, using his foot to shove the chair beside the desk toward her. "Might as well. You certainly made yourself at home walking in here without being asked."

"Evidently I'm not the only one who makes herself at home around here," she snapped.

He snickered, eyebrows raised. "But with a difference, wouldn't you say? I am family."

"You're right," agreed Lily, sorry she had let him get to her even briefly. "So I'll just leave you to whatever you're doing alone here in your wife's office and come back when she's here."

"Yeah, you do that," he called out. Lily could tell without turning around that he'd gotten up and followed her to the door. "Or better yet," he said in the same belligerent tone, "why don't you just bring whatever's so damned important straight to Jack. That's your usual modus operandi, isn't it?"

Lily came to a dead halt and turned to face him. "What did you say?"

"Modus operandi," he said again, enunciating the words as if she was a lip reader. The liquor on his breath lingered in the air. "Your pattern. The way you get to where you want to go. You did it at Goddard's, milking old Drew for whatever he was worth, not that he had any complaints about your...technique, I'm sure."

"You don't know anything about my work at Goddard's," Lily lashed out, trembling with anger. This time he'd struck where she was most vulnerable, and she wasn't going to back down and run.

"I know as much as everybody else, that all was well as long as you were working on Drew, but that when he went, so did you. His sisters must not be as susceptible to your charm. Why is that, I wonder?" His lips executed a sneer that left little doubt about why he thought it was.

"What the hell gives you the right to stand there and insult me?" she cried, driven closer to him by the rage that had the blood pulsing like liquid fire through her veins. "Never mind the things you're implying about Drew, the most decent, honorable—" She broke off, pushed nearer the edge by his laughter. "You're weren't even man enough to say these things to his face. You'd rather take on a woman ... or a child."

"Well, you're the expert on men, honey. First Drew, now Jack. Lucky for you the boss has an eligible son, huh?"

"Jack and I are friends, period. He has nothing to do with my working here. Nothing, do you hear me? Wherever I am, I made it on my own, damn it."

"Yeah, I've got no doubt about you making it," he countered with a sly edge in his voice. "As for that 'just friends' garbage, I know my son, and if he isn't getting it off you, you haven't got anything worth getting."

"That's enough."

Kay's voice whipped through the air; a split second later she was standing between them, two broad red blotches staining her cheeks.

"This is too much even for you," she said to James through clenched teeth. "I've had it with you and your petty jealousies, your drinking and shooting your mouth off whenever and wherever you please. I tolerated your interference, even when that Japanese fiasco you orchestrated threatened to wipe out a full year's profits. But I will not—will *not,* do you hear me?—tolerate your interfering in Jack's life."

"I don't know what you think you heard," James said, "but I—"

"I heard more than enough to turn my stomach."

"Oh, really? Then you've got a pretty weak stomach, and a pretty short memory, if the talk of a little outside action gets you all hot under the collar."

Kay blanched, but Lily noticed that her jaw remained thrust just as far forward, her shoulders just as square.

"I'd like for you to apologize to Lily," she said in a calmer tone, "and then I'd like you to leave us alone so that I can try and repair whatever damage you've done."

"What if—"

"If you have anything else on your mind," Kay broke in, "I'll be happy to discuss it with you later, at home."

"Right," he said, with a grunt of amusement. "See you at home, sweetheart." He stopped close beside Lily on his way to the door. "Sorry for any misunderstandings."

"I didn't misunderstand anything," Lily said coldly. She held her clenched fists pressed to her sides as he gave a negligent shrug and walked out.

As long as Lily's anger was propelling her forward, she was all right. Once James left and Kay had shepherded her to a chair in her office and brought her a glass of water, she collapsed, physically and emotionally.

Cupping her face in her hands, she battled tears for a few minutes. When she finally had them under control, she blew her nose on the tissue Kay handed her and managed a rueful smile.

"I can't believe I let him get me that upset."

"I'm sure you had more than ample provocation," Kay assured her, lines fanning from the sides of her pinched lips. "Lily, what can I say, except that I am deeply sorry for what just happened, and to tell you what I'm sure you've already deduced, that James does not in any way, ever, speak for me or for this company?"

"I do know that. I just can't understand why he would attack me that way for no reason."

"James has a tendency to take others' success as a personal affront. Just be assured that anything he said was the product of a small, vindictive mind, and don't give it another thought."

"I'll try." She stuck her hands in her pockets and found the crumpled papers that had brought her here. Smiling weakly, she tossed them onto the desk. "My presentation notes for the morning. I thought you might want to check some of the details for accuracy."

"I'll take a look later," Kay said distractedly. "Lily, are you sure you're all right?"

"Positive." She got to her feet and smoothed her hand over her hair. "I think I'll just go home and eat a pint of Heath Bar Crunch ice cream."

Kay nodded solemnly. "Sounds like the appropriate response."

They both managed a small laugh.

"Lily," Kay said, her tone hesitant, "I know you're too professional to let anything James said interfere with our work, but, well, I hope you'll be just as sensible on a personal level. I'm talking about Jack," she explained when Lily glanced at her quizzically. "I hope you won't let James's disgusting insinuations come between the two of you."

"There's nothing to come between," replied Lily, feeling like a broken record. It seemed she was always trying to convince others—and herself—that Jack was no more than a friend. James's ugly accusations only added one more reason to keep things that way.

"Yes, that's what he says, too, when he says anything at all, that is. The man is a positive sphinx where you're concerned." Kay gave a sheepish shrug. "I confess, I'm as nosy as the next mother, and being a mother I couldn't help noticing that you and Jack have seen less of each other lately than you did over the summer."

"I'm busier now than I was during the summer."

"Of course. I just hope that's all it is, and that you won't let one man's ugly suspicions cause you to overreact."

Lily stood with her hands shoved deep in her pockets, trying to decide how much to tell Kay. "You're right," she said finally. "I have been finding excuses to see less of Jack. I'm only telling you that so you won't think it's a result of what happened today."

"But why? I thought you were getting along so well. I'd hoped—" She broke off, shaking her head. "Now I'm the one who's interfering, I suppose."

"It's understandable. You want Jack to be happy, and so do I. That's why I've decided not to go on monopolizing his time. Jack deserves a woman who can give him what he needs."

"I think my son would say that you are that woman."

Lily shook her head firmly. "No. That's impossible. There can never be anything more than friendship between us. Jack knows that, and he knows why."

"You make it sound so final."

"It is final."

Kay circled the desk to rest lightly on the corner nearest Lily. "Lily, I won't lie to you. The fact is that nothing would make me happier than to see you and Jack together permanently. But not just because I'm concerned for Jack. I think it would be good for you, as well, and, I admit it, for Delaney Silver. I've accepted that Jack has no interest in the business, but if he were to marry a woman with your natural talent and instincts, it would be a breath of new life for this company... and this family."

Her hands loosely clasped in her lap, she added, "And it would be a personal blessing for me to know that the future was in good hands, that everything I've done hasn't been for nothing."

"I'm sorry, Kay, truly I am."

"Don't try and tell me it's because you're not interested in Jack. I've watched your face when you're together. I know that look, Lily. Please don't throw it away lightly."

"It's not lightly, and it's not easy. I think it's the hardest thing I've ever had to do."

"Then maybe you should ask yourself why you feel you have to do it."

Lily sighed, feeling a rush of sympathy for Kay, who was no doubt thinking about her own doomed love for Drew. "Kay, what's between Jack and me isn't some frivolous misunderstanding. It goes back a long way."

"But he's only been home—"

"It goes back to before he ever went away," Lily interjected. Kay fell silent, her expression bewildered.

"It goes back to the night of my father's accident."

As quickly checked as it was, Lily couldn't miss seeing how Kay stiffened and recoiled at the mention of her father.

"What about that night?" she asked, a new undercurrent of tension in her voice.

"Well, for starters, my father wasn't a drunk, if that's what you've thought all these years."

"Lily, I never thought that. I had great admiration for your father."

"He never even drank. The only reason he was drinking that night was because of me."

Kay stood suddenly, putting the massive mahogany desk between them before responding. "What makes you think he was drinking because of you?"

"I suppose because that was the fastest, easiest way to forget that his daughter was a failure, and an embarrassment to him."

"Lily, you were only a child."

"I was old enough to know better."

"To know better than what?" Kay asked, her tone gentler now, in spite of the rigid way she was sitting with her elbows planted on the desk, her chin resting on the tightly clenched web of her fingers.

"You probably don't remember, but the accident happened just a couple of nights after your birthday party."

"You're wrong. I do remember."

"Do you also remember that Jack brought me to that party?"

Kay nodded. "You left early."

"Very early. I left because..." Lily shrugged. "Why I left doesn't matter now. What matters is what happened afterward." She paced a few feet to stare out the window behind Kay at the parklike grounds surrounding the building. "After we left, Jack and I took a walk on the beach and... God, I can't believe how hard this is to talk about even now. We had been seeing a lot of each other, more than you probably knew at the time, certainly more than my parents were aware of, and we had become very close. But that night was the first time that we ever..." She hesitated awkwardly. "The point is that we were caught in what's known as a compromising position."

"Caught by whom?"

Lily shrugged. "I don't know exactly, only that it was the relative of a classmate who happened to be driving along the old dirt road above the dunes and recognized us. Whoever it was called the principal of my school, and then she called my father. By the time I was summoned to her office, he already knew...everything."

Lily tossed her head back, her arms folded tightly across her chest. "It was horrible, sitting there, the look on his face, as if he couldn't believe it, as if he was waiting for me to say it was all a mistake. But I couldn't say it. I couldn't look him in the eye and lie, not even about that."

"Oh, Lily, how awful for you."

"It wasn't just how ashamed I'd made him and my mother. Because of what happened I lost out on the scholarship we were counting on to pay my college tuition."

She heard Kay's sharp intake of breath.

"Until that night," Lily went on, "my father had always been so proud of me, so sure I would be the first one in the family to make it to college. And I let him down. That night that I made love with Jack on the beach, I let him down. That's why he was drinking," she said, her tone growing more taut and hurried. "And that's why he's dead. And that's why I can't ever let myself be with Jack again. It's a matter of honor. I owe that much to my father's memory." She didn't say that it was also a matter of fear.

Whirling toward the door, Lily purposely avoided Kay's gaze. "Look, I've got to get out of here."

"Lily, wait."

It was more of a plea than a command, stopping Lily at the office door.

"Please," Kay said.

Lily slowly turned to find her ghostly white and looking as emotionally terrorized as Lily felt.

"You've been very honest with me," Kay said, her voice cracking beneath the strong surface. "I think maybe it's time I did the same."

She quickly closed the door and faced Lily. As if, thought Lily anxiously, she was afraid if she didn't act quickly she would change her mind. What on earth . . . ?

"The accident that took your father's life wasn't a result of his drinking and losing control of the car. It was just made to look that way." She took a deep breath. "As far as I know, your father wasn't drinking at all."

"What do you mean?" Lily demanded, confused. "How do you know all of this?"

"I've always known," Kay replied, squeezing her eyes shut briefly. When she opened them, they were filled with tears and remorse. "I know because James was the one responsible for that accident. He was the one who had been drinking. He drove head-on into your father's car as Rusty was turning out of our drive.''

"But even the police said . . ." Lily trailed off as Kay shook her head with an anguished frown.

"Somehow he got them to lie for him," she explained, "bribed them, blackmailed them. James has ways of getting what he wants. He had his car towed away so no one would ever know he'd been involved. Then they planted those beer cans in your father's car to make it look as if he'd lost control because he was drunk.''

Dazed, Lily gazed past Kay, struggling to put the pieces together in a way that made sense. "But why?''

"Why?" Kay echoed when she hesitated. She gave a bleak laugh. "Because my husband is a coward. He doesn't like taking responsibility for his mistakes, and I'm afraid that he seldom ever has to.''

"But you— You knew. . . .''

"After the fact," Kay added, "But yes, I knew. And I went along with it, because I accepted James's reasoning that there was nothing to be gained by his going forward, that it wouldn't bring your father back. And because I wanted to avoid a scandal.''

"You wanted to avoid a scandal?" Lily countered, disbelief slowly giving way to anger. "My father was dead. I thought he died because of something I did. I've lived every damned day of my life since that night thinking that, believing it, and you kept all this a secret because you didn't want a scandal?''

"Oh, God, Lily," Kay cried, reaching out, then abruptly dropping her arms to her side when Lily jerked away. "I had no way of knowing any of what you just told me, no idea of what was going on in your family at that time, or of how you would blame yourself.''

"And you didn't really care, did you, Kay? The only family you cared about was your own. It wouldn't do to have your husband's name plastered across the front page as a drunk and a murderer. Oh, no. So you let my father take the rap. Why not? He was only the hired help," she cried, her voice cracking. It felt like she was on fire inside. "You let him go to his grave with everyone thinking he was nothing but a poor, stupid drunk.''

"No, I . . .''

"Yes, you did. As long as we're being so honest here, admit it."

"All right, I admit it. What I did was wrong," Kay said. "I knew that then, and I know it now."

"Well, it's a little late," shouted Lily. "About twenty years too late for me."

"I'm sorry, Lily, I'm so sorry." Tears streamed down Kay's cheeks through creases the years had carved into her face. "I was wrong to lie, wrong to cover for him the way I did, wrong to make the choices I made. I put pride and the reputation of the Delaney family ahead of everything and everyone else."

"You still do," noted Lily, her eyes narrowing in suspicion. "So why are you telling me now? What's in it for you?"

"Nothing. You have to believe me, Lily," she said, ignoring the scoffing sound of disbelief that Lily made. "When I heard what you had to say I knew that no matter what happened, I couldn't keep silent any longer. My God, Jack would—"

"Of course," Lily cut in. "This is all because of Jack. Because now it's time for Jack to get what he wants, right? Or is it because you've decided we should be together? Or is it simply because that's what's in the best interest of Delaney Silver? Which is it, Kay?"

"Please, Lily, I told you now because you deserve to know the truth. You've always deserved to know, of course, but I found the courage to speak up now because I didn't want you to live one more day blaming yourself for something that you had nothing to do with. Your father may have been disappointed in you, Lily, but you should at least know that he spent that last evening working in the greenhouse, not getting drunk."

Lily dragged her fingers through her hair and grabbed onto a handful, welcoming the pain it caused at the top of her skull. It was a different kind of pain than she'd been carrying around inside her for so long. This pain she could make stop hurting whenever she chose to.

"But mostly," Kay continued quietly, "I'm telling you so that you won't go on making the same mistake I once made, putting some foolish, mistaken notion of pride ahead of the man you love."

"The man I love? Or the man you *want* me to love? What is that? The Delaney family motto? If you can't buy or steal what you want, marry it?"

"Lily, I want you to know that I understand your anger completely."

"How noble of you."

"I deserve that. I know how you feel and I deserve whatever—"

"Don't," Lily ordered. "Don't you dare patronize me, damn you. You have no idea how I feel or how angry I am or how much I hate you at this moment. You could never know. You've never had to stand and watch your father being buried, thinking that you were the reason he was dead. You've never had to watch your mother grow old all alone because of you. You've never had to give up everything . . . *everything* . . . and then work and scrimp and drive yourself to make it, to become somebody, because that's the only way you could even begin to redeem yourself."

Kay's hand trembled visibly as she reached to touch Lily's shoulder. "Lily—"

"No! Don't touch me. Don't even say my name. There's only one more thing I want to hear from you. Tell me how much of this Jack knows. Or has he been in on the whole thing all along?"

Kay shook her head, her expression stricken. "Oh, no, Lily, you have to let me explain . . ."

"I don't have to do anything for you, ever again. And since I can't believe a word you say, anyway, I guess the only thing for me to do is to ask Jack myself."

THIRTY-NINE

Lily leaned on Jack's doorbell, and the vintage chimes that were among the old house's many hidden charms pealed in response. It was too damn melodious a sound for her state of mind. Raising her fist, she pounded on the front door Jack had painstakingly stripped and refinished, heedless of its irreplaceable stained glass window. Lots of things were irreplaceable, she thought bitterly.

In cartoon fashion, she kept pounding as he swung the door open and had to catch herself from landing on top of him.

"Lily," he exclaimed, his eyes lighting with pleasure at the unexpected sight of her on his doorstep. He was wearing faded jeans and a paint-splattered sweatshirt with the arms torn off. As she stood there, her breath dragging in and out, he held up a brush covered with yellow paint. "Caught in the act."

"Caught," she agreed tersely, "that's for sure."

"Come on in," he invited, turning and heading inside as if for her to follow, still oblivious to the fact that this obviously wasn't a social call. "Let me stick this brush in some water and slap a cover on the paint can. I decided you were right; the dining room should be painted yellow. Liquid sunshine. I ripped out the paneling like you suggested and underneath—"

"Jack, I came here to talk to you, not discuss decorating tips."

He took one look at her face and tossed the wet brush aside, leaving the can uncovered. He rubbed his hands along his thighs, the way she'd noticed he did when he'd been working too hard and his legs bothered him. "So talk."

Driving there, her mind had frantically spun through a half dozen ways of setting him up to reveal what she wanted to know. Now, like a swordsman with his back against the wall, she abandoned subtlety and simply lunged.

"What do you know about the night my father died?"

He started, his eyes crinkling in confusion. "Your father? What's to know? I—"

"I'll tell you what's to know. You could know, for instance, that it was *your* father, not mine, who was drunk that night. Your father who drove into mine, killing him, and then fixed it to look the way it did...bribing cops, planting beer cans. *Your* father who was responsible for everything that happened. Everything."

"What?" He raked his fingers through his dark hair, which had grown longer over the summer. "What are you talking about? Who told you all this?"

"You mean who broke the family code of silence? Your mother, that's who. Kay told me. She went along with the cover-up. She knew. All this time, while I've been blaming myself and driving myself and hating myself for making a mistake my own father couldn't forgive...all the time she knew and never said a word."

"Is this true?" Jack asked in a strangely distant tone. "He caused the accident?"

Funny, thought Lily, he seemed fixated on James's role in this, while so far she'd given James the least thought. Maybe because she expected the worst from him. It was the sense of betrayal, layered on top of anger, that had her trembling inside, and that was reserved for Kay. And for Jack, if this surprised reaction turned out to be an act.

"Do you have any idea what this means?" he asked her.

Lily laughed harshly. "More than you'll ever know."

"No," he shook his head, his jaw clenched. "I know."

"No, you don't," she cried. "Why does everyone suddenly think they know all about me and how I feel? How could you know what it feels like to have your father die ashamed of you? And then living with it..." Her voice trembled, but Lily refused to permit tears to come. "Living with it all these years, having a single stupid mistake hang over everything you do—" She broke off, clutching her forehead with her outstretched fingers. "Everything and everyone."

She heard Jack move and looked up, prepared to shove him away if he dared to touch her, but instead he was moving past her toward the door.

"Where are you going?" she demanded.

"To see my father," he said, putting a cynical twist on the word *father*.

"Why?"

"Do you really have to ask?" he shot back in a tone she'd never heard before.

The red haze of anger enveloping Lily split apart, pierced by a sudden flash of concern for Jack and what might happen to him if he walked out there in the mood she suddenly realized he was in. His posture was rigid with anger, and when she instinctively reached out and touched his arm, his skin was damp, his muscles clenched so tightly it felt like a solid steel shaft.

"I didn't come here for that," she said.

"No?" he countered, only his head turned toward her as his body remained aimed determinedly at the door. Lily could feel his impatience. "You didn't think that telling me this was going to get a reaction of some sort? You don't know me well enough by now to realize what that reaction would be? What did you expect, Lily? That I'd say let's let bygones be bygones? Everybody makes mistakes? All's well that ends well? What the hell did you come here expecting from me?"

She stared at him, the words that were locked inside vividly reflected in the questioning, entreating, condemning expression on her face.

Now he did turn to her, slowly, his expression incredulous. "You didn't come to tell me at all. You came here because you thought I already knew. You thought I was part of it, just like my mother."

"I . . . I wondered . . ."

He made a sound that caught deep in his chest, then glared at the ceiling. "I don't believe it."

"It's not so farfetched. You lived in the same house with them. They're your family, for God's sake."

"He's nothing to me." Jack tossed his head back, his temper lacing the air in the room like the early rumblings of a volcano. Without warning he grabbed a cane chair they'd found at an antique fair and hurled it against his sunshine-colored wall. It crashed to the ground in two pieces, leaving black streaks in the wet paint.

Moving closer, he brought his face to within inches of Lily's. "How the hell could you think that? How could you ever think that I would do anything to protect that son of a bitch? For any reason, but especially if it meant losing the only woman I've ever loved?"

"What did you say?"

He grimaced, the movement of his hand impatient. "That I love you. You know that."

"No."

"Yes," he said, his tone just short of a roar. "You have to know. Your own mother knows, hell, my mother knows, the whole damn world probably knows, how could you not?"

"I believed you loved me once," Lily explained, her heart pounding under a fresh onslaught of conflicting emotions and desires. "But that was a long time ago."

"What did you think these past few months were all about? All the waiting and taking it slow so I didn't spook you? Never touching you even when it felt like if I didn't touch you I was going to die? When all I wanted every second we were together was to grab you and drag you off to the nearest bed and make love to you for the next twenty years to make up for the twenty we wasted?"

Lily flinched, half afraid he intended to grab her and do exactly that, half of her not afraid at all. "I knew you wanted me," she admitted.

"Wanted you? Lady, wanting doesn't come close. Do you know what it's like to keep yourself alive with one thought, one goal in mind, and then make it back, only to be told that the only thing you want is the only thing you can't have?

"But I could take that," he continued as Lily stared at the hardwood floor, awash in misery. "I could take it because I understood your reason. I hated it, but I understood. So I did the only thing I could do. I backed off and waited. When you said you wanted me to be your friend, I waited. And all those times you'd dance closer, making me crazy with wanting you, only to pull away again, I waited. Because I understood."

He reached out and took her chin in a firm grip, forcing her gaze to meet his. "But I can't understand how you could come here today thinking that I was any part of what drove you away from me in the first place."

"I was just so shocked when Kay told me, I wasn't sure what to think." She stiffened at his rough sound of disbelief. "I knew you wanted me. I... Maybe I wanted you, too. But it's so much more complicated now than when we were kids. Maybe you wanted me because I *was* the one thing you were told you couldn't have, or maybe, subconsciously even, because you were after revenge. It seemed safer to—"

"*Safer?*" he interjected harshly.

"I just thought—"

"You know, that's always been your problem, you think too damn much and don't feel enough."

Lily nervously moistened her lips with her tongue, a gesture that seemed to momentarily distract and mesmerize him. The fingers gripping her jaw slipped lower, to tease the sensitive skin beneath her chin.

"I know what I feel," she said softly, bravely and very inaccurately. At the moment she wasn't at all sure of what she felt or how to separate the tangled strands of pleasure and apprehension and relief to begin figuring it out..

"Do you?" he challenged, slowly sliding his hand lower, until it rested over her collarbone, his fingers tracing the neckline of her silk T-shirt. Shivers cascaded down Lily's spine. "Tell me, Lily, when was the last time you felt passionate about something other than your work? The last time you got really excited by something besides a hunk of raw silver and a blowtorch?"

Lily fought the urge to arch her neck in response to his maddeningly light caress. "I . . . don't really remember."

"How could you? When you keep at arm's length any man who makes the mistake of starting your juices flowing." Somewhere along the way, his voice had shed its anger and slowed, lowering until it was as much texture as sound, a caress of a different sort.

Lily sucked in air. "Just because I don't choose to—"

"Admit it, Lily," he said, easily overriding her tremulous protest. "It wasn't only your guilty conscience standing between us. You're not the cool, single-minded career woman you like to think you are. The truth is you're afraid. You're scared to death to let yourself feel what you're beginning to feel right this second, because you don't know where it might take you."

She shook her head, even as she quickened with excitement caused by his finger straying beneath her shirt, finding the satin strap of her teddy and following its trail lower. "No, you're wrong."

"Prove it."

He waited, watching her face expectantly, his fingers still and heavy at the top of her breast.

"No?" he said finally. "Okay, then. I guess I'll have to prove it to you."

"What are you going to do?" she asked warily.

"Just this," he replied, putting both hands on her now. His touched was light, devastating. "I'm going to take you inside all the unfulfilled fantasies I know you must have locked away up here," he said, running his fingers through the long red-gold waves of her hair. "I'm going to make you so hot you won't even remember all the reasons you don't do this sort of thing, until all you want, all you can think about is surrender. And I'm going to prove to you that the world won't fall apart if you do."

There was barely time for a shiver of anticipation to dance along Lily's spine before his mouth was on hers, hard and hot and devouring. There were years of hunger driving Jack, and he let her feel every second of it in the rough, swirling thrusts of his tongue.

Lily kept her hands stubbornly clamped to her sides, but her well-forged instinct to resist lasted all of a half a minute before crumbling in the face of the desire he was unleashing, and the simple fact that there was no longer any good reason to resist. That reason had been swept away by Kay's revelation that Lily wasn't, had never been, responsible for her father's death. Along with it had gone guilt, leaving her feeling dazed with relief. Open and new.

Now all that was left to battle was the fear Jack had accused her of, fear that if she let go and let the crosscurrents of sensation carry her away, if she didn't plan and control every single move she made, disaster would follow. It was, Lily discovered as Jack tipped her head back to deepen the kiss, hard to hold onto fear, or even a healthy caution, when everything inside her was moving toward a heated, steadily building pulsing at her core.

Jack made no pretense at slow, measured seduction. Instead he seemed intent on rushing her senses, on overwhelming her with pleasure, and it was working, she thought, as he slid his hands down to cup her bottom, binding her mouth to his with only the insistent pressure of his kiss. She could hardly breathe, much less think.

Pulling her up and against him so that her belly was caressing the hard, unmistakable bulge at the front of his jeans, Jack lifted his head. His eyes, nearly black in the waning light, were aflame with raw, undisguised passion.

"Give me your tongue, Lily," he said, delivering the blunt command in an erotic rasp that sent excitement rippling through her.

Dipping his head, he stabbed at her lips until she parted them slightly, then dragged the tip of his tongue back and forth across the scant opening she allowed, wetting, cajoling, battering her with delight.

"Come on," he urged, "you'll like it. We'll both like it. Please, Lily."

The magic word. Hesitantly, Lily stuck our her tongue and touched his lips, and was dazzled by their softness and heat. His breath mingling with hers, Jack opened his mouth wider, tempting her with the softer, hotter secrets within.

Lily released a hushed whimper as she abandoned her grip on the fabric of her skirt and at last wound her arms around his neck, clinging to him as her tongue dared exploration of his mouth. It was like licking fire, and she felt the shower of sparks all the way to her toes. When she started to withdraw, Jack resisted, capturing her with an unhurried sucking motion that caused small swells of heat to progress rhythmically down the center of her body and left them both gasping.

Curling his fingers around the lapels of her black linen suit jacket, he peeled it off her shoulders and let it drop to the floor before pulling her into his arms. He bent his head and nuzzled her throat, raking his teeth against her soft skin until she shivered in response.

In her decidedly limited experience, Lily had never been loved with anything resembling roughness, probably because she sent such clear warning signals that no man had ever dared. Jack dared everything, and it shocked Lily to learn how thrilling it could be. He wound one hand through her hair to hold her still for his kiss, while the other moved over her back, caressing her from shoulder to thigh.

Tugging her shirt loose, he plunged his hand underneathe cursing softly when he encountered more silk in the form of her teddy.

"You wear too many damn clothes," he grumbled close to her ear.

"Sorry," Lily whispered distractedly, drifting on a gently undulating wave of pleasure that insulated her from concern about such things as clothes or how he was going to deal with them.

"Don't be," Jack said, with a soft laugh. "Sometimes the right clothing can be very exciting." Lifting her arms over her head, he tugged her shirt off with one swift motion. "You definitely wear the right clothing."

She stood before him, her chest rising and falling provocatively, in a lacy raspberry teddy and short, black knit skirt, her hair tumbling over her shoulders. With her face flushed and lips swollen, Lily could imagine the picture she presented and had no doubt about why he stared at her so hard for so long before drawing her close once again.

The miracle of it was, she wasn't ashamed or afraid to have him look at her that way. She didn't feel the need to protest or explain or clarify all the things she didn't want and couldn't do. She simply felt like a woman. Jack was making her feel like a woman, and it felt wonderful.

This time when he took her into his arms, he lifted her off her feet and put her back to the wall, letting her slide slowly lower until her feet were once more on the ground. "Don't worry," he whispered against her lips. "This wall's dry."

"I don't care," she murmured, amazed that it was true.

She was beyond caring, past protest. When he lowered his head and ran his tongue along the lace bordering her breast she trembled in response, then clutched his shoulders for support as he moved over her with his open mouth, his breath moistening the silk and scorching the flesh beneath. Just as she thought she would go crazy with anticipation, he took her silk-covered nipple in his mouth, kneading it firmly between his lips, thrumming it with his tongue, until it was ripe and full. He did the same to her other breast.

Bracing his hands on the wall on either side of her, he moved lower, kissing and nibbling, the sheer barrier of silk only enhancing the eroticism for Lily. He was right. Sometimes clothes added to the excitement.

If she wasn't already convinced almost past endurance, she was when he slipped his hand between her legs and palmed her, the sudden gush of heat threatening to make her explode. With a soft cry of longing, she twisted her head back and forth against the wall.

Jack increased the pressure slightly, pressing and releasing, pressing and releasing, cranking the glorious tension up another notch, then another. With one finger, he plucked at the lace border and Lily, yearning to have him touch her, really touch her, twisted to give him better access.

Jack shook his head and nipped playfully at her belly, his muffled words drifting up to her as he went down on his knees. "Not yet, sweetheart. There's more. Much more."

But she couldn't take much more, thought Lily as he held her hips and kissed her through the strip of silk between her thighs. He caressed her with his breath, and with the sweet stabbing pressure of his tongue, so that she was wincing with need, her breath coming in short rapid pants by the time he ripped open the snaps holding the fabric together, taking them slowly, one at time.

Lily felt the cool air, then finally he touched her, sliding his thumbs over the soft swollen petals. She quaked as he found her center and captured it.

She knew now what he'd meant by surrender, and how complete and total he wanted it to be. And at last, after sucking in her breath and holding it for as long as she could before it broke from her in a soft whispered plea, she gave it to him. Hearing her whimper, Jack pressed deeper still and sent wave after wave of pleasure crashing over her.

All her rationalizing had been for naught, she thought as the throbbing slowly calmed. Time and imagination had distorted nothing. Her memory had been achingly accurate. This man, and only this man, had the power to steal control of her senses, to take her higher and send her crashing harder than should be humanly possible. It wasn't fair, but it was real, and she was tired of fighting reality.

Straightening slowly, Jack gathered her against him, his embrace gentle for all of the second and a half until their lips met and lightning struck all over again. Lily was amazed; she'd expected to feel full and replete for days, or at least hours. Instead, he touched her and this crazy hunger for him flickered once more.

"Right now, I'd like nothing better than to pick you up in my arms and carry you off to my bed," Jack said, his tone laced with regret. "But..."

"But?" she prompted, fighting disappointment. Sure the earth had moved for her, but what about him? Had she been too slow? Too fast? Too passive? She was so concerned with self-protection, she had no idea of what pleased a man. Cursing her ridiculous level of inexperience at her age, she braced for the but.

"But I'm afraid if I dropped you, it might break the mood."

It took a second for his meaning to penetrate, then Lily laughed with relieved abandon.

"You don't mind a short unromantic walk to my bedroom?"

"Not at all," Lily told him, the joy reflected in her eyes telling him more than words ever could how much she wanted to take that walk with him.

The layout of the cottage necessitated passing the living room and the kitchen to reach the master bedroom, which overlooked the ocean from the back of the house. Outside, the sun had given up for the day, but left behind enough of a glow reflecting off the water for Lily to see the changes Jack had made since the first time he'd brought her here.

The thoughts of the cottage renovations never made it past the bedroom door. Stopping her just inside, Jack tugged gently at the straps on her shoulders.

"Pretty as they are, I think your clothes have outlived their usefulness." He slipped them down, only to be stopped short at the elbow. "The only problem is that my vast experience with female fashion doesn't include anything quite like this." He glanced at her with wry amusement. "Help."

"First tell me, just how vast was it?"

He bent one dark brow. "My experience with women's fashion?"

"I don't really much care what the women were wearing."

"Ah."

"I know I have no right to ask," she added hurriedly.

His expression sobered as he lightly placed his hands on her shoulders. "You have a right. I spent nearly twenty years in the military, Lily, surrounded by men ninety percent of the time. When I had time to kill, I usually chose to kill it with someone not wearing the same boots and stripes I was."

"I understand," she said, wishing she hadn't asked and brought this crushing disappointment on herself.

"But," he said, framing her face with his hands, "I meant what I said out there. Lily, you are the only woman I've ever loved. I loved you then, and I love you now. And whatever happened in between doesn't mean squat compared to that. Okay?"

"Okay."

"Good. Now close your eyes." He leaned close to whisper, "And tell me the fastest way to get these off you."

Laughing softly as their hands bumped and indulged in irresistible side explorations, they undressed each other. When her silk stockings and his faded jeans lay entwined in a pile on the floor, Jack eased her onto the mattress. The sight of him above her, gloriously naked and aroused, brought a jolt of fresh desire.

"I can't believe it. You're as beautiful as ever," he said, caressing her with his gaze.

"That's funny, I think you're even more beautiful now."

He grimaced, glancing down at his battered body as he joined her on the bed, at the crisscrossing scars Lily hadn't missed as she undressed him. Overcome with emotion she pressed her lips to a jagged one high on his chest, thinking of all the pain she'd caused him, and of all the pain she hadn't caused but hadn't been around to help ease.

When she told him he was beautiful, she wasn't thinking about the beauty of smooth skin or broad shoulders or even the inspired arrangement of bone and tissue that made his face stand out in a crowd. She was thinking about what kind of man loved with such endurance and inspiration, loved enough to know when to take no for an answer, and when not to.

"You have a strange concept of beauty," he told her.

Lily shook her head. "No, just a wiser one," she said, reaching for him, wanting him more at that moment than she wanted promises or safety.

Jack bent and kissed her lips, balancing his weight on one elbow as he gently parted her legs, caressing her inner thighs and between them until they were both on fire once again. Reaching between their sweat-dampened bodies, Lily took his arousal in her hand, glorying in his trembling response and in the dewy evidence at the swollen tip, proof that he wanted her with the same ferocity she wanted him.

Groaning, he turned away briefly in order to protect her. When he rolled back, Lily encircled his waist with her arm and guided him to the part of her that his touch had made moist and ready. With a sharply drawn breath, his gaze holding hers the whole time, Jack slowly sank against and into her body.

The first long, deep strokes wiped away the past for both of them. The rest were purely for pleasure, a rare, exquisite form of pleasure that united their spirits in a place outside of themselves, a place neither of them had ever found without the other. Excitement arced between them as they climbed higher and higher, matching each other's pace, first Jack leading the way, then Lily. They reached the summit together as well, climaxing with an explosion of sensations that echoed back and forth between them long after their cries of exultation had faded into the night.

Jack awoke hours later to find the bed beside him empty. First he panicked, then he noticed the flickering blue-white light of the television in the living room.

Hauling himself from the bed, he fished his jeans out of the pile on the floor and followed the light to where Lily sat curled up on one end of the sofa.

Circling behind her, Jack leaned over the back of the sofa to rub her shoulders. The late news was on, reminding him that he was usually still hard at work at this time. He did his best to knock himself out so that when he finally did allow himself to turn in he could find sleep. Tonight, for the first time in a long time, he hadn't had to court sleep.

It didn't surprise him that Lily was too restless to sleep, however. She had been dealt a massive emotional blow a few hours ago, one that called much of her adult life into question. Sex had flowed from her anger, delivering an exhausting but temporary reprieve. Now that she had burned off the first, raw rush of emotion, she had a lot to deal with.

He stood by silently, not sure if she was listening to the newscaster as he told of a long-lost bag of mail that had been discovered buried away in a neighboring town. Obviously not, because she looked up at him after a minute, her smile transparent.

"Couldn't sleep?" he asked.

She shook her head. "I didn't mean to wake you."

"You didn't." He hunkered down closer to her. "Were you thinking about your father?"

"Yes." Sighing, she loosely hugged her bent legs. "It seems as if this should make everything easier, you know? Make me feel better. And I guess I do in a way. But where before I was filled with guilt, now I'm filled with anger."

"I'd say you have a right."

"I don't care if it's petty or vindictive, I want them to pay for what they did."

"What do you want to do about it?"

"What can I do?" she exclaimed, standing as if propelled off the sofa by the force of her frustration. She paced across the room, a distracting sight in his sleeveless sweatshirt. "I'm sure the statute of limitations ran out years ago, so there's no way James could be charged with anything...even if I had any idea of how to gather evidence against him."

"I'm sure your brother Ben would know," said Jack. "He's been a state trooper for a lot of years."

"I thought of that." She shrugged. "When I first came out here I almost grabbed the phone and called him. But I realized that even if I involved Ben, there's still a chance that it's too late to do anything about it and I will have stirred it all up again for nothing. I can't put my mother through that."

"What about all that you've been through? Don't you think you need some sort of resolution?"

"Yes, damn it, but there are times when you have to put other people's needs before your own. That's what being a family is all about." She rubbed her arms as if she was cold, triggering Jack's instinctive urge to go to her and protect her.

"Besides," she said, not resisting as he pulled her against his chest. "My mother and brothers made their peace with what happened long ago. Learning the truth now will only make them feel as bitter as I do, and I don't wish that on anyone."

"God, I love you," Jack whispered, rubbing his cheek against her silky hair.

"And it's not as if it would change anything for me," she continued, talking to herself as much as to him. "They never blamed me for what happened. I blamed myself. I'll deal with it."

"How can I help?" he asked, clamping down on his own murderous urges toward his father. What had she said? That being a family sometimes meant putting someone else's feelings before your own? That's what he wanted for Lily and him.

"I don't expect you to help," she said, taking him by surprise. "I believe now that you didn't know anything about this before today, but Kay and James are still your parents."

"I've told you how I feel about him," Jack said, the tightening of his gut that always accompanied thoughts of his father stronger than ever. "With my mother, it's different. I can't believe . . ." He shook his head. "She was never the mother I wanted her to be, but I always felt she was the best mother she knew how to be . . . if that makes any sense at all."

"It does. It's funny, though, Kay was always exactly the mother I wanted. So beautiful and glamorous."

"And selfish," Jack added dryly. "Don't get me wrong, she's a very kind and loving person in her own way. But my mother always has her own agenda, and that always comes first. I'm sure that was the case with this. She decided it would cause the family embarrassment if the truth got out, and so she made sure it didn't."

"She admitted that," Lily told him. "She told me she wanted to avoid a scandal. I guess she was doing the same thing I am, hiding the truth to protect her family."

"Except that where the Delaney's are concerned family isn't people. It's something else, something I never really understood." He hugged her tighter. "As far as I'm concerned, they were wrong all the way. But even if they weren't, I'd be in your corner, Lily. I'll always be there."

"That helps," she told him, and Jack felt her relax against him for just a split second before the restless tension returned. "But this has always been my problem. It still is, and sooner or later I'll find my own way to settle the score."

They returned to his bed and made love again, and this time Lily slept afterward. When she woke, sometime around dawn, it was as if someone had come during the night and left the solution to her problem under her pillow, the way the tooth fairy used to leave a quarter there when she was younger.

She had the perfect way to take revenge. She would hit Kay where it would hurt most—Delaney Silver. Just thinking about it brought Lily a slow burn of anticipation. It was not only perfect, and something she alone could pull off, it had a satisfying ring of poetic justice.

James Terrell had been responsible for her father's death, and Kay's treacherous compliance had stolen from Lily years of happiness and left her feeling that she had broken her father's heart. She recalled the day of his funeral, when Kay had come to the house with her *generous* offer to help and her check. Blood money, Lily thought bitterly.

Yes, it was fitting that the Fleur-de-lis line, the designs that captured her father's dream so beautifully, the designs that Kay and Delaney Silver needed so desperately, should be the instrument of her revenge.

FORTY

Jack found the note taped to the bathroom mirror.

I told you I'd find a way to settle the score. I just didn't expect to find it so soon. L.

He rubbed his eyes with the heels of his hands, wishing she'd left the note in the kitchen, where he might at least have had time to make coffee and have a cup before finding it. What did she mean she'd found a way to settle the score? For just an instant, his heart wrenched with the fear that maybe her note wasn't meant to inform so much as to gloat. Maybe walking out on him again after last night *was* Lily's way of getting even.

Jack shook his head to clear it. He really did need a cup of coffee. Lily had meant it when she said she believed he hadn't known anything about the cover-up until she told him. This was something else. Somehow, in the few short hours since he'd finally left her alone so she could sleep, she had come up with a plan.

They'd made love again and again during the night, sometimes with a desperation bordering on aggression, sometimes with a lazy sweetness that washed away everything that was wrong with his life and filled him with the desire to do the same for Lily. That would take longer, he knew, and he was prepared to be patient.

However, he was no longer prepared to go on avoiding words that he'd been afraid to use in her presence, words like love and forever. To his satisfaction, she hadn't protested, not even when in the early morning darkness he'd finally opened up to her about his longing to start a family of his own. He'd also finally gotten around to giving her the necklace that had been delivered to him by Goddard's months ago. If Lily hadn't understood that day they'd worked on it together that she was the only woman he had in his mind and in his heart, Jack made certain she understood now.

The woman was amazing, he thought, missing her already. Altogether too early a riser, but amazing just the same.

Even an amazing, beautiful, loving woman like Lily, though, was no match for James Terrell. His father never played fairly or by the rules, especially someone else's rules. If Lily's plan involved confronting him in any way, Jack wanted to be there. And if it meant seeing that James finally got what he had coming, he definitely wanted to be there.

Mary was sitting at the kitchen table when the sun came up. She'd been awake all night, ever since learning that bags of lost mail had been found in an old shed nearby. She'd sat there hour after hour, worrying, remembering.

Scenes from the past had come out of the darkness to haunt her, like bloated bodies rising to the surface of a still lake. She'd relived the night that Dolly Martin had died after being visited by James Terrell then giving birth to his child, Lily. And she thought about her confrontation with Dr. Lagasse afterward and the horrible day in his office when he'd looked at her with that twisted and accusing expression on his face, his black eyes empty. Even now, just thinking about it made her shiver.

After a while, she'd relived some of the happy times, too. You could do a lot of thinking if you sat in one spot long enough. She'd recalled the good years, after they'd brought Lily home to stay, when the kids had been young enough to keep safely under her wing and Rusty had once again been the lighthearted, loving charmer she'd fallen in love with. And she had almost believed that everything might work out for them after all.

A lot had happened since then. Rusty was gone, she thought with a sadness that never dulled, but there were grandchildren to take up her time now, and watching them helped keep alive the memories of when her own were young. One thing hadn't changed in all that time, however. No matter how it came about, she had never for a second regretted making Lily one of her own. Lily was as much a part of her heart as any of the boys.

She didn't regret it now, either, even if it did look as if a stitch she'd dropped a long, long time ago was finally going to unravel her entire life. Or at least what was left of it. Mary didn't need a crystal ball to know that at this point, there was more behind her than ahead. It was Lily who concerned her now, and

Lily's future happiness was more important than protecting secrets from the past.

Of course adding Jack Terrell to the soup only complicated matters enough to make Mary's heart begin to race all over again. She quickly brought it under control. She didn't have time for that now. For years she had tried to protect Lily with threats and warnings and subtle pushes in any direction that would take her away from Delaney Place and the Terrell family. After her talk with Jack a few weeks ago, she'd accepted that the time for that was past.

For all that she wanted to think the worst of him, her heart saw things differently. In a way, Jack and Lily reminded Mary of herself and Rusty. They'd made their share of mistakes and had their share of misfortunes, too, but they'd always come through for each other in the end. Remembering that made her decide to step aside where Lily and Jack were concerned and let things take their course. Last night she realized that wasn't good enough.

Her letter to Mrs. Terrell might turn out to be in one of those mailbags, and it might not. It didn't matter. Even if it didn't turn up now, it could someday, maybe someday after Mary was dead and gone, when there'd be no one around to tell Lily what only Mary could tell her—the truth. The letter existed. It was somewhere, waiting, a bloated body ready to bob to the surface of Lily's life.

The difference was that poor Lily didn't even know it was down there. She had to be told, and Mary was determined that she was going to be the one to tell her.

Checking the kitchen clock for the hundredth time that morning, she was relieved to see that seven-thirty had finally arrived. She washed and dressed as quickly as she ever had and made the short drive to Delaney Silver, counting on Lily to do as she always did, arrive early enough to have some quiet time to herself before the actual workday began.

The guard at the front gate admitted her when she identified herself and implied it was an emergency, but after that Mary was on her own. She had visited Lily's office only once in the months she'd worked there, and it was hard to find her way there through the maze of stark look-alike hallways.

She did remember that it was a very nice office and when she came to a row of very nice offices, she decided she must be on the right track. None of the brass nameplates on the closed doors bore Lily's name, though, so when she arrived at one that was ajar she crooked her neck to read it, hopeful that this might be the one.

As she focused on the name, she heard a pained grunt and from the corner of her eyes caught the motion of someone lumbering to life from a sofa inside the plush office. The disheveled form of a man levered upright, and then stumbled closer, stopping right in front of her to rub at his eyes.

"What do you want?" he mumbled, squinting at her as if it was still dark in the room instead of bright enough to see everything with absolute clarity.

Mary shook her head, panic sweeping through her like a glacier, freezing everything inside so that she could neither speak nor move. It was exactly the way she'd always known it would be when she finally came face to face with James Terrell again.

For a few seconds he seemed not to recognize her at all. Then something, maybe her stricken expression, triggered his comprehension of exactly who she was. His mouth formed an ugly curl, so different from the dashing smile he'd bestowed on a gullible young nurse all those years ago, and somehow, miraculously, Mary found the strength not to flinch, inside or out, as their gazes locked. . . .

Kay was in too much of a hurry to eat breakfast. This morning's critical meeting with sales executives and department heads was scheduled for ten, and she wanted time to speak privately with Lily beforehand. She had tried phoning her at home last evening, but to no avail.

Lily had been very upset when she stormed out of her office, and with good reason, Kay acknowledged regretfully. There were a great many things she regretted this morning, most of which she couldn't do anything about. She could, however, bend over backward to make amends to Lily, and she intended to do just that.

The possibility that Lily might have gone running straight to Jack both pleased and frightened her. Kay had debated calling to warn him of the situation, but had decided against it. However unintentionally, she had interfered enough between the two of them. She had faith they would survive this together, much more faith, in fact, than she had that either Lily or Jack would be able to forgive her for the horrible mistakes she had made.

The clock in the hall chimed eight, spurring Kay to move even faster. She pulled open the front door just as an unfamiliar mailman was reaching to ring the doorbell.

"Mrs. Terrell?" he inquired.

"Yes."

With a smile he held out a stack of envelopes. "These are for you. Special delivery. Very special, actually," he added in a somewhat wry drawl, "considering that they're thirty-eight years overdue."

"For heaven's sake," Kay exclaimed as she took them from him. "I heard something about this on the news last night, but it never occurred to me that any of that mail might be coming here."

"Yes, ma'am. Most of it's going to you and a hundred or so of your neighbors. I've been instructed to deliver these along with the apologies of the postmaster general and his assurance that it won't happen again."

"Yes, I suppose this qualifies as a once-in-a-lifetime experience."

"Let's hope so, ma'am."

Kay smiled her thanks before hurrying toward the waiting car. Seated in the back, she thumbed through the envelopes. She could use a distraction. What good would it do to rehearse her meeting with Lily when she had no way of knowing the younger woman's mood now that the dust from Kay's bombshell had had time to settle? She was bound to be bitter, and rightfully so. She might well be angry enough to quit, and Kay was prepared to apologize, cajole and bow to any demand she made in order to stop that from happening.

She glanced at the return address on one of the envelopes that was addressed to her parents, noting that the senders, like her parents, were now dead. The sad irony of that touched her in a special way this morning. The past doesn't die, she thought, only people do. The past lives on in words and deeds, some so indelible they might as well be written in blood. And some actually were, she thought miserably.

To occupy her hands, if not her mind, she began opening the envelopes, most of them addressed to her parents and containing Christmas cards that looked and felt like something time had left behind. There was a letter from a distant aunt and a card sent to her and James by a couple she hadn't seen in years. The final envelope bore no return address and was addressed to Kay.

Curious, she slit it open, barely glancing at the formal greeting printed above the now faded Christmas wreath on the front before flipping the card open to see who it was from. She was surprised to find a rather long note scrawled inside.

"Dear Mrs. Terrell," it began. "We've never met, but I'm a nurse on the obstetrics ward at Our Lady of Hope Hospital . . ."

She read quickly, thinking it had to be a hoax. A joke of some sort. A very tasteless joke. Not until she finally read the signature on the back of the card did she accept it as truth. The heavy churning that had begun down low in her stomach stopped suddenly, leaving behind something cold and hard and permanent.

For the rest of the drive, Kay stared out the window without seeing, the coldness inside growing stronger all the time, spreading until it killed off the last traces of any old feelings that might have contradicted or challenged it. And it was still intensifying, reflected in her eyes and her determined stride, when she left the car and headed for the office where her husband had chosen to spend the night.

Jack missed Lily at her place, where she had obviously gone to don the crisp business armor she was wearing when he finally caught up to her in the parking lot at Delaney Silver. Not, he noted as he left the Landrover, that the surprisingly conservative black suit and white blouse in any way muted his memory of her more abandoned appearance in his bed only a few hours ago.

Lily smiled the second she saw him, in spite of the tense and drawn expression that very quickly reclaimed her beautiful face. It was as if joy was something she was too tired and too preoccupied to sustain this morning. Jack could only partially regret his role in her obvious exhaustion. The fact that she considered the sight of him reason to smile in the midst of her pain made him feel young and indestructible.

He kissed her before he allowed her to say a word, showing more restraint than he would have liked due to their public surroundings. He wished the morning could have started differently. Someday, he promised himself, someday very soon, he was going to teach Lily the singular pleasure of spending a full twenty-four hours in bed.

"Now tell me about this plan of yours," he said.

"You got my note."

He nodded.

"Calling it a plan to even the score wasn't quite accurate," she told him. "The way I feel right now, I don't think anything short of murdering James will really satisfy my need for revenge. But I have to accept that I can't hurt him without hurting people I love in the process. And since I'm convinced he is personally incapable of feeling sorrow or humiliation, I've decided the only surefire way to get at him and Kay is through Delaney Silver."

When Jack glanced at her quizzically, she explained. "The Fleur-de-lis line, the line Kay herself told me she considers a life preserver for the company, a project she's climbed out onto a very risky limb for—financially and professionally—isn't going to happen."

"What are you talking about?"

Lily quickly explained her intention to exercise her legal and artistic rights over the Fleur-de-lis line by stopping its production. When he expressed doubt that the rights Kay had permitted her to retain extended to halting production after the company had invested so much money and manpower in the project, Lily calmly agreed that Delaney Silver would no doubt prevail in a court of law.

And if Kay wanted to fight a court battle, with all the attendant bad publicity and who knows what sort of unflattering revelations about the parties involved, Lily would oblige her. But she was betting that Kay wouldn't fight. While it wasn't close to the perfect revenge, she would at least have the satisfaction of taking from them something that they wanted.

"I know just how badly Delaney needs a winner like Fleur-de-lis promises to be, and I'll be damned if I'll let them have it without a fight. The meeting Kay called for this morning will give me an opportunity to tell her so," she concluded.

"Perfect," said Jack. "The meeting will have only one minor addition—me."

Lily shook her head. "Absolutely not, Jack. This is my fight...and I just happen to be fighting your family. It isn't fair to involve you."

He stood before her wearing last night's jeans, his fresh white shirt contrasting dramatically with his face, which had been burned bronze during the long days they'd spent beneath the summer sun. He'd been compliant then, Lily recalled, willing to shelve his own wishes in deference to hers. The stubborn thrust of his jaw told her that things had changed. His lack of socks and a belt and his finger combed hair gave him the look of a man who'd left home in a hurry and with more on his mind than collecting a good-morning kiss.

"I want to be there, Lily," he said, his quiet determination harboring an explosive she didn't have time to try to defuse. "In a way, this is my fight, too. Please, don't shut me out."

"Do I have a choice?"

"None at all."

She tightened her grip on the leather briefcase containing her copies of the agreement she and Kay had signed. "In that case, let's go."

FORTY-ONE

"What is this?" James demanded in a surly tone. "A damn social hour?"

He didn't like the way the Saville woman and Kay had stepped outside for a brief private chat, only to return, sandwich themselves in his office door and stare at him like he was something they stepped in at a petting zoo.

And he didn't like the clawing feeling in his gut that being trapped there with them was giving him. Not that he wasn't used to it. It was a feeling he had more and more lately and which no amount of vodka ever really numbed. It was like being eaten away from the inside out.

Kay finally spoke. "There's nothing social about this, James. Far from it. Mary tells me she came here looking for Lily. I came looking for you. But under the circumstances, it's appropriate that the three of us are here together."

"Really? What circumstances are those?" he asked with a show of nonchalance, while all the time the claws bit deeper.

"The circumstances surrounding this." Kay held up an envelope. "This letter from Mary was in this morning's mail."

"So you're pen pals," he said, noticing that Mary Saville didn't look all too thrilled with this development. Actually she looked a little queasy. Maybe he ought to offer her a drink, then join her. "I'm happy for you. Now would you mind giving me some privacy so I can get cleaned up?"

"There's not enough privacy on the planet for that to happen," countered his loving wife. "You might be interested to know that this letter is postmarked 1953."

"Complain to the post office. I don't deliver the mail."

"Neither did the post office, in this case. If you'd been in any condition to watch the news last night, you would know that."

"I'm sure you'll fill me in on all the details."

Turning his back to them, he crossed to his desk, taking his time about it as he recovered from that last curve she'd thrown him—1953. He didn't know exactly where this was headed, only that 1953 cut much too close for comfort.

"Mary wrote this letter to me thirty-eight years ago," Kay said, moving to stand in front of his desk, while the other woman hung back. "But because of a twist of fate, it was never delivered. Until today. I found it fascinating reading. I think you will, too." Letter in hand, she glanced at the woman behind her. "Mary, do you mind?"

Mary shook her head. "It's time it was all out in the open."

Wanting that drink more and more, James took the letter Kay held out to him, then sat there staring into her eyes. If there was a way out of whatever this was, it would be there, a flicker of lost love or pity or whatever it was she felt for him these days. A theme he could expand upon. But there was nothing. Kay's eyes were a flat, lifeless green.

"Read it," she said. When he continued to stare at her, she slammed both fists on his desk. "Read it, damn it."

He let another few seconds pass, then read. In spite of the fact that his worst nightmare was unfolding on the page before him, he did his best to project only growing astonishment, shaking his head, hissing through his teeth a couple of times. It didn't work. When he finally lifted a carefully injured and outraged gaze to meet hers, Kay conveyed with a shake of her head that she believed the letter and not him.

All right, thought James, *think fast.* There still had to be a way out of this. There was always a way out. All he had to do was think fast and talk faster.

"How could you?" she asked, her expression contemptuous. "Until a moment ago I wouldn't have believed that even you were low enough to father a child then abandon both the mother and baby, not even stepping forward to claim the child after the poor woman was dead."

"What the hell are you talking about?" he demanded, waving the card in the air. "This is garbage. The ravings of a madwoman."

"Mary doesn't look mad to me," Kay said. "And she had no reason to lie about what's in that letter. Then or now."

"Of course, she did. The best reason in the world."

"And what is that?"

"Do re mi, sweetheart. The Savilles never had two cents to rub together. Everybody knows that. This was probably some sort of a scheme to blackmail us."

"It wasn't that at all," protested Mary. "I wrote the letter because it's the truth. Every word of it. I know what I saw that night."

"Well, you sure as hell didn't see me knocking up some broad, did you? You've got no proof of that." He turned to Kay, reining his voice in to a more reasonable range. "Her husband was probably behind the whole thing. He dreamed up this get-rich-quick scheme and then got cold feet and never followed up on it. She—"

"No," Mary cried, finally coming out of her huddle by the door, her face going from sickly white to scarlet as she shot forward to confront him. "How dare you talk like that about Rusty? He never in his whole life took a dime that wasn't his. And maybe we never had two cents to rub together, like you said, but at least we always took care of our own. Which is more—"

"Shut up, you damn busybody," James shouted, standing and looming over the desk at her. "Don't try and tell me—"

"What the hell is going on in here? We could hear you all the way down the hall."

The three of them turned as one as Jack came into the office, closely followed by Lily. Her jaw dropped when she saw Mary.

"Mom, what on earth are you doing here?" She glanced from one angry face to another, finally zeroing in on Kay. "What is it? What have you told her?"

"Nothing," Kay said, her eyes reinforcing that message. "This has nothing to do with you or our discussion last night. Or with you either, Jack. I think both of you should leave us—"

"No," interrupted Mary.

Lily shot a surprised look at her mother, whom she expected to be intimidated beyond speech in such a situation. Her fiery urge to protect Mary was edged aside a little by curiosity.

"Let them stay," Mary said. To Kay, she added, "This concerns Lily more than you know, and unless I miss my guess that means it concerns Jack, too."

She glanced at the two of them and received nods of agreement from both.

"All right," said Kay, wondering how this could get any worse and afraid it was about to. "Please close the door, Jack." When the door was shut, she said, "Maybe we should all sit down and try to get to the bottom of this in a rational fashion."

No one, including Kay, moved.

"All right," she continued. "Lily, your mother feels you should be in on this, so I'll tell you what I know—"

"Wait, Mrs. Terrell—" Mary broke in again. "Please, if you don't mind, I should be the one to tell Lily."

"Of course." Kay backed up half a step, leaving Mary and Lily facing each other in the center of the room.

"I'm so sorry, honey," Mary said to her. "I wanted to get to you first, to prepare you somehow..."

"Prepare me for what, Mom? What's this all about?"

"Most of it is in a letter I wrote to Mrs. Terrell a long time ago, but that she never saw until today."

Kay interrupted only to explain about the newly discovered mailbags.

"You can read the letter later if you want," Mary said to Lily. "Right now, I just want to tell you in my own way."

She spoke haltingly at first, her voice gaining control and conviction as she went, as if she drew courage from the simple act of speaking the truth.

For Lily, listening, the room was pared down to just the two of them. She forgot where she was or that others were even present as she listened to a tale that was too outrageous to be digested all at once.

Mary, too, forgot the others as she told her about James Terrell's visit to the hospital that stormy December night thirty-eight years ago, about Dolly's crying and pleading for her baby and about the impulsive promise she had made to the frantic young woman, a promise that had changed her life forever. Finally she spoke about the baby girl born that night and left motherless and defenseless, condemned to an orphanage by papers Mary was certain in her heart Dolly had never signed.

Her words were as plain and direct as she was, and yet they painted vivid pictures in Lily's mind. Knowing Mary, it was not difficult at all for Lily to accept how her heart had gone out to that baby or how she'd been driven to do something to try to help her. Or how, when her desperate letter to Kay went unanswered, she did the only thing she could, made room in her own family for the baby nobody else wanted.

Images culled from old black-and-white snapshots flickered in Lily's mind as Mary told her how blessed she and Rusty Saville had felt to finally have a little girl of their own. Pictures of her father beaming as he cradled a ruffled bonneted infant in one powerful arm, of a little girl who was all long legs and toothless grin sitting atop his shoulders, of five stair-step children lined up in new Easter outfits paid for with money saved, a dime here and a nickel there. The story of her life, suddenly brought into a different, sharper focus.

Of course she knew long before Mary actually said it how the story would end. Still, the words rocked her in a way that made her feel like running and running until she reached some place where none of this could ever find her.

"Lily, you were that baby," she said.

"What the hell?" she heard Jack mutter, simultaneously with Kay's shocked gasp.

All Lily could do was stare at her mother, the only mother she had ever known—who was suddenly not her mother at all. Her mother was some woman she'd never even seen, who had died giving her life, and her father...

Lily shuddered violently and against her will her gaze went to James Terrell, who was watching and listening to it all with a look of blatant contempt.

"We wanted you and we loved you like you were our own. No matter what," Mary was saying now, in the same granite tones she'd once used to tell Lily she could not have a cookie before supper or stay out after the streetlights came on or smoke cigarettes in her house no matter what everyone else was doing. "And no matter what happens today, nothing will ever change that."

Lily slowly turned to her, only faintly aware of the support of Jack's hand on her shoulder. "Why didn't you tell me before now?"

For the first time since she'd started, Mary faltered. She felt her face color and heat at the memory of her visit to Dr. Lagasse's office and the baby she'd let him destroy. If it would help Lily, she would tell it all. It would certainly help explain why she had kept silent all these years. The truth would almost be a relief.

But, on top of everything else, did Lily really need to face the fact that the woman she'd thought was her mother had such sordid secrets in her past? Mary didn't think so. She'd borne that weight alone for years now. She supposed she could go on shouldering it for whatever time she had left.

"Maybe we should have told you," she said at last, "but things were different back then. Not as free and open as today. The boys were young enough that they never questioned but you were their new baby sister. After a while it just didn't seem to matter. You were ours, plain and simple. Can you understand that at all?"

"I don't know. Maybe. What I can't understand is how you could not tell me about—" Her gaze hardened as it slid past Mary to James. "You knew, all the time you knew that he . . ." She took a few steps toward him, putting her back to the others. "If you're right, then he's my father."

James stared at her, his expression cold and sullen. "There's no need to look at me that way," he said. "I assure you I'm no more eager to be your father than you are to have me. Fortunately, neither of us has to worry. This whole thing is a farce, and I, for one, am through listening."

"Oh, no, you're not," said Kay, stepping directly into his path as he moved toward the closed door. "You'd like nothing better than to just shrug this off and walk away. No matter that people's lives are involved here, their feelings, their futures. For God's sake. Doesn't that mean anything to you?"

Kay stared into the black void of her husband's eyes and shook her head. "No, of course it doesn't. It never has. But this is one time you're not going to walk away," she said with a quiet vehemence he couldn't help but understand. "This time you're going to stay and face the facts . . . whatever they turn out to be." She waved her arm toward Mary and Lily. "These people deserve the truth. And this time, by God, they're going to get it."

James glared at her. "The truth is that I didn't do anything."

"I know what I saw," Mary insisted from behind Lily.

"What you *think* you saw," snapped James, his face darkening to the color of dried blood. "It was nearly forty years ago."

"Not at the time she wrote this letter," Lily reminded him. "There's that to consider. And of course, the fact that you are a liar."

"And you're a little—"

"Watch it," warned Jack, suddenly at Lily's side. "The last time you insulted Lily, I walked away, I won't make that mistake twice."

Lily thrust her chin higher to confront James's gaze. "If my mother says you were there that night, you were there. She wouldn't lie, not about that or the rest of it. I think you got that woman pregnant and then you had to find some way out of it. You must have been scared to death that Kay would find out," she said scornfully. "That would have ruined the good thing you had going here, wouldn't it? So you went to the hospital to try to force the woman into giving the baby up, and when she wouldn't, you panicked. Tell me, how much did you pay that doctor to forge those adoption papers?"

"This is your show," James replied, his mouth twisting into a smile. "You tell me."

Lily felt herself tense; hatred like she'd never felt before pulsed through her. "How do you live with yourself? How did you sleep at night knowing you had just walked away and left her there all alone? Did you ever bother to check on her afterward?" she demanded, hearing her voice rising and unable to control it. "Did you even know that she had a baby girl? Or that she'd died giving birth to her...to *your* daughter? Did you ever try to find out what happened to her baby? Your baby? Your own flesh and blood? To see if she was cared for or happy or loved?

"I suppose that's a foolish question," she went on as he endured her bitter tirade in silence. "After all, why would you care? There wasn't any advantage in acknowledging an illegitimate daughter...then or now."

Lily stared hard at him, unable to believe that her words didn't elicit even a glimmer of response from him. She was shaking with anger, with hatred, from the sheer trauma of having her whole life torn out by the roots and tossed down in some place she didn't want to be, and he was just standing there, cool, calm and collected. Totally unmoved. As if she and this entire scene were some sudden storm and he could simply wait for it to pass over.

"No," she said suddenly, the word firing from somewhere deep inside her. "You are going to acknowledge it, damn you. You are finally going to do one thing for that woman, and for my mother, and for me." And for Rusty Saville, too, she thought, fighting for control. She'd decided to keep secret the truth about his accident, and she would continue to do so. But she'd be damned if she'd let him off the hook again.

"For once," she said, "you're going to own up to what you did. I want to hear you say that you're my father, just once, and then you can go back to your stinking lies and choke on them for all I care."

"Go to hell," James snapped.

Lily flinched instinctively, coming up hard against Jack's shoulder as he suddenly leaned over the desk to grab James by his rumpled and sweat-stained shirtfront, his cane clattering to the floor as he used both hands to jerk James forward. "Say it. For some godforsaken reason she wants to hear you say the words, and you're damn well going to give her that much."

Kay quickly moved to grab Jack's arms, but he shook her off.

"For God's sake, James, say it," she urged. "For once in your life, be man enough to tell the truth."

"The truth?" he chortled. "I already told you the truth. That's not what you want. You want a damn confession. One more nail in my coffin. One more thing to twist and turn against me and hang over my head. Well, this time you're not getting it."

Jack yanked on his shirt so hard that James's midsection slammed into the wood desk with an audible thud.

He winced. "What the . . . Are you crazy?"

"Yes," retorted Jack.

"Well, get your hands off me. You're hurting me."

"Not nearly as much as I'm going to hurt you if you don't start saying what Lily wants to hear." He jerked him against the desk again.

James grunted. "All right, all right, you want the truth, I'll give it to you." Jack eased his hold slowly. When he was finally free, James pulled at his shirtfront and said, "First I need a drink. I mean it," he said when Jack looked ready to lunge again. "This is no picnic for me, either. I'll tell you what you want to know, but I need a drink first."

Jack crossed to the bar and poured a shot of vodka into a glass.

"Make it a double, will you?" James requested, with the first hint of emotion Lily had seen him display.

Jack thrust the single shot at him. "Say what you've got to say, then you can swallow the bottle whole, for all I care."

"Some son," James drawled as he tipped the glass up.

"Some father," Jack countered.

Lily could guess how this was tearing him up inside, as well, rousing all kinds of bad memories. It was a nightmare for everyone in the room, but it was too late to turn back now.

"You all want to hear the truth," James said finally, wiping his mouth with the back of his hand, "I'll give it to you. But it's not what you think."

He looked at Mary. "You're right, I was at the hospital that night. And I did try and talk Dolly Martin—at least I think that was her name—into giving the kid up for adoption. It was the best thing she could've done, believe me. She was no more than a kid herself. But the *truth* is I hardly knew her. I sure as hell wasn't the father of her kid."

Lily laughed with disgust. "You expect anyone to believe you went there to see a woman you hardly knew?"

"I don't expect anything from any of you," James told her. "I did it for a friend, an old Navy buddy of mine. He knocked up this girl, then he got shipped out. He asked me to keep an eye on her, so I did."

"You never mentioned a word about any of this to me," Kay said.

He shrugged. "It was no big deal. I slipped her a few bucks from time to time. Saw to it her rent was paid, let my buddy know how she was doing, stuff like that. Just goes to show it doesn't pay to be a good Samaritan?"

"Somehow the image of you as a silent benefactor of the downtrodden doesn't wash," observed Jack harshly.

"You wanted the truth," James reminded him. "That's it."

"So you're saying that if the doctor forged those papers, he did it all on his own?" Lily asked him.

"Must have."

"But why?"

James shrugged. "Beats me."

"All right," she pressed, "what about after the baby was born? Did you ever let this friend of yours know that he had a daughter who needed him? Or that the mother had died?"

James again wiped his mouth with the back of his hand, but this time it was sweat, not vodka, beaded there. "I tried. But I kind of lost track of him."

"Come off it," groaned Jack. "You lost track of a man in the United States Navy?"

"All right, all right," James conceded, nodding so forcefully that drops of perspiration flicked from his forehead, carrying the smell of fear across the desk to Lily. "I guess I could have looked harder. But when I found out the Savilles took the kid in themselves, I figured she was in good hands." He made a small snorting noise and gestured at the letter on the desk. "That's the thanks I get for all my trouble."

"What was his name?" Lily asked.

James gaped at her. "His name?"

"Right, this man, this old Navy buddy of yours, the one who trusted you enough to look after the mother of his child. What was the man's name?"

"It was, ah . . ." He licked his lips and darted a glance toward the empty glass. "Baxter. That was it, Rick Baxter."

"No," Lily murmured, shaking her head. "That's all wrong. You're still lying. I know it."

James glared at her with disdain. "Look, honey, I'm sorry if you don't like the name Baxter as much as you do Terrell. It's been obvious for a long time that you're dying to worm your way into this family . . . Maybe get your own cushy thing going, huh? But just because you can't make it on your own back, don't try getting there on mine."

Jack was across the desk before any of the others reacted, rage and adrenaline overcoming any physical limitations for the moment. He landed a punch on James's jaw, knocking him off his feet, then bent and dragged him upright, shoving him backward into the custom-built case holding dozens of the bottle-enclosed ships that were his passion.

"You lousy, lying bastard," Jack growled, hitting him again as one glass-panel cracked and the entire six-foot-high case shook.

James stiffened, his eyes wide as he twisted to glance fearfully over his shoulder. "Stop," he shouted. "Get away from there. Don't you see what you're doing? Those ships are worth a—"

Jack shut him up with a quick jerking movement that brought them face to face with only inches between them. "I don't believe it," he panted. "You care more about those damn ships than about your own flesh and blood?"

Why am I surprised by that? Jack wondered. He suddenly recalled the morning they learned Drew Goddard had died, how broken up his mother had been and how all James had on his mind was the ship he'd just acquired. No matter who was born or died, or who lost what, he remained unruffled. *His collec-*

tion, Jack thought bitterly, was the only thing he'd ever shown any real heartfelt emotion for.

"You know, *Dad,* you're absolutely right," he said, releasing James with exaggerated care. He straightened his shirt for him and even fixed his collar. "These ships are much too valuable to mess around with. What do you figure just one of them is worth? Thousands? Tens of thousands?"

At first Lily was stunned by Jack's abrupt change. Now she watched with growing anxiety, wondering how it was possible to feel any more tension than she already did. The air in the room seemed to hum with it. There was something too measured, too controlled about Jack's tone and his manner. Something frightening. Looking on, she thought of the eerie stillness that comes with the eye of a hurricane, and she curled her hands so tightly her nails bit into her palms.

"Even more than that?" Jack asked, appearing genuinely interested in the value of the ships.

James looked as apprehensive as Lily felt. "Some of them, I suppose."

"No kidding?" Jack whistled through his teeth. "Like which one? Show me."

"I don't know," James replied, running his fingers through his hair, not even glancing at the display case. "Look, this is—"

"Show me," Jack repeated in a soft, terrifying voice.

James's hand seemed to tremble as he gestured toward a ship on the second shelf. "There, that one. It's a one-of-a-kind replica of a British tall ship, over a hundred years old. Now are you satisfi—"

"Let's take a closer look at it," Jack suggested.

James shook his head, his eyes as bright and darting as a cornered animal's. "No. I don't have the key on me."

Jack smiled agreeably. "No problem."

There was a collective gasp as he suddenly swung his arm and sent his fist crashing against the door so that the already cracked glass showered to the floor. The ships inside rattled on the glass shelves and James stood in front, waving his hands in the air as if to catch them should they fall.

"You crazy bastard," he cried. "What the hell are you trying to prove?"

"That even *you* care about something. Maybe not your wife or your son...or your daughter," Jack added pointedly. "But something. I don't know exactly what price you put on the truth, but I'm willing to bet I'll hit on it before I finish emptying this case.''

All of them, even James, watched in silence as he reached through the broken glass doors and picked up a bottle containing the ship James had pointed out. Probably, Lily realized a few seconds too late, because no one could believe he would really do it.

Jack held the ship before him and glanced negligently at James. ''Let's call it an even ten thousand.''

He tossed it aside with enough force to send it crashing against the desk. The sound of shattering glass and splintering wood filled the room.

He looked at James, who glowered at him, his jaw thrust forward, his temples lined with purple veins that pulsed visibly.

''Not high enough?'' Jack asked. ''All right.''

He reached for another bottle, this one containing a smaller, more delicate ship with her sails unfurled. Lily wanted to cry when it fell to the floor in pieces.

''Twenty thousand,'' said Jack.

James watched him reach into the case again. ''Who the hell do you think you are?'' he shouted. ''To come in here and try to blackmail me with my own things? You think I'll crack for you, you two-bit tin soldier?''

''I think if I push hard enough you'll crawl,'' Jack shot back. ''I also think we have to pick up the pace a bit or we'll be here forever.'' He lifted a ship in each hand and sent them flying across the room one after the other.

Lily heard her mother moaning softly and turned to find her patting her chest. She hurried to her side and put an arm around her. ''Are you all right, Mom?'' she asked.

Mary nodded. ''It's just so awful. Such an awful waste.''

Lily nodded. ''Jack, maybe this has gone too far.''

He seemed not to hear her. It was as if he and James were alone in the room. Just the two of them and all those remaining ships.

Spotting his cane, Jack used it to smash the other door of the cabinet, reached inside for one of the largest bottles perched on the top shelf, and smashed it against the wall beside him. He glanced around. ''That has to be close to a hundred thou in shipwrecks,'' he observed calmly.

"More, you idiot," cried James. "You just broke the *Santa Lucia* ... I spent over ten years looking for her. I spent over fifty thousand dollars tracking her down."

Jack glanced at the remains. "You got taken."

James made a whimpering sound as he fell to his knees and tried to gather the hundreds of tiny pieces together. The broken glass cut his fingertips until they dripped blood and still he kept at it. Listening and watching his shoulders heave, Lily suspected he was crying. Finally he stopped and stared at Jack.

"You would really do this? Destroy a man's lifetime work?"

Jack shook his head. "You just don't get it, do you? That people matter more than things. Yeah, I would really do it. I'll smash every last one of them. Then I'll come after you again."

"For what?" James gasped, as if he really didn't get it. "For me to say some words that mean nothing?"

"For a name, that's all. The name of Lily's father, whatever, whoever that is." He waited, but James remained silent, his face a stiff mask of hatred, until Jack turned to the case.

"I think it's time we went for the grand prize," he said, grasping the top of the case with both hands.

"No," James screamed. "Not all of them, no, please, no, no more. I'll tell you what you want to know, I swear. The truth this time ... You can check it out if you want. There are tests, ways to prove it. I know there are."

From his position on the floor, he turned to look first at Kay, then Lily. "I'm really not your father," he said to her. "And the part about doing it for someone else was true. What I didn't tell you before was that the friend I was talking about was ..." He wet his lips and slid his gaze toward Kay. "It was your brother. Ted was Lily's father."

FORTY-TWO

Lily whipped around to look at Kay, who was visibly shaken by James's revelation.

"Ted?" Kay echoed, incredulous. "Ted was Lily's father?" She stared aghast at her husband. "My God, all this time you knew and you never said a word.... Why?"

"Why? Because if Ted had found out that his little tramp was pregnant, that he was a father, he'd have come running back here and settled down with her and—"

"And you would have been bumped down a rung at Delaney Silver," Kay finished with disdain. Her chin quivered until she bit her lip to bring it under control. "But what about after Ted died? Why didn't you tell anyone the truth then?"

"Then it was too late. Your old man would have figured out what I tried to do and sent me packing. It was too late." His head sagged against the wall. "All I wanted was to have her out of the way. Instead she's haunted me every day of my life. This hasn't been easy for me, either, you know. In fact, it's been worse on me, knowing and not being able to say anything and—"

"Shut up," Kay snapped. "What kind of monster are you?"

"Kay, listen to me—" he began, somehow getting to his feet and staggering a few steps until Kay stopped him in his tracks. Blood trickled from the corner of his mouth where Jack's punch had landed and stained his shirt where his bloody hands had touched it.

"No, I'm through listening," she said, "I'm through tolerating, I'm through with you, period. I don't care if you have to crawl on your hands and knees, I want you out of here now, and out of my life entirely by the end of the day."

He stared, as if trying to decide if she was serious, and evidently concluding that she was.

"You won't get away with this," he snarled, but the wince of pain that accompanied the threat gave it a hollow ring. "Getting rid of me will be the most expensive thing you'll ever do."

"And worth every penny," Kay countered. "Now get out."

"This is my office," he reminded her.

"Not anymore."

As Jack wordlessly, but pointedly, walked over to open the door for him, James's gaze limped around the room, pausing on each of them in turn. His glassy, bloodshot eyes were filled with hatred, but the slope of his shoulders inside the expensive, hand-tailored clothes that were now limp and stained conveyed his defeat.

He's nothing to me, Lily thought with joyful relief. *Nothing at all.*

At the door, James seemed to regain a speck of his old cynicism. "A match made in heaven," he tossed back to the room in general. "You deserve each other."

Did he mean her and Jack? wondered Lily. Or her and Kay? Or maybe he meant that they all deserved each other. It was easy to be confused. Her mind was a jumble of overlapping and crossed signals, her thoughts like puzzle pieces scattered across a table. But her dazed, shell-shocked brain kept touching two thoughts together and producing the same emotional spark. If this was true, she was a Delaney. Lily found the prospect amazing and horrifying.

From the corridor outside came the sound of someone exclaiming over James's battered appearance. Someone else said something about calling the company nurse, then the door closed, leaving the four of them alone.

Kay spoke first. Lacing her fingers together, she clasped them beneath her chin and gazed at Lily with an expression of wonder. "Of course. I can see it so clearly now. Oh, Lily, you're so much like him. Your hair, the way you laugh, even the way you sometimes hold your head. Maybe that's why I've always been so drawn to you, even when you were a child."

Lily recalled Drew once saying something very similar to her, only of course he hadn't known at the time that she was the daughter of his best friend. They still didn't know that for sure.

"What if James was lying about this, too?" she asked Kay.

Kay shook her head with a tremulous smile. "He wasn't. Not this time. There are DNA tests that will prove that to you, but I already know that you are my brother's child. My own niece."

"I have something here that might help," said Mary, in a hesitant voice. "There might be pictures . . . something."

She pulled a square box from her handbag. A yellow label on one side read Dolly Martin—East Three.

"It's Dolly's belongings from the hospital," she explained. "Seeing as she had no next of kin—except for Lily, of course— it would have been thrown out." She looked directly at Lily. "That didn't seem right to me, so I took the box home and it's been in the attic ever since. I didn't expect to ever be standing here, doing this, but, well, here it is."

She held out the box to Lily. "I never looked inside. You ought to be the one to do that. If things today have made it so you can't think of me as your mother anymore, well, then, I at least want you to know all you can about the woman who was."

For a long time Lily stared into Mary's eyes, unable to move. It was as if her life was one of those childhood slates, where you lift the cellophane top sheet and everything is erased, wiped clean. The revelation that Ted Delaney was her father had torn the top sheet right off.

It meant her mother wasn't really her mother, her brothers not really her brothers. Sisters-in-law, nieces, nephews. Suddenly with it all in danger of slipping away, Lily understood how very important her family was to her. How did you go from being a Saville to a Delaney in a matter of seconds?

As Mary finally thrust the box into her hands and turned as if to go, Lily knew that answer. You didn't.

"Mom, wait," she cried.

The name came instinctively, rising straight from her heart. She wasn't sure if the feelings inside her at that moment were instinctive or learned—learned through years of kindness, guidance and sacrifice that had been spent raising her—and she didn't care. She loved this woman as a mother because that's what she was, what she would always be. Gathering her into her arms to hug her, Lily told her so.

"I love you, Mom. Nothing can ever change that."

Mary's tears flowed freely then. "Oh, Lily, I was so afraid you'd blame me for everything."

"Blame you? Mom, I have to thank you. More now than ever." She drew back and smiled at Mary through her tears. "I think you are the strongest, most wonderful woman in the whole world. I've always been lucky to have you for my mother, I just never knew how lucky until today."

Mary shook off the praise, uncomfortable displaying her emotions so freely here.

Lily understood. "We'll talk later, okay? At home."

"Yes." A smile lit Mary's face. "At home."

"I might have questions," Lily warned softly.

"I'll tell you everything I know."

Lily hugged her once more. There would be a lot of talk about later. And of course, the news would have to be broken to her brothers. She wanted no more secrets, even though, after last night, she understood why it was sometimes necessary to protect those you loved by keeping the truth from them.

She would be strong enough to keep her secret about the accident, just as her mother had been strong enough to keep hers. And like her mother, if the time ever came when it was right to tell, she would be strong enough for that, too.

She glanced at the box in her hands.

"Open it," Kay urged quietly, even as Lily debated waiting until she was alone to do that.

This was hers, and frankly she felt no desire to share it with Kay. DNA be damned, she certainly felt no bond with the other woman. She had once, without even knowing they were related, but that had all been changed. Finding out the truth about the accident had changed it. She no longer felt the admiration and respect and affection she felt for Kay for so long, since she was a child, in fact. She refused to feel it. And she refused to share this moment with her.

Except when Lily turned to tell her so, Kay's wistful expression stopped her. In spite of the worry lines and creases, she suddenly reminded Lily of a child. The image haunted her, and she found herself shrugging. What difference did it make if Kay saw what was in the box? It wouldn't change anything.

Lily placed the box on a corner of the desk and easily snapped the old string securing it. As she lifted the lid, she was struck by the sadness of a woman's life, her entire legacy to her daughter, being reduced to a single small cardboard box. Seeing the few ordinary items inside only made it worse.

There was an unopened box of Heaven Scent dusting powder, a tube of red lipstick now shriveled and dried, and a small, dark blue glass vial of Evening in Paris cologne, evaporated past any hint of scent. A comb, a crochet-edged handkerchief, a red wallet and a few pieces of tarnished jewelry, and that was it.

Lily reached for the wallet, giving in to a compulsion to count the money inside. For some reason it seemed very important to her to know that Dolly Martin had set off from home that night with six one-dollar bills, two quarters, two dimes and seven pennies. Perhaps because there was so little else to know.

Unsnapping a leather flap, she looked through the cellophane picture enclosures that cracked in spite of the fact that Lily handled them as reverently as she would a priceless heirloom. There was a magazine photo of Cary Grant, a few torn ticket stubs and a lock of reddish-brown hair very like her own. Movie stars and ticket stubs and locks of hair. It was the sort of stuff she'd filled her wallet with in high school, thought Lily sadly. It occurred to her how very young Dolly Martin had been when she died. More child than mother.

What would her life have been like if Dolly had lived and raised her, alone, an unwed mother in a time when that was considered a sin of the highest order? That led Lily to thoughts of what might have been if James's plan had failed, if Mary's letter to Kay had been delivered when it should have been, and if she had gone to live at Delaney Place. All her old fairy-tale dreams and fantasies came flowing back to her, and for just a moment Lily was filled with a sense of loss.

Then she lifted her head to look across the room at Jack. He had grown up in Delaney Place, and his childhood had been far from the stuff of fairy tales. There were big holes inside Jack that should be filled with happy memories of all the small, seemingly inconsequential events that make up a life. Family picnics and birthday parties and times when you feel like you haven't got a friend in the world, and your mother comes and sits beside you on the curb and stops the ice-cream truck to buy a Popsicle for you, just for no reason, and you suddenly know that you have a friend after all, and that you'll always have one, no matter what.

Those were Lily's memories, and because of them there were no black holes inside her. She was suddenly overwhelmed with the desire to spend the rest of her life creating enough happy memories to fill Jack to overflowing.

What had he said last night, about wanting a family before it was too late? She felt a stirring deep inside. Thank God it wasn't too late for them. And thank God for putting her in the home He had. If she'd been raised at Delaney Place, with Kay and James for surrogate parents she would have had everything she ever dreamed of, and nothing that really mattered.

Instead, she had it all, a wonderful family, a man she loved desperately and who loved her, and the good sense and humility to appreciate and hang on to it all, no matter what.

She sent Jack a smile that drew a broad, relieved one in return. Are you okay? his eyes asked. Lily nodded, then turned to the final enclosure in Dolly's wallet and looked into the eyes of a laughing young woman captured years ago by the camera in a dime-store photo booth.

"That's her, Lily," Mary exclaimed, coming to stand by her side. "That's Dolly. Oh, she was pretty."

Kay quickly joined them, standing on Lily's other side. "And that's Ted," she said, the sound she made both a sob and a laugh.

There were four snapshots altogether, all of them taken with Dolly seated on Ted's lap, their grinning faces cheek to cheek. From the hint of mischief in his eyes and the surprise in Dolly's, Lily had a hunch he was tickling her out of camera range, and a warm feeling spread all through her.

She studied the grainy images intently. Ted Delaney. Her father? Unbelievably young, with kind eyes and high cheekbones very like the ones she dusted blush on each and every morning of her life. She looked again at Dolly. Her mother. Staring, willing something from the two of them, or maybe from the heavens above, some sign, some ethereal sensation of spiritual blending that these two attractive young people, so obviously in love, were indeed her parents.

There was nothing. Dolly and Ted were forever sealed there behind the cellophane, alone together.

With a sigh she returned the wallet to the box and lifted out a tarnished silver chain and medallion.

"That was Ted's," Kay said softly. "It's one of a pair of medallions. I have the other. Ted never took it off."

The obvious fact that he had taken it off to give to the woman he loved seemed to suddenly bring all Kay's emotions to the surface.

"Oh, Lily, there's no doubt that you are Ted's daughter. And you have no way of knowing what that means to me. It's a blessing, an omen. I can't find the right words to tell you what I'm feeling."

She paused to draw a deep, shuddering breath, cupping her fingers around her mouth briefly as she struggled for control. Finally she opened her arms to Lily, stretching forward as if she were drowning and Lily was a lifeline just out of reach. "You are a Delaney, and that makes everything I've done—all of it—worthwhile.''

Now, thought Lily, now was her chance. By simply turning her back on Kay she could accomplish what she'd climbed from bed at the crack of dawn to do, punish her for her role in Rusty's accident. That was part of the everything Kay was referring to that Lily's very existence was somehow supposed to sanctify. Giving up Drew had been another part of it, she was sure. Yes, she could see that Kay needed a reason to believe it had not all been for nothing.

It certainly must look that way to her at times, with Jack not interested in the family business and that business perched at the edge of extinction. Now Kay saw that the business she fought and lied and sacrificed everything to preserve had a future after all, and that future's name was Lily.

All Lily had to do to give Kay peace of mind was reach out her hand. All she had to do to get revenge was walk away.

The room was so silent it was hard to breathe. Or maybe she was just afraid to breathe. This instant seemed so important, a turning point really, the start of the future for all of them. Lily felt her mother's presence by her side, and Jack right behind her. Neither of them said a word. She was on her own, but not alone. Kay wasn't so lucky; she was alone.

By her own choice, a steely inner voice insisted, but something else inside Lily resisted, and suddenly she knew why she'd found Kay's vulnerable, almost childlike expression a few moments ago so haunting. The child Kay had reminded Lily of at that moment was herself. Briefly her gaze was drawn to the floor and the shards of broken glass and she thought of other broken glass, and of another ship broken on another day.

That small mishap paled beside this debacle, but at the time it had seemed like the end of the world to her. She remembered sitting in the greenhouse afterward, miserable and alone, and how the only person who could possibly have made things better had taken the time to reach out to her.

Yes, she thought, Kay was alone because she had chosen to be, and that was punishment enough.

Lily slowly lifted her hand and reached out to Kay, seeing the tremble of relief that passed through her as she grasped it, and their hands locked around the pendant that Ted had given to Dolly so long ago.

* * *

"Why did you do it?" Jack asked her much, much later.

It was nearly midnight and they were sprawled across his bed, enjoying their first chance to speak privately since the tumultuous events of the morning. The day had been consumed with endless discussions and explanations, and the evening spent at her house where, amazingly enough, her niece's birthday party had gone on as planned.

The get-together had given Lily a chance to speak with all her brothers at once, and also to plant the idea in their sometimes stubborn heads that they would be seeing a great deal of Jack from then on. It had made for a lively evening, which, all things considered, went more smoothly than she anticipated.

They had finally returned to Jack's about an hour earlier, but talking—about any subject—hadn't been the first thing that leaped to mind when the door clicked shut behind them, Lily thought, remembering with delight their heated, sex-starved, inspired journey from the door to the bed.

"Why did I come home with you when it was obvious that your intentions were dishonorable?" she teased.

"No, it's obvious you came *because* my intentions were dishonorable."

"This is true," she said, turning in his arms to rest her head on his chest, idly running her fingers over the ridges of muscle and bone.

"I meant why did you let Kay off the hook this morning?"

"Oh, that."

"For a minute there, I thought you were going to go for the jugular. You did leave here this morning hell-bent on revenge."

"I guess I decided that justice is preferable to revenge, and as far as I'm concerned, the agreement we reached later is just."

"You mean using the name Saville for the new line?"

Lily nodded. "It's a small enough tribute, but I think my father would be very pleased and proud." The soothing motion of his fingers on her skin added to the feeling of serenity that had been slowly building in her for hours. "But I guess when it came right down to it, I let Kay off the hook because she did the same for me."

And more than once, thought Lily. But telling Jack about that day and the broken ship would only add to his bitterness toward his father. She didn't particularly care about James, but she cared very much about the emotional well-being of his son.

Jack had suffered from all the lies and treachery almost as much as she had. It was time for the healing to begin.

He looked at her quizzically. "In what way?"

"Last night," she explained. "Regardless of her involvement, she did finally tell me the truth about the accident. Knowing Kay, it wasn't easy for her to admit what she had done, but she did it because she didn't want me to go on blaming myself. She did it for me, and for you. I owed her for that." She looked at him through the darkness. "If she hadn't told me, we might not be here right now."

Jack tightened his hold on her, as if the words alone were a threat to their newfound bliss.

"I think Kay was braced for retaliation," he said. "And she's just grateful it didn't happen. I know she's grateful that you're staying on at Delaney Silver."

"Your mother is very resourceful. No matter what she says, she and Delaney Silver would go on without me. But I have to admit," she added sheepishly, "it is exciting to be a Delaney, sort of like a dream come true."

"Speaking of dreams come true, has it occurred to you that when we get married, I'll be the one marrying into the Delaney family instead of you?"

Lily lifted her head. "Are we getting married?"

"Do you think I'm crazy enough to let a Delaney get away?"

He stopped her laughter with a deep, unhurried kiss that left her shimmering with passion and love as he continued to dapple kisses along her throat.

"So everybody gets their happy ending. With the possible exception of my mother," she added, sighing.

Jack stopped kissing her long enough to ask, "Why isn't she happy?"

"Because now she has more things than ever to worry about. For instance, she knows we spent last night together and right this minute she's probably worrying that you won't marry me because why buy the cow when you can get the milk for free?" Lily continued over Jack's groans of laughter. "And if you do marry me, who's going to walk me down the aisle? And where will we hold the reception? And what on earth will she wear to a Delaney wedding?

"Plus," she said, turning serious, "I really haven't had a chance to talk with her alone for very long and reassure her. She's bound to lay awake all night worrying that everything isn't going to work out all right after all. First thing tomorrow—"

"Tomorrow," Jack agreed, his warm lips finding hers, his hands moving insistently down her body, starting a slow pulse of pleasure deep inside that made tomorrow seem a lifetime away.

Her mother, thought Lily, while she was still able to think coherently, had only been partially right about the perils of being a dreamer. And Lily suspected that deep down, Mary knew that. Any woman who would defy logic and practicality to take in a baby she couldn't afford believed in dreams big time.

Dreams could be dangerous, to be sure. They could even break your heart. But some dreams were worth any risk, any sacrifice. And sometime, she thought, wrapping her arms around Jack, they could even come true.

Just a few miles down the road, Mary suddenly stopped in the act of tossing her robe over the bedpost and smiled. The sounds of creaking floorboards and hissing radiators surrounded her, as comforting to her as an old friend's laughter. How she loved this old house. Feet first, that's how she planned to leave this place, and she didn't plan on it being any time soon, she thought, as she climbed into bed and turned out the light. After all, she had a wedding to plan.

In December 1992, look for Patricia Coughlin's next Silhouette Special Edition, GYPSY SUMMER, only from Silhouette Books!